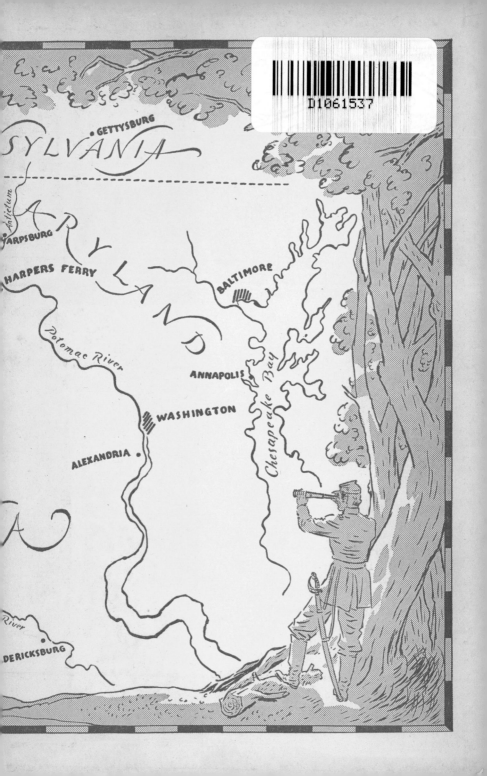

Date Due →

Books returned after date due are subject to a fine of 5 cents per library open day.

ILLUSTRATED BY

JOHN ALAN MAXWELL

★

BOOK DESIGNED BY

GEORGE SCHLINING

HANG
MY
WREATH

BY WARD WEAVER

MCMXLI

WILFRED FUNK, INC.

NEW YORK

CL

PRINTED IN THE UNITED STATES OF AMERICA

To my old friend,

FRANK C. HENRY,
and
to those soldiers, Northern and Southern,
who though often defeated
were yet ever victorious in their
courage and patriotism.

AUTHOR'S PREFACE

TO WRITE about the Civil War or, as some prefer, the War between the States is yet a delicate matter. Among the traditions of some of our older American families certain biases, hatreds and illusions are still to be found. This book is written in an effort to demonstrate how erroneously some of these ugly memories came into being.

Otherwise the author has endeavored simply to tell a lively, swiftly moving tale with no pretentions to anything but entertainment. Military movements, historic figures, dates and even weather conditions are accurate however.

The locomotive chase herein described is based on a raid which took place on the Georgia State Railway during the year 1862. The author has, of course, changed the locale and altered the ending.

All opinions concerning the enemy and the conduct of the war should be considered those of the character who utters them—not of the author. The Cary and Duveen families are wholly imaginary.

AUTHOR'S PREFACE

The author is deeply indebted to Charles P. Golding of South Dartmouth, Massachusetts, for his generous co-operation in editing details concerning the railroads of the time and their operation; to his mother, Mrs A. Ward Weaver, the author owes a debt of gratitude for her tactful aid in criticizing this volume.

Whatever success this volume may achieve must, the author feels, be shared in great measure by his good friend, John Alan Maxwell, who executed the wrapper and the sketches for this book.

WARD WEAVER

CONTENTS

PART I

CONTENTS

PART I

The Valley

1862

CHAPTER ONE

SHENANDOAH

ONCE his patrol came to a halt Captain Hubert Cary, First Rhode Island Cavalry, sat quite still looking out over the Shenandoah Valley. Brown, green and yellow billows of treetops rolled away for miles over a succession of minor ridges and hills. Cary guessed he had better keep an eye on himself—this time he was entering Loudoun County as an invader.

On this September afternoon the valley looked even lovelier than he had remembered it. Heavily, the sun was plating with gold wide fields and pastures opening here and there to either side of the rutted road along which he and the reconnaissance patrol had been advancing since noon. It was scarcely a road at that, more of a trace winding across the Blue Ridge Mountains.

The lean, long bodied Federal could see further stretches of this yellow-red road coiling downward toward the lush floor of the valley. Most of it, though, was hidden in woods which might very well harbor whole brigades of the rumored gray- and brown-clad troops his reconnaissance patrol was attempting to locate.

The noise of a horse forcing its way through a tangle of laurels prompted Cary to turn in his saddle in time to see his lieutenant ride up. The young man's features were flushed and crisscrossed with dull red branch marks; both he and his horse looked hot and disgusted.

"No sign of the enemy, sir, other side of this spur."

"At ease, Mr Blake." The red-haired captain's manner relaxed and he grinned at his subordinate. "We'll catch our breath before we descend any further. Well, Tom, like to be back in Harpers Ferry?"

"Hell, no!" Eyes narrowed, the lieutenant viewed the valley so green and blue below. "D'you think some of old Stonewall Jack's boys are restin' in the shade of the trees down yonder?"

"Maybe." Cary swung off, eased the girth of the restless black gelding serving him as charger. "You can figure the rest of the Rebs sometimes—but not Stonewall."

He ordered his detail troopers to dismount, to rub their horses' legs and to let air under the saddlecloths. Blake meanwhile picked bits of twig and bark from hair falling

[4]

almost to his shoulders. Next he dusted a short shell jacket
and his dark blue saddle cover.

How much longer would the sun remain hot? Cary
wondered. His face was so coated with sweaty dust it felt
leathery and stiff.

"Say, ain't *that* a view for you?" When young Blake unhooked his collar and ran a finger along the inside of it
yellow velvet of his officer's shoulder strap gleamed.

Cary smiled, swallowed a pull of luke-warm water from
a blue-covered canteen slung from his pommel. "It's the
prettiest country in America, to my way of thinking; but
it won't do to daydream—not with Jeb Stuart patrols out
God knows where."

For some moments the two officers stood beside their
chargers carefully studying the countryside.

From a nearby pine a mockingbird cocked a bright
inquisitive eye, and deep in the woods a jay screeched
strident protests against the presence of these dusty blue
cavalrymen.

Captain Cary's wide set gray-blue eyes traveled slowly
back and forth over the panorama below and high lights in
his red hair shone like dull copper when he trained field
glasses on a distant bridge. Next he scrutinized the length
of the ridge opposite.

"Don't like the looks of it—too blamed quiet to be true.
Those buzzards are circling low over there."

"*If* there *are* any Johnny Rebs down yonder, they're damn
well hidden," Blake grunted. He pulled off his kepi, blew
a layer of dust from its crown, then straightened the crossed
sabers ornamenting its front.

From the shade of a clump of hickories came the nasal accents of Cary's first sergeant, "Give me a New England fall fer choice. Here 'tis September, but you'd never guess it to look round you."

From beneath the cracked patent-leather visor of his kepi Sergeant Jeremiah Tatnall was, with obvious contempt, viewing this green and amber valley.

"What's wrong with a Virginia fall?" drawled a gaunt corporal stuffing a corncob pipe.

"Wrong? Why, ain't a mite o' snap to the air, and look at them there leaves, will you; green like 'twas May."

Disgustedly the bronzed first sergeant spat into the dusty underbrush. The troopers' mounts hung their heads, tiredly switched at flies which promptly came swarming out of the woods.

"Only a ignorant, frozen-toed Yank would gripe over these nice warm nights," remarked a bandy-legged cavalryman wearing a sergeant's broad yellow chevrons. He fixed on the first sergeant a hostile gaze. "And it 'll be warmer yet if we blunder into a mess o' Fitz Lee's hoss thieves."

" 'Tain't natteral," somberly persisted the New Englander. "I tell ye, Raines, the Lord God meant His autumns to be snappy-like."

"You go to hell, Tatnall," drawled the other sergeant. "Any half-witted boogie knows the butt end o' Maryland is wuth fifty o' Rhode Island."

The first sergeant's face, resembling an old saddle both as to texture and color, turned a shade darker.

"I'll remember that there opinion, Raines," he promised

[6]

slowly. "You talk a sight too secesh. Why the cap'n brung you along stumps me."

Captain Hubert Cary meanwhile closed the case of his field glasses with a snap, then glanced at his watch. Um. Nearly three o'clock. He guessed he'd better get his patrol down on the plain and reconnoiter in the direction of the railroad. He said so.

"Just five minutes more," Blake pleaded. "The men need it. Horses too."

Blake was quite right. They did need rest. The rank and file of the First Rhode Island Cavalry wasn't much to look at these days. Cary had to admit it whether he wanted to or not. His troopers, mostly fresh from the North, handled their ungainly mounts in a fashion which would have broken the hearts of Lee's cavalry officers.

"Very well."

"Thanks." In fumbling for his tobacco pouch young Blake brought out a well-fingered dance program.

Captain Cary saw it, chuckled. "You and Jeb Stuart seem designed by Nature to flutter the dovecotes of America."

The lieutenant grinned, reminiscently fingered the gay little dance card. "Cavalryman's privilege. Notice you ain't so unhandy yourself."

"And of what city is this a token of bright moments in dark corners?"

"Baltimore." Blake's grin faded.

"Ah, still another maid bound to the conqueror's chariot wheels?" suggested Cary, pulling tangled grass from his charger's bit.

"Wish to God you were right," sighed the younger

[7]

officer, slapping at a fly. "Best I could manage was a couple of dances."

"Do you good to get taken down a peg," Cary commented.

"My God, Hubert, you should see her! She's the most divine, the most——"

"——The most exquisite, the most talented, the loveliest, the best dressed." Absently Cary considered a lone buzzard rocking high in the brazen-blue sky. He began to enumerate on long, sunburned fingers. "Let's see—that also describes Peggy Clark of Providence, Cornelia Van Wyck back in New York, Betty Sanderson languishing in Washington, Genevieve——"

"Lay off it!" The lieutenant glared. "I thought so at the time; but damn it, man, this girl's different. A regular stunner, with wits to match. Wait 'til you see Diana—the Golden Diana."

"I can hardly wait—— Eh!" Cary's red head snapped about. "D'you say her name was Diana?"

"I did." Mockery entered the lieutenant's expression. "Can't be that an old campaigner like you——"

Cary rubbed a squarish jaw and, bending, picked up his

[8]

charger's near foot. "Hate to disappoint you, but I've never even laid eyes on the lady.

"Heard of her though," he admitted, dislodging a bit of gravel from under the shoe. "They say she's spoiled to death. Anybody called a 'Golden Diana' would be. Bet she can't so much as boil water. Oh, I know the type." Over his shoulder he called, "Get ready to mount, you men."

Blake swung stiffly up into his saddle. "I don't fancy you——"

"Never mind me, Tom," Cary smiled. "Go ahead, worship

your heartbreaker. I'll stick to fair-to-middling pretty gals with fine figures."

"Who are you to talk? You, who got half the dear things in Washington aflutter, then rode off like a—a damned French hussar!"

The cavalry captain chuckled, swung into the saddle, eased his holstered revolver. "Had me a elegant time, Tom."

"Don't brag. I'd admire watching you try your maneuvers on a stunner like mine."

At Cary's laugh his charger swung back delicate ears. "Never fear, my lad. When two people who are used to getting their own way come together—well, the fur is apt to fly. And I don't particularly enjoy rows."

Blake, still resentful, gathered reins in gauntleted hands. "You'd come off second best. Ten dollars on it!"

"Listen—I——"

"I'll see you presented, next leave to Washington."

"How would I prove I'd won?"

"Kiss her without getting slapped. Of course if you aim to play safe——"

The captain grinned. "I see your game—but I'll take you if we get the chance."

The balance of the reconnaissance party, having mounted after adjusting buckles, quarter straps and cinches, looked restlessly about. Would a dust cloud presently climb into the sky to substantiate that rumor which had sent a chill of apprehension through Harpers Ferry?

ATROCITY

CURB CHAINS JINGLING and saddlery creaking gently, Captain Cary's detachment set off in a column of twos. Sunlight, beating through trees along the dusty track, unrolled for the riders a dark blue, green and gold carpet.

"How come you're so confounded sure of the roads hereabouts?" Lieutenant Blake presently demanded.

"Ought to be," came Captain Cary's brief reply. "Cousins of mine live less than twenty miles from here."

Blake nodded. "Funny, all along I've been thinking Cary was a Southern name."

"When my family first came over from England they settled in these parts," Cary explained, gaze fixed on the next bend in the track. "They say that 'round 1752 a tremendous family row took place. What about, I don't believe anybody knows."

"Some girl, shouldn't wonder," grinned Blake. "You Carys beat all in that direction."

"Go to hell, Tom," Cary suggested amiably. "Anyhow, my branch of the family migrated to New England. Around thirty years ago Pa figured the row had lasted long enough and came down for a visit at the old place— Philomont, it's called. My brother and I used to visit there too."

A grin widened faintly reckless lines about Hubert Cary's mouth. "Hang this war! It would be elegant to stop by and say hello. You'd fall for Melissa like a thousand of brick; Cousin Craig too—great fellow, sportsman clean through. Damned pity he's a reb. Naturally would be, of course. Great man in the hunting field."

Moodily Hubert Cary studied the familiar countryside. How lovely and mellow it seemed. Such a far cry from the grim holly- and creeper-choked tangles of the Wilderness; from the gloomy, treacherous bogs on the Peninsula. The First Rhode Island Cavalry hadn't taken much pleasure from that dismal campaign under "Little Mac."

A fork abruptly divided the sun-speckled road. Cary raised his hand and immediately the patrol reined in, brass ornaments dully agleam. With carbines slung across their shoulderblades the fourteen troopers sat their horses, looking expectant and a trifle apprehensive.

Cary spoke succinctly but in low tones, "Sergeant King and Corporal Fallon will fall out to accompany Lieutenant Blake.

"Lieutenant, you will reconnoiter the right fork of this road for a distance of three miles. Maintain a sharp lookout for dust columns or any traces indicating the recent passage of troops. Don't fight unless surprised. Rendezvous is at this spot within an hour."

Blake saluted and moved off along the right-hand track. Carbines slanting, his detachment disappeared under a lazy haze of dust. His long-limbed black set up a nervous dancing as Cary turned to face his own men.

"If Jackson's forces are in the valley, we should collide with a reb detachment before very long." His gaze traveled over all their faces, steadied them. "Remember, we're here to take prisoners. Unsling your carbines and keep four feet from head to croup. I don't want anybody kicked."

Imagine entering Loudoun County like this! Last time he'd traveled this trace it had been to race 'Lissa and Craig. Um. What would 'Lissa be like now? Petite, lovely and dark, probably—most of the Southern Carys were.

Suddenly Cary reined in. The men followed his example without command. Once the jingle and clank of equipment had died away the Federal leaned forward in his saddle, listened intently.

Faint as though let in by a pin point on the horizon, he heard the cry again. A thin wail which seemed to rise from a minor valley sloping off to the right.

The sunburned troopers in short blue jackets heard it too, exchanged curious glances. When for a third time a shuddering cry of pain arose beyond this green tangle young Denby, rawest recruit in the troop, nervously passed his tongue over dust-coated lips.

"Seems if someone down yonder don't feel so pretty good," Sergeant Tatnall muttered and, bending, secured his saber scabbard lest it click against his cinch ring.

"Mought be only a catamount," suggested Raines, the Maryland sergeant. "They's a few left in these here hills."

Captain Cary spoke over his shoulder, "Quietly now. As foragers—ho!"

The patrol began to deploy with great care, but their clumsy, dull-coated nags made a terrible racket.

Cary, thinking back, seemed to recall a farm in this direction. What in hell was going on? One of the farmer's kids getting a whipping? Or was some woman having a baby?

Though it became increasingly difficult to guard his eyes from low-flung branches, the Federal watched his men pick their way among the tree trunks. Not a bad advance for men who'd never ridden more than a farm horse 'til six months ago.

That Denby boy, however, couldn't ride worth shucks and he never would, not with thighs round on their insides as any girl's. How stupid the government was to mount raw farm boys on coarse-bred nags and expect them to match up with Stuart's lean, well-seasoned and beautifully mounted troopers.

The First Rhode Island, however, was learning this business, improving every day. Tatnall and the other sergeant were riding where they should be—on the extreme right and left of line.

Gradually the woods thinned until the Federal captain could see a yellow field of second-growth hay shining ahead. In response to his arm signal the patrol halted just inside the woods and studied the situation. Yonder lay a farmhouse, barn and some outbuildings.

Cary's heart jumped like a scared deer. Somewhere had sounded the distinctive clash a curb chain makes in brushing a stirrup iron.

There was cavalry down there. Whose? He was still wondering when, in the farmyard, a horse whickered.

Corporal O'Leary immediately swung off and, tightly gripping his mount's ear, pulled the animal's head low. Three other blue troopers also mounted on "talking horses" did likewise.

Young Denby's horse raised his head, cocked ears at the farmhouses.

"Quick, boy, grab his ears!" Cary ordered the wide-eyed recruit.

The bewildered recruit only gaped foolishly.

"Grab what, sir?"

Before Sergeant Tatnall could reach the boy's rawboned bay the animal had sent an answering neigh beating across the pasture.

As if a mine had been touched off, the afternoon's stillness instantly became shattered. Equipment clashed, then followed the stamp and trample of many hoofs and the sound of heavy booted feet running.

"Mount up! Mount up!"

"Out o' my way!"

"Where's my hawse?"

"Hell's fire, where are they?"

"Dra-a-aw pistols!" Low-pitched but penetrating came Cary's command. His wiry figure collected itself, bent low over the pommel. Snatching out his own weapon, he gave Eclipse a gentle pressure with his calves.

The eight troopers hurriedly reslung their carbines and jerked out heavy Colt .44s, carried them in the "ready" position.

"All right, men! Follow me and for God's sake keep together."

The crackling of underbrush grew louder as the patrol broke into a trot slowed by fallen logs and tangles of laurel and Virginia creeper.

A branch snatched at Hubert Cary's hat. Was this only a foraging party? Or part of a cavalry screen thrown out before Jackson's rumored advance? Colonel Miles, holding Harpers Ferry, was desperately anxious to know.

As they burst from the edge of the wood the patrol raised a long, deep-chested shout very different from that shrill, yelping cry known as the Rebel Yell. At a hand gallop the Federals pounded out over the hayfield. Waving revolvers, they bore down on a plain, two-storied frame farmhouse.

Before the dwelling a small tangle of horses and men were milling in furious disorder.

"Oh, damn!" Cary straightened, uncocked his pistol. Yonder cavalryman who was vaulting into the saddle of a rearing gray horse was a Federal. More bluecoats appeared on the run, hastily mounted up and retreated rapidly down the valley.

A surge of disappointment swept Cary's being.

"Trot, ho! Walk, ho! Close in."

"Hi!" Tatnall began to yell. "What you buggers scared of? Come back, you dumblocks! Come back!"

Nevertheless more of the strange Union troopers, half

in and half out of their saddles, went racing off out of the far end of the farmyard. Their horses' hoofs left woolly yellow puffs of dust hanging in the still sunlight.

Even though Sergeant Raines trotted some distance down the road and kept waving his kepi in friendly salute, the surprised blue riders only increased their pace until they became lost to sight around the bend of a little rutted road leading down the valley.

A single horse remained hitched outside the farmhouse, and, just as Cary's patrol trotted up, a sergeant ran out and vaulted into the saddle. As if only now aware that the new arrivals also wore blue, the N.C.O. checked his obvious impulse to flee and, cantering up, saluted smartly.

The N.C.O. was huge and wore such a huge black beard that it quite eclipsed his top tunic buttons.

"Heyo, Captain. Sure scared the lights out o' us, sir."

"So I notice. What regiment are you?"

"Ninety-ninth Pennsylvania, sir. On reconnaissance duty."

A wide red scar running down the sergeant's cheek was clearly visible as he jerked his head toward the road down which his men had vanished.

"If you'll excuse me, sir, I reckon I'd better go and fetch 'em back."

"Very well," the red-haired captain nodded curtly. With disgust he noted a general disrepair of the Pennsylvanian's uniform. Some of his insignia, too, were missing. "What made you run like that?"

The strange sergeant's blue eyes shifted uncomfortably.

"Wal, sir," said he apologetically, "heard tell they's a lot of rebels hereabouts wearin' blue. I reckon the boys didn't figger on takin' no chances."

"Who was that yelling just now? Sounded pretty bad."

"Hawse fell on Ben Parker, sir; one o' my boys. Broke his leg. We was settin' it for him. They generally hollers a bit."

Cary dismounted and turned toward the pleasant vine-covered farmhouse. "Bring your men back directly."

"Yes, sir."

"Messy critter," growled Tatnall. "Still I allow even a good soldier can git tolerable messed up durin' a long campaign."

Once the rattle of the Pennsylvanian's hoofs died away down the road the patrol relaxed. Raines, dismounting, led his horse over to an object gleaming in the trampled dust.

It proved to be a heavy sterling-silver soup spoon. "Say, Cap'n, them boys seem to have takin' ways," grinned the Marylander.

"Bring that here." Frowning, Cary fingered the spoon. "What kind of business . . ." His voice died away. From behind a row of sunflowers back of the house had come a whimpering moan.

Slipping the spoon in his pocket, the Federal led his charger around into the farmyard. There a mongrel dog was snarling, lunging wildly at the end of his chain.

"My Gawd!"

"Mother o' Mercy!"

"God Almighty!"

Suspiciously regarded by a pair of fat Plymouth Rock

hens, a twelve-year-old boy with sunburned hands and legs awkwardly outflung lay sprawled face down in the thick yellow dust of the farmyard. From a deep wound in the top of his tawny head a shiny rivulet of blood was creeping toward a rut a few inches away.

Choking, Cary noted that one of the boy's bare heels was sagging slowly sidewise. Beside it a dusty blue kepi presented damning evidence. Everyone could see the trefoil insignia of the Second Corps of the Army of the Potomac stitched to its sweat-marked top.

For a full minute Cary's patrol gaped paralyzed, then a long-drawn wail from within the farmhouse roused the Federal captain and he barked an order which flung about the dwelling a cordon of men.

"Kaskel, you hold my horse," he directed a sandy-bearded Rhode Islander. "Take Tatnall's too, but mind Eclipse don't kick him."

Colt in hand, Captain Cary strode back across the sunlit yard, his wide mouth robbed of its gay half-smile.

"Please take care, sir," the first sergeant urged in a hoarse whisper while his broad thumb drew back the hammer of an issue Colt. "Something's mighty wrong in there, sir."

Cary made no reply. His attention was concentrated on a reek very like that of badly scorched steak.

"Oh God! O-Oh God!" From a half-open window at the back of the house floated such a cry as set the hairs on the back of Cary's neck to itching furiously.

"Kill me. I—— Oh-h-h—in the name of—merciful God— someone—kill——"

Coldly calm, Cary took up a position at one window,

signaled the N.C.O. Tatnall, pale brown eyes alert and anxious, flattened his angular body to the house and, with revolver raised, approached a second open window, his long Chicopee saber trailing behind him like an awkward third leg.

"Now!" Cary called and suddenly put his head through the window. At what he beheld his teeth locked with an audible click. He spun about.

"O'Leary! Thomas! Dismount and come here!" he barked. "Rest of you look lively. Shoot anybody who tries to get away."

To his last hour Hubert Cary never forgot the trembling old man they found lashed onto a heavy kitchen chair. When his tortured eyes fell on the blue shell jackets of the newcomers the ancient called down a stream of curses such as the Prophets of the Old Testament might have laid upon their enemies.

"Mother o' Mercy!" gasped Corporal O'Leary.

White as death beneath his tan, he helped lift the old man's charred feet from the pot of glowing coals over which they had been securely lashed.

"Unto the seventh generation may you and yours be accursed; may all that ye touch blight and wither away."

O'Leary crossed himself, warned, "Take care, ould gaffer, 'tis bad cess to call down curses on the innocent!"

The old man's head seemed bowed by an invisible overwhelming weight but he raised quivering eyelids, stared up into Cary's rigid features.

"So ye've come back, ye sons o' Satan!" A ghastly croaking laugh cackled. "It's to waste yer time again then. Ye can burn me by inches, but ye'll never learn where my money's hid."

The smoky, foul-smelling kitchen rocked before Cary's eyes. There were hard and cruel men in both armies, but this passed belief. If only he himself hadn't seen those damning blue uniforms.

Sergeant Tatnall, prominent Adam's apple moving forward and back, hacked at the binding ropes and then strode over to a wooden bucket to fill a dipper and hold it to the old man's twitching lips.

A look of bewilderment came over the graybeard's pallid, pinched features, and then mercifully he fainted.

Leaving O'Leary applying lard to the unconscious victim's feet, Cary prepared for a more careful search of the property.

"Must be one of 'em still round, suh," Sergeant Raines hurried in to report. "They's a hoss ready saddled in the barn, suh."

"Hope so. Come along—a couple of you."

Tormented by visions of that blue kepi beside the murdered boy, Cary cautiously made his way up a narrow stair. With boots creaking faintly and the rowels of his brass spurs making a little jingling sound he peered up onto the landing of the second floor.

A swift glance informed him that all the doors stood open save one. Pausing on the landing, he could see that the nearest bedroom was a scene of wild and senseless destruction. Furniture lay overturned in all directions. A slashed mattress had shed a litter of straw over the floor; bed sheets and a patchwork quilt formed a fantastic hurrah's nest in one corner, and a shattered stoneware pitcher still dripped its contents onto the floor.

The second and third bedrooms revealed similar scenes. There remained only one door—the closed one. Avoiding a possible line of fire, Cary tested its latch. It was locked.

"Anybody in there?"

Though there came no answer, Cary caught a subtle sound. Unmistakably someone *had* moved inside.

"Open this door or I'll break it down!"

From beyond the door panels still only a single small noise. The metallic *click-cluck!* of a firearm being cocked.

"Sergeant, come up here." Cary's gray-blue eyes narrowed and he wetted his lips. "Stand to the right. Kaskel, take the left. Raines, you cover the door."

"Hold on a minute, Cap'n," came Sergeant Tatnall's whispered plea. "He'll likely shoot through the panels."

Hubert Cary shook his head as he cocked his Colt then, bending low, he launched his full weight at the door. Under the impact of his shoulder the lock broke with such unexpected ease that he went stumbling headlong inside.

CAPTIVE

GRANTED a split second's warning that a figure had materialized in line with a window, Captain Hubert Cary instinctively flung up an arm. Nonetheless his face was buffeted by a blast which singed his brows and eyelashes. Powder particles stung his hands and cheeks. Dazed, all but deafened, and coughing heavily among fumes of burnt powder, he reeled back. Tatnall's rasping curses rang loud.

Must get in a shot, he knew, before the murderer could fire again. Half blinded by a swirl of smoke, he leveled the big Colt in line with his assailant's head.

So dimly seen through the billowing smoke was a crouching shape that Cary could never explain what stayed his finger on the trigger.

"Cap'n's hit!" yelled Kaskel as he and Sergeant Tatnall simultaneously burst through the door. They hampered each other so that neither could, for an instant, do anything.

Kaskel began tugging at his saber. "Lemme by! I'll kill that son of a bitch!"

"Out of my way, you fool," snarled the first sergeant. "I'll drill——"

"No! No!" Cary cried. "Don't shoot!"

"No? Why not, sir?" Tatnall panted. Then, "Well, may I be——"

Powder-blackened officer and dusty troopers alike remained panting in breathless astonishment. Sunburned heads outthrust, all three were staring into the eyes of a white-faced girl.

She stood pressed flat against the further wall with a tangle of pale yellow hair falling over her face. Her hair, reaching nearly to her waist, mingled with remnants of a white cambric blouse which hung in ragged tatters about her neck and arms. She seemed quite unaware that one shoulder and a breast were completely exposed and scarlet scratches were marking her forearms.

One hand hung at her side, still clutched a clumsy single-shot pistol. From its barrel blue-gray curls of smoke crept upward, clung to a wide black riding skirt.

"'At hellcat harm you, Cap'n?" demanded the first sergeant.

"I—all right——" But for all that, Cary's head was spinning and his ears ringing. By an effort Cary pulled himself together and stood gazing incredulously on that figure which seemed to be all white face and blazing black eyes.

"Why—ma'am, what did——" Mechanically Cary uncocked the Colt and fumbled the weapon back into a long holster over his right hip.

No reply came from the girl across the room.

Cary passed an uncertain hand over his scorched and blackened features.

"Hey, what's up?" Boots clattered on the stairs and a dusty blue and yellow wave surged into the room.

The girl's dark red lips writhed suddenly. "Get back!" she choked. "Don't any of you dare lay paws on me again!"

Cary motioned his men back. "You are mistaken, ma'am. We mean you no harm." As his head cleared still more an uncertain smile came to Cary's lips and a less deadly gleam shone in his gray eyes.

What a picture she presented, all disheveled like that. Yonder breast was a regular little rosebud, and what a lovely oval shape to her face. Slender, wide-parted brows seemed to hover over two of the stormiest brown-black eyes he had ever beheld. There was breeding in her bearing too.

He checked himself, jerked a stiff bow.

"We'll not harm you, ma'am. The—the others have gone. Believe me, they will be punished for this. My word on it. In the meantime——"

Aware of several red and brown faces grinning, crowding in the doorway, he caught up a towel from a washstand; he advanced, one placating hand outheld.

"Put this over your shoulders—your blouse—er—is——"

"Stand back, you—you *Yankee!*"

Curiously the yellow-haired girl seemed to grow taller and whiter—if that were possible.

"Stand back, I warn you!"

"Really, ma'am, you mistake——"

Barely in time Hubert Cary ducked as she flung the empty pistol at him in a final desperate gesture. The heavy weapon whirled past Cary's ear and, flying on across the room, shattered into a hundred tinkling fragments the glass of a polychrome "Rock of Ages" lithograph.

As the girl in the riding habit lunged toward a lamp with the obvious intention of hurling that also, Cary sprang at her. In an instant his arms were full of surprisingly strong softness. Her eyes, shaded by bluish lids, rolled and teeth, singularly even and white, glistened with her efforts.

"My Gawd! ain't *she* the little 'coon cat?" demanded a delighted voice from the doorway. "Watch out, Cap'n, she dun't chaw yer thumb."

"Please, don't be a fool!"

Cary imprisoned both of his captive's wildly clawing hands in one of his and found himself looking down into brown-black eyes dilated in stark terror. The scent of gardenias beat in his nostrils—warm gardenias.

Over his shoulder Cary snapped, "Tatnall, get these men downstairs—post pickets! Others may get reinforcements —come back. Be right down."

"Yes, sir."

The sound of the girl's spasmodic breathing became lost in a clumping of heavy boots on the stairs.

"Now, ma'am"—Cary's gray-blue eyes were very earnest and he spoke soothingly—"I know what you're thinking, and I can't blame you for it at all. However, you must believe me. I simply can't explain that first lot—and what they've done. You're making a mistake about us—we drove them off."

"You lie. You're all beasts! No decent woman can trust a *Federal!*"

His cheekbones suddenly gaunt and sharply outlined, Cary said quietly but without relaxing his grip, "You're judging nigh on two million men mighty hard, ma'am."

[27]

"I have reason to. Let me go."

Red hair grazing a ceiling of dull white plaster, Captain Cary gave a little shrug which lifted his shoulder straps an inch or two and stepped free. The gardenia fragrance of her hair, he noticed, still lingered among the brass buttons of his tunic.

He jerked out his Colt, deliberately presented it butt first. "Possibly you'd like to try another shot?"

Her hand shot out, hesitated and then drew back.

"The outrages which have occurred," he repeated gravely, "I simply cannot explain. I can't believe that regular Federal cavalry could commit such atrocities."

"Nevertheless they have," the girl replied in a toneless voice. Still ignoring the towel, she attempted to readjust the shreds of a fine cambric blouse. Listlessly she then pushed bright strands of hair away from her eyes, but not once did her glance leave the powder-blackened features of this square-jawed officer who seemed to fill so much of the room.

"Though I can't imagine you'll believe me," Cary resumed in a final effort to carry conviction, "I know absolutely nothing of what happened before we rode up. I am Hubert Cary, ma'am, commanding a detachment of the First Rhode Island Cavalry. We are on reconnaissance duty from Harpers Ferry."

"On reconnaissance!" Incredulity wrote itself large over the girl's ghastly pale features. "The same wretched lie your other Yankees told me. On reconnaissance for loot, plunder and——"

Cary cut her short with an impatient gesture. "Nevertheless, ma'am, I speak the truth. I promise you we'll stop at nothing to catch and hang the men who did this."

Her pale gold head jerked back in contempt. "That is easily said. Prove it by letting me mount my horse." The vivid lips tightened. "I believe your friends tied him in the barn."

"Very well."

"Better not do that," warned Tatnall from the foot of the stairs. "Please, Cap'n; this here valley's alive with rebs. She'll set the hull o' Loudoun County on the warpath inside o' half an hour."

"That will do, Sergeant."

Alarm raised the New Englander's voice. "But, sir," he urged, "we ain't yet spied hide nor hair o' Jackson's corps. If——"

Hubert Cary stalked to the door. Damn! Of course Tatnall was right. Yet—wasn't it wiser to free this girl and balk the spread of a tale of atrocity?

"Sergeant, fetch this lady's horse out of the barn. Kaskel, see if the old man has come to. I want to question him."

"Yes, sir."

On the landing below the two saluted and, leaving behind the aroma of horses, sweat and damp wool uniforms, they swung out into the drowsy afternoon sunlight. Perfectly audible in the sudden stillness was Tatnall's grumbling comment:

"Hanged if I'd mind anyone else. Lettin' that woman loose is the same as puttin' our goddam necks into a noose."

Silence continued in the bedroom. Cary stooped, mechanically righted an overturned chair.

"If I let you go," he inquired stiffly, "will you promise not to raise the country?"

The brown-black eyes glittered and color rushed back into smooth cheeks. "I will promise nothing. I only hope I'll live to see you and every other Yankee barbarian hanged higher than Haman."

Hubert Cary suddenly grinned, wiped the powder from his forehead. "That 'll call for a lot of trees, ma'am. Please consider yourself invited to my hanging. I'm told I hang very neatly."

She mustered a wavering smile. "I am being absurd." Bitterly she added, "Nevertheless, after today I shall never cease to hate everything Northern!"

The red-haired captain shrugged, strode over to the window.

"I see your horse is ready. No one will prevent you from riding away. I've only one suggestion. If you can find a doctor for the poor old——"

"Old Mr Calthorp," she supplied coldly. "I will try."

Cary caught up his sword in his left hand, and the spurs on his dust-speckled boots jingled when he turned to the door. At the threshold he bowed slightly and said, "I'm mighty sorry, ma'am, that you continue to hold such a bad opinion of us."

Long lashes swept down as she passed and she caught up the towel.

For the first time he saw the round black hole her bullet had made in the door jamb. It hadn't missed him by much, or Tatnall either. Queer. Unexpected little scrapes like this could kill a man as dead as a great smashing battle like Bull Run.

When he strode out again into the warm sunshine the chained dog, a shaggy black-and-white mongrel, snarled and snapped at him, but the hens went on scratching at a manure heap back of the red barn.

Vaguely he could hear Kaskel and Denby working over old Mr Calthorp, soothing him, trying to convince him that the First Rhode Island was guiltless.

"That ain't no proper way to store corn," Kaskel was stating. "Damned rebs don't know the first thing about farmin'. Now at my place down to Saugus——"

The girl's mount, a neat little cob, was dancing before the front door. How the devil had she, so obviously a lady, come to be locked, disheveled and terrified, in the farmer's upstairs bedroom?

Dismissing further conjecture, Cary busied himself with a quick examination of his patrol.

Under the captain's searching eye passed every shaggy hoof, fetlock and worn shoe.

"Saving Eclipse, sir, they look right tuckered," Sergeant Raines dubiously informed him. "Pore, cold-bred stock. Ain't no hot blood into 'em at all."

Gloomily Captain Cary nodded. "You're right, but I suppose an army horse contractor has the bounden right to get rich."

"Denby"—he turned to the recruit—"how's the old man?"

"As well as may be, sir, 'til a doctor comes. But—I—I'll see those feet 'til I die! What orders now, sir?"

"Ease your cinch and slide that saddle a mite further forward, two fingers behind the shoulder blade. Now, before the pickets come in, we'll water. By sundown we'll have a look into Snicker's and maybe Ashby's Gap, then——"

The sentence remained incomplete. The blonde girl had suddenly mounted and now was racing out of the farmyard. At a dead run she disappeared down the valley road.

"Plenty of nerve," mused Cary, eyes following the whirling dust. "What wonderful hair! Might have mentioned her name, though, after my *very* gentlemanly behavior."

Though the troopers grinned, the expression on Sergeant Tatnall's wrinkled brown visage would have soured milk.

"Ye've made a mistake, sir. I'll vow you have," he muttered. "She'll raise the country 'gainst us in short order."

Captain Cary abruptly aroused himself. "Somehow I don't fancy she will—when she cools down she'll see the right of things, shouldn't wonder.

"O'Leary, ride up and take a look over the end of yonder ridge. Raines, throw an eye into the next valley. Rest of you sponge out your horses' mouths and nostrils, wipe off their backs. In fifteen minutes we move."

Cary was well aware that coarse-bred horses, having covered twenty-five miles since dawn, should rest longer, but a stench of scorched flesh clung, leechlike, to the farmhouse. Over yonder the murdered boy's bare feet, projecting from beneath a log-cabin patchwork quilt, had become a focus of interest for hundreds of bluebottle flies.

Where, he demanded of himself in an effort to shake off a persistent uneasiness, would General Thomas Jonathan

Jackson's lean battalions likely be marching on this ninth
of September?

Colonel Miles, commander of the uneasy garrison at
Harpers Ferry, had heard them rumored now at Hagerstown, now at Martinsburg and again at Leesburg. Where
the devil were they *really?* Colonel Miles very much
needed to know. Since Lee's crushing victories at Fair Oaks
and Second Bull Run the Union commanders had remained mighty worried.

Leading Eclipse to a watering trough, he slipped off the
charger's bridle. Thank God, in less than five minutes the
patrol would be clear of this ghastly scene.

Would that yellow-headed girl raise an alarm or send a
doctor? Had she finally admitted that the second party
of Federals might have had nothing to do with the
first?

Kneeling, Hubert Cary vigorously massaged Eclipse's
slender legs, wondered what scouts from the Sixth Pennsylvania Lancers—on a similar reconnaissance—were finding north of the Blue Ridge. Surely, either he or they must
that day collide with some of the enemy.

At the sound of O'Leary's horse clip-clopping back from
the hillock his spirits rose. Someday that little Irishman
would make a jim-dandy sergeant. If only he could think
half as well as he rode.

"The valley, sorr, is quiet—like a churchyard at noonday.
There's niver a reb to spoil the scenery."

"Good. Sergeant, have the men mount up."

But even as Tatnall bawled, "Stand to horse!" and the
troopers prepared to swing up into rawhide-covered Mc-

Clellan saddles, a flat, staccato report rang out, echoed briefly among the mellow hills.

Raines was plunging back down the mountainside in a headlong hurry. At the top of his lungs he was yelling, "Get away! Whole troop o' rebs just over the ridge."

Already the patrol could hear a steady snapping of branches and the crackle of trampled underbrush.

"Didn't take that blasted female overlong," grunted Tatnall, but Cary was too busy to hear.

"Scatter!" Cary called instantly. "Scatter! Meet at the rendezvous!"

His patrol was so heavily outnumbered it could not possibly stand and fight with any hope of success, nor could most of these scrubby troopers' mounts win in a test of speed.

Young Denby, the recruit, stared about in round-eyed indecision. "Please, somebody—what shall I do?"

"Follow me, ye damned numskull—you can't fly away."

Whereupon Sergeant Tatnall set an excellent example by spurring off down the valley road at a dead run. The lazy air became filled with high-pitched yelping cries from the enemy as the blue scouts dashed off, some up the ridge, some across fields and a few down the Valley.

Conscious that his was the best horse and hopeful that by attracting the attention of the onrushing Confederates he might let more of his patrol escape, Cary reined in, remained in the center of the barnyard.

Weighing the consequences of each passing instant, the Union captain sat his mount and listened to the Rebel Yell grow louder.

Quivering, anxious seconds flashed by as he waited for a first glimpse of the attackers. He'd no intention of permitting this, his first expedition into the Valley, to end in disaster.

Gathering himself in the saddle, he watched something flash beyond a birch thicket. Followed a violent swaying of branches, then, as suddenly as if propelled from a gun, a bearded figure in a gray shell jacket burst into sight.

Supple-waisted, the Confederate—he looked like an officer—leaned so far forward that a rusty black plume whipping out behind a broad-brimmed felt hat mingled with the mane of the chestnut he bestrode.

"Surrender!" he shouted. "Stand and surrender!"

Hubert Cary delayed a few seconds longer, watching the other's headlong descent. How sharply a white blaze on that chestnut charger's face showed up among the green leaves and dark tree trunks.

"Give 'im the spurs, Johnny!" he hailed, standing in his stirrups. "Can't wait for you all day."

"With you in a minute, Yank," yelled the enemy officer.

"Sorry, you're too slow!" Copper-hued hair shining in the sunlight, Cary raised a yell, whirled Eclipse about and, settling well forward in the saddle, put his long-limbed charger at a snake fence enclosing the farmyard.

Eclipse cleared it with feet to spare and raced across a pasture between a couple of stupidly staring red cows.

"Hi! Hi! Gone awa-a-ay!" yelled the gray officer as though coursing a fox. Hubert Cary, risking a glimpse over his shoulder, saw that a stream of riders in gray and butternut jackets also were jumping the fence. They were bent low over their pommels, like jockeys.

His blood warmed, began to surge in his ears.

Reassured by Eclipse's easy, powerful stride, Cary sailed a rail fence bounding the pasture's far side just as the brown-bearded officer's chestnut pounded past the cows.

"Harkaway! There he goes! Ride him down!" Another, another and another of the pursuers jumped the snake fence and entered the field.

Mindful that he must not retreat too rapidly, lest these well-mounted Confederates seek easier quarry, Cary increased pressure on his reins.

His thoroughbred blood well heated, Eclipse bitterly fought restraint. When a rock ridge showed ahead Cary elected a road which went threading upward through a narrow gorge gouged from the side of the Catoctins.

Louder rose the yells of the pursuers, but Eclipse settled down, went surging along as though fresh from the stable. Furiously he fought for the bit.

"We'll let the Johnnies come a little closer," Cary gasped, "then show 'em what a Diomed can do."

Cary fled on between reddish rocky walls towering ever more sheer to either side until Eclipse checked so suddenly he was almost hurled from the saddle. A rock wall loomed ahead.

Wild-eyed, the Federal hunted an outlet. Hell's jangling bells, *there wasn't any!* He had ridden into a quarry, a cul-de-sac from which there could be no escape.

Even if he deserted his mount there wouldn't be time for him to scale the jagged walls penning him in.

To try to shoot his way out would be suicidal. Accordingly he reined in and with one hand was stroking the stallion's crest when half a dozen breathless gray troopers clattered into the cut.

An officer, the brown-bearded fellow on the blazed chestnut, spurred forward.

"Take it—suh," he panted, "that you wish to surrender?"

"I've no choice." Hubert Cary's tight smile successfully masked his rage. "Seems to be a few too many of you gentlemen."

The Confederate leader, a sad-eyed, middle-aged individual, nodded but kept his eyes on Eclipse.

"That, suh, is a mighty fine mount. Regret our little race got spoiled." The lieutenant, who wore a red-and-white-checkered shirt beneath his half-buttoned shell jacket, held out a hand.

"As it is, I will trouble you for that pistol."

Cary quickly noticed a difference from the expected soft Virginia accent even before the bearded leader announced quietly, "I, suh, am Lieutenant Coleridge Moss of Cobb's Geo'gia Legion. Whom have I the honuh of addressin'?"

Hubert Cary gave his name and regiment.

"Fortunes of war, suh," smiled the Confederate. "That is a trite consolation, I reckon, but it is the best I can think of right now. We all had better get back to that farmhouse. I must learn whether mah boys caught any more of you all."

THREE NOOSES

THE BEARING of Hubert Cary's captors underwent an abrupt transformation once the leather-faced enemy discovered the delirious old man, saw the evidence of torture. It didn't help matters either when old Calthorp began moaning, babbling disjointedly.

"Leave me, you Yank devils—ain't goin'—get money—— Oh Gawd! Gawd! My feet. Don't hurt me no more—can't tolerate——"

Stony-eyed, the Georgians pinioned Cary, paid not the least heed to his confident, then desperate, explanations.

"Misto', hangin's a heap too fine fo' you," rasped a gangling sergeant in an old beaver hat. "Rightly oughter give you the same dose as you gived the pore ol' man."

Hands tightly tied before him, the Federal was led before the bearded lieutenant. He sat rigid on a ladder-back chair with one hand grasping the handle of a large bowie knife. Somberly he ordered:

"Le's make no mistake, boys. Search him."

[38]

Wade Hampton's gaunt troopers searched him and laid on the marble-topped parlor table the silver spoon he had recovered in the barnyard.

"Suppose you explain that?" growled the Georgian.

"Oh, don't be fools!" Cary protested when a burly corporal grabbed him by the collar. "Neither I nor my men did what you think. Listen, for God's sake, listen! I tell you we only came across this farm twenty minutes ago—we drove away the brutes that did this."

"Hush yo' fuss, Yank. 'Tain't no use to lie," snarled a gap-toothed corporal, propelling Cary toward the door. "So come along to the party. We got two more o' you murderers dead to rights."

Cary wrenched loose, ran over to Lieutenant Moss. His sad eyes had turned a hard black, deadly in their expression.

"Sir, I demand to know. What do you intend to do?"

"What's generally done with murderers, I reckon," came the impassive response.

"Hang us?"

"You all deserve a heap worse," was the Georgian's impassive verdict. "I never did credit half of what I've heard against you Yankees—'til now."

Beads of horrified sweat began pricking Cary's forehead. Hang? He, Hubert Cary, was doomed to choke slowly, to die at the end of a rope? Preposterous! This Georgian could be, *must* be convinced of the truth.

Fighting down a sudden panic, Cary glanced out of the parlor window and could see Kaskel and a man called Cunningham being dragged, struggling, cursing and terrified, into the barnyard. Both were hatless, bruised and stripped to undershirts.

The dust flew about their legs as they fought to postpone the inevitable, but already their hands had been bound behind them. How brightly the sunlight glanced off the rebel sabers and carbine barrels. Half the Confederates remained astride their sweaty mounts.

The Georgian heaved himself to his feet. "Take this houn' dawg out, Corporal. Reckon we better get this business over with. We've got a long way to——"

"In God's name, sir," Cary burst out in fresh revulsion, "if you can't believe me—I—we—we are at least entitled to a trial—to a court-martial. You can't murder us in cold blood! Why, I——"

The big corporal's horny hand slapped him viciously across the mouth.

Lieutenant Moss said, without turning his fine shaggy head, "Hush yo' fuss. I've got eyes in my haid. I saw that spoon come out o' youah pocket."

"But it was found on the ground in the barnyard—my men picked it up before I went into the house."

Lieutenant Moss merely grunted. "Bring that polecat along, boys. Shut his lyin' mouth and string him up."

Only pitiless determination showed in those sharp sunburned faces about him. The long hair and tangled beards of the motley-uniformed riders accentuated their air of savagery.

The Georgian lieutenant, forcing a way through his mounted detachment, indicated a huge white oak shading the barn.

"Digby, boy, just you all shinny out on that limb. Lige Hunt, rig me some nooses. Corporal, you and fifteen men stand guard over these here murderers."

The swiftness with which Lieutenant Moss's orders were executed nourished Hubert Cary's despair. Of course all this was an illusion, a hideously real optical illusion.

Yet it was not.

A taste as of sulphur entered his mouth. He felt as though something unclean had crawled into his stomach and had died there.

Hemmed in by these fierce, stringy-bearded Georgians, there wasn't the least chance for escape.

He steeled himself to face reality. Inside five minutes he'd be swinging, shuddering below that oak limb; ambitions, hopes, dreams forever at an end.

Outrage darkened his wide cheekbones. This was an abomination. These men had no right to kill poor honest fellows like Kaskel and Cunningham. They'd committed no crime. Kaskel had a wife and three children.

"For God's sake, Lieutenant, don't murder my men!" he burst out in a desperate appeal. "We're none of us guilty. I swear we aren't. But if you must find someone to hang——"

"Stow yo' gab, Yank." A hatchet-faced sergeant cut him short. "You're all as guilty as Judas an' caught red-handed."

With an invisible hand squeezing his heart the red-haired captain watched a young Confederate hitch out along the oak limb. His gray breeches had been patched on the seat with Union blue, and he'd a rope's end gripped between his teeth.

Bits of bark came loose, fell in a small rain onto the dusty earth. The hens, interested, came waddling over.

What a foul, miserable way to perish. To die in the thick of a crashing cavalry skirmish was at least a shining way to go. No one could live forever. But this——

A chicken intently dusting itself squawked on barely escaping the progress of a barrel being rolled across the yard by a trooper whose toes were leaking out of one of his boots. Queer that during the final moments of his life a man should notice such foolish trifles.

Nothing romantic about this last act.

Accepting at last the certainty of death, Cary cast a glance at Cunningham and Kaskel. Kaskel, he noted, had been wounded. His shirt's left shoulder was soggy with bright red blood.

Tense in every muscle, the ex-farmer stood quietly now. He was looking steadily out over the gentle blue-green hills raising such a pretty barrier down the valley. Was he, in spirit, back on his own farm in Rhode Island, waiting for nothing more serious than the arrival of his cows to be milked?

Cunningham must be praying; Cary could see the soldier's ashen lips fluttering, though no sound could be heard.

"You've done nothing to be ashamed of," he called out when the further of the troopers swayed a little.

The doomed trooper looked up, managed a rigid grin. "I'll be all right, sir. I ain't feared o' no parcel o' nigger-murdering rebels."

"You'd better be!" snarled one of the gray executioners. "We're sending you to hell."

Trying to forget the efforts of that man astride the limb, Cary tried to fix his mind on the cavalrymen ringing him about. They weren't very soldierly appearing, these silent troopers. Their armament was exceedingly varied—for all they appeared to be a regular Confederate cavalry regiment. Into broad leather belts was tucked a weird assortment of bowie knives and pistols. For sabers these lean, brown-faced riders carried everything from Highland claymores to navy cutlasses.

Now three nooses were rigged, and dangled, reddened by the setting sun, like serpents uncoiled from the limb above.

The young trooper astride the limb tested his knots for a last time, and now he scrambled down and began dusting off his hands.

"Heyo, Misto' Moss, which one first?"

"That wounded one. Reckon he's fittest."

Lieutenant Moss moved over to stand erectly beside the barrel which had been set on end directly below the nooses. He drew his revolver.

"I'm sure mighty grieved and 'shamed," he stated in a low voice, "to know that Americans could commit such crimes. Proceed, Corporal."

"My God, Captain!" Kaskel strained toward Cary. "Make these fellers understand, can't you? Ain't there no way? Maria can't handle that farm alone; the kids are too little to——"

A blow in the mouth silenced the gray-faced trooper.

As through the shimmering fabric of a dream, Cary watched a pair of Georgians haul Kaskel to the upended

barrel. They had set a lard tub before it to serve as a step.
"Into Thy hands, O Lord."

A peaceful look suddenly relaxed the ex-farmer's sweat-bathed features. The setting sun wrought a glory upon them.

When tne burly corporal dropped a noose over Kaskel's head, began to adjust it, revolt seethed in Hubert Cary. A powerful semicircular swing with his shoulders tore his captors' hands from his arms. Raising a deep-chested yell, he charged.

Shouts rang out as Cary kicked one horse in the belly, then another. Outraged, the beasts reared and plunged. For a long instant no Confederate made a movement to check him.

Tight as his ropes had been tied, the red-haired captain was able to pick up a dropped carbine by its barrel. Clubbing it, he rushed about in a despairing fury. Headlong he hurled himself at the mounted groups, and they dared not fire for fear of killing each other.

He whirled the heavy piece over his head and brought its stock crashing down on the head of the Georgian who leaped toward him with a bowie gleaming blue-gray in his right hand.

Snarling, the graycoats closed in but as quickly leaped back. With his back to the farmhouse, Hubert Cary had become an elemental creature struggling for existence. Eyes deadly as bayonet points, hair tumbled over his forehead, the Federal gasped:

"Got lead in your boots? Come on."

A trooper in a frogged jacket sizes too small for him

dropped on one knee, sighted a carbine at the cornered captain.

At once Lieutenant Moss shouted, "Don't shoot—tek him alive!"

A shifting pattern of mouthing faces, sun-bleached beards, gleaming teeth, panting lips, wavered before Cary's eyes. By twos and threes the Confederates started forward but ducked swiftly aside when, with wide, terrific sweeps, Cary whirled the heavy Sharps' carbine at them.

Occasionally the Federal felt his weapon jar, strike some yielding object. Vaguely he sensed that figures were writhing on the ground.

"Get back!" Incisively Lieutenant Moss's voice dominated the melee.

Sweat stung, obscured Cary's eyes. His arms, with their circulation so hampered, felt as though hot wires, not muscles, manipulated them. He knew the Rebs would get him soon now. Then they'd hang Kaskel and Cunningham. But first he'd cost them some broken heads and arms and he'd put up the best fight possible. When the panting troopers gave back in obedience to their officer's command he momentarily lowered his carbine, stood glowering and fumbled to let some blood into his cramped wrists. As quickly he got an inspiration.

This carbine was loaded; must be! As the gray troopers gathered for a final rush he cocked and reversed the carbine. Holding it pistolwise in both hands, he leveled it at Lieutenant Moss's belly. The Georgians halted, frozen into odd, awkward attitudes.

"Take my man off that barrel!" Cary directed.

Lieutenant Moss shook his head. His eyes were clear, deadly, like a hawk's.

"Go ahaid, boys. Then hang these hyar butchers."

Rather splendid, that Georgian. Took a lot of nerve to talk thus looking down the muzzle of a desperate man's carbine.

Not a man of Moss's command stirred.

A yellow-bearded sergeant drawled, "Sho, Marse Coleridge, ain't no use seein' yo' killed for the sake o' hangin' three wuthless buzzards. Am I right, boys?"

"Sho' are, Lige."

Almost everybody looked down the road. A picket was galloping in, waving his hat. Where was Tom Blake? The rest of his men? Maybe they were mustering—if he could hold out a little.

"Friendly cavalry a-headin' this way, suh," he called. "An' comin' like a house afire."

More of the enemy! That last faint spark of flickering hope in Hubert Cary's being went out like a candle in a gale. Of course these other Confederates wouldn't be bound by the same consideration for Lieutenant Moss.

The Georgian must have read his thoughts.

"Reckon you all know what this means," he cried in harsh accents. "The Lord fails not to see the wicked punished——"

"Stand still!" Cary rasped. His hands were beginning to feel weak. He couldn't hold that carbine up much longer. He tried easing its butt against his thigh.

The rattle of hoofs on the valley road grew louder. Four

Confederates riding in advance of the main body came racing across the fields, their clean-bred horses skimming fences with the ease of jack rabbits clearing a fallen branch.

In desperation Cary clung to his feeble advantage, and held the Sharps' front sight waveringly on a tarnished breast button of the Georgian's weather-beaten gray tunic. They'd kill him in the end, of course, but by God, he'd take Moss with him. Subconsciously he was aware of newcomers reining in, yelling queries.

"What the blazes is this?" By his accent a Virginian was speaking. "Damn me, Tom, this don't look like the second act of a melodrama. Yank, you better put down that carbine. You might hurt someone an' get us mad."

Cary never moved at all, kept the terribly heavy carbine leveled at Moss.

All at once the flank of a bay horse became interposed between the Sharps' front sight and that twinkling button.

Hubert Cary let the Sharps sag—couldn't have held it up any longer anyhow.

The newcomer who had ridden his horse in to shield the Georgian was young, very dark haired.

Cary got a blurred impression of a sensitive young face outlined against the afternoon sky. It swung toward him, assumed an expression of ludicrous astonishment.

"My God! Am I seein' things or ain't I?"

"Suh, you will be seein' a hangin' right soon," cut in Lieutenant Moss curtly. "I will trouble you, please, to stand clear of my prisoner!"

The Virginian, sitting easily on his restless bay charger, made no move.

"I regret the necessity, sir, to remind you of yo' manners. It seems as if we have saved yo' life."

The Georgian flushed, bowed just a trifle. "Yo' pardon, suh. You are quite correct."

The voice was lost as more gray cavalry came clattering into the farmyard. A young authoritative voice demanded, "What's all this mean?"

From his position, half hidden among the Georgians, Hubert Cary could only tell that the latest arrival sat a gold-chestnut thoroughbred, that his uniform was new and fitted like a glove. On his head a black slouch hat sported a rakish jet ostrich feather which swayed to every movement of the rebel's high-strung charger.

The dark-haired officer laughed briefly. "Well, Craig, I'd venture this heah looks like a necktie party. Come heah an' take a look. It's the queerest thing ever. Cuss my eyes if this heah damn' Yankee don't favor that portrait in yo' house."

"Vance, reckon you been drinkin' again," replied the soft voice. A hand flickered up in salute.

Moss fell back, returned the courtesy.

"Afternoon, Lieutenant; see you've taken some prisoners. What corps?"

"They ain't soldiers, suh, just common killers—they done murdered a boy heah and tortured his grandsir." Moss called a command. Hubert Cary, disheveled and dirty as any tramp, was pushed forward.

"God in heaven!" gasped the Confederate in the new uniform. "Why—why—*you're Hubie!*"

The prisoner forced a pallid grin. "Just barely. How are you, Cousin Craig?"

[48]

The officer called Vance swore, slapped his thigh so hard that dust sprang from it. "No wonder he's the spit and image of old Colonel Redspurs!"

The officer Cary had called cousin jumped off his horse and ran forward.

"Hubie! You ornery old duck-dusker." Craig Carey flung an arm about the other's shoulder. "Good to see you back in the valley."

Gaping troopers of both commands grinned, scratched their heads and stared to see enemy officers vigorously pound each other on the back.

When Lieutenant Vance Chambers dismounted Craig Carey beckoned him.

"Vance, this reprobate's my cousin Hubie. He's all wool and a yard wide, even if he is a Yankee."

Sensitive features expressing a lively curiosity, the young lieutenant ripped off a gauntlet, offered his hand.

"Surely am honored, Captain. I've heard a lot about you, an' I trust——"

"How is Cousin Lovelace?" Craig Carey broke in.

"Last heard of, he was doing all right. He's serving as a shavetail in Rush's Pennsylvania Lancers. Might meet up with him someday."

The Southerner's smile faded. "I most certainly trust not. Though I'll admit we all have been wondering how a lance would stack up against saber and pistol."

"I wouldn't worry," Cary told him. "This country is too thick for lances—not like Europe—'specially in these parts."

"Yo' pardon, gentlemen." Lieutenant Moss, mighty

puzzled and definitely annoyed, came swinging forward. His weirdly garbed troopers, gathering in a determined knot about the other prisoners, eyed the well-dressed Virginian cavalrymen with disfavor.

"Suh, I greatly regret to convey news which I sense will be painful."

"Painful, sir?" Gold braid gleamed on Captain Craig Carey's forearms. Dark brown hair falling to his collar glowed as his head went back and his small spare figure stiffened. His chin lifted. "Nothing my cousin would do could cause me pain."

"Nevertheless, suh," Moss said steadily, "I must info'm you that this fellow and his command have committed some dreadful crimes."

"*Crimes?*" The Virginian captain's manner was painfully correct. "I fear, Lieutenant, you are laboring under a misapprehension."

Craig Carey nodded in the direction of the valley road. "A guest of ours we met riding down the road yonder has conveyed to us the fact that this, my cousin's patrol, surprised certain jayhawkers in a raid."

The Georgian's bearded jaw sagged. "Jayhawkers?"

Craig Carey remained coldly official. "Captain Cary freed her a few moments before you captured him."

"Then this heah Yank has been tellin' the truth?" Moss burst out.

"I reckon so, Lieutenant. This outrage has been committed by jayhawkers. Seemed to have adopted Yank uniforms this week—'twas ours last month. Over in Maryland there's been hell to pay and us to blame. We've had word Luke Archer has crossed over from West Virginia last week sometime."

His checked shirt bright in the afternoon sun, the Georgian stumped forward, flushed and embarrassed. Gravely he saluted Hubert Cary.

"I'm mighty sorry and I regret my error, suh." He stood straighter as he returned the Federal's revolver. "Rest assured, suh, I stand quite ready at once to afford you the satisfaction one gentleman owes another."

Hubert Cary's grimy visage relaxed.

"No, Lieutenant, that would be a damned unsporting way to accept a gentleman's apology." He hesitated, then added, "However, if you still feel you owe me er—a—well, reparation, I'll ask a favor."

"Name it, suh," earnestly invited Lieutenant Moss. His aquiline features more resembled those of a preacher rather than those of a warrior.

"Permit me to surrender my men and myself to my cousin's command."

The Georgian's long black hair swayed over the sweat-stained yellow velvet decorating his collar. He bowed with quaint old-world dignity.

"It will be an honuh and a pleasure, suh, to make so triflin' an amend fo' my error." He saluted again. His men looked resentful when he added, "I shall be glad, suh, to include yo' side arms an' that noble-lookin' hoss."

He cast a quick glance at Craig Carey. "I reckon I must keep these troopers' mounts and equipment. We-uns are pow'ful sho't."

"You're welcome to the mounts," Hubert Cary said

with a short laugh. "You're not getting much. Won't you untie my men? They won't try to get away."

So promptly were Lieutenant Moss's orders carried out that the Georgian detachment was ready to resume its march by the time Captain Craig Carey's command had dismounted.

CHAPTER FIVE

THE PLANTATION

TO CAPTAIN HUBERT CARY, U.S.A., it seemed
weirdly familiar to stand once more in Philomont's
oak-paneled library. Yonder were the familiar portraits
and the rich, gold-tooled calf bindings of hundreds of
books. Not a few of them had been brought from England
by the first Lovelace Carey who, back in 1677, had fought
to carve for himself a barony among the wilds.

How many pleasant memories were not conjured by
these soft Virginian voices saying, "Your very good health,
suh"? Old Jonadab filled a succession of slender-stemmed
glasses so rapidly it seemed that the cellars of Philomont

[53]

had not yet felt the effects of a blockade which must soon curtail so many pleasant things.

The gray, gold and yellow uniforms, the bright sashes and brighter spurs of these latter-day Cavaliers, however, struck a discordant note to his memories. For all their eye-filling glitter, uniforms didn't belong in the serene and comfortable pattern which was truly Philomont.

Let this glitter flash as long as it could, Hubert Cary reflected; if the struggle lasted another year, there would be precious few smart uniforms, fewer rich wines and no more savory roasts for Virginians.

Already the bloom was off the adventure of war. Around the sideboards of a thousand similar plantations old men's eyes were beginning to peer out of young men's faces.

Strange, Cary mused, absently fingering an ornately bound volume of Washington Irving's *Sketch Book,* he had always felt more at home here at white-pillared Philomont than in Pa's neat brick mansion on College Hill. Why?

Maybe Esek, his sober elder brother, was right when he had observed, "Hubie, I declare you're a throwback to the Cavaliers. There's not a practical notion in your whole head."

As he lifted the cover of a Lowestoft bowl of potpourri and sniffed its sweetly acrid odor it struck him as amazing that Cousin Craig, 'Lissa and Little Grandma Suzanna had succeeded so thoroughly in making him forget that he was a prisoner.

Their reception had warmed, had raised his bitter mood. Always he would remember Little Grandma Suzanna's gray moiré silk rustling across the Aubusson carpet. Frail, blue-veined hands had extended themselves from frills of fine lace to draw him close. Why, she'd been as cordial as if he'd been really near kin rather than a distant Northern relation.

"You are always welcome, Hubert, no matter the color of yo' regimentals."

Fine gold chains around the old lady's neck and a pair of very long pendant jet earrings had quivered.

Melissa had lingered, obviously aware of the charming picture she made poised between tall white columns flanking the entranceway. There had been tears in her great eyes though, and she'd looked very sweet in a sky-blue taffeta gown banded in narrow black velvet.

"That was all fo' you, Cudden Hubie," she'd confessed, smoothing a matching blue bowknot in her dark hair. "Ain't you flattered?"

"Lord, 'Lissa, I'd clean forgot how pretty you girls grow in the Valley," he'd cried as she rushed down onto the drive to clasp hands about his neck.

For a little Craig's sister had laughed and cried and "carried on" as Little Grandma had declared. Then, quite the young lady all at once, Melissa had drawn back to arm's length, had examined him, made eyes.

"You ain't changed a mite. My, but you're handsome, Hubie. Reckon you did pick the right color fo' yo' uniform. Blue certainly sets off that red head of yours better than gray."

"Auburn, my dear," mildly corrected Little Grandma.

Then she had turned to greet a succession of lithe, sun-burned young officers who came riding up.

"It is red," insisted Melissa, making a small *moue*. "Tell me, Hubie, has this awful war changed us very much?"

"Only for the better," he'd declared. "Little Grandma looks younger, you're a sight prettier—and perter. Only Craig looks—well, different."

"La, Craig *is* changed," Melissa had sighed, rolled her eyes. "You know what love is—or don't you?"

"'Course Hubie does," sniffed Little Grandma. "It's written big as life all over the gawky length of him."

"What! Craig's in love?"

Leading the way indoors, Craig had flushed, had shaken his head. "To no avail so far. I entertain hopes, however, that the lady someday must weaken."

"Hopes are all that Craig ever will have," Melissa had added. "You're a sight too sobersides, honey. Too gentle, if I do say it. What Lenore wants, needs, is a—a——" She fumbled for the word.

"Beau sabreur?" was Little Grandma's prim suggestion.

"Yes, that's it," Melissa giggled. "Somebody romantic, somebody who—who'll rush her off to the parson!"

Craig hadn't liked that much, Hubert recollected.

"Reckon Miss Duveen's too schooled, too experienced fo' a Virginia farmer——"

"Planter," Melissa corrected.

"Same thing."

"You'll see for yourself, Hubert, before long."

Yes, the warm affection of his cousins had made this pause at Philomont so pleasant, so natural that he felt, in effect, an honored guest rather than an enemy and a prisoner of war.

Mustn't delude himself though. To the rest of this hard-riding gentry he was just as much a prisoner as Kaskel, Cunningham, Sergeant Tatnall and poor little Denby, who also had been rounded up by Cousin Craig's wiry troopers.

And still Jackson's men hadn't been located. Great God! Back in Harpers Ferry the C.O. would be having fits. *Where was* Jackson? Neither Moss nor his cousin seemed to be under Jackson's orders.

For the present there was nothing to do but be pleasant. Maybe when the great white and yellow mansion grew still he'd make a stab at trying to reach that corncrib in which his Rhode Islanders lay imprisoned. It didn't help matters that the crib was located near the center of the rebel bivouac.

When he wandered into the billiard room Cousin Craig and the officers of Troop B, Third Virginia Cavalry, seemed wholly absorbed in a discussion of some obscure skirmish. Attracted by the twilight's cool, he stepped out onto the deep carpetlike lawn of a terrace back of Philomont.

A catbird was calling drowsily from a row of magnificent boxwoods, a lonesome dog barked down in the quarters and, nearer at hand, crickets chirped among the rose roots. Now that Jonadab was circulating a second bowl of bombo, voices in the billiard room sounded more argumentative, higher pitched.

Why hadn't Craig demanded his parole? Was it cousinly consideration, or did he imagine the escape of a lone Federal impossible?

Troubled and once more immeasurably depressed, Cary moved out over the terrace to where the old mansion's upper windows sketched a succession of bright emerald-hued squares across the grass. Wearily he sank onto a stone bench, felt the chill strike through his breeches. What he'd give for a real bath, a change of linen and twelve hours of unbroken sleep.

Down yonder, behind the stables, sounded the familiar noises of a cavalry troop preparing to mess. Lost in thought, Cary did not at first notice the slender, full-skirted figure which appeared, remained framed in a doorway opposite.

He jumped up suddenly as if the stone bench had started to collapse under him. It couldn't be! Yet it *was* the girl of Calthorp's farm.

Even while he gaped incredulously she, quite unaware of his presence, stepped out onto the terrace. After all, was it so strange that this stately blonde girl should be here? Philomont was the center of social life in this part of the county. There were no villages, no resorts.

Cary remained motionless and could have cursed when some slave lit a lamp indoors which, with its yellow-red glare, picked him out of the darkness.

A slim hand flickered to the cameo pin at her breast. "Oh, please excuse me—I—I didn't see you at first."

"I'm sorry to have startled you," he apologized, smiling. "When I first saw you come out I was so surprised I, well, I couldn't speak."

"Surprised? Why should you be?" she demanded curiously. Wide skirts asway, she advanced, peering at him through the dusk. A firefly circled about her head, lit in her hair, clung there—a pallid starlet.

"I imagine you can't have recognized my uniform, ma'am —or me."

Another lamp began to flare inside the house, to cast its sudden radiance across the terrace. It revealed his faintly sardonic expression and picked out her face framed by pale golden hair. A straying curl gleamed amid the gloom bright as the buttons on the Federal's shell jacket.

He heard her breath escape with a short rushing sound. "You!"

Beneath his tan Hubert Cary flushed. Tall and dignified, he made her a little bow, started to turn away.

"Why are you leaving?" she inquired in a low voice.

"I believe my presence cannot be agreeable to——" he stated formally, then realized how idiotically pompous his explanation sounded.

She ignored the implied question. A distant mocking-bird began to imitate a song sparrow's notes as, crossing the terrace, she halted by a rosebush to finger a great pallid blossom.

"Tell me, Captain Cary," she queried suddenly, "do you really fancy being alone?"

"Why do you ask, ma'am?"

He saw her teeth flash. "Because I have heard to the contrary."

His wide mouth parted in a smile; quite a girl, this with her poise, her dignity. The way she carried her small bright head was fascinating.

"Not as a rule, ma'am," he admitted, moving to maneuver her into the lamplight. "I guess I was trying to get used to the idea of being a prisoner. You see, it isn't exactly a familiar feeling. Feel stupid, ashamed——"

"There is no cause for that," she interrupted quietly.

"I wasn't really clever," he insisted, "or I wouldn't have been taken. Feel kind of, well, inferior with no side arms—no——" He left the sentence unfinished.

The girl in white sauntered over to the edge of the terrace, bent a graceful neck to sniff a white rose no paler than the fingers with which she steadied it.

"I understand. This terrace *is* conducive to meditation. Why not continue?"

He took a step toward the door, then paused. It was the condescension in her tone which checked him.

"You are very gracious, ma'am. Under the circumstances, however, I can imagine two good reasons why you might prefer to be alone."

He felt brown-black and faintly oblique eyes seek his. He sensed, rather than saw, her small bright mouth tighten in a quizzical half-smile.

"Indeed, Captain, why should I?"

"First, and most obvious, I am an enemy. Contrary to Cousin Craig, I have no reasonable claim on your sympathy. You *are* Miss Duveen, aren't you?"

She nodded, remained quite still a moment studying the dancing fireflies. "And this second reason?"

"What happened this afternoon. I scarcely imagine you can have forgotten the incident."

A small hand, tied at the wrist with a narrow black velvet ribbon, flashed upward in an involuntary gesture.

"Of course not." Her rich voice quivered. "I'll never forget today 'til I die." She looked away suddenly. "It was sickening—horrible!"

Again he marveled at her self-possession, was amazed the she should have appeared at all. Most girls would be in bed right now, indulging in hysterics and surrounded by distracted relatives, anxious doctors and spirits of ammonia.

Suddenly she faced him and said softly, "Please believe me I feel dreadfully about having misjudged you."

She held out her hand and Cary bent low over it. He was greatly tempted to kiss it, but New England was too strong in him. "You had sound reasons to think as you did."

The escaped curl on the Duveen girl's neck glistened when she shook her head. "If I hadn't been so upset I imagine I would have realized the truth in a minute. So

[61]

you are wrong, Captain, on at least one count." Her eyes met his steadily. "I—I don't hold this afternoon against you. On the contrary——"

For the life of him he couldn't tell whether she meant something more than her words implied.

"Thank you," he replied gravely. "Unfortunately you still can't deny that I'm a Federal—and therefore an enemy."

"Dear me, Captain"—she turned again to the rosebush—"you seem almost determined that I shall hate you." A laugh rich as the ring of a gold coin dropped on a marble floor rippled out. "You are wrong in that respect also."

"Eh? You're not Northern? Can't be!"

"No, Captain, I am English."

Warm relief flooded Hubert Cary's being. Lord! Here *was* a piece of luck!

"English!" He hesitated. "Look here, you're not funning me? You don't talk like an Englishwoman—not much, that is."

Lenore Duveen laughed lightly and, amid a swirl of wide skirts, seated herself on a broad stone wall overlooking the lily pool.

"I presume it is because I have lived almost all my life in America. Papa is a tobacco buyer. He conducts a business near Sharpsburg—a village in Maryland. Affairs keep him in the States the better part of each year."

Said he, tanned features gilded and in strong relief, "Officially, then, we won't have to hate." He grinned.

"I really couldn't have—not after you saved my life."

Wide-set brown eyes for the first time regarded him with uncertainty.

"I *saved* your life? Why I did my level best to—oh dear—to kill you!"

He seated himself on the stone wall beside her. The lamplight created sudden coppery high lights in his hair and touched with fire the gold buttons of his campaign jacket. It also brightened a broad yellow stripe descending breeches of light blue.

"True enough," he admitted lightly. "On the other hand, if you hadn't galloped off to tell Cousin Craig about the affair, I'd have been most unpleasantly hanged by an obstinate Georgian who dispersed my patrol just after you —er—left."

Finger tips crept up, pressed her cheeks. "They—they were going to *hang* you?" she demanded, round-eyed.

"Yes. Seemed very earnest about it too." He laughed a little. "Funny, remember I invited you to my hanging? Hadn't figured on the entertainment so soon though. Anyhow, Cousin Craig arrived and spoiled the party."

"War is so—dreadful, so ugly. And I used to think it all brass bands, smart uniforms, parades and cotillions."

A fresh burst of laughter from inside the great house seemed to belie her statement.

"Ever notice," he asked, picking a half-opened flower from the stone wall, "that 'most everything enjoyable in this life is a direct contrast to something we don't enjoy?"

"In other words, '*Chaque médaille a son revers!*' Deep philosophy for a captain of cavalry," she mocked, smoothing the billows of her white skirt. "It seems that the cavalry, as well as a medal, has its reverse side. Oddly enough I have always pictured cavalrymen as bold, reckless fellows never thinking seriously about consequences or anything else."

Cary jerked a little bow, confessed, "You're pretty near the mark at that, Miss Duveen—so beware."

"Should I?"

"Well, we've just been through a mighty unpleasant six weeks down on the James, and most of us are fairly starved for the sight of a lovely girl."

Unsuspected mischievous glints sparkled in her brown eyes. "Sight? La, sir—if you're satisfied with that much, you Federals must be different from the Confederate cavalry."

"That was only a *pourparler,* as the French say." He bent, offered the flower. "Really, Miss Duveen, it's quite extraordinary. Why, when I first laid eyes on you——"

"You were half blinded with smoke." She jumped up. "Heavens, you *are* a real cavalryman. No pretty speeches—not before dinner at least."

"Fair enough." Hubert Cary hesitated and then burst into a chuckle. "Good lord, do we have to go indoors?"

"In a moment, surely."

Hubert Cary tried to keep his voice casual. "By the way, Miss Duveen, do I understand correctly that you and Cousin Craig are—er—contemplating?"

Lenore Duveen's slender brows rose, met.

"Were you not Craig's cousin, I should consider that an impertinence." She twirled the flower, held it up for a firefly to settle on. "But since you are, I will tell you we are excellent friends—but for the moment no more." Pursing soft dark-tinted lips, she blew away the insect.

"Yes," she sighed, "I am fond, very fond of Craig—but that is all—*merci*. Therefore I can still tremble before, and defy, your cavalry tactics as much as I please. Unfortunately I am at the end of my visit with Melissa."

"But," he protested, "you can't go. How am I to develop my grand strategy?"

"No, *Monsieur le Chasseur,* I must go," she declared softly. "I really must, though I don't want to. I am to visit distant relatives of Mama's in Salem—provided the railroads are still running."

"Then my campaign must be quick and direct."

She burst into sudden laughter. "I declare, Captain Cary, you do me a world of good! Why is the art of nonsense so near unknown in the South? La, how very solemnly these Southern gallants vow and protest a dreadful eagerness to die in all kinds of horrid ways—just to win one smile."

Opening, a french door flung a flood of light across the terrace. Melissa Carey came out with her brother swinging along a step or two behind.

Melissa rushed forward, slipped her arm through Hubert's. "So here you are. Laws! Craig was beginning to fear you had run off with Lenore."

Golden braid on Craig's light gray sleeves sparkled as he bent to kiss Lenore Duveen's tapering fingers.

" 'Pears like you and Cousin Hubert have explained matters," said he. "We could hear you all laughin' 'way inside the house."

Lenore Duveen flushed a little. "Success came late. At

first I was having a dreadful time to prevent your cousin running away from me."

"From *you!*" Craig chuckled. "That sure 'nough stamps Hubie as a E-less Cary."

"E-less?" Lenore demanded. "What do you mean, Craig?"

Melissa giggled. A jest of long standing seemed to be forthcoming.

"You see, Lenore, 'way back in 1759 when our great-great-granddaddies got mad at each other, Lovelace Secundus Carey went off up to Boston. Took on Yankee ways, of course, and got stingy-like; he dropped the E out of his name." When he sighed the odor of good corn whisky became mingled with the drowsy rose perfume. "That's how you can always tell a Northern Carey from a Southern. But I will admit as far as Hubert and his brother go, it's the only way."

"A neatly turned compliment." Lenore Duveen clapped hands. "Old King Carey himself couldn't have turned a prettier." She checked herself, peered intently at the Federal as he stood teasing Melissa about her hair-do.

"My word, Craig, I—why, I've *just* noticed! Doesn't your cousin look the image of that portrait of King Carey, the one they called—— Oh, bother! What is his nickname?"

"Colonel Redspurs," Craig replied.

"Why Redspurs?"

"I expect 'twas on account of he rode so hard playin' the devil with the British and—the ladies. Vance Chambers just now spoke of the resemblance too. Strikin', ain't it?"

"An' from what I hear, Cudden Hubie takes after Gre'tgrandpa in more than looks," Melissa declared. "I declare, Hubie, you surely are old Redspurs come back to earth. Jenny Fraser from Washin'ton has written tellin' us 'bout the cruel way yo' made their poor hearts flutter."

"Colonel Redspurs? Um-m." Lenore Duveen tested the name, tilted a pale gold head to one side. "I do believe, Craig, the name suits Captain Cary to a T. Personally, I shall use it—what with all you Careys about Philomont it's hard for a girl to remember which one is which."

Hubert Cary's shoulder straps glinted faintly as he bowed.

"I shall be deeply honored, Miss Duveen. But suppose I can't do the original Redspurs justice?"

"Don't you listen," warned Melissa. "Really, Lenore, you should have heard that gabby Jenny Fraser gossip about Cudden Hubert's doin's."

"I wonder, Craig." Melissa arched questioning brows. "Do I detect a soft light in Lenore's eye?"

"Only a light to dazzle her victim," Craig chuckled. "And now come on, all of you. Vance Chambers is gettin' ready to sing 'Jine the Cavalre-e-e,' so I reckon dinner's about ready."

As Craig tendered his arm to the Duveen girl a voice, loud with liquor, rang across the wide shadow-ruled terrace.

"Damn it, you're wrong, Joe! You're all wrong, I tell you. I ain't on 'Beauty's' staff without knowing."

"Nonsense," another voice contradicted. "I tell you Jackson *must* cross at Point of Rocks——"

Craig Carey checked his loose cavalryman's stride, turned, began a joke—but the people inside talked too loud.

"No, dammit," the first speaker was heatedly insisting. "Jackson's to swing down from the North—by way of Martinsburg. I saw the orders, I tell you. McLaws and A. P. Hill have been ordered to carry Maryland Heights. Walker's to——"

Little icicles stung Hubert Cary's temples. Good God! He tried to listen over Melissa's soft chatter, heard a third voice, sharp with annoyance, cut in.

"Quiet, Chew, yo' are talkin' out o' turn."

Instantly Hubert Cary was brought tumbling back to realities. Quite evaporated was that bright spell with which Lenore Duveen had lulled his bitterness. Must pretend not to have heard. Craig was studying him mighty hard.

He said, "'Lissa, you should have seen the French ambassador's wife! Looked like a green salad when Mr Stanton inquired whether they'd bathtubs in France!"

In letters of fire Chew's words burned themselves into Cary's memory. He could visualize the simultaneous onslaught of those magnificent gray divisions; right now the finest soldiers that had ever trod the soil of North America. Jackson rushing down on Harpers Ferry from the North; McLaws and A. P. Hill surging up from the South and East; Walker—from what direction would his veterans strike?

Great God above! Harpers Ferry was about to be cracked in a steel ring. He must get away.

Laughing, teasing Melissa all the while, he began to plan. When they approached the door and the ladies preceded them Craig Carey fell back a step.

"Maybe you overheard what Billy Chew said, maybe you

didn't," he muttered. "I regret I must warn you that if you try to escape—my pickets—well, they have already been ordered to shoot *any* prisoner who attempts to escape.

"I trust, Hubert"—the sensitive features quivered momentarily—"yo'll not put them—or me—to such a—such a necessity."

CHAPTER SIX

THE PENNSYLVANIANS

CONVINCING, if mechanical, was the interest with which Hubert Cary followed the lighthearted conversation flickering across the fine old mahogany dinner table. When they were not lingering on Lenore Duveen Cousin Craig's eyes were forever studying him, asking silent questions. The English girl, gay as if no danger had ever threatened, directed the conversation of these hard-bitten young men to safe neutral channels.

Jackson, McLaws and A. P. Hill; Jackson, McLaws and A. P. Hill. In a compelling, harrowing refrain the three names beat at Cary's brain. He must get away somehow.

God above, he *must*. The fate of thirteen thousand Union troops might well lay at hazard.

Inexplicably he sensed that these soft-spoken officers were well aware that he'd overheard Captain Chew's incautious statements. His ears, well trained to such details, presently detected the sounds of pickets being posted in a double cordon about the plantation house.

Cousin Craig, it seemed, intended to be as good as his word.

Jackson, McLaws and A. P. Hill.

While replying to Melissa's lazy raillery he decided that Little Grandma Suzanna—Craig's and Melissa's great-grandmother—was the only entirely comforting person in this gleaming, time-mellowed dining room. To his relief the ancient lady's humor remained sharp and bright as a new knife. Fragile and petite in gray moiré silk and rose-point fichu, she seemed wordlessly to converse with him.

"My dear," she declared to Lenore Duveen, sitting at the prisoner-guest's right, "I vow I will never forget the first visit Hubert made to Philomont. He was the biggest, longest-legged, reddest-headed rascal a body ever laid eyes on." She beamed across the napery. "Blessed if he wasn't dead-set to straddle every colt on the place right off; nearly broke his neck doin' it. Course 'Lissa set her cap for him then and there——"

All six gray-clad officers threw back their heads and laughed; Melissa blushed to the roots of lustrous blue-black hair.

"La, Little Grandma, you'll be makin' me out a regular heartbreaker, and I'm not, am I, Hubie?"

[71]

Hubert, making the expected reply, became aware of the Duveen girl's secret amusement.

"Nonsense, 'Lissa," continued Little Grandma, taking a sip of madeira, "you've been a flirt and a shameless trifler ever since you could stand up in your crib."

She turned faded gray eyes on Hubert again. "Yes, yes, you remind me a heap of your uncle George. He was a throwback to the E-Careys too." She sighed a little. "Dear George always drank too much, gambled too much and ruffled too much; but he was a sweet boy, and everybody down here doted on him. I trust he is well, Hubert?"

"He's tolerable, Little Grandma, and he often speaks of you."

Jackson, McLaws and A. P. Hill.

"Good lord, Mis' Suzanna," broke in Chambers with a wry smile, "yo' don't seem to set much store by the E-Careys. Soon you'll have Miss Duveen, heah, thinkin' we don't do anythin' in Loudoun County but race, gamble and enjoy life."

"I don't reckon you do," came the old lady's placid admission, but her smile robbed the assertion of any sting. "You do those things right well though. Eh, Miss Duveen?"

"Most charmingly!" Lenore Duveen's white teeth flashed. "I have been wondering, Colonel Redspurs, where you found that handsome horse of yours? Didn't—er—lift him down on the Peninsula—along with all those poor girls' hearts?"

Hubert grinned. "Not Eclipse. Uncle George gave him to me."

"Eclipse?" Amid a perceptible stir Lenore Duveen studied him with fresh interest.

Captain Chew burst out, "Eclipse? Sho'ly, suh, he don't trace back to American Eclipse who raced back in '23?"

"He does, Captain, straight back. I have his papers in Boston."

Jackson, McLaws and A. P. Hill!

My God, what can I do? When? How?

Little Grandma settled back in her Chippendale chair, fragile, blue-veined hands gently caressing the lustrous mahogany of its carved arms. Two spun-silver locks of hair trembled over her wrinkled temples.

"Eclipse? Eclipse? Mercy, how that name does carry me back! Wasn't it American Eclipse old Colonel Ambler fetched down from the No'th to race against Sir Henry?"

"Yes ma'am," agreed a chorus.

"If an old lady's memory still isn't tricking her, weren't Eclipse and Sir Henry both descended from the peerless Diomed?"

A handsome young captain with black hair falling to broad shoulders pushed back his chair. He raised a glass and bowed to Little Grandma.

"Ma'am, ladies and gentlemen, I rise to offer a toast to which we can all drink—to Diomed, greatest thoroughbred that has ever put hoof to the sod of the United—er—to the sod of America!"

Braid flashed, buttons glinted, faces bent forward, became briefly gilded by the candelabra's waxen cluster. The seven officers drained their glasses.

Jackson from the North, McLaws from the East, A. P. Hill from the South, Walker *from whence?*

"Sho' now, Craig," 'Lissa exclaimed, "you must remem-

ber? Yo' Moon Gold is descended from Sir Henry. Laws!
Ain't it funny that Eclipse and Moon Gold should be
stabled in the same barn?"

"It's a cryin' shame we can't race 'em," complained
Vance Chambers. "Why does there have to be a war?"

"Yes, why?" sighed Lenore Duveen. Then deep red lips
curved in a provoking smile. "If they could race, I should
bet on Colonel Redspurs."

Melissa sat up, stuck out her tongue. "No, you don't! I
won't let any other girl bet on Hubie. Only me!"

Little Grandma laughed, thrust aside a Coalport dessert
plate. "I declare, 'Lissa, you *are* a brazen piece. And as for
you, Miss Duveen, I don't know as I fancy yo' callin' Hubert
after wicked Colonel Redspurs. By all accounts, he was
nothin' but a rake and a devil with the ladies. Now Hubert——"

"—Is only a chip off the old block," supplemented Craig.

Hubert Cary flung up hands in a gesture of surrender.

"One more toast!" called Vance Chambers, pushing
back his chair. "Gentlemen, please fill yo' glasses."

Melissa, Craig and one or two others looked uneasy.
Would Chambers be tactful? The usual concluding toasts
were not of a nature generally pleasing to such a guest's
ears.

"Gentlemen"—young Chambers arose, lifted his glass—
"I give you our charming English guest, that queen of
hearts, worshiped throughout Virginia and Maryland.
Gentlemen, to the Golden Diana!"

Six figures in gray and one in blue leaped up, raised
sparkling goblets. Cary's hand quivered as he set lips to

the fragile glass. Tom Blake's angry voice came back to him. The Golden Diana! Well, he'd be damned and double-damned. Wasn't at all as he'd pictured her. No wonder she'd dashed so many hopes with a self-possession such as hers.

Didn't this beat the Dutch? Blake was right. She seemed a mighty cool and distant proposition. Ten dollars? But as she herself had said, she "understood nonsense." A kiss with her, then, didn't mean a be-all and end-all as to a Southern girl.

At an imperceptible signal from Little Grandma the young ladies rose amid a silken whisper of skirts and petticoats. In passing, Cary wondered whether Lenore Duveen did not cast him a swift smile as she swept out into the living room.

Still grouped about the table, the men relaxed, lit long black cheroots and, after sedulously avoiding the topic for a

few minutes, drifted inevitably into a comparison of Union
and Confederate cavalry tactics, equipment and functions.
Twice Craig Carey tried to steer the talk to a safer subject.

"Last time I saw you, Hubie," he remarked, long legs
thrust out before him, "you were tellin' about a fellow who
wanted to duel you."

"Duel me?"

"Yes. A classmate or something. You know, the fellow
you beat out for cadet captain at the Point."

Hubert Cary stared away over his wineglass.

"You mean Joyce MacKenny." He nodded to himself.
"Well, we never did duel—he got ordered away."

The Northerner spread broad brown hands. "Pity Mac-
Kenny's so all-fired ambitious he acts a little cracked when
anyone gets in his way."

"When a mean man gets set with a mean notion I notice
it's damned hard to pry one loose from the other," observed Captain Chew in semi-drunken solemnity. When,
heavily, he crossed his legs the rowels of his spurs clinked
faintly; he eased belt buckles and buttons.

Chambers asked curiously, "You've seen this MacKenny
since the w—er—the trouble started?"

"Not 'til last month," Cary replied. "It's the irony of
fate, I suppose; but he's my brigade adjutant just now."

Jackson, McLaws and A. P. Hill.

"And he's a major, just to help matters."

A silence fell, and presently the conversation reverted to
a discussion of the respective armies. In detail men argued
those costly battles fought earlier in the year along the
James and amid the tangles of the Wilderness.

Again and yet again Jonadab filled the glasses, passed dainty crackers which tasted well after long weeks of hardtack.

"I will admit we have the horses of you, suh," Lieutenant Chambers remarked, absently tugging at a short black mustache, "and the bulk of our troopers have ridden since boyhood. On the other hand, suh, yo' service can find five horses to replace every one that is lost. Again, yo' troopers carry breech-loadin' carbines and plenty of fancy equipment of all kinds."

"True." Hubert inclined his ruddy head. "We have better equipment, but most of us line officers would trade it all for a handful of leaders who understand the proper functions of the mounted arm." His eyes questioned the earnest semicircle facing him.

"Right now we have to gamble on our general officers. I can tell you firsthand, gentlemen, it's damned thin fun to ride into a battle feeling your life may be tossed away because some higher-up doesn't understand his business."

Apparently such a problem had never occurred to the slim young gentlemen in gray.

"Reckon it *would* require a heap of courage," slowly admitted a short blond lieutenant. "A lot of our folks would most likely refuse to follow orders 'lest they knew Jeb Stuart, Stonewall Jack' or Marse Robert was givin' 'em."

"I'd never thought of it that way either," Craig Carey drawled. "I reckon we all have been too busy with our own troubles—powder shortages and these infernal jayhawkers—to look at your problem that way.

"Thank you, Jonadab," he smiled. "Captain Cary's glass

[77]

is deplorably empty. Hubie, I wish to God you'd describe those jayhawkers as closely as you can. We've orders from our department commander to catch 'em and hang 'em on sight."

Hubert put down a tiny glass of brandy.

"Didn't get to see much of them, but Miss Duveen can doubtless give you an excellent description. The only one I saw I'd know anywhere. Brute stood near six feet, had a ragged black beard and a long pointed nose. Um—and he'd a red scar slanting across his left cheek."

The black-haired captain nodded slowly. "D'you know, I reckon Archer and his sort are to blame fo' a heap o' the bitterness in these parts?"

"That's right," Vance Chambers agreed over his poised glass. "Old man Calthorp will swear to the end of his days 'twas Yankees tortured him and murdered his boy. Worse yet, there's plenty of fools ready to credit his tale—just as Union folks over in Kentucky will take their Bible oath it was our cavalry robbed their homes last spring and stole their stock and burned their barns."

"How about one last brandy—some of the 1801?" suggested Craig. "I fear the ladies——"

Chairs had begun grating back over the glossy dining-room floor when everyone present froze into rigidity.

Somewhere, not very distant, a carbine had cracked in the darkness. Brutally, its staccato report ripped through the peace of the purple-black night, echoed among the out-houses and hills. There followed a fusillade, a muffled yelling. More musketry crackled until it sounded as if some giant's boy were splitting kindling.

"Jayhawkers, b'God!" mumbled Chew.

"No—a Yankee raid!" rasped Chambers. "Jayhawkers would never dare tackle Philomont."

Hubert Cary glanced at his cousin, hardly knew him. The well-loved cousin had vanished, leaving in his place a strange, hard eyed enemy.

Jackson, McLaws and A. P. Hill! And Walker—*where?*

Cary remained motionless, listening to the rattle of a rapidly developing skirmish. The stately old mansion roused itself from the calm of years, resounded to feverish activity. For the moment ignoring the Federal's presence, the gray officers rushed about yelling questions and commands.

His horse at an extended gallop, a trooper appeared rounding the circular driveway, flung himself off and clattered up front steps.

"Cap'n Carey, suh! Cap'n Carey!"

Dwarfed by four great pillars guarding the entrance to Philomont, Carey spoke, "Well? Speak up, I——"

Craig Carey's voice was lost in the brazen notes of a trumpet which began braying breathlessly in the direction of the barns.

Sleepy shouts arose.

"Hey, what's up?"

"Where are they?"

"Out o' my way!"

Seated in the now deserted dining room, the Federal tried to sense what was happening, what would happen. No use going off half-cocked, wasting his chance. Distinctly the messenger's gasping voice beat in from the porch.

"Heavy patrol o' Yank cavalry headin' this way down Berlin Pike, suh."

"How heavy?" Craig snapped. Cary could see his cousin jerking at the buckle of his sword belt. "Speak up!"

"Cain't nowise tell, suh. Hit's powerful dark out yonduh."

"Ride like hell, order Sergeant Pegram to mount up half the troop—other half will stand ready to repel attack. I'll be there in a minute."

In the distance were rising fierce yells and the hollow clatter of hoofs. Slaves began to scream. Clamor filled the house.

"Oh, Laws! Laws! Yankees comin'—hide de silber! Hide de hams! Run! Run!"

Little Grandma's serene accents penetrated the din.

"Hush yo' fuss, you addled idiots. Never did see Negroes with less sense. Mister Craig won't let them harm you."

All at once Philomont seemed very empty and deserted.

Hubert Cary guessed he'd better make sure the ladies weren't molested by a sudden influx of raiders. His uniform in the parlor should form an effective deterrent.

He found the ladies forming a pale island amid a dark mass of round-eyed, patently terrified house slaves.

"It is very good of you to come here, Hubert," remarked Little Grandma Suzanna. She was sitting very straight in her Hepplewhite armchair. "Daresay some of Craig's friends will be sobering up in a hurry."

The old lady continued sorting the colors of her embroidery wool as if nothing more serious than a childish squabble threatened the firefly-filled night outside of Philo-mont.

"It appears that your partisans are closing in, Captain," Lenore Duveen said, making an effort to imitate old Mrs Carey's calm. Her eyes, however, were wider, her breasts rising sharply beneath the wide-skirted white gown.

Steadily the distinctive sharp *crack!* of carbines sounded louder, closer—more deadly. When a wounded horse shrieked all the colored people groaned, hugged each other tighter.

"Oh-h—look!" choked Melissa. Fearfully she was peering out over the wide moonlit lawn. Across it a riderless horse came galloping, stirrups flying, nostrils flaring.

A Confederate, bareheaded and kicking viciously at his limping mount, next appeared. "Get away quickly!" he bawled. "They's a million Yankees comin' down the pike!"

Through the parlor's tall french windows Cary watched a scattering of dislodged outposts come tearing into sight. They had their sabers out and saddlebags pounding heavily at the flanks of their Virginia half-breds.

Jackson, McLaws and A. P. Hill!

At the far end of the long driveway appeared a dark blur. *"There* they are," announced Lenore Duveen, fists clenched at sides. "Quite a lot of them, too."

Melissa began to whimper, "Oh, Granny, wha—what's goin' to happen to us?"

A very short officer named Thorne had dashed upstairs for his side arms and now came clattering downstairs. Features flushed, he paused in the doorway to call out:

"Don't fret, ladies. We'll tend to these sassy Yankees and

be back directly for our coffee!" He started to turn away but saw the figure in blue.

"Captain Cary, I reckon you have been overlooked. I must request yo' parole."

Cary's eyes kindled. "I can't give it, sir."

Melissa darted to his side. "Please give yo' word, Hubie. They—they might hurt you else!"

"No, 'Lissa, that's impossible."

Melissa gave a little scream when the young Thorne jerked out a long-barreled revolver. The assembled servants squeaked, covered their eyes, their heads.

Little Grandma said sharply, "Such melodrama is hardly required, Mr Thorne. Pray put that ugly thing away."

The little bowlegged officer paid not the slightest attention.

"Stand where you are, Yank!" warned the Confederate. "Don't make a motion!"

"Shouldn't dream of it. Lieutenant Thorne, do you notice that there are ladies here?"

Cary's gaze flicked over Little Grandma. "Don't you think you might be a bit safer upstairs, ma'am?"

Brief streaks of orange red had begun to stab out of the undergrowth beside the driveway. The hollow *thock! thick!* of bullets hitting the house were plainly audible.

"I have survived two wars," declared the old lady placidly, "and I once shot an Indian myself. I reckon it will be amusin' to watch a war from my own parlor window."

"Miss Duveen, 'Lissa—I beg you to go up."

"Indeed I will not," replied the English girl decidedly.

[82]

"This sight of Federal cavalry doesn't frighten me. I am quite accustomed to it."

"Please! Lieutenant Thorne, won't you persuade——"

The balance of Cary's plea was drowned out by a chorus of hoarse yells rising to the north of Philomont. A straggler in gray was cutting across the lawn; his mount was moving along on wavering legs.

Just as the animal reached a flower-ringed fountain set in the circle of the driveway it halted. For a long moment the animal stood there swaying, then its legs gave way with ludicrous suddenness. The rider stepped off as though this was a well-rehearsed act.

Moonlight glanced off the barrel of the carbine he whipped up. Settling the butt into his shoulder, the Confederate sighted at an indistinct mass of horsemen charging up the drive. He fired.

"Oh, my God!" Melissa screamed shrilly when a ragged fusillade of carbine shots punctured the night with a series of incisive reports.

In the living room a pane of glass was shattered. It made a high tinkling sound.

The unhorsed rider swayed, uttering a piercing scream, then toppled over to lie half submerged in the lily pool. His legs began jerking with dreadful spasmodic lunges.

"Oh—oh, look! Oh, look!" Lenore gave a breathless gasp and with one hand clutched her throat. "He—he's been killed!"

Little Grandma, sitting straighter than ever, selected a shade of embroidery wool. Said she, "My dear, when men are fools enough to fight many of them get killed."

More shots clattered, made the windows rattle; another pane was splintered by a bullet which came whistling *zw-e-e* through the lamplit room to shatter a Dresden shepherdess on the mantelpiece.

'Lissa fainted comfortably, genteelly, on a couch as a line of shadowy horsemen appeared leaping over a box hedge at the far edge of the lawn. Lieutenant Thorne cursed softly, stood undecided.

Cary gaped too. Good lord, was he seeing things? The moon was glimmering on long shafts, on a flicker of pennons. Lancers, of all things!

Never mind that. What would they do? Ride by the mansion, most likely, and attack the surprised, hastily mounting Confederates. Of course this patrol couldn't be aware that they were tackling a full troop of the enemy.

He was gathering himself when Thorne's crisp voice warned, "Steady, Captain. Stand still!"

Sharp indecision tore Cary's mind. His chance of escape would, of necessity, be brief. The Federal raiders, outnumbered, must in their turn flee very soon.

Damn! If Lieutenant Thorne's revolver weren't so obviously ready. What to do? He *had* to get back to Harpers.

"Miss Duveen," he called, "that poor devil by the fountain is still moving. Can you see whether his head is under water?"

Cary's heart began to pound. Very well he understood that the step he contemplated would forever alienate him from the Southern Careys. But what did private affairs amount to?

Lenore Duveen drew near, white bouffant skirt asway as she advanced toward the window.

"I'm not sure, but I'm afraid he's——"

Her voice became lost in a startled gasp. Hubert Cary had caught her by the elbows, had swung her between him and the gaping lieutenant in gray.

"Halt! Or I——"

The Confederate leveled his revolver, found Lenore Duveen over his sights. Quite effectively she screened the blue-clad officer as he went leaping through the hall door.

"Halt!" Thorne yelled. "Halt, you blasted coward!" Elbowing aside the speechless English girl, he raced through the front door, bounded out onto the wide veranda. The prisoner was snatching at the reins of a riderless trooper's mount.

Silhouetted against the yellow rectangle of Philomont's front door, Thorne sighted carefully at the fugitive's broad back but, from a group of azaleas beyond the fountain, a finger of flame reached toward him.

"Oh, my God!" choked Lieutenant Thorne. His poised revolver fell, slid across the veranda until it tumbled into a bed of pansies.

Slowly the stricken officer sank to his knees then began to cough violently. All at once he slumped sidewise and lay flat, his gay gold buttons reflecting the wavering lights of the Waterford chandelier.

Only Lenore Duveen saw Hubert Cary whirl himself into the saddle and spur furiously for the stables.

"Turn back!" he was shouting as he vanished. "For God's sake, Union, turn back!"

[85]

CHAPTER SEVEN

CATOCTIN CREEK BRIDGE

NERVES CRISPED, Hubert Cary snatched out a saber he found thrust through the cinch strap of the horse he had captured.

Shouting queries, he searched for officers of the rescuing detachment. Meantime he tried to fit this chaotic situation into some sort of a pattern.

Chunky blue troopers, with lances lowered and red and white pennons whipping, raised triumphant yells as, like medieval men-at-arms, they charged gray stragglers seeking shelter among the moon-silvered barns.

Behind the long row of stables shouts marked a rally of the surprised troops.

Anxiously, Cary peered about. *Where* in hell were the

[86]

lancer officers? Must find them, warn them how heavily their detachment was outnumbered, that they should retreat immediately.

While spurring across a flower bed beyond the front lawn he peered about. Yonder shone the distinctive glimmer of a shoulder strap. He urged his horse ahead.

He waved his sword, trying to attract attention.

"Come along, Cary!" shouted a short, heavy-bodied lancer captain. "Blake found us—said damn rebs had gobbled your patrol." The stranger's voice sounded hoarsely through a crackle of carbine shots.

The staccato report of revolvers and a distinctive shiver of steel meeting sword blade so filled the September night that Cary had to yell at the top of his lungs:

"Clear out! Full troop's here—forming back of barns!"

Panting, the lancer captain reined in, his bearded face bright with sweat. "The hell you say! Perkins, blow recall!"

A bugler at his elbow whipped out his instrument and began to sound a recall.

Cary grabbed at the lancer captain's sleeve.

"Some prisoners—my men—in corncrib! Know this place. Lend me some men?"

There was cavalry recklessness in those eyes below the stranger's wide-brimmed black felt hat. "Sergeant Callahan, take two squads—follow Captain Cary. Rally point— bridge across Catoctin Creek!"

"Thanks," Cary gasped, wrenched his mount about.

"Best hurry, sir, thim rebels behind the barns is thicker'n fleas on a dog."

Cary's detail yelled defiance and closed up once they

glimpsed horsemen swarming on a training track behind the stable.

"Follow me," Cary yelled. "Don't scatter. Keep four horses near me—strong enough to carry double."

"Yes sir." Sergeant Callahan called off some names then, with a whoop and a yell, the rescue party charged around a great white-painted barn and dashed headlong at the dark outlines of some corncribs.

Like the eyes of blinking monsters, abandoned Confederate watch fires dotted the center area of the training track, filled the air with a ghostly drifting smoke. Yonder a dark mass of rebel troopers was forming with ominous steadiness.

Cary rose in his stirrups. "Tatnall! Where in hell are you, Tatnall?"

"Here, sir," roared a voice from a huge crib on the far edge of the group. "But fer God's sake don't try to git us! The rebs will cut you off fer sure!"

In a compact swirl all eight lancers bore down on the row of corncribs. A hound, trampled on, went ki-yiing off into the dark. Flinging lances back on their arm loops, the Pennsylvanians drew pistol and fired point-blank away at a dark double line of horsemen on the training track.

Like a wave which, far offshore, gathers itself for a furious assault on a breakwater, the Confederates hesitated, closed up, then began to come on.

Cary flung himself to the ground and, slipping the reins of his terrified horse over his left arm, ran over to that crib from which Tatnall's voice seemed to have come. Desperately he wrenched at a peg securing the crib's hasp lock for a dull thunder of hoofs told him that the Confederate countercharge was gathering momentum.

Flinging back the door, he panted, "Mount up behind first four men!"

Bullets commenced whining by as Sergeant Callahan and his men wheeled and, bent low over their horses' manes, came pounding back.

"Howly Mary," the sergeant gasped, "be quick! There's a full squadron o' rebs down—— Och!"

In a queer convulsive movement the Irishman's thick figure snapped backward. Because his hands were locked in reins the stricken N.C.O. pulled his mount over on top of him when he fell out of the saddle.

More bullets. Cary could hear them smacking against the corncrib with a noise like that of enormous hailstones striking a barn roof. One of the rescued prisoners, Kaskel, gave a single dreadful scream and collapsed half in, half out of the crib door—his farming days forever done.

All became noisy confusion. From the corner of his eye Cary glimpsed Tatnall stepping astride Callahan's horse as it scrambled to its feet; little Denby was hauled across the cantle of a powerful bareheaded lancer; Cunningham was scrambling awkwardly onto the back of an enormous brown gelding.

Roars. Shouts. Shots. A shower of sparks marked the contact of two hard-swung sabers.

A horse, screaming like a woman in agony, went plunging toward the yelling gray troopers.

Hopeful that his last man was mounted, Hubert Cary scrambled into the saddle. Without wasting time to find

stirrups he wrenched his horse about, tried to cover the retreat of a laggard Pennsylvanian.

Too late. Cunningham and the man who had rescued
him were cut off by a quartet of Confederates. Briefly heavy
sabers flashed in the moonlight like windmills of steel. As
the Federals dodged and tried to fight back, cries of pain
and terror arose; they sagged earthward.

His was a strong horse, Cary realized. He was glad of
that when he wheeled and, following the survivors of the
rescue party, raced for the protection of the main lancer
body. They were drawn up in a heavy double rank across
the broad deep lawn before Philomont. When the dark
ranks of rebels came on, the Pennsylvanians couched lances,
raised a ringing cheer and spurred furiously at them.

Once his rescue squad had merged with the main body
Cary raised a ringing fox hunter's whoop and wheeled to
join in the renewed skirmish. With battle surging through
his veins he forgot that Craig Carey must be among those
yelling rebels. Lord God, how those Virginians could swing
and slash!

Yielding to relentless pressure, the Federal left commenced slowly to fall back through that same box-bordered
garden in which Hubert and Craig had played as children.
Now lances were abandoned in favor of revolvers—weapons
far better suited to such a close melee as was rapidly developing.

By a freak of battle the two forces abruptly separated as
if parted by the hands of an invisible Titan. Somewhere in
the moonlit dark Craig Carey was imploring his men to
fall back, to re-form.

The thick-bodied lancer captain also was shouting a command for the remnant of his men to close up. Wounded, powder-blackened, the Pennsylvanians lined up. Veterans among them hastily reloaded their revolvers, examined their horses for injury. The greenhorns merely yelled a hoarse, wholehearted defiance.

"Must get back to the Ferry," Cary panted to the lancer captain once they began a retreat along the drive. "Important intelligence."

"Rebs going to follow us?"

"Bound to. Can stop 'em though, maybe. Send twenty good men ahead with me. Know a good place for ambush —Catoctin Creek Bridge." Cary's face was bright with the heat of the fight. "You retreat down road—when rebs get onto bridge we'll charge in from the flank. Ought to shake 'em—right?"

The Pennsylvanian jerked a nod. "All right. Take Carter's platoon. It forms my left. Your friend Blake and the balance of your patrol is with 'em."

Under a clump of swaying lances Cary glimpsed Tom Blake.

"What orders, sir?" he shouted. "Carter's been knocked out. I'm in command."

"Quick! Form these men—column of twos," Cary rasped. "Try ambush 'em at creek bridge. Who's C.O. of this outfit?"

"Fellow named Walters—from Philadelphia."

In disjointed sentences the two conversed while the dim ribbon of the Berlin pike unrolled under the detachment's hoofs. Dark clumps of trees rushed by as the column clanked along at a hard gallop.

On glancing over his shoulder Hubert Cary felt his heart lift at those unfamiliar pennons flaunting beneath the moon. For an instant he felt he was living in another age— a feudal baron, leading his men-at-arms, might have seen such a sight.

At his heels rode perhaps twenty men, silhouetted heads bobbing rhythmically up and down. Sparks struck by flying horseshoes vied with the fireflies.

Could an ambush succeed? Cary, cooling from the skirmish, was suddenly sobered. They'd all have to fight like hell. Come to think of it, the fate of near twelve thousand men was at stake. Aye, perhaps more than that. Suppose Lee's hosts became able to turn the right flank of the great blue armies guarding the line of the Potomac?

He had scarcely devised a plan of action when a stone bridge loomed ahead—massive, moss-grown and narrow.

"Trot-ho! Walk-ho! Halt. This is it, boys."

The lancer detachment clattered across Catoctin Creek, then stuck useless lances into the ground, dismounted and surrendered their badly winded mounts to a quartet of horse holders. These promptly trotted off, disappeared around a bend in the moonlit turnpike.

Among laurel thickets crowding up to either side of the pike the bareheaded Federal and his lieutenant disposed men so pitifully few that Cary's heart sank. Worse yet, only a small part of the Pennsylvanians were equipped with carbines. Still, the cover was so thick that a dozen-odd heavy Colts might do effective work.

The breathless ambushers had only just begun to slap mosquitoes when shots and yells sounded from the direction of Philomont. Presently all the sweating, dusty men above the bridge recognized the furious drumming of a single horse's hoofs.

"Capt'n Cary! Capt'n! Where are you?" A bugler rode into sight, his gray horse pounding along at an extended gallop.

Cary stood up briefly and through cupped hands yelled, "Here! All ready?"

"Yes sir. Mah Gawd, but ye're well hid. We'll be along in a minnit."

Having identified the ambush, the bugler wrenched his beast about and dashed back toward the rear guard.

"Get set, boys," Cary called and heard Blake repeat the warning across the road. "Wait for my whistle, then cut loose; but be sure you see who you're shootin' at."

"Jeeze, hope they'll hurry," complained the heart of a willow thicket. "Mosquitoes round here run two to the pound!"

Like an omen of disaster a riderless officer's charger appeared, reins dangling loose; another; then a stream of wildly fleeing lancers.

Whether Captain Walters rode among them Cary could not tell. Once the Federal main body had passed over the bridge and had begun to form a line of sorts the leader called:

"Hurry, you fellers! Git them goats o' yourn movin'."

"Can't. Mine's shot through the guts," a straggler yelled back.

A lancer alongside Cary shouldered his carbine as the yells from the pursuers rang louder. "Here they come, sir. Sounds like they's a million of 'em."

Breath halted in Cary's lungs and he shrank lower among the dewy leaves. Down the road a heavy column of horsemen came surging into sight. Their uniforms showed up pale in the half-light, left no doubt of their identity.

Where was Craig? An artery over Cary's temple commenced to throb painfully. He hoped Craig wouldn't be in front!

Slowly the Federal leveled his revolver and, over its sights, watched the foremost Confederates start over the mossy old bridge.

When the enemy saw their quarry halted, even waiting for them, they slowed, became jammed together.

Weapons aglitter in the moonlight, the pursuit swept up the bridge under a miasma of heavy dust.

"What's the matter up ahead?" excitedly yelled a corporal standing in his stirrups. "Keep after——"

A shiver flickered the length of Cary's spine as he drew a deep breath. His whistle shrilled like the scream of a harpy. There went the lives of a good many men.

The laurels bloomed with gigantic golden-red flowers. The air quivered while, with terrific effect, the Federals in ambush fired into the thick of the enemy formation jammed up on the bridge.

Stricken horses fell, lay kicking wildly, tripping those behind. Jammed together, the gray troopers could move neither forward nor back nor properly handle their weapons. Some lashed their horses, trying to ride over their fellows until they themselves went down in the plunging, tangled mass of men and beasts.

At this moment the lancers who had been fleeing closed up and poured in a volley, blasting to the earth such Confederates as had struggled across the bridge.

The scene on Catoctin Creek Bridge became appalling. Desperate gray riders jumped the mounts off the bridge sides, fell threshing into the stream; but others, able to check their advance before reaching the bridge, grimly began to put their horses at the none-too-steep sides of the road. Snarling curses at the thin blue line above them, they came bucking, lurching up, waving sabers.

"Steady!" Cary called out. "Steady! Hold fire a minute more!"

He had caught a glimpse of Captain Walters' force back on their horses and hurriedly couching their lances.

"Forward! Come on!" he shouted. With a scattering of dismounted troopers at his back he charged down to meet the Confederate advance.

Yammering, the Pennsylvanians followed him through the shrubbery, shooting their revolvers as they went. The enemy horses would not face such an uproar and went plunging back to the road.

A rebel officer on the near side of the bridge saw Cary. Reining about, he grabbed a revolver from a saddle holster, took a snap shot.

The gray officer's charger shied, however, when a carbine blazed almost in its face, and his bullet merely hissed by Cary's head. Badly hampered by spurs which seemed designed to catch every root and shrub, the Federal continued down the slope.

The Confederate leveled his weapon for a second shot, but by now Cary had lined up a cluster of gold buttons over his Colt's front sight. Craig? Couldn't tell. The doubt stayed his finger. War might be war but—— Something rapped his right shoulder so hard that he reeled.

Dimly he saw his enemy jerking at his sword grip. Pistols and carbines were crackling like burning hickory logs. Recovering, Cary raised his revolver once more.

The Confederate was aiming his sword point. With legs braced far apart the Federal took careful aim. He had this reb dead to rights—and the reb knew it. It *was* Craig! Once before he'd seen such a look in his cousin's eyes—an unbroken colt had run away, had rushed headlong toward a stone wall.

The Federal knew he should squeeze the trigger, also that Craig Carey should have lunged at him. But they didn't, either of them. Craig surged by and was lost to sight in the melee.

A split second later Cary found himself trading shots with an immensely long-limbed Virginia sergeant who, snarling like a trapped wolf, stood astride a dead horse. Wide yellow chevrons rippled when the fellow shot. He missed and ducked low, but Cary's second bullet took the sergeant in the shoulder. Its impact spun him half around. The Virginian tripped and fell backward. Before the matter could be settled a riderless mount, appearing from nothingness, sent the victor reeling aside.

He scarcely realized that the Confederates, assailed from

[96]

three sides and terribly punished, were scattering in retreat. At once stubby little Captain Walters sang out:

"Led horses forward! Where in Christ's name are those horse holders? Get 'em out! Quick!"

The led horses of the ambushers appeared at a run. Meantime the victors conducted a hasty search through the grisly tangle heaped at the center of Catoctin Creek Bridge. A recruit, nauseated by the musty odor of spilt blood and the reek of torn entrails, began to vomit.

Once he had remounted Cary gasped at Walters, "Goin' ahead. Got to get back to Ferry!"

Wearily he stooped and readjusted his stirrups leathers for the long ride ahead.

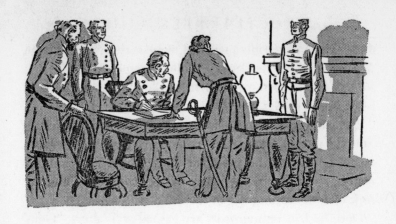

CHAPTER EIGHT

STAFF ROOM

COLONEL DIXON MILES raised severe, heavy features above a map spread on the table before him. Lines of worry engraved on his face became emphasized, more deeply etched, by the light of a pair of smoky lanterns.

"Then, Captain, there is little possibility of General Jackson's division having entered the valley?"

"Very little, sir."

"You searched methodically, of course?" Major Mac-Kenny's sardonic expression seemed to imply a doubt on the point. "You didn't, for instance, allow your love of skirmishing to run away with you?"

"No, Major." Cary fought to down a rising resentment, kept his eyes on the commanding officer. No doubt now that MacKenny hadn't changed a bit; he'd still his knife ready for the man who'd beat him out for the cadet captaincy.

A silence fell, remained unbroken by the staff officers standing in varying attitudes of anxiety about the stone-walled staff room.

"Did you discover signs of other enemy corps in the valley?"

Cary, standing very straight before the council table, shook his head. He hadn't even taken time to wipe off an accumulation of dust and grime.

"No sir. We found nothing beyond casual troops."

"Casual troops?" barked the colonel's adjutant. "Be more specific, Captain."

"Just a troop here, a platoon or a company there."

"How large would you say these units were, Captain?" Colonel B. F. Davis of the 8th New York Cavalry wanted to know. He kept tugging perplexedly at a fine pair of sand-colored sideburns.

"As I said, sir, never more than a company or a troop; nothing important."

"Well, then, why the deuce, Captain, d'you take up my time?" growled Colonel Miles and took a sip of steaming coffee from the battered tin cup an orderly placed at his elbow. "Why did you tell Major Corliss it was imperative that you see me? You did, didn't you?"

"Yes sir. That matter has nothing to do with my original mission, sir," Cary explained. "While held prisoner at Philomont Manor I overheard a statement——"

The colonel nodded, glanced up irritably. "You may go,

Captain Cary. With matters as they are I've no time for sifting rumors."

Obviously harassed by the dangerous predicament of his post, Colonel Miles arose, commenced to shift bright-headed pins on a map before him.

"Davis, give us that late despatch—the one from General White."

MacKenny's pale eyes held a glint of satisfaction. "In the future, Captain Cary, we trust your reconnaissance work will prove of greater value. You may go."

"Just a minute, Colonel."

Major Corliss, commanding Cary's squadron, thrust his solid bulk to the fore. "During our ride in from the outposts Captain Cary spoke to me about this information. I believe it to be of serious significance, sir."

When several staff officers nodded Colonel Miles flung down his pencil and emitted an irritated grunt.

"Well, get on with it; but I forewarn you, Major, I set small value on chance gossip overheard in a rebel camp."

Cary, flushing from his grimy collar to the roots of his rusty-red hair, said in a level voice, "Sir, I believe what I heard was more than gossip. The person who let fall these remarks was a staff officer of General Stuart's."

"Eh? On Stuart's staff? What was his name?"

"Chew, sir. Captain Chew."

The dark blue knot of staff officers looked up, abandoned whatever they were doing.

"And just how did you come across this precious item of information?" Miles fixedly considered the dusty figure before him.

"I was on a terrace outside of the billiard room. Some rebel officers inside got into dispute. One of them, Chew, got angry and raised his voice. This, sir, is what he said——"

Silence in the staff room became broken only by the heavy shuffling tread of a sentry walking post below the window.

"Well, get on with it."

"He said, sir," Cary spoke slowly, impressively, "that Jackson's corps is ordered to attack Harpers Ferry from the North."

"Eh? How?"

"By swinging down from the direction of Martinsburg."

"From the *North?* What utter damned-fool nonsense! He can't be up there. We'd have heard."

"But he seems to be, sir, all the same."

Major MacKenny rustled his papers irritably.

"Captain Cary means well, Colonel, but isn't he taking up valuable time? You'll recall, sir, that our last information before the telegraphs went out this evening was that Jackson's corps is on the Maryland shore and bivouacked just outside of Frederick."

Excited conjecture filled the room. Cary said nothing, only considered the probable consequences of driving a hard right into MacKenny's pink moon of a face.

"Go on, man, go on," ordered Colonel Miles. Testily he surveyed the cavalry captain's haggard, sunburned features. "Proceed with this quaint rumor of Captain Chew's."

"Chew also stated that the corps of Generals McLaws and A. P. Hill have been directed to storm Maryland Heights."

"What of Loudoun Heights?" demanded a thin, black-mustached colonel of field artillery. "That's our weakest spot."

Cary made a negative gesture with a hand yet spattered with the blood of some trooper hurt during the fight at Catoctin Creek.

"About that I don't know, sir. Captain Chew started to say something about General Walker's corps, only he got stopped. That's all, sir."

"All! I allow you've told us plenty," came the acid comment of Colonel Cameron, commanding the 15th Indiana. He turned a grim, lantern-jawed face toward the commanding colonel. "As I've maintained all along, sir, there's only one thing to do: *clear out!* If what this gentleman says is so, Harpers Ferry ain't nowise tenable."

"But his report mayn't be accurate," MacKenny argued.

"I think it is." Gaunt and sardonic Colonel Maulsby of the 1st Maryland also foresaw disaster and added his support to Colonel Cameron's view.

The smoky little staff headquarters room became a battle-ground for conflicting opinions. Various brigade and regimental commanders offered tentative solutions to the problem until at last Colonel Miles brought his open hand thumping down on the table with a violence which made the lamps' wicks flicker.

"Quiet, gentlemen. That will suffice. If this intelligence Captain Cary reports proves to be correct"—he shot the dusty figure a searching glance—"we cannot, even though re-enforced by the regiments of General White's command, hold out against four full Confederate divisions."

He swept the hot, red-faced group before him with a somber look. "MacKenny, fetch me that telegram I received from Washington yesterday."

Shadows, thrown blackly gigantic on the walls, hovered, seemed ready to pounce upon the officers grouped about the council table. Major MacKenny produced a sheet of paper from the bulging portfolio he carried under an arm. In silence he passed the blue and white form to his superior.

"In compliance with orders," Miles explained wearily, "I have not previously made this public. Please listen:

"Washington, D.C.
Colonel Dixon H. Miles,
Harpers Ferry.

Our army (McClellan's) is in motion; it is important that Harpers Ferry be held to the latest moment. The government has the utmost confidence in you and is ready to give you full credit for the defense it expects you to make.
                    H. W. Halleck, General in Chief."

As Colonel Miles's nasal accents died away a stunned silence reigned until a cavalry colonel with the long black chin whiskers burst out passionately.

"God's bloody bones! Doesn't old Brains know *that all of Lee's army* is marching between us and McClellan?"

Silver eagles stitched to Colonel Miles's shoulders glimmered briefly as he shrugged, made a gesture of helplessness.

"I presume he does, Colonel. These, however, are his orders."

Under cover of a furious debate which immediately ensued Cary found himself merged with the background. There he bolted surreptitiously a piece of bread and cheese brought by an orderly.

Bone-weary, he would have given years off his life for a few hours of unbroken sleep. Also he wanted to escape recollection of Lenore Duveen. He needed also to readjust himself to the fact that he had forever cut himself off from Philomont and all who dwelt there.

Still, he figured, he'd done what he'd ought—Miles had been warned, and now the matter was out of his hands. Or was it? An idea set him to staring fixedly at a yellowed Hagerstown Almanac hanging from a string above the orderly's desk.

Damn MacKenny! The fellow was downright vindictive. What hard, calculating eyes he had in that baby face of his.

Had Craig survived the fight at the bridge? Chewing mechanically, the travel-stained cavalryman wondered. So many had not.

He recalled how Denby, the little recruit, had gone backward off his horse, his skull split by the hissing sweep of a Virginia saber. He still could see a sub-lieutenant's handsome young face twitching as he clutched at a left sleeve gone dark with blood. He still heard those kicking, screaming horses, the howling of wounded men trampled underfoot.

Once more Colonel Miles's rapping forced unwilling silence.

"Gentlemen, General Halleck's order has left us no choice but to defend this post. This we will do, though I fear our position is desperate."

"Of course it is," said the black-bearded colonel, "if Lee is ordering four corps against us."

"Damned if I understand why he's sending so many," growled Colonel Davis. "Two corps should be ample."

Colonel Cameron tugged at his ragged beard. "Means only one thing, of course. Capture of Harpers Ferry and the arsenal here must be the first step if Lee really means to invade Maryland."

"But why is Harpers Ferry so important?" demanded Colonel Davis. "Lee can just as easily cross the Potomac at a dozen other points."

During the long ride back to Harpers Ferry Hubert Cary had been mulling just that question. He drew a deep breath and reapproached the map-littered table.

"Colonel Miles, sir?"

"Well, Captain?"

"Ever since I overheard Captain Chew's remarks I've been trying to find a reason for General Lee's setting such an importance on this post. Why has he ordered such an overwhelming concentration on Harpers Ferry? I believe an answer is clear."

Heavy gray head outlined against a window which predicted the imminence of dawn, Colonel Miles looked up, brows merged.

"Well?"

"Excuse me, please." Cary bent over a map of the region, his sweaty shell jacket showing dark in the lamplight.

"I believe that, unless there have been later dispositions, General Lee's line of communications with Richmond still runs through Rapidan station." He indicated that point on the map. "Then through Manassas and on up to Frederick."

"To the best of our knowledge that is so, Captain. What of it?"

"I don't pretend to be a tactician, sir," Cary hurried on, "but it seems fairly obvious that by permitting his communications to follow the line of the Potomac General Lee exposes his supplies and supports to the risk of capture by our cavalry."

Said Major Corliss quietly, "Your reasoning is correct, Cary. The rebels certainly must have Harpers Ferry if they're to establish a new line of communications."

"To amplify Captain Cary's great discovery," coldly interrupted the Union commander, "I will add that ever since this invasion began General Lee has wanted to change his line of communication with Richmond to a safer route —namely to one running through Winchester, Staunton and Harrisonburg.

"By capturing Harpers Ferry the rebels cannot only make use of the Winchester & Potomac Railroad but also the B. & O. as far as Martinsburg. From there it is an easy wagon haul into Hagerstown, Sharpsburg and Frederick.

"Perhaps it dawns, Captain, just why General Halleck has ordered this post held to the last?"

Cary was flushing under his superior's irony when Mac-Kenny burst out, "But, sir, we haven't half enough men to hold the Ferry; and help from General McClellan can never reach us in time. This garrison is as good as lost— unless we evacuate."

"Not necessarily." Cary risked his official head, said

sharply: "Suppose, gentlemen, that the Winchester & Potomac Railroad could be crippled, seriously disabled? Then Harpers Ferry would no longer be of such major importance to the rebels. General Lee would be forced to stick to his old line of communication and there would be no necessity to crush this garrison——"

"That will do, sir! I do not recall having invited your opinion."

Once the redheaded cavalry captain had stepped back Colonel Miles announced the council to be at an end. Grave-faced, the officers filed out with the exception of Cary, Major Corliss and MacKenny.

The commander turned on Cary.

"You and your talk about destroying the Potomac & Winchester! Where am I to find a force strong enough for such a task? From up my sleeve? You will report back to your troop and, in the future, please confine your brilliant ideas to scouting!"

MacKenny got quickly to his feet. "You heard what the colonel said—"

Quivering, the gaunt Rhode Islander remained where he was.

"Suppose, Colonel, it *were* possible to cripple that railroad without risking more than a handful of men?"

Colonel Miles, too outraged to speak, started up, cheeks rounded with anger.

"Just what do you mean?" quickly inquired Major Corliss. "You aren't being clear."

"It *is* possible." Lean features lighting, Hubert Cary spoke hurriedly. "I know of five important bridges on the

Winchester & Potomac line between here and Mount Jackson. Suppose these were destroyed? The W. & P. could be
made useless for at least two weeks."

"Eh? What's that?"

"It might be possible, sir, to destroy those bridges."

"You aim to blow them up, I presume? Bosh! How could
you carry enough powder?"

"No need to use powder, sir. We could burn them!"

Colonel Miles slapped a mosquito from the back of his
neck so violently that MacKenny jumped. "What you sug-
gest is idiotic under present conditions. You couldn't ride
five miles out of Harpers Ferry."

"Not in uniform, sir."

Colonel Miles caught his breath with a click and some
of his hostility departed.

"Then you propose to enter Virginia in civilian clothes?"

"Yes sir."

"You realize what will follow if you are suspected and
caught?"

"Yes sir." Cary smiled a tight smile. The idea wasn't a
pleasant one. "I realize that we would be treated as spies."

"We have had to execute two spies only recently. Hanging is a dreadful death, Captain."

"Undoubtedly, sir. But isn't the risk—well—isn't it justi-
fied? Besides, I don't expect we will be caught."

The commandant pulled at fluffy chin whiskers, made no
further comment. Presently he arose and made his way to
a large well-thumbed scale map tacked to the staff room
wall.

Picking up a lantern, he held it close and for many minutes intently studied the route of the Winchester & Potomac. At length he put down his lantern, faced the two cavalry officers.

"Success in such an attempt seems so unlikely, Captain, that I—I——" Colonel Miles paused, at a loss for words, then went uncertainly on. "Well, I won't—can't—*order* a single man to go with you.

"However, this garrison is in so—so dangerous a situation here that if you can secure sufficient volunteers"— Colonel Miles dropped his voice—"we will consider the plan. You may go."

He turned abruptly to MacKenny. "Now then, Major——"

Heart pounding, Cary drew himself up, clicked his heels and saluted the harassed commandant.

"Thank you, sir." On the way to the door he was aware of MacKenny's half-closed eyes.

In the deserted orderly room of headquarters Cary paused to gulp a drink from a tin dipper. He was just setting it back on its nail when Major Corliss strode in.

"Hope you manage this, Cary," said he heartily. "Calls for considerable daring, but your plan seems strategically sound enough. Miles appreciates that—otherwise, I believe, he would never have consented." Corliss stepped closer and added in an undertone:

"If you do go—I—I—would you do me a personal favor?"

After Corliss' support in the staff room Cary, genuinely grateful, could only nod.

"Of course, Corliss. What can I do?"

The major's expression softened. "My sister moved South

before the war. Last word I received was that she's still living near Staunton." He hesitated, looked uncomfortable.
"Hate to bother you with personal details, but, well—
Nancy's husband was killed fighting for the Union—in Kentucky. Nancy wrote that she is almost destitute.

"Nobody down there will even speak to her. It's hard,
mighty hard because—well, they've a child—a little
girl——" He pulled an envelope from the front of his tunic.
"Here is a letter addressed to her and containing some
money. The letter is of only personal importance." He
paused, added gravely, "You have my word on that. All
I ask is that you mail this for me if and when you penetrate
the rebel lines."

"It will be a pleasure."

"I don't like to ask this of you since it may prove dangerous," Corliss went on. "If you——"

The door of headquarters opened as Cary said, "That
will make no difference, Major. I will do it."

Major MacKenny's pudgy features peered out.

Corliss offered his hand.

"Well, good luck, Cary, and give 'em hell."

Turning toward the door, Cary wondered briefly at Mac-
Kenny's sardonic smile.

CHAPTER NINE

WINCHESTER & POTOMAC

STILL SHARP in Captain Hubert Cary's memory was that moment when, two hours earlier, the raiders had separated on the banks of Opequan Creek. Because they had all ridden quietly out of Harpers Ferry at five of the morning, he guessed not many people had seen them leave that pretty little town. Sturdily it climbed a hill above the junction of the Potomac and the Shenandoah.

They'd made a varied group. Among them had ridden half a dozen stalwarts in homespun jeans. These had elected to masquerade as Maryland boys on their way to enlist in Jeff Davis' army. Also present had been four "guards" in rebel uniform. They carried scrupulously forged travel orders and talked in low tones with six Federal "prisoners" who, stripped to shirt and breeches, were so dirty and unkempt as perfectly to counterfeit the genuine article.

Among these shabby pseudo prisoners had been Sergeant Tatnall, lantern-jawed and caustic as ever, the irrepressible Corporal O'Leary, who with Blake had led the Pennsylvanians to Philomont. The Confederate "guard sergeant" was that soft spoken, loose-jointed Marylander, Sergeant Raines. Three others beside Cary were posing as civilian army contractors on their way to Richmond.

It had been a breathless, mighty solemn moment for the twenty adventurers when their escort had ridden back toward the threatened citadel. Left alone under ominous gray skies, the adventurers had tried to appear confident, cheerful as they shook hands all round.

According to plan, the "guards" and their "prisoners" were to proceed to a water-and-wood station called Knolls Forks and there wait for the 8:15 A.M. local for Mount Jackson to come by. The station had not long been evacuated by Federal troops.

All "recruits" were directed to separate and to board the train in Winchester. Meanwhile, with an expert fireman and a pair of tobacco-chewing ex-locomotive engineers who spoke a convincing Kentucky dialect, Cary would proceed on foot to a stock ramp on a siding, a spot dignified with the name of Bellews Crossing.

It was an immense relief to Cary's group that when they boarded the pathetically dilapidated local the six "prisoners" and their four "guards" were already aboard. Scratching themselves, smoking and dozing, they occupied one end of a coach already crammed with refugees, invalided gray soldiers and Confederate officers traveling on detached duty.

No more than a curious glance did Tatnall and Raines bestow on the four prosperously dressed "contractors" who, gold watch chains ostentatiously aglitter, came swaying through their car in search of seats. No more did any of the other five blue-clad "prisoners" interrupt a fervent cursing of their luck.

Conversation between the "contractors," except of the most innocent sort, was forbidden. At times, however, the clatter of the W. & P.'s appallingly bad equipment made it possible for Cary to exchange a word with First Sergeant Brady, chief of the raiders' intended engine crew.

"How far to Winchester?"

"About two miles now, I reckon," drawled the Kentuckian. " 'Pears like we all are havin' luck so far."

Cary peered anxiously through a rattling and very grimy window. "We will if it don't come up to rain. How's your courage?"

"Fine, suh. Clayton looks kinder down in the mouth though."

And well might Clayton take a dark view, Cary reflected. At this moment he was one of twenty spies riding steadily further into a violently hostile countryside, a valley which swarmed with enemy troops. Let but one man among the raiders betray himself or lose his nerve——

A trifle uncertainly Hubert Cary's hand crept up to rearrange a flowing, polka-dotted blue tie sprouting from the front of his none-too-clean paper collar. Um—a rope wouldn't be half so comfortable. The memory of the three nooses adangle at Calthorp's farm sent an icy trickle down his spine. That had been too damned close to be funny. Another time his luck might break.

He wrenched his mind from that train of thought. The uneven rails jolted horribly, and dust and smoke beat in the open windows as the local lurched southward. At least his present anxiety kept him from dwelling on Lenore Duveen. He had been deeply, seriously impressed, very puzzled by that calmly aloof English girl.

Being a woman, Lenore Duveen probably would never forgive him, even if admitting that his ungallant act had been prompted by a sense of duty. Craig Carey, already in love with the Golden Diana, would be no more prone to listen to excuses or explanations. All would believe he'd been coward enough to thrust a girl's body between danger and himself.

Curious, one and all would condemn him, would ignore the fact that he had risked his life to preserve hundreds— possibly thousands of lives—Northern *and* Southern. Gloomily he switched his thoughts to the present, stared absently at a row of incredibly blue hills looming off to his right.

[114]

Clickety-clack! Clickety-clack! The coach wheels bumped and thumped over the Winchester & Potomac's uneven and long-unrepaired roadbed. A fat old woman across the aisle slept noisily. Her immense double chin quivered visibly to every jolt. In unison vibrated an impossible purple geranium stitched to a straw hat tilted at an angle over her eyes. Beside her an aristocratic gray-haired major of artillery dozed, hands crossed over the tang of a long old-fashioned sword.

Anxiety began to eat rat-like at Hubert Cary's peace of mind. They would reach Winchester in a few minutes. Would the balance of his party have reached their destination? Two of those "recruits" were expert firemen, the other four past masters in the gentle art of lifting a rail from its crossties. Very deftly they could twist a rail into curves which could only be removed by a foundry.

"Reckon it ain't over half a mile to Winchester, suh." Brady spat at an overflowing cuspidor set in the aisle with the accuracy of a veteran artilleryman.

"Stop saying 'sir,' you idiot," Cary whispered savagely. Then somewhat louder, "You certainly know this line."

"Oughter. Run her, fireman and engineer, near five years."

Further conversation was prevented by a shrill blast from
the locomotive's whistle. Couplings clattered and clashed
like a cartload of scrap falling down a chute; the coaches
groaned more heavily as the local began to slow.

"Win-ches-tuh! Win-ches-tuh!"

A brakeman with a tobacco-stained gray waistcoat and
imposing side whiskers opened the door, stood already
twisting the brake wheel. Gusts of wood smoke went
whirling down the aisle.

The conductor, resplendent in a red-and-white-checked
shirt, an old plug hat and blue jeans stuffed into cowhide
boots, came swaying along. Skillfully he avoided the
mounds of luggage stacked in the aisle. He paused to stare
down at Cary and his companion.

"Say, friends, let's take a look at yo' ticket."

What was wrong? A tiny cold barb of fear pierced the
young man with the short red sideburns. What could have
gone wrong?

"Mount Jackson, eh? That's the end o' the line."

The conductor went over and prodded the fat old woman
with the end of his punch.

"Here you are, ma'am. Better step lively; we all don't
tarry pow'ful long."

A row of shacks and rough houses flashed into sight only
to be obscured by a string of dingy B. & O. boxcars. At a
crossing an old man in a ramshackle buggy was trying to
soothe a frenzied horse. More houses—children playing on
some muddy artillery caissons parked alongside the track.
A sentry with sad, houndlike eyes stared at the train with
hands crossed over the muzzle of his musket.

"Win-ches-tuh!"

Creaking and rattling like a barn door in a gale, the train came to an abrupt and panting halt. A curious assembly crowded the platform: many soldiers in butternut and gray, most of them bandaged or limping; women in flowered bonnets craning their necks, hands in lace mitts waving good-by; ragged little Negroes vending pies and candied yams. Very numerous also were the ubiquitous railroad station loafers. These lounged about, surveying the scene with detached indifference.

Once the locomotive whistled a warning of imminent departure the local's brakemen released the brakes of each car.

Hell's bells! From where he sat Cary had seen no sign of the "recruit" party. His own group was becoming apprehensive when they spied the six missing men settling themselves in the first car behind the locomotive.

With that weight off his mind Hubert Cary returned to his seat and fell to counting the bridges over which the southbound train was speeding.

Kernstown and Newtown flashed by. When the local rattled across an enormously long bridge over Cedar Creek Brady abruptly aroused himself, nudged his superior.

"This here is one o' the main ones," he whispered. "Take the rebs three weeks or more to rebuild it."

At Strasburg Junction Brady got out to stretch his legs, carelessly surveyed the locomotive Pocahontas, which was hauling the train. Tatnall also wandered out to watch a gang of loose-jointed Negroes replenish the engine's supply of wood and water. Brady exchanged the time of day with the locomotive's oily and unshaven crew.

Once the journey toward Mount Jackson was resumed Brady leaned over and murmured, "Learnt the schedule for the Manassas Gap line, sir, along with the reg'lar schedule on this route. Say, what's the matter?"

"Look!" Tight-featured, Hubert Cary pointed at the windowpane. Rain was commencing to draw irregular pale lines through the dirt encrusting it; it looked like that fine, persistent rain which heralds a prolonged downpour. "This better let up soon or we'll be in a bad way."

"Yep, I've noticed wet wood don't burn so well," one of the ex-firemen observed somberly.

On down the lovely, rolling Shenandoah Valley the Pocahontas drew her train of four rickety coaches and three boxcars. Gradually the number of passengers diminished until only a scattering of weary travelers remained aboard the jolting local as it crept almost gingerly out over a high trestle.

When the rain diminished to a heavy mist Cary felt as if a too-tight belt about his middle had been eased. He glanced at his watch, saw it was nearly eleven o'clock.

"This heah's North Branch Bridge, suh," Brady whispered, lean jaws working with excitement. "Oughter be our first job."

Before Cary could reply the coach was plunged into a sepulchral gloom for, like another bridge already crossed, it was covered. He took advantage of the darkness to shift his revolver from his trousers to a coat pocket. His fingers, closing on that cool greasy surface, tingled. The rest of his men were fidgeting, chewing extra hard on their cuds of tobacco. He guessed they, too, were getting their revolvers ready.

Too bad that, outside of the muskets of the four "guards," it had been impossible for the would-be raiders to carry long-range side arms.

Once it re-emerged into daylight the train ground around a long curve. The engineer whistled "down brakes," whereupon the local's three "screws," as Brady termed them, ran out into the smoke and rain to take up the brakes.

"Be in Mount Jack' in just a minute now," Brady whispered.

Hubert Cary watched a succession of dripping telegraph poles flicker past and gradually became aware of a tight feeling at the base of his stomach. In a very few minutes now the sheltering cloak of disguise must irrevocably be thrown aside. The nearest haven now lay seventy long miles away. Seventy miles which must be traveled despite rain, pursuit or interception. Seventy miles within which three major and several minor bridges should be burned.

The top-hatted conductor appeared carrying a pair of live chickens in one hand.

"Mount Jackson!" he bawled. "Mount Jackson! End o' the line! Everybody off!"

Creaking loudly, the local clacked over a switch, turned down a siding to the right and came to a halt before a big freight shanty. Surrounding it was a desolate scattering of unpainted houses hemmed in by gloomy pines.

Hubert Cary's fingers curled when, descending, he beheld four Confederate sentries on the platform. Leaning on bayoneted rifles, they were at the same time carefully eying the crowd and cursing the rain. Now it had steadied into a relentless downpour; like febrile fingers, big drops drummed on the shanty's tin roof.

The first thing Cary did was to cross to a letter box and in it deposit Major Corliss' letter. Good old Corliss, he'd been aces.

As prearranged, the three groups of raiders quite ignored each other. Sergeant Raines, swearing with remarkable fluency, demanded the whereabouts of the provost to whom he must surrender his prisoners. The "recruits" meanwhile mingled with passengers setting out for a saloon behind the station.

Sergeant Tatnall, shivering in his shirt sleeves, cursed his guards and blasted the Sunny South from Florida to Maryland with such a ready flow of profanity that a passing mule skinner halted his team and listened, lost in admiration.

"Will you listen to that damn Yank swear," he chuckled to a gap-toothed companion. "Uster reckon I could cuss kinder fancy, but he sho' puts me back 'mongst the ama-choors."

Cary lingered on the platform with Brady at his elbow. In silence they watched the big bell-funneled locomotive swing around a loop, then stop to refuel.

A tight feeling in Cary's throat increased when, through the grayly slanting rain, he at last beheld the Pocahontas' headlight bearing back toward the station.

"You say when. You know what they ought to do," Cary said.

"When her crew gets down to liquor up and eat will be

our best chance," the engineer murmured, scarcely moving his lips.

From a little shack beyond the locomotive some train-men sauntered out. One of them yelled up to the Poca-hontas' engineer:

"Have a good run, Gus?"

"Tol'able. Ol' Pokey hain't a bad enjine, but she ain't a-goin' to like the return trip; wet iron makes the haulin' mighty hard on that Woodstock grade."

The conductor and his three brakemen, their lunch pails swinging, clambered down from the train and started for the saloon. Presently the engine crew did the same. Panting like a tired horse, the locomotive and its train stood quite deserted.

Brady's elbow nudged Cary. The red-haired cavalryman nodded imperceptibly, pulled from his pocket his little silver whistle. He sounded one blast. Then, in the vicinity of the Mount Jackson station, things began to happen in rapid succession.

CHAPTER TEN

THE LOCOMOTIVE POCAHONTAS

STARTLED CRIES, bewildered shouts, arose on the rain-sodden platform. Without warning the six "prisoners" and their "guards" hurled themselves upon the unsuspecting Confederate station guards. All but one of these were promptly disarmed, but he, leveling his musket at Tatnall, fired hastily. He missed, and his musket ball flew on down the platform and into the breast of a young woman in a plum-colored hoop skirt. Without a sound she collapsed on the wet bricks, her hoops arching absurdly. Her small round hat rolled out onto the track.

Meanwhile the six gawky "recruits" drew revolvers and came bounding back across the road while the civilian population of Mount Jackson looked on a moment in helpless, wide-eyed amazement. Under the threat of the six Colts the inhabitants scattered like a flock of chickens at the approach of a hawk.

Three of the raiders lunged into the telegraph office and, using revolver butts, smashed every key within sight. The operator, white to his lips, stood backed against a wall, staring down the barrel of a fourth man's revolver.

Brady, accompanied by the two firemen, immediately ran across a series of tracks to the Pocahontas, scrambled up into her cab. At their heels dashed the "guards" and "prisoners." These, having disarmed the station guards, had locked them in a tool shed.

"Cut her in the middle, Collins!" yelled Brady, leaning far out into the rain. "Tatnall, you keep that train crew in the saloon!"

The engineer spun about to check the steam pressure and to test the water try-cocks. Cary meanwhile directed the rest of the raiders.

Ever-swelling tumult reigned in Mount Jackson. Shirt-sleeved shopkeepers appeared at their doors brandishing old-fashioned horse pistols. All they accomplished, however, was to terrify the recently arrived passengers.

Pelted by a lashing rain, Cary signaled with his revolver, directed the uncoupling of the last four day coaches. This left only the three freight cars attached to the Pocahontas and her tender. Spurred by the certainty that each passing second increased the possibility of failure and disaster, Collins and his men were working frenziedly to release the brakes.

Cary set the whistle to his lips, blew two blasts summoning the raiders still engaged in wrecking the telegraph office. Why didn't they come? They were fools to risk everything for a little destructive fun. Instants dragged by on leaden feet. He whistled again.

Damn! He'd have to leave them. Down the muddied main street was advancing a menacing mob of soldiers on furlough, angry villagers and boys armed with every sort of weapon.

Far more disturbing to the redheaded leader was the sight of a man on a powerful horse splashing off down a road which, for a short distance, paralleled the tracks of the Winchester & Potomac. To Cary there wasn't a doubt in the world but that he was heading for the nearest military telegraph station.

"Hurry! Hurry! For God's sake, hurry!" Cary yelled.

"We've got to pull out right away!" Brady warned from the cab window. His bald head was gleaming and his brown beard quivered.

The last of the "prisoners" and "guards" went scrambling into the rearmost boxcar while others of the raider's number leveled revolvers at the train crew which had run up to line the right of way. Their mouths were still full of lunch, and some swallowed as hands were obediently raised in air.

What in hell was keeping those fools inside the station?

The Pocahontas puffed, emitted a blast of steam and then, amid a banging of link-and-pin couplings, the train

commenced to move. A ragged fusillade banged from behind the station and bullets shattered several coach windows. The "recruits" came pelting across the platform.

"Hey! Wait!" They were carrying a varied assortment of
stolen crowbars and pickaxes. Hands reaching down from
the boxcar doors hauled the tardy ones aboard. That much
Cary saw before he swung up into the shelter of the locomotive's cab.

Slowly the train gathered momentum. More shots were
fired, and the crowd started running along the track in
pursuit, with the dispossessed crew in the lead. They were
shaking futile fists.

"Get goin', Joe, open her up!" pleaded Collins, the relief
engineer, wiping sweat from an Indian-like face. Brady,
eyes fixed on the rain-dimmed right of way, inched back his
Johnson bar and widened on his throttle—a volcano of
smoke and sparks was spouted from the huge bell-shaped
smokestack. The Pocahontas shuddered violently as her
driving wheels, accelerated too quickly, lost traction on wet
rails and began spinning uselessly.

Braver now that the enemy was in flight, the clamoring
mob began to close in.

A ragged line of infantry appeared down a side road,
halted and fired. Like deadly hailstones their musket balls
clanged against the iron sides of the locomotive and tender.

Cursing, Brady, kneeling on the floor of the cab, throttled down and this time applied the steam more gradually.
Like a dog shaking itself the train quivered and over again
commenced to roll forward.

"Made it, by God!" exulted Cary as with the two firemen

he crouched amid the firewood. Shots were still crackling spitefully.

Steadily the Pocahontas gathered speed until her cab commenced to sway with that sharp jolting motion which, though alarming to the novice, tells an engineer that his engine is hitting off a steady, space-eating speed.

The last Hubert Cary saw of Mount Jackson was the dark mob to the one side of the station shanty and the deserted, rain-shiny platform on the other—and that crushed-looking body sprawled upon the wet bricks. The dead woman's hoops were stirring a little in the wind.

Faster and faster revolved the heavy five-foot driving wheels of the Pocahontas. Gusts of hot, pitchy-smelling smoke swirled out of the firebox to obscure the steam gauge whenever the two firemen fed pine slabs into it.

The smokestack gushed sparks which, like clouds of tiny meteors, went whirling back over the swaying boxcar tops.

"Got us a fair start, Cap'n." Brady grinned in relief. "But, Holy Jesus, I like to died of old age when them drivers began to race."

"So did I." At considerable cost to his natty gray civilian suit, Cary braced himself against the cab's violent jolting, cupped a hand and raised his voice. "Since we know there's no locomotive behind, I suppose there's no sense in tearing up the track yet?"

"No, but we'd better cut the telegraph in a minute," the engineer bellowed over the crackling roar of burning pine slabs.

"Collins, you take the throttle. Brady, tell me what we're to expect along this line."

Wiping his forehead with the sleeve of his blue flannel shirt, the engineer leaned close. "Gotta meet a down freight t'other side o' Woodstock Run. That'll be below Strasburg. Gotta beat this freight to the passing track there so's to let her go by. Above Strasburg we meet the twelve-thirty out of Charlestown."

The bald man's reddish eyes narrowed. "Shouldn't meet no trouble if only this blasted rain will let up."

Cary's earlier apprehensions returned. Suppose the bridges got too wet to burn? Suppose that horseman quickly got to another wire?

Like the ruffles on a drum, sheets of rain beat against the cab's windows. Suddenly Cary's spirits rose; after all, the adventure had begun well enough and the rails were clicking out a reassuring song. A succession of dripping hills rolled past.

"A little more luck, Brady, and we'll do it, by God! Throttle down; we'd better cut the wires."

"That's a right good notion," Collins agreed nervously. "Might be somebody in the station back there find an extry key."

Twice the Pocahontas' whistle screamed for brakes. The jolting lessened, and presently the little train came to a panting halt.

From beneath the jacket of a "recruit" appeared a strong cord equipped near one end with a steel hook; a foot above the hook was fastened a lead weight.

"Get to work," Cary called, "and shake a leg about it."

The fellow needed no urging. Watched by his nineteen companions, he leaped down to the ballast and twice whirled the weight above his head before, with an expert cast, he sent a light but strong rope hurtling over the three bright strands of wire.

A little cascade of water shook loose when the rope slid over the wires. Promptly the line thrower snapped the hook back about his rope. It formed an effective noose.

"All set!" A jet of steam burst from the safety valve on top of the Pocahontas' hivelike steam dome. As the train lumbered forward the hook skittered along the taut wires, while he who had cast it scrambled back onto the last car.

Once the train had traveled a few yards, with the other end of the rope lashed to a brake beam, all three wires gave a sharp, harplike *hum-m-m,* went curling back on themselves. They had been very neatly ripped down. The whole operation had not required a delay of thirty seconds. The raiders grinned delightedly.

Again the doors of the dirty red-painted car slid shut and, to all intents and purposes, the train was a harmless special freight with convincing white flags fixed to its pilot, rattling on through the downpour.

"What's next?" Cary inquired after studying his watch. It did no good to sit there silently damning this rain.

"They's the covered bridge, suh. It spans the North Fork River."

CHAPTER ELEVEN

THE POWDER SPECIAL

IN AN ENDLESS PANORAMA of scattered farmhouses and dog-run cabins the rain-veiled countryside rolled by. In this district most of the dwellings looked poverty-stricken and sheltered a collection of most disconsolate-looking cows and some sheep.

"There she be!" Collins yelled in evident relief. "We sure are makin' time!"

Cary, leaning out, glimpsed the black entrance to a covered bridge.

"Brady, we'd best stop in the center," he directed. Soon the stolen train plunged under the shed and the world grew dark. It became filled with wood smoke. Light, beating up from under the sleepers, afforded barely enough illumination to work by.

"All out! Get moving!" Boxcar doors slammed back, and the noisy gloom became peopled.

"Grab wood from the tender, boys," Cary directed above the asthmatic panting of the engine. "Stack it alongside the shed walls. When we pull forward set a fire in the center of the track too."

Half a dozen men in their shirt sleeves sprang up to help. Cary and the firemen passed down dozens of pine slabs. The engineers, Collins and Brady, improved the moment to grab tallow pots from their shelf on the boiler head, where the tallow was kept warm and liquid, and hurriedly lubricated various vital valves and brass bearings.

Heart thudding, Cary presently drew Tatnall aside and both became veiled amid clouds of steam.

"We'll come to Woodstock next. There Brady says we will have to wait on a siding." He spoke crisply, earnestly. "Jam those boxcar doors on the inside so they can't be slid back. No one is even to whisper. Remember, it'll cost our necks if the rebs catch us," he reminded. "We're counterfeiting a special powder train on its way to supply Jackson's army. Understand?"

"Yes sir." Even Tatnall's long Yankee face looked ghostly, unreal amid this shifting steam.

"If things come to a showdown, I'll sound my whistle— one short and two long blasts. Then you'll throw open the doors and shoot—no missing. Understand?"

"Yes sir," nodded the brown-faced veteran. "But, dag nab it, I wisht we was a-horseback."

Five minutes later the Pocahontas went puffing out of the far end of the covered bridge. In the wake of the train coiled a heavy wave of blue smoke. Cary, by craning his neck, could see flames, generated by the heap of firewood, beginning to lick up along the dry inside of the shed. One bridge, at least, was out of the way—but it was the least important.

Try as he might, Hubert Cary could not quite rid himself of qualms aroused by the rider who had gone galloping out of Mount Jackson. He was still conjecturing on the fellow's destination when he thought he heard, faint and far away, the screams of a locomotive whistle.

Brady listened hard, swore and turned, gray-faced, to admit that his superior was right.

"Christ in the foothills," he growled. "Them goddam graybacks *would* schedule an extra!" There had been some change in the already disorganized schedule of the Winchester & Potomac! Cary could read fear written large on Collins' Indianlike visage.

"Slap the wood to her, boys," Brady urged over an oil-stained shoulder. "We better beat that extra to a passing track, 'cause they ain't nowise expecting an uptrain now. They'll run smack into us."

As he spoke he grabbed the whistle cord, sent two long and one short blasts echoing over the green, gently rolling foothills.

Ensued a nerve-racking period during which Brady coaxed the stolen train to a speed so dangerous that Clayton, the boss fireman, turned a dirty gray and, clinging to a handrail, screamed:

"Joe, for Christ's sake, slow her down! We'll jump sure! This ain't no sixty-pound iron we're on!"

Clickety-clack! Clickety-clack! chanted the rails, and the pine slabs crackled so loudly that if the other train had whistled in reply Cary could not hear it. Momentarily the possibility grew greater that the two trains would crash head on around a long curve which, skirting the base of a mountain, grew tighter and tighter. He felt his hair squirming at the back of his neck as, holding hard onto the swaying cab's handrails, he peered anxiously ahead.

Then to ease his tension he joined in hurling slabs into the smoke-spewing firebox of the Pocahontas.

Once more Brady jerked the whistle cord. The stolen train thundered steadily on toward the North and toward its own inscrutable fate.

The most imminent peril faded when, at the end of a long curve, a little telegraph station and freight shed loomed into sight. At once Brady whistled for brakes.

"Remember now," Cary warned the engine crew, "keep your nerve; let Brady and me do the talking."

Once the train slowed, Clayton, the boss fireman, sprang to earth and, running ahead, threw over the siding switch.

That those in charge of the Woodstock station were astonished was all too evident. Defying the driving rain, half a dozen individuals in greasy jeans and overalls came out onto the platform when the Pocahontas puffed alongside. At their head stalked a tall old man with a tobacco-stained white beard and sharp, suspicious eyes. To make matters worse two squads of Confederate infantry in butternut-dyed homespun stood taking shelter from the rain in the baggage shed.

"Is Bill Meeker gone plumb crazy?" roared the station agent, the brim of a floppy straw hat wagging his indignation. "How come he dispatched this heah 'thout sendin' narry a train order? I sho' admire to see his hide tacked to a barn door fo' this."

"Sorry, pardner," grinned Brady. " 'Tain't no fault o' mine.

Mebbe the wire is out. Jayhawkers been thick in the valley heah anyhow. This heah is a powder special. Meeker had his orders to cl'ar this track fo' us clean through to Charlestown."

"We didn't get no order," grumbled the other. "Where did this powder come from?"

"Feller said 'twas by wagon from Harrisonburg," Cary supplied.

He swung easily down to the platform and turned up his coat collar against the rain. He could feel the eyes of the squad in the baggage shed searching him.

"Where at's Johnnie Faulkner? He's Number Six's regular hogger," demanded the old man.

To Cary's intense relief Brady also descended.

"Johnnie? Oh, he's back to Mount Jack'. Got took with a chill on the down trip. They stuck me on fo' the up trip."

Doubt was in every line of the station agent's seamed face as, with a faded Federal overcoat flapping loose about his legs, he strode the length of the "special," peering intently at each car. Sight of Raines and the other "guards" in gray uniforms, however, seemed to allay a certain amount of the stationmaster's suspicion.

"Heyo, Pop," grinned the Marylander from his post in the first car behind the tender. "You all ought to collect double fares on this heah line."

The station agent blew his nose on a blue bandanna. "Double fares? What's yo' meanin', Bub?"

"Why, on the W. & P. don't a feller travel two ways? He goes as far up and down near as much as he travels forward."

[133]

"Smart, ain't you?" snarled the station agent. "Wal, mebbe you all won't be so peart when them Yanks gits a crack at you."

Like music lulling Cary's anxiety sounded the faint screech of a whistle.

"Number Twelve's late," grunted the station agent as he turned away through the silvery downpour. "And it's damned lucky she is. Had you all met her below heah, the buzzards would be feedin' fat tomorrow."

Blue coattails flapping, the old man stumped back across the platform, stopped and, while ostensibly blowing his nose on a blue bandanna, muttered a few words to a telegraph operator. Cary saw the surprised youth glance up, then bend over his instrument. His fingers were fairly flying as he began tapping out a message.

"Think he's caught on," Cary murmured. "Shall we jump him?"

"Can't," Brady replied. "Switch ain't clear yet. I'll send Donaldson—he's in reb uniform an' can read Morse."

While turning to watch the approach of a huge locomotive with four-and-one-half-foot drivers he saw Donaldson saunter across the platform, his musket lock held under his armpit. He needed to keep it dry, all right.

Brady caught his breath sharply and his hand closed tight on Cary's wrist. "Oh, sweet Jesus!"

"What's wrong?"

"Them green flags to her pilot!"

"What of them?"

"They mean there's *another train* behind this one. We're likely to be held here God knows how long!"

[134]

PURSUIT

CARY LIVED a thousand years during the following few minutes. Curiously the newly arrived train's crew came wandering over to gaze at the powder special. Its engineer, frowning perplexedly, asked Brady:

"Where at is Johnnie Faulkner?"

"Got took sick," Brady grunted as with dripping tallow can he oiled the side rod bearings and valve links.

"Sick?" The other stood tugging at untidy chin whiskers. "That's funny. He looked all right to me this morning."

"Well, he's sick now. He caught a chill."

Cary meantime, every nerve humming, lingered outside the telegraph office in company with Donaldson, the "guard" who was also an expert telegrapher. Apparently over-intent on avoiding this persistent drizzle, the latter listened to a steady tapping of the Woodstock operator's key. Presently he nudged Cary, said out of the side of his mouth:

"You're right, sir. They *are* suspicious about something.

That feller's trying to reach Mount Jackson by a relay through Strasburg, Manassas and Richmond."

The "contractor's" heart sank. "Let me know the minute he gets an answer."

Cary climbed up into the cab. "Brady, things are getting a bit tight. That break in the wire has been noticed."

"Mebbe so," Brady grunted, "but there ain't a thing we can do but pray for that second section to come up quick."

Ten, fifteen minutes dragged by before the second section, a long train of empty boxcars, clattered into sight. Soon, Cary mused, those empty cars would be hauling supplies for the Army of Northern Virginia.

Would that endless train of cars never clear the switch? Hubert Cary dismounted again and through the window watched the white-whiskered station agent. He was sitting beside the operator and pretending to check waybills. A child could have told, however, that his whole attention was on the clicking sounder.

Donaldson caught his breath, spat into the rain: "Richmond reports he's clearing the line," he muttered. "You'll have to do something quick."

Into the station strode Cary, blue-gray eyes hard as agate. "You been clearin' the road ahead fo' us?" he flung at the station agent. "General Gorgas will sho'ly have yo' head if you ain't."

"I'm sendin' off a couple of wires first," the old man admitted sullenly.

"Why, yo' damn' ol' bugger." Cary tried to mimic Raines. "You drop what you're doin' and wire them route orders to Strasburg right now! Order the dispatcher to keep this line clear 'til I report from Winchester."

A glance out of the rain-lashed window revealed that the long freight now was all but clear of the switch. It was going to stop for wood and water—but it should clear the switch.

"Keep yo' hair on, Bub," the agent grumbled. "Ah'll tend to yo' business in a minute."

"In a minute, hell!" thundered Cary. "Yo' weak in the haid, man? This powder special is the most important train on this line. Mister, you'll send that order *now,* understand?"

The station agent wavered and finally nodded. After all, to interfere with the powder supply for Lee's army might prove a serious offense.

"All right, Hank." The station agent blew a long red nose in his blue bandanna. "Ask Strasburg to hold Number Fourteen in Rectortown." Then he glared at this well-dressed civilian. "Ye needn't have been so danged ornery, mister."

"Sorry, Grandpap; it's important we ain't delayed." And this, Cary felt, was no less than the truth.

"Misto' Cary! Misto' Cary!" Brady was beckoning vigorously from his cab. "Track's clear. Let's go!"

"So long, Grandpap," Cary drawled and, forcing himself not to move too fast, clambered up into the locomotive's cab.

Just then the sounder began to rattle again, and Donaldson lingered under pretense of retying a bootlace. He delayed even when the Pocahontas had commenced to roll forward at considerable speed.

"Hi," he yelled, "wait for me!" and came running over the platform.

"Brady, get going *quick!*" gasped Donaldson. "Get us around that bend in a hurry! We've got to cut them wires! Mount Jackson is tellin' 'em 'bout our stealin' the train!"

Though the driving wheels turned faster and faster, in Cary's imagination they crept along at a snail's pace. Ages seemed to elapse before the stolen train halted. Again the wire-cutting squad went into feverish action, but the Pocahontas had barely started again when behind them they heard the halted freight train's whistle set up a sudden furious screaming.

"They've caught on! Oh, God help us!" Collins lifted a scared, sweaty face from his efforts at the firebox. "If only we'd cut that line a minute earlier!"

"Let 'em catch on," Brady snapped. "It'll take that hogger on Twelve plenty of time to get shut o' them boxcars of hisn."

"But *will* they?" demanded Clayton, purple-faced from exertion.

"They've got to," Brady reassured. "That freight hog can't back all them boxes fast enough to catch us—not in a month o' Sundays. We can break the track long before he c'n get started."

The flight commenced in earnest. Not a man of the raiders but knew that the alarm had been given and that the hunt was up. A mile down the track the stolen train halted. Tatnall and his crew labored frantically to lift out a rail.

It was hard work since they had few rail-lifting tools.

[138]

They toiled mightily, however, with long iron crowbars stolen from a tool shed at Winchester. They had freed one rail from its bed and were attacking spikes securing the other when from down the track sounded the hoarse, triumphant scream of a locomotive's whistle.

"God in heaven, but they got clear quick!" panted Brady. "Thought we'd have at least ten minutes more."

"Abandon work! Get aboard!" Cary snapped to those men who, stripped to their shirt sleeves, toiled in the driving rain. "Don't leave that crowbar, Grogan; we'll need it later." The passage of every second before reaching Winchester immeasurably reduced their chances, Cary felt. Had that wire been pulled down in time?

"Let her roll, Brady!"

The Pocahontas had barely begun to move on, with the wrecking crew scrambling head over heels into the last boxcar, when around a distant bend appeared the smoke of a locomotive. It was, for a fact, the big freight engine seen at Woodstock.

The giant fairly roared into sight less than a quarter of a mile back, traveling in reverse and pushing before it a pair of dirty red-colored boxcars. These looked to be overflowing with armed men. At surprising speed the pursuers came on.

For better view Cary clung to the outside of the cab, felt hard-driven drops sting the back of his neck.

"Stopped 'em, by God!" Brady shouted. "Listen to that!"

The other locomotive's engineer saw the loose rail and stopped very suddenly. A sudden high white plume of steam shot from the pursuer's safety valve. The Confederate train had come so close that Cary could distinguish details in the equipment of the troops who came tumbling out of the cars. Perhaps a dozen dropped to one knee and opened fire. A few stupidly brandished guns and began running along the right-of-way track as though they expected to catch the fleeing Pocahontas. The more level-headed began to pull the loose rail back into place.

"Close," Clayton muttered, sucking a skinned finger. "If only word ain't gone up ahead, we'll maybe be all right."

"It'll take 'em quite some time to fix that rail," Brady announced. "Slap the wood to her, you boys. My God, why does it have to rain like this?"

On clattered the stolen train. Through a succession of rain-drenched hamlets and villages it sped, white special flags whipping in the wet wind. After every station the raiders grudgingly delayed to cut wire.

"It all depends," Brady pointed out, "on whether that there old whiskered goat at Woodstock got his message through to Strasburg before we snaked down them wires the second time. We'll know pretty soon."

"And ain't that the truth?" Clayton sighed.

The men in the cab joked as men will at such times, raised uproarious laughter over any attempt at humor. But they couldn't disguise the mortal anxiety looking out of their eyes.

A team of mire-splashed oxen waiting at a crossroads lifted heads and, with strings of saliva drooling from their jaws, gazed stupidly at this train passing amid a spindrift of rain and flying smoke.

A long column of field artillery, plodding along a muddy road, hardly lifted their eyes. How tired the gunners looked and how wearily the gaunt teams lifted their muddied hoofs.

Scattered houses flashed into sight.

"Strasburg," Collins announced, dashing the sweat from his forehead. "Now we'll know—for sure!"

Did a clear track or a battery of artillery trained along the right of way wait up ahead? Brady's lumpy jaws began working fast and hard on an imaginary quid of tobacco. Sleeve aflutter, he reached for the whistle cord. Two long and two short blasts split the gray daylight.

For better or for worse the Pocahontas commenced to slacken speed as a freight yard and some loading platforms appeared up the track. The wet roofs of Strasburg gleamed dully; empty streets stretched away; a mule stood tethered to a well-gnawed post, ears canted earthwards.

"Thank God, she's clear!" Cary exulted and felt a crushing weight fall from his back. "The line at the junction's free!"

"Hey, look over there! See that big engine—the Resolute—on yonder spur? Means the Rectortown train must have just pulled in," Brady announced stonily.

Clayton, the pessimist, added dejectedly, "Hell and blazes! This hog's headed right to chase us."

Brady glared. "Shut up, else I'll slap your goddam noisy jaws!"

Clayton subsided.

Confidently the Pocahontas and her three freight cars rattled across a double set of switch points and rolled past the station where guards waved a greeting from the shelter of the dripping eaves.

Once the houses had thinned Cary ordered the wires cut again. The now overheated engine resumed its flight toward the long and critical trestle over Cedar Creek.

"What d'you think, Brady?" Cary questioned. "Had we better take time to rip up track?"

"No sir," the engineer said without turning his head. " 'Twould waste a lot of time, and ever'thing seemed quiet at Strasburg. Ought to sight the bridge in a minute now, and once that's afire we'll be in no danger from Strasburg."

The Cedar Creek Bridge was not covered. Only then did the raiders fully appreciate the disastrous effects of the rain. Even wood from the Pocahontas' fast-diminishing fuel supply refused to be coaxed into a blaze. It would burn only feebly even when, in desperation, Cary's men held coats to shelter the spasmodic flames.

"No use," Tatnall growled, then ran up to the engine. "Hey! Kin you spare us some tallow?"

"Half a gallon, maybe, but I can't loose no more firewood."

Tight-jawed, Cary got an inspiration. "Use your crowbars, boys, and wreck that last boxcar. Quick, now!"

The car, none too strongly built, yielded to the assault of the panting raiders. Promptly they knocked out the rear end and one of the sides. Fed with splinters, a fire commenced to grow and billow. Eye-stinging gray smoke went beating down to hang over rain-swollen Cedar Creek some sixty feet beneath. But almost at once the flames withered.

"Consarned stuff jest won't burn, sir," complained Tatnall as, using a crowbar, he strove to stir the sullen flames to life. "Can't catch a real holt in a frog-drowndin' rain like this."

"It's no use," Cary admitted at last. "We'll stand a better chance with the West Branch Bridge; that's covered."

"Yeah," put in Clayton, his long flat face shining with wet, "*if* we get time. We've wasted near half an hour."

"I'm going to pull forward," the engineer called down from the cab. "They's a stack of ties ahead. You maybe can use 'em for fuel later on."

Once the shattered boxcar was uncoupled the Pocahontas rolled up to a big pile of ties conveniently stacked by the right of way.

As though controlled by a single wire, every head snapped to the rear. Faintly, but unmistakably, the puffing of a locomotive laboring up a grade came beating up the valley.

"They're after us again!" quavered a pitch-smeared "recruit." "Oh, my God, why won't this damned bridge burn?"

"Enough ties!" Cary yelled. "We can stop them even yet!"

"Mebbe the smoke will keep 'em off Cedar Creek Bridge," Tatnall suggested with more hope than conviction.

Collins nodded vigorously. "Yeah, even them rebs will think twice 'fore riskin' a sixty-foot drop."

Once his train began to jolt onward Cary made his way back to the last freight car. "Six of you grab a tie. Batter a hole through the end of this car."

[143]

It chanced that the Winchester & Potomac's right of way ran straightaway nearly half a mile beyond the bridge over which they had wasted so much irreplaceable time. Accordingly the raiders for a while were able to watch the progress of the pursuing locomotive. Everyone agreed it was the Resolute from the Rectortown train; they saw it was dragging only one dull red freight car. A long streamer of flame licked back from its stack. A feather of steam from the Confederate engine's safety valve suddenly changed to a white plume soaring high in the air.

"Stopped 'em, by Gawd!" Tatnall grunted. " 'Lowed they wouldn't dast face that smoke."

Cary, soaked and smoke-blackened, peered tensely through a great splintered hole punched in the boxcar's end.

One of the younger men passed a quivering hand over his forehead. "Thank God!" he breathed. "They're backing!"

"Yes! They *are* backing!"

"No! Look! Look!"

A loud-pitched groan echoed over the bumping and rattling of the last freight car. The Resolute, after backing a short distance, suddenly commenced to come on again. Courageously her engineer set out over the trestle. Long cowcatcher projecting five feet ahead of the breastbeam, the pursuer plowed right into the smoldering fire. With superb ease the cowcatcher spilled a cascade of smoking timbers over into Cedar Creek Ravine.

Once across the trestle the pursuers sounded a triumphant blast, came pounding along. Slowly, surely, the Confederate train commenced to gain though Brady and his crew recklessly sacrificed their fuel supply.

What to do? What in blazes to do? Cary knew he'd have to think of something, or twenty men—those in civilian clothes and rebel uniforms in any case—would hang. Having run over fifty miles at a speed for which she had never been designed, the Pocahontas was steadily losing ground to the huge black Resolute. There could be no doubt of that.

Inspiration seized him. "Heave some ties through that hole, boys. Try to drop them square on the track. One might derail her."

Eagerly the order was put into execution. When six sleepers had been dropped the round-eyed Federals paused, watched.

"They're stopping," Tatnall panted. "Don't dast risk derailing."

"Drop one tie every quarter mile," Cary ordered, then made a perilous trip forward over the madly swaying box-car tops.

"We're gaining, man, we're gaining!" he cried and clapped the engineer on his sweaty shoulder. "They've got to stop to pick those ties off the track!"

"Sure, it's slowin' 'em. By gobs, we've gained ten minutes already!" Collins was almost hysterical with relief. "Maybe if that shed on West Branch gets lit, the rebs won't dast run through it."

"Stop to get a bridge lit? Like hell we will!" snorted Brady. "We're runnin' for our lives now, you fool!"

Nevertheless, Cary felt, they must make sure of at least

one vital bridge. So far the expedition had accomplished next to nothing. True, the Woodstock covered bridge would, in all probability, be completely destroyed, but the Cedar Creek trestle was only slightly damaged.

Savagely the cavalryman beat his fist against the cab's hard green seat, yearned to howl curses at that sullen, unconquerable rain. It and it alone was snatching victory from their hands. How MacKenny would laugh when he heard the news! Twice more, yellow sleepers slanting across the rails forced the pursuers to stop. The Pocahontas began to gain.

"Think! Think! You must think!" Frantic voices clamored in Cary's brain.

Suddenly he jumped up. "Keep her going, Brady, but stop in the West Branch Bridge shed—got an idea going back."

"We *can't* stop, sir! This heah engine's brasses are heatin' fast. I can't keep up even this speed much longer."

"Slow down, then; we'll only need a minute——"

"Only a minute?"

Cary gave a reckless laugh. "Yes, I've a good idea—a *damned* slick idea!"

Far behind, the pursuer's whistle screamed like a hungry bird of prey.

STRATAGEM

MINUTES LATER the Pocahontas' grimy crew beheld Hubert Cary, coatless and smoke-blackened, clambering back over the car tops. Collins, glancing back to watch him, emitted a startled yell. A dense pall of smoke was hanging over the right of way.

"Good God! Train's afire!"

"Only our last car," Cary corrected, crawling over the last of the fuel. "It's what ties are left. How far ahead is West Branch Bridge?"

The engineer thrust his bald head out into the rain to study the landscape. Cary mopped a face decked with a confident smile—which was wholly counterfeit. There was something inevitable, something ominous about the persistency of the pursuers.

Twice the Federals glimpsed the Resolute toiling up a long grade, pushing before it the Pocahontas' shattered boxcar. Pulling a single boxcar, the Confederate train was gaining with dismaying speed.

[147]

The smoke-streaked faces about him had reason to look taut and anxious, Cary guessed. Brady's voice jerked him back to immediate problems.

"West Branch ain't but a quarter of a mile ahead, sir."

"How much of a lead we got?"

"Fifteen—twenty minutes."

"Why'd you set that car afire?"

"We'll leave it in the middle of the West Branch Bridge," Cary said, red hair whipping about his face. "Our lead ought to get that shed well afire before the rebs come up. Figure to block the car's wheels so's they can't push it clear."

"Gawd, Cap'n, you shore got yourself a jim-dandy idea," panted Clayton, feeding logs into the firebox. It glowed red hot around the edges. "Mebbe we'll win time enough to pull out a rail. You shore got that car agoin'!"

Soon the stolen train pulled out onto the West Branch trestle and became lost in the gloom of its shed. As quickly the dark walls glowed to the ruddy glare of the burning freight car. Once the dangerously overheated engine had halted, hissing and breathless, near the middle of the bridge, Cary led his men in leaping down to the ties. Silhouetted and shielding their faces from the orange-yellow flames, they worked madly to jam the wheels.

Veiled with smoke and fantastically lit by the dancing flames, they suffered numerous burns in their efforts to pull the coupling pin on the burning car and to thrust ties between its wheels.

"I allow *that* ought to hold 'em," Raines choked as with the others he scrambled into the last of the three boxcars.

[148]

"Damn well better." Cary's eyes were streaming; a dozen minor blisters stung his hands, wrists and face.

Suddenly he recalled a beetle he had once seen trying to climb out of a jar. Again and again the insect had toiled laboriously upward until, a fraction of an inch from the top, it had encountered a glazed area. Then it had fallen back into the jar, only to try again.

That burning car would form an effective block, Cary tried to assure himself. In a short while West Branch Bridge would be reduced to smoking embers.

So assured of success was the wearied, nerve-racked crew that a quarter of a mile beyond the bridge Cary ordered the engine halted for a final time to lift a rail.

"Heave-yo! Heave-yo!"

In unison "guards," "recruits," "prisoners" and "contractors" heaved and strained with that strength Nature lends to creatures in peril of their lives.

One end of the first rail had been loosened and gasps were rising from the red-faced toilers when the furious blast of a locomotive's whistle froze them in their several attitudes.

"It's them!" groaned Tatnall.

"Only a minute more," Cary pleaded; but there was no time.

"God damn, they is still coming!"

Sickened, Cary led a rush back to the loose and worn-out Pocahontas. When the engine commenced to move again it clattered dryly, ominously.

"We all will soon have to take to the country," Brady predicted with fatalistic calm. "I can't run fast now. Even

if this heah engine was fit, which she ain't, one car behind
don't steady us much. I don't dast hit even thirty miles—
we'd jump the track."

"Keep her going," Cary choked. His reddened, sunken
eyes flickered back to the pursuer so aptly christened Resolute. By God, those men in her cab were no weaklings!
Pushing the blazing car before them, the Confederates
must be scorched, bitterly stung. Doggedly the great black
engine was driving before it the shattered car abandoned
at Cedar Creek.

Though Brady skillfully, desperately coaxed every possible revolution from the Pocahontas' chattering, red-hot
bearings, the pursuing engine closed in foot by foot, yard
by yard.

"It's no use," the engineer said. "Just listen! Ain't half a
mile more in her. What'll we do?"

"Stop when we've got to," Cary said. "Then you'll reverse your engine. Might wreck 'em. Meantime we'll jump
and scatter—every man for himself."

So this was the end of the adventure. Almost. If only
the rain—— No use thinking about that—twenty—thirty—
forty miles to Harpers Ferry. A slim chance for anybody.
It wasn't right. Coolly, deliberately these men, Tatnall,
Collins, Brady, O'Leary, Clayton and the rest, had offered
their lives—because they believed that in America there
should be no jealous, petty, bickering statelets. Slavery?
To hell with the rights and wrongs of that problem! His
men were riding this crazily jolting, doomed train because
in their inarticulate way they felt that Europe's madness

should not reseed itself in America. Oh, it was so utterly, damnably unfair that the rain should have come.

Sullenly the engine crew were watching Brady's hand close over the worn brass throttle when the unexpected happened. Frame timbers of the blazing car suddenly disintegrated. Flaming boards, smoking stanchions and braces flew through the rain in every direction.

The bottom of the freight car fell to the rails, and its trucks jumped the track. In a twinkle it derailed the Resolute. The Confederate locomotive lurched on, splintering ties, spilling its fuel. In terrifying violence the Resolute catapulted its crew right and left. Ultimately the engine toppled over amid blinding clouds of steam.

Hysterical cries of triumph burst from the raiders' throats, diminished the surging of the Pocahontas' boiler, the dreadful clatter of her bearings. Cary almost collapsed on the engineer's seat.

Safe! Safe! No drumhead court-martial, no hangman's noose!

"Oh God, I thank thee!" babbled Collins, and the two firemen pounded each other with blistered hands.

Safe! *Safe!* SAFE!

Anxious lines faded from their set faces. Brady throttled down. Stopped. Reoiled. Everybody shook hands, pretended they hadn't been scared—and fooled no one. It wasn't safe to delay—word *might* have gone still farther ahead.

At Kernstown a single passenger car, left on the main line by a local engaged in switching, was unceremoniously picked up. Despite the startled yells of the passengers the

Pocahontas started triumphantly on toward the last and most important bridge.

"We'll give 'em the ride of their rebel lives," Brady chortled.

"When can we get rid of that blasted car?" Cary rasped. He could see scared white faces on the passenger car's platform.

"We can drop 'em outside of Winchester," exulted Brady. "There's a spur there."

Everyone was talking now, waving derisively at the civilians in the passenger car. They didn't know what had happened.

No more pursuers, an open road. Best of all, the rain was letting up!

Cary felt like singing. Once more life was an adventure. The effort hadn't been in vain. His mind's eye saw the all-important bridge over Opequan Creek reduced to ashes. To rebuild it would require two weeks, ten days anyway. No supplies for Lee from this direction, not for ten days anyway.

After stopping to cut wires the Pocahontas comfortably entered the last stretch of her run. Up, up the engine labored through the foothills of the Blue Ridge. Dripping woods came down closer to the track. The weary engine labored like an overladen beast of burden.

"Top this grade in a minute," Brady cried. "Then it's only seven miles to Opequan. Bridge's covered so——"

Brady never finished. The Pocahontas surged upward— the gray sky resounded to a deafening, heart-shaking crash.

Bodies were flung against each other as woods and sky

wheeled dizzily about—screams, the snarling sound of splintering wood and, fleetingly, the brittle jangle of smashing glass were recorded in Cary's ears. Like a speared fish the locomotive floundered off the track, plowed across the rear end of the Kernstown car, ground it into the ballast, smashed it into the sodden earth.

Hubert Cary was hurtled into space, rolled furiously down the embankment away from a hell of spurting steam and crashing timbers. Amid a blinding blaze he sank into oblivion.

CHAPTER FOURTEEN

LUKE ARCHER

A REEK of burning wood smoke stung Captain Hubert Cary's nostrils, set him to coughing feebly. The world seemed veiled as if seen through a white woolen muffler. It had looked like that when a New England zero gale was stabbing every exposed inch of his face. He heard groans, cries. Were those shots?

A heavy tread shook the ground near his head, then a hoarse voice drawled:

"'At's one daid, Gurney. Mount up, Cash; we-uns best be high-tailin' outta these parts."

Sulphurous oaths accompanied someone's assent. "By the devil's hoof, they's sumpin' queer 'bout all this."

"Yeah. Warn't no *up*train due."

Feet trampled again. Somewhere a woman cried out in pain.

Gigantic, muddied boots filled the world of Cary's vision.

"Heyo, Cash, this feller hain't daid. His eyes is open. Playin' possum, b'Jeeze. Git back!"

"No. Ah gits his watch."

Cary felt his watch snatched away, then there ensued a scuffle followed by a snarling curse.

"Jest you lay yore dawg's paws off 'n hit. I saw hit fust."

"Hey!"

A boot prodded Hubert Cary's inert form. He couldn't move; his insides felt all cold and queer. Then he remembered what had happened. He was captured—and *out of uniform*.

Too bad he hadn't died in the wreck. These rebels would hang him out of hand. He hoped he'd find courage to make a good end.

The foot kicked him back of the ear.

"Git up, Yank—you ain't foolin' nobody."

Cary struggled to raise his head, but an overpowering nausea forced him to relax again on the wet leaves.

"He's too hurt to take along," grunted the voice of the man addressed as Gurney. "Knock him off, Cash."

[155]

The metallic *click!* of a revolver being cocked accomplished miracles.

"No, no!" Cary choked. At the same time he made vague negative motions with his hands.

"Oh, so y' wuz playin' possum. Git up, yu wuthless houn'!"

Another kick under the shoulder made his teeth rattle. The world reeled crazily around and around, but he clutched a young birch and succeeded in raising himself.

Gradually his vision cleared, revealed a sight beyond description.

Soldiers in gray uniforms, both afoot and ahorseback, swarmed all over the debris-littered right of way. They poked at the wrecked Pocahontas, which lay on its side, still sending gray feathers of steam wavering skywards.

The boxcar which had contained Tatnall and his men was ablaze despite the chilling downpour. Perhaps two dozen lanky individuals in butternut or gray uniforms were braving the low-hanging smoke to explore the shattered passenger coach picked up at Kernstown.

A ragged volley made the dizzied Federal choke. God above! The Confederates weren't losing any time executing their prisoners. But then an obvious spy must expect short shrift.

Almost under the smoking muskets of a slovenly firing party composed of infantry, artillery and cavalrymen Raines and two of the "prisoners" lay, their bodies slowly, hopelessly contorting themselves.

"Don't murder me, gentlemen. For Christ's sake, *don't*— my wife!" Collins, the assistant engineer, was trying to crawl off into a laurel thicket. He was trailing a badly broken leg that sprouted bits of bloody bone. He reminded Cary of a crippled dog he'd once seen.

After Collins trampled a grinning, hulking giant in a gray artillery uniform. He carried a cocked revolver in one hand. This he alternately leveled and lowered, threatening the terror-stricken captive.

"Beg, damn you, beg!"

Raines raised supplicating hands. "Please, mister, *don't*— I ain't——"

The man in artillery uniform roared with laughter, squeezed the trigger. Under impact of the bullet Raines's body was jolted flat. A bright scarlet trickle began to slide down from the Marylander's half-open mouth.

"You damn butchers!" Futile revolt poisoned Cary's brain.

Were these the chivalrous Southerners of history? God— how could they murder helpless wounded men like this, even if they were spies?

Yonder half a dozen privates were tugging, hauling at a row of limp and lifeless civilians scattered beside the steps of the derailed, but not upset, coach.

A small vicious fellow with deep smallpox pits scarring his features callously explored the petticoats of a woman, searched her stocking tops. Finding a roll of greenbacks, he exhibited it in triumph.

Other men in rebel uniform stood taunting a knot of disheveled, dripping prisoners. It included four women and half a dozen men.

Of the raiders less than a half-dozen still lived. Among

these were Tatnall, Brady and Clayton, the pessimistic fire-man. Of the women one was weeping hysterically and hiding her head in a dull green shawl. The others stood staring in numb, rigid horror.

Still too shaken to perceive matters clearly or to conjecture upon his probable fate, Cary nevertheless became aware that this body of Confederates had two leaders.

One of them said, "Reckon we all got to separate!"

"Yep, my fust choice though."

"Yo' choice this time, Joe. Whar 'll we meet next?"

"At the crossroads come Sunday."

Suddenly the question obtruded itself. Why were these fellows taking women and civilians prisoner? For hostages, maybe? Both sides recently had adopted the pernicious practice.

His brain moved sluggishly as a mass of cold glue. What was wrong about this business? Something was wrong— very wrong indeed. He was still attempting to reason it out when a mounted squad, with brutal thrusts of their carbine butts, divided the prisoners into two groups. To Cary's dismay Tatnall and other survivors of his party were allotted to another gang.

He tried to edge over to join them, but a bony artillery private freed a foot from its stirrup and kicked him. "Git back thar! Git a move on."

Once the Confederates had divided the prisoners into two parties of equal size they loaded some pack horses with miscellaneous plunder and mounted up. One detachment immediately moved off down the track, but Cary's captors started driving the prisoners up a path leading toward forbidding pine woods which seemed to rise in unbroken gloom to the very summit of the Blue Ridge range.

Suddenly nausea assailed and so weakened the semi-dazed cavalryman that, to keep from falling, he clutched at the shoulder of a powerful middle-aged fellow prisoner.

"Help me," Cary choked.

"Help *you?*" snarled the other. "Only thing I'll enjoy about this mess is watching you hanged, you goddam Yank spy."

A younger well-dressed fellow, however, caught the reeling Federal by his elbow. "Lean on me. If you fall back, they'll shoot you."

Fighting a blinding nausea, Cary stumbled, was barely able to follow the trail. Luckily he kept bumping wet branches. These drenched him again and again, helped to clear his aching head.

If he could only forget Raines and those two other men choking out their lives on the wet weeds beside the right of way.

A little steadier, Cary tried to smile his thanks to the man who had helped him, but the young fellow looked quickly away. The other men prisoners simply glowered. As for the two women, they were led at the end of this long slender column.

Cary began to study his captors as they rode along with carbines held ready. They kept peering restlessly about like ranging bird dogs. Most of them were very thin, Indian-visaged and hawk-nosed. Almost without exception these enemies wore their hair down to their shoulders. Many boasted great tangled whiskers which more resembled the manes of animals than the beards of human beings.

At the head of this slow, rain-drenched column rode a hulking individual on whose sleeves glimmered the broad red stripes of a Confederate artillery sergeant. Alternately cursing the weather and his stumbling, shivering prisoners, the leader now bent low in his saddle, now parted the branches with vicious thrusts of tremendously long arms.

All at once Cary began to think, to be sure, that he had seen the leader's wide shoulders before. Where? At Philomont? Down on the Peninsula? Where, then? Maybe if he could glimpse the other's face he'd remember.

His clumsy efforts to remember were interrupted by a gasp, the faltering voice of a woman:

"Oh—oh, please—kind sirs, I—I can't walk this fast any longer."

"Like hell you cain't—keep movin'. Yer ain't traveled

[160]

half a mile. Pick up them feet!" Her guard used the flat of a heavy Federal saber, and the woman gave a weak little squeal like that of a trapped rabbit.

Cary slugged on, clutching the young fellow's arm.

In a deep ravine the column halted and collected under a clump of slowly dripping pines; some furry horses stood picketed there, nibbling at grain scattered on the earth. A trio of guards as wild and unkempt as those who had wrecked the Pocahontas shambled forward waving wide-brimmed hats.

"Heyo! How wuz the pickin's?" bawled a horse guard. He trotted through the pines.

"Wa'n't wuth the trouble," complained the broad-shoul-dered leader. "Some damn Yank raid wuz on. Didn't git to the Rectortown express."

Hubert Cary suffered a major shock when the leader, reaching the floor of the ravine, turned about and pulled off his wide-brimmed felt hat to beat it free of raindrops.

In a flash returned visions of a horse tied outside of Cal-thorp's pleasant little farm, of a black-bearded giant in the uniform of a Union sergeant.

Yonder stood the same man; scar, long nose, black beard and all. But this time he was wearing a Confederate artil-leryman's regimentals. What was his name? Craig Carey had mentioned it. Abers? Aber—— Couldn't remember. No—Archer, that was it!

"Wal, now let's see whut we've got." Mounting up, Archer kicked forward his horse and, bending in the saddle, scanned a damp heap of booty collected by his followers.

"Slim pickin's fo' all that trouble," he growled.

The jayhawker turned, studied the prisoners moodily, then stiffened suddenly. "Wal, sting my britches! Ain't you—*sho'* you are. Wal, wal, Goldilocks, fancy comin' up with you again. Miss Duveen, you sho' air welcome to my eyes."

Cary wheeled when a woman uttered a stifled gasp. Because of several mounted jayhawkers crowding about their leader, he could not see the Duveen girl. How? Why? Then he recalled their conversation at Philomont. Her saying, "Yes, I am going south to Salem soon—provided the railroads still are running."

Recollections more painful, more vivid, returned. He visualized the English girl as he'd first found her—two or was it three days back?—in that bedroom of Calthorp's farm. Could see her torn waist fluttering, her pale hair streaming.

Dazedly he tried to assure himself that all this nightmare was some trick of the imagination. It could not be she.

How monstrously ironical that the fleeing Pocahontas should have found in its path a single coach, had, of necessity, propelled it to disaster and its passengers into the hands of these human wolves.

Licking a cake of mud and dried blood from his lips, Cary got a glimpse of the Duveen girl. Her lovely features now were rigid, and a dull red bruise marred one cheek. So far, it appeared, she had not recognized him. Small wonder when he came to think of it. The remnants of his civilian clothes were ripped and snagged, and his face was stained with engine oil, dirt and clay.

Apparently Archer also had failed to recognize him. He wondered what Lenore Duveen would say, and do, when recognition came. He guessed she would rate him no higher than these barbarous marauders.

What stung Cary most was that Archer had, at the very last instant, snatched away his hard-earned chance to burn that all-important Opequan Bridge. Now only God knew what would happen to Colonel Miles's garrison. Maybe they could hold out—maybe not.

"Mount up! Mount up!" roared the jayhawk leader. "Tie these hyar prisoners onto the mules. Fo' yore sakes, you gals better know how to ride."

Archer sent his horse surging toward where Lenore Duveen stood. In muddied dark green her lissom figure stood outlined against a holly thicket.

"Gawd boil mah body, but I'm pleased to find my Goldilocks again. Look, Scroggs, remember her?"

"Sho' do. Watch out," warned the lieutenant. "She was a reg'lar hellcat when we took her down in the valley."

Archer reined in, grinning; his pale brown eyes narrowed slowly. " 'Til now I reckoned I had won a powerful po' pot with this hyar hand, but blamed if I don't hold the wild kyard after all."

The jayhawker's scar flamed as, with a sudden swoop, he bent low and hauled Lenore across his pommel.

"Wal, honeybee, how you doin'?"

"Let me go. You will be paid, well paid," the Duveen girl promised.

"Shucks, honeybee, ain't 'nough gold in America to pay for a kiss o' yourn. So I reckon I will jest have to *take* it."

The assembled marauders made the pine woods echo with deep guffaws as Luke Archer bent and rained kisses on the quivering face. Long legs and arms flailing, Lenore Duveen twisted, pounded and squirmed in futile rebellion.

There wasn't much he could accomplish, Cary guessed, but it wasn't in him to do nothing. He staggered forward suddenly.

Frightened, Archer's big bay horse commenced to rear and plunge as Cary grabbed the animal's bit and forced the startled mount to rear up—up. To avoid sliding from

his saddle Archer was forced to release the girl. Her pale hair was loosed, fell tumbling over her shoulders.

"Hell's roarin' bells! Somebody stab that son of a bitch!"

Leaping in from behind, a jayhawker got a strangle hold on Cary's neck and tried to wrench him over backward. The Federal, however, reaching back, got hold of his assailant's collar and jerked him overhead in a wide somersault.

The thrown jayhawker's fall forced back his companions. Cary lurched forward, got the fellow's revolver. Over its front sight he placed the furious distorted features of Luke Archer.

Archer knew what impended, flung out a futile fending hand. When Cary squeezed the trigger there followed a dry *click!* Archer's stained teeth flashed in a diabolical grin.

Like deerhounds the jayhawkers pulled their prisoner down. Hands clawed at Cary, gouged the skin over his throat; then a knife blade glimmered before his eyes. From the ground Cary glimpsed Lenore Duveen staring at him in stunned amazement.

"Leave him be!" Archer's horse, violently spurred, scattered Cary's attackers in all directions. Steel shoes momentarily flashed past the fallen Federal's face. "Cash, jist put away that goddam knife. There's a hell's mint o' fun to be had of this Yank 'fore I'm shet o' him."

They stripped the Federal to a blue-checked cotton shirt, then bound his hands behind him so tight that a few instants later he commenced suffering an exquisite torture. Next, the bewildered, battered cavalryman was lifted astride a rangy gelding. It wore no saddle and galled its rider with a backbone sharp as the Blue Ridge itself.

[165]

Cash, a young sandy-haired fellow in a round civilian's hat and a gray shell jacket stolen from some murdered Confederate, tied Cary's ankles beneath the gelding's lean belly.

"That's jest so's to make sure ye ain't turnin' up missin' at the doin's."

"But"—the prisoner protested—"suppose—he falls—narrow trails—can't——"

"You'll fall with him," chuckled the marauder. "Mebbe you'd be better off." The sandy-haired ruffian dealt his prisoner a stinging cuff. "Jest to clear yo' haid."

That gratuitous slap went far to reinstill revolt in Cary. 'Til now he had been too crushed at the apparently complete failure of his raid, too depressed by the death of his companions to accomplish much consecutive thinking.

Refreshed by the thinning rain, he managed to turn. The outlaws were lifting Lenore Duveen and another young woman astride a pair of horses. In sullen obedience they hitched up petticoats and skirts. The jayhawkers guffawed and offered bawdy comments on the exposed legs.

"Wal," Scroggs called out, "may I be dipped in slops, Luke, if we hain't miscounted! Short one hoss."

The young fellow who had helped Cary looked nervous—and with reason. Luke Archer rode over, peered down at him.

"Wal, Bub, 'pears like yu are in luck. We hain't got 'nough hosses."

"Y-yes sir, but I can walk fast," the prisoner stated, his features ghostly pale.

"Not near fast enough ter keep up with these here

hosses." Archer scratched meditatively under his red-bound collar. "But don't you worry, Bub; we hain't goin' ter hurt yer. We aim ter turn yer loose."

"Turn me loose!" Incredulous joy lit the young fellow's rain-streaked features. He began to tremble. "Oh, thank you! Thank you. God bless you, sir."

"They's only one condition," the outlaw qualified. "That ye'll not say nawthin' to nobody 'bout what we-uns was wearin' or whar we-uns is headed."

"Oh-h—no." The prisoner lifted a radiant face. "On my sacred word of honor, sir, I won't say a word. Save for me, my ma's got nobody. On her account I was afraid——"

"All right, Bub." Shifting his revolver, Luke Archer leaned down, extended a huge hairy hand. "Wal, we'll shake to show there hain't no hard feelin's."

Once they had shaken hands Archer gathered his reins; the other jayhawkers commenced to grin. The two young women, trying to rearrange their skirts, looked a little more hopeful. Maybe Archer had a few decent impulses.

"Now, Bub," the jayhawker said, "you better run like hell outen this hyar ravine. Mought change my mind."

The prisoner needed no urging. He wheeled and, turning off at right angles to the line of horsemen along the trail, commenced to sprint. His brown-clad figure was sharply silhouetted against the dark underbrush.

"Faster, Bub!" advised the man called Cash.

Cary, in helpless horror, watched the guerrilla turn, grinning, and level his big navy-type revolver.

"Mark this, Scroggs," Archer announced. "I'll drop him fust shot once he passes that there spruce root."

"Five greenbacks yer don't," drawled the jayhawker's fox-faced lieutenant.

"Take yer. Watch!"

A flat, incisive report made horses rear all along the line. Lenore Duveen's companion screamed shrilly with a rising note of hysterical terror.

Some fifty yards away the fugitive seemed to trip; convulsively his arms flew skyward. Twisting, he fell heavily onto the wet dead leaves. Slowly, painfully, the victim rolled over, then collapsed, lay with face turned up, oblivious to the sifting rain.

Above the murderer's head a woolly patch of grayish smoke lingered like a sinister halo.

"Hya! Hya!" he bellowed. "C'mon, Scroggs, fork over that five. Yer know what folks say 'bout a fool an' his money."

CHAPTER FIFTEEN

THE CAVERN

IT SEEMED that an agonizing century elapsed before the rain-soaked column came to halt in a rocky ravine high amid the Blue Ridge range. At one end of this retreat gaped the cavern which must have served as a more or less permanent base for Archer's marauding expeditions.

Before the cavern's entrance a pair of bandaged guerrillas had a fire going. These arose to greet the straggling expedition with hoarse inquiries.

A scattering of rough lean-tos, built amid a magnificent stand of pines to the right of the cave's mouth, afforded a further shelter for the men. Cary found it significant that the guerrillas' horses were protected by a carefully constructed shed which had been partitioned off to prevent the animals from kicking each other.

The other male prisoner forgot his hostility long enough to mutter in Cary's ear. "Thank God, the rain has stopped. I'm mighty near frozen."

"So am I."

Once he stood on the ground again, the cavalry captain's teeth began chattering loud as the bones of a Negro end man. There wasn't much warmth or protection in a thin cotton shirt. As he stood under the dripping pines Cary's bound hands went absolutely numb.

The female prisoners were to be better treated, it seemed. Two jayhawkers emerged from the cave bearing grimy blankets in their arms.

"Heah you is, gals," one of them called out. "Tuck these about yourselves and keep yo' bottoms warm 'til Luke decides kin you all go inside."

"Yeh, wrap yerselves up tight," grinned another. "We-uns ain't got airy use fer cold wenches."

"Pleasant swine!" Cary chattered. "Hanging's too good for 'em."

"My name's Kernan, Hobson Kernan," the other prisoner began. "I'm a grain dealer, was on my way to Richmond when your train picked up my car."

Kernan's eyes bared whitely through the gray and cheerless twilight. "Why in hell did you do it?"

"It's too long a story to tell now," shivered Cary. "They leave anything sharp on you—a penknife, perhaps?"

"Nary a thing." The grain dealer sighed, blowing a drop of water from the end of an oily-looking pointed nose. "'Pears like we're in for it, Mister Yank. In for it good and proper. What do you reckon they'll maybe do with us?"

"Try to make you pay ransom, shouldn't wonder."

"Me? Why not you?"

"You saw what I did before we mounted up. Besides, Archer has an older score to settle with me."

"Then you've seen this God-damned bushwhacker before?"

"Sure. I know enough about Archer to hang him a dozen times over."

The prisoners lapsed into a miserable silence, sullenly watched the motley-clad jayhawkers rub down their horses then kindle fires before their lean-tos.

About fifteen in all they were, without exception leather-faced, loose-jointed men such as the Alleghenies breed in numbers.

"Reckon you all kin git up an' move around," grudgingly remarked one of the younger jayhawkers. " 'Tain't no use for you all to ketch a never-git-over."

Cary presently limped over to where Lenore Duveen sat comforting the hysterical young woman who was her only companion. He stood before them in silence.

The English girl's skirt was in thorn-ripped tatters. Split from hem to waist, it revealed long legs in torn stockings. Bruises and scratches marred their smoothness. Her hair hung in lank strings to her shoulders, and her nose was pink and shiny.

What would the fire-eating beaux of Baltimore have thought of their cherished Golden Diana in such a state? Odd, Baltimore lay little over two hundred miles away.

Although she must have been aware of his presence, Lenore Duveen made not the least effort to acknowledge his existence until he spoke.

"Seems I am fated to cause you unhappiness," he muttered, trying to still the chattering of his teeth. "Anyhow, I want to tell you that I am sorry—dreadfully sorry—for what has happened; though I imagine nothing I can say will make any difference."

Her look flicked him like a whip. Had he been a complete stranger she could not have been half so coldly impersonal.

"Your assumption, Captain Cary, is quite correct," said she in level tones more withering than blazing invectives. "Please leave us alone. Mrs Ross is exhausted."

"You loathe me," he muttered. "You think with good reason. You're wrong. If you'll co-operate, I will try to get us all out of this."

She raised a face drawn and somehow refined by weariness. "I don't imagine you will understand why, Captain, but I would rather perish than to accept help from you."

In a gesture of unmistakable finality she turned her back, drew a blanket higher over her companion.

Cary nodded. He had expected such a reaction and yet he had not. He had hoped that Lenore Duveen of the sharp wit and the clear insight might understand—might see into the underlying motive of his act at Philomont.

Numbly he turned aside and saw Archer talking to the grain dealer. The jayhawker was standing before the fire with threads of steam climbing from his sodden breeches' legs.

"I want five thousand greenbacks," the jayhawk leader was declaring. "Not one cent less."

"But, Misto' Archer," cried Kernan desperately, "I ain't got even two thousand dollars to my name."

Archer tugged at his great fan-shaped beard. "You had better find it, else we'll stake ye out on the mountingside and let the buzzards at you.

"As fer you"—his scar flamed as he turned on Cary—"I bin thinkin' 'bout ye. Kain't quite decide jest which idyah's best." He leveled a gnarled forefinger at the cave's entrance. It yawned like the maw of some mythical monster. "Get in thar! The hull kit an' boodle of ye."

Presently all four prisoners were squatting on piles of moldy hay.

Despite urgent pleas the captors kept the hands of both men bound behind them. At the cave's mouth squatted a quartet of long-haired jayhawkers. These held ostentatiously cocked Spencer carbines across their knees. In the heart of the pine grove a large fire flared continually, outlined the guards in its ruddy glare.

"Oh, my Jesus, hell will bust loose before long," quavered Kernan in a scared whisper.

"Why?"

"See that moonshine?"

Grimly Cary watched a demijohn of corn whisky beginning to circulate among the marauders. Before the outlaws had half cooked their supper Scroggs, Archer and half a dozen other figures in muddied uniforms began to bawl out a mountain ballad concerning certain obscene happenings "Down in the Lehigh Valley."

Presently Jed, the young jayhawker who had told Cary he might move about, entered the cave carrying two bowls of stew.

"How can we eat with our hands tied?" Kernan protested. "Say, Bub, suppose you turn us loose, long enough to eat leastways?"

"Reckon I cain't. Hit's agin Luke's orders. Better git

them gals to feed ye. Mebbe you kin make these hyar bowls a sort o' lovin' cup."

Sniggering, the jayhawker shuffled back out to the fire. The outlaws were now eating noisily, redly outlined by the fire.

Cary stared intently out into the darkness, forced himself to forget the agony of his pinioned wrists and his apprehensions that gangrene might already have set in.

Odd, the flames of the fire made the thin flat faces of the guards glow as though fashioned of molten iron rather than flesh. What vicious, stupid, brutish faces those were out there. Was there the least chance of escape in that direction? At present there certainly seemed no way out. Damn, those shaggy devils out there were working at the demijohn again.

He was recalled to the present by hearing Lenore Duveen's soft voice:

"Please, Mrs Ross, you must—really must—swallow a bit of this stew. If you don't keep up your strength, there's no hope for you."

"Strength for what?" whimpered the other, lifting a face which, though grimy and quivering, was still pretty.

"Oh—I—I—want to die. Oh, Lord Jesus, save me. Don't I know what they're going to do to us pretty soon?"

Lenore looked aside hurriedly.

"Maybe they won't. They're humans."

The smaller girl shuddered.

"They will. If I have less strength maybe I'll die quicker. Oh, Lord, save this poor sinner."

The distracted young creature fell to mumbling snatches

of prayer until Lenore took her firmly by the shoulders, lifted a spoonful of stew to her lips.

"You stop your nonsense," she commanded sharply. "Eat this. There *is* hope so long as we keep courage. I—I'm just as badly off as you and—I—look at me eat!"

Cary, fascinated by Lenore Duveen's poise, watched the Ross girl, a petite brunette of twenty, yield. She commenced to eat, slowly at first, then hungrily.

Presently Mrs Ross must have felt better, for she pushed some strands of sodden wet hair from her eyes, murmuring, "I—I'm so sorry, Miss Duveen. I—I'm afraid I am not overly brave."

Rallying, she sat up, dragging the blanket about her shoulders. "I will f-feed Mr Kernan—you f-feed the—the other g-gentleman."

Occupied by a particularly agonizing twinge in his swollen wrists, Cary was not aware of Lenore Duveen's approach until her slender silhouette eclipsed the firelight.

"Since your hands are tied, I suppose I shall have to feed you," observed the English girl, her face a pallid mask.

The injustice of her attitude stung him into a childish retort.

"You aren't obligated to do a thing for me. I'd rather you didn't." He turned aside to stare out at the campfire. He heard her gasp of surprise.

"But really!"

"I've gambled and lost," he rasped. "I prefer not to be reminded of it, and I'm in no mood for contemptuous false pity."

"Mock heroics!" Her tone was cutting, but there was a

changed light in her anxiety-widened eyes. "Here, you'd better eat this." She might have been speaking to a sullen child and so infuriated him more. As she bent over him a faint odor of gardenias raised harrowing recollections.

"Thank you, no." He fixed a pain-brightened look on her. "For God's sake, be consistent! You despise me. Why be kind?"

Lenore Duveen's dimly seen face went whiter than ever, her large eyes more shadowed, her mouth more appealing.

"About your finer feelings I don't care a rap. However, I do know that you should eat. After all, there is Mrs Ross to consider. The poor thing has only been married a month. You must get her away from this horrible place."

Not a word of fear or concern for herself. Cary suddenly became annoyed with his petulance.

"Possibly you are right," he agreed.

Eagerly he gulped his share of a coarse salt-pork stew which she dipped up with a battered pewter spoon. Not once, however, did she meet his eyes. He might have been an infant or a Negro.

"Thank you," he said simply. "You must eat yourself."

Lenore Duveen nodded, got up and, reseating herself a few feet away, finished the second half of the stew as calmly as if it had been one of those dainty dishes served at Philomont.

Greatly refreshed, Cary sank back on the damp hay. Dear God! No wonder he was hungry. He hadn't eaten since leaving Harpers Ferry half a lifetime ago.

So this was Tom Blake's feather-headed, volatile Golden Diana! The nickname, at least, was apt. If ever a modern girl's figure had been formed on the lines of the fabled huntress-goddess, it was that of Lenore Duveen. Richly golden, too, were flashes drawn by the fire in hair she hastily had plaited into a braid.

What would the jayhawkers, Archer and all his crew, decide to do? What would she—all of them—suffer before that darkening sky grew light once more?

He found no reassurance in the fact that another jug of liquor was brought up. Voices by the campfire were becoming pitched to a second and a third drink.

Common sense and some familiarity with the local mountaineers warned him what to expect.

Could anything be done to forestall an impending tragedy? There could be no doubt that these outlaws were working steadily toward a more bestial mood.

Stratagem after strategem he debated and discarded as hopeless. The conviction grew that perhaps *there was no way out!* With sweat pouring down his back Cary lay staring into the darkness.

Minutes dragged by. Beside the fire the demijohns circled more quickly. Nasal, whining voices' accents grew louder, more argumentative. Something decisive would happen very soon now.

Archer, gigantic amid the drifting smoke, was rumbling,

"Never in my bawn days hev I seen a gal so fetchin' as that yaller-haid. Declar', boys, I feel like, why dammit, like she was 'most good enough to marry."

Scroggs, the vulpine lieutenant, held up the liquor jug. "Marry? Best licker up, Luke—yo're still sober. Besides, it's share and share alike."

Archer's hand flew to his bowie. "You, Scroggs, shet yer trap!" He glared about. "Jest one o' you billies dast look cross-eyed at my Goldilocks and I'll shorely spill his guts onto his boots!"

"What—what was that he said, Captain?" Kernan whispered.

"Nothing," Cary lied. "He's just making a brag."

Mrs Ross must have heard though. Her wide horror-filled eyes kept staring out past the guards at the cavern's entrance. These also were now taking a turn at the demijohn.

The bride began shivering violently beneath her blanket, Cary noticed, then shut her eyes and pressed hands over ears in a futile effort to deny realities.

Indescribable obscenities commenced to pass among the marauders. One of them jumped up and, contriving a caricature of a skirt, commenced a grotesque parody of a dance. It was the *hodiadah,* a licentious *pas seul* which field hands had brought over from the jungles of the Ivory Coast.

Rocking their bodies and clapping hands, the carousers warmed to their merriment; one of them caught up two fagots and commenced to drum on an upturned bucket.

"Sho' now, hain't Jerry got the orneriest wiggle to his bottom?"

"Wiggle's all right," hiccoughed another, "but he's sho' got a figger like the breakup o' a hard winter 'long the Potomac."

Scroggs swayed to his feet, bandy bowlegs blackly outlined by the leaping flames.

"Of all the hawg-stupid fools in this world," he wheezed, "you billies watching that fool Jerry shore wins the cake-walk." He flourished a horny palm in the direction of the cave. "Hain't we got the real goods in yonder?"

"Now hain't Joel the sly old he-coon?"

A terrified moan burst from the Ross girl's lips. "Oh, dear Father in heaven, d-don't let those—people come in here." She raised shaking hands toward the cave's roof.

Cary, utterly helpless, watched Lenore Duveen assume a pose of resignation. Her face became calm, a lovely tragic mask.

A swarm of gap-toothed jayhawkers, food-stained gray uniforms unbuttoned and flapping loose, advanced sway-ing toward the cavern.

"Sho', sho', le's have a real dance. Le's strip 'em, birch 'em, make 'em strut lively."

"Hold on, you billies." Archer pitched away the chop bone at which he had been tearing. Wiping fingers on beard, he momentarily barred his advancing followers.

"Go ahaid an' have yer fun, boys. Sho', take the dark wench ef yo're so minded, but I'll shorely skin alive the first son of a bitch lays paws on my Goldilocks."

"Hi-yah! Ain't stripped a gal in the longest time."

Like creatures in a nightmare the malodorous throng came tramping in, darkened the cavern's entrance.

"Step right in, Joel," invited the guards. "Help yo'self to as sweet a——"

"No! No! Mother! Oh, God, save me!" The Ross girl fled, whimpering, to the blank end of the cave. Head shielded in arm, she crouched like a rabbit terrified at the approach of a fox.

"Shore, Gawd don't nohow need to save you, honey," mocked Archer's bandy-legged lieutenant. "We ain't goin' to hurt you, sugar. Come along, pet, and amoose the boys awhile."

Reeking of the corn liquor, Scroggs grabbed at the girl's shoulder and tore her sleeve. Suddenly Kernan sprang up with a cry of, "Leave her alone!" and butted Scroggs so effectively that he went reeling back among his fellows.

"Yer ornery——"

Grimacing horribly, the jayhawker called Jerry drove his fist smacking against the captive's jaw. Because Kernan's hands were tied he lost his balance, went over backward and fell heavily onto some loose rocks strewing the cavern's floor. Obviously stunned, he lay quivering while the outlaws kicked and trampled him in drunken ferocity.

Cary would have sprung up but Cash, his earlier persecutor, promptly bore him back to earth and, winding fingers in the cavalryman's hair, pressed the edge of a bowie to his throat.

"Make a move," Cash snarled, "and I'll shorely nick yer gullet!"

Raising a series of soul-shaking shrieks, the Ross girl struggled but became pinioned by four joyfully shouting jayhawkers. They carried her past Cary exactly as though she were a deer—one man to each limb. Her head sagged so low that her dark hair trailed on the ground. Though she continued to scream, she kept her eyes tight shut.

Once they had passed, Lenore Duveen sat as before,

hands rigidly clasped before her. For all the life in her face, it might have been fashioned of wax.

"Bind that polecat's laigs, Cash," Scroggs snarled when the man who had been seated on Cary's chest made ready to rise. "Luke wouldn't fancy gettin' butted in the slats when he comes a-callin' fer Goldilocks."

Scroggs paused to squirt a stream of tobacco juice into the face of the ghastly pale and stertorously breathing Kernan then, hitching his pistol belt higher, he swaggered out into the firelight.

"Hya! Hya!" he called. " 'At's a way. Always pick a dove clean."

Despite himself Cary couldn't help watching the wild play of the Ross girl's limbs as in savage eagerness Archer's men ripped away her clothing until she cowered at last, sobbing, disheveled, wholly nude, in the dancing firelight.

"Dance, honeybird, dance."

"Oh-h, I can't—really, I——"

"This 'll help ye l'arn!" Scroggs snatched off his belt, hit her with it; a dark line materialized across her buttocks.

Irresistibly attracted, the guards arose and wandered out to stare on that tortured figure which, under the threat of birch switches, staggered wearily back and forth beyond the fire in a pathetic mockery of a dance.

Later the night was made hideous with vain cries and entreaties for mercy.

The liquor made itself felt in other ways; two outlaws suddenly commenced to fight for no visible cause. Knife blades glittered and flashed until one of the antagonists, doubled up and moaning, staggered off toward the underbrush, pursued by his infuriated comrade who pitilessly slashed him again and again until he fell.

Inside the cave, however, ruled silence. Only Kernan's labored breathing formed a small island of sound. Lenore Duveen sat as before, rigidly waiting.

Captain Cary lay on his side studying various actors in the saturnalia taking place beyond the fire.

The Federal felt clearer headed now but began to curse inwardly because the fire was being allowed to burn so low. He could no longer count the number of times the stone jug was circulated.

Three, four, half a dozen outlaws had, in drunken slumber, collapsed onto the wet earth. Mrs Ross was no longer dancing, but from the depths of the pines issued sobbing, dreadful whimpers—whimpers which evoked only obscenities and drunken laughter. Presently Cary counted only Archer and four others still on their feet.

Of the guards at the cavern's entrance one was nodding; the other had gone swaying off to that pine grove in which the ultimate outrage was being perpetrated.

"Miss Duveen," Cary begged in a hoarse whisper, "come here—quietly."

Apparently Lenore Duveen did not or would not hear him.

"Lenore Duveen! For your own sake come here—listen."

The girl's head, ghostly in the uncertain light, swayed up. She stared dully at him an instant, then set her lips and began crawling toward him on hands and knees. It had grown so dark he could barely distinguish dark smudges where her eyes should be.

"Yes, Captain?" She held her head so close he smelled the faintest suggestion of perfume.

"Untie my hands."

Perforce she worked with dreadful slowness. He could feel her cold fingers slipping as they wrenched at the knots. Eventually the rope eased its agonizing pressure and, locking his teeth against an excruciating pain, he beat his deadened hands together. Meanwhile the English girl crouched flat beside him, unbuckling the belt securing his ankles.

"Don't take it off," he muttered. "Leave it loose."

Because a wild song, loud and off-key, made hearing difficult, she stooped so near that her ear almost touched his lips and the softness of her hair brushed his forehead.

"Archer will be coming for you before long," he breathed. "When he does, keep him here as long as you can."

Lenore recoiled, lay on her back and fixed horrified eyes on him. "I—I can't. You ask too much."

"You *must*." His voice was savage. "Play up to the brute. Let him take you all the way back into the cave."

Her breath quickened before she said in lifeless monotone, "Go on, please."

"Struggle just a little; he'd be suspicious else. Let the swine think you might be coaxed to give in. Can you do it?"

In the uncertain gloom of the cavern which smelled like a long disused cellar he read doubt, fear and disgust in her glance.

"I—don't know," she whispered, "but I—I'll try. If you expect any reward from me, don't risk your life. I loathe and despise you and always shall."

"I expect you will," came his cold reply, "but I owe as much to any girl in your place." He rolled back into his former position. In silence she crept back to lie on her pile of moldy straw.

Twenty minutes later Archer's huge figure outlined itself against the glow of the coals outside. Only two voices babbled and muttered. The snuffle and stamp of horses on the picket line could be clearly heard once more.

Feigning sleep, Cary watched Archer's approach. He moved unsteadily past the guard who only glanced upward then, unluckily, stirred the fire.

"Heyo, honeybee," came the thick whisper. "You look good to me, Goldilocks."

Damn! The jayhawker had tripped over one of Kernan's laxed arms.

Lenore Duveen made no reply, but Cary caught the click of her sharply indrawn breath.

"Don't be scairt. Ah may look kinder rough, but Ah don't aim to hurt yer none." He paused, swaying.

The intruder's shadow projected across the fire-tinted roof of the cave, towered Titan-like above the prostrate cavalryman. Suppose the jayhawker stooped to investigate his lashings. Cary's blood seemed to halt, to flow back on itself.

"Oh—oh—Mr Archer, please don't—do anything dreadful. I—I can't bear it."

So convincing was Lenore Duveen's terrified sobbing that Cary wondered whether she was indeed iosing her nerve. He prayed she had not; everything would be lost.

"Sho' now, honeybee, come outside. Hit's nice and warm by the fire."

"Oh no. Please! I can't stand all those—those people looking at me; don't take me outside."

The sound of faint struggles, Archer's deep breathing and the scuffling of feet lasted several moments. "Please, I'm—I'm really afraid of your men. If you'd——"

"If I'd *what,* Goldilocks?"

Even lying a good ten feet away, Cary smelled Archer's sour body odors mingling with the smell of horses and the pungent reek of whisky. Small wonder if Lenore Duveen lost her self-control.

"Whut wuz you a-goin' to say?" inquired Archer in surprisingly gentle tones.

"I—why, I thought we could be—more comfortable, more private in here." Every word seemed to be dragged from the girl's lips by an invisible windlass.

"Say, ain't you gals the devil?" Eagerness entered the jayhawker's tone. "Ah was fearin' you'd git fractious. Give us a kiss, a real nice kiss, jest to prove you ain't foxin'."

A loud smack and a faint gasp of, "Don't, please don't," reached Cary's ears.

Listening hard, the cavalryman remained quite motionless on the moldy hay. As long as he lived he'd never forget that odor. Aye, and how long would that be?

"Wal now, you shore got sense, Goldilocks. Yer mighty purty—like a dogwood in the spring. Know somethin'? Ah got took with yer time we met t'other side o' the mountings.

"Yep, Ah bin thinkin' a heap about yer."

"And I about you," came Lenore's deep voice. "If you hadn't frightened me then, we might have become friends. I dote on strong men, the mastering kind, though I don't generally admit it. Tonight you are——"

"Tonight, honeybee?" A new, almost awed note had crept into Luke Archer's hoarse voice. "Do y' really like me?"

"Oh yes. Yes. You see, it *is* more comfortable back in the cave—and this hay is warm."

"Wal, Gawd boil mah body an' bones." The jayhawkers' leader emitted an enormous belch. Delightedly he went on. "You sho' foxed me what with yer high and mighty ways. Ye won't be sorry, Goldilocks, fer favorin' me. Ah'm rich, and Ah'll be richer still 'fore this war ends. Yep, Ah got me a bagful o' diamond rings, earbobs, real gold necklaces and such; all waitin' fer a pretty gal like you.

"Funny, since sundown Ah been figgerin' on how ye'd look. Won't be no gal in all the valley will dress nigh so fancy as Luke Archer's woman."

Archer bestowed more kisses. A muttered conversation took place in the rancid gloom, but so low pitched that Cary couldn't hear what was said. Presently footsteps receded as Archer and his companion groped into the further recesses of the cavern.

Cary lay not moving a muscle but with every nerve on edge. What was happening outside? The fire, poked into activity by Archer's arrival, revealed a single guard nodding at the cave's mouth. Kernan's breathing was so stertorous Cary guessed very likely the whole back of the grain dealer's head had been crushed.

From the depths of the cavern came Lenore's voice, muffled but protesting:

"Lay easy, honey, easy. Ah ain't goin' fer ter hurt you——"

Silently, careful as a ranging ferret, Cary began to creep into an almost tangible blackness shrouding the depths of the great cave. Slow work. The guard's fire had died down again, but here and there an outline yet was recognizable.

Body pressed very flat to the clammy rock floor, the cavalryman squirmed on. He could distinguish them now; Archer seated with back turned to the fire and Lenore Duveen lying drawn across her captor's chest. She was fighting off his busily ranging hands, her eyes very large.

Clutching a stone, Cary rose abruptly to his knees, then brought the rock crashing down on Archer's head with furious force—just as any cave man.

CHAPTER SIXTEEN

THE MOUNTAINESIDE

CROUCHED over the lax, malodorous form of Luke Archer, Hubert Cary was aware of Lenore Duveen staring at him from wide horror-filled eyes, of the guard rising at the cavern's mouth. Trying to fight down his gasps for breath, Cary watched the blanketed outlaw, all shawled in a blue army blanket, kick together the ends of the fire. Once it flared up it would certainly illumine the whole length of the cave.

"Lie down beside Archer. Keep still," he urged. Then, giving her a mechanical smile, he scrambled back to assume his original position. Good God, if Tom Blake could only see his Golden Diana!

For the first time in his life he hoped he had killed a man—war was different. You had to kill or be killed.

The guard, cursing his drunken companions, sought firewood. From the depths of his being Cary marveled at the English girl's courage. She had stretched out beside the unconscious jayhawker.

Archer lay on his back, clumsy spurred boots and yellow-striped gray legs flung wide apart. The fire picked out contours of the ruffian's throat. His great tangle of beard was pointed upward at a sharp angle.

Lying in enforced inaction, Hubert Cary estimated the likelihood of escape. Buckled outside of Archer's gray uniform were his long navy revolver and a bowie knife. Knives were very common among Confederate irregulars. That knife suggested possibilities.

If he and the English girl did get away, how far could they expect to travel before daylight? The jayhawkers, of course, were expert trailers—they couldn't afford to let anyone get away. Behooved him to make his bid in a hurry. It must be well past midnight.

If only Kernan would stop that dreadful, lagging breathing! Of the pine grove he couldn't bear to think. If she was lucky the Ross girl wouldn't survive.

Cary's conjectures ended when the guard came shuffling back, yawning and swinging a wooden canteen in one hand. Absolutely incurious, the outlaw seated himself and presently hunched forward with elbows around knees and a carbine slung across his lap. Sleepily the jayhawker shoved a shapeless gray kepi back on a shock of yellow hair.

Save for drunken snores the camp seemed still. Cary rolled over on his side, facing Lenore Duveen and Archer. Motioning for silence, he secured the unconscious outlaw's knife and revolver.

An owl began hooting down the ravine as he commenced a stealthy advance on the nodding guard. By now he had slumped a little sidewise with one hand lying lax at his side.

Cary calculated his thrust. He aimed the point under the outlaw's left shoulder blade.

Gradually he advanced the steel until its point poised against the gray cloth; then, teeth clenched, he put all his weight behind the heavy, razor-sharp blade.

Heat drenched the Federal's hand. A long sigh, escaping the guard's lips, was the only evidence that he had died. Hardly a tremor marked the outlaw's slow slumping sideways. A soft noise, very like the noise of paint poured from a bucket, entered the cavern.

A sickish-sweet, musty odor grew stronger.

Before he beckoned forward Lenore Duveen Cary hesitated; he went over to examine Kernan.

The back of the grain dealer's skull was a shattered, shapeless mess. He would never rouse from his coma.

"Any hope for him?" came the English girl's shaken query.

"He's dying. Come."

Catching skirts and petticoats garter high, with long legs agleam, Lenore Duveen followed him toward the cave's entrance. Nevertheless her movements were so hampered that Cary grabbed up an armful of clothes drying beside

the watch fire. With revolver ready and probing every shadow, the cavalryman took her hand, led her past the collapsed figure of the guard. Cary paused long enough to appropriate the dead man's haversack.

Picking every footstep, silent as wind-blown seeds, the fugitives made their way toward the picket line under the pines. It was a dangerous but necessary move. Everywhere figures lay sprawled, sleeping on heaps of hay.

For the first time Lenore Duveen's self-possession betrayed signs of cracking. What shook her was the discovery of the portions of the Ross girl's clothing on the pine needles of the grove's floor. As dim white splashes, blouse, petticoats and other garments lay scattered all about.

"Oh-h!" Lenore clutched Cary's arm, stood swaying, shuddering.

The Ross girl lay a few feet away, her slim form a nude, pallid outline under the raw night wind. She was obviously dead.

"Don't look."

Too utterly weary to think a great deal, Cary merely wiped his sticky right hand until it felt cleaner, then conducted his companion into the further depths of the pine grove.

From the bundle under his arm he selected a pair of breeches, a coat, and thrust them into her hands.

"Put these on," he ordered, struggling into a civilian coat at least a size too small.

The command did her a lot of good, shocked her into protest. "Oh no, they're filthy!"

"Put 'em on!" he insisted. "You'll never get through these woods in a dress. Do you want what she got?"

Without a word the English girl commenced to tear at her dress hooks. Carefully Cary reconnoitered that clearing in which coals still blinked sleepily.

For the first time he perceived that the rain had, at long last, ceased.

Slipping into a long lean-to stable, he bridled a pair of what seemed to be strong, clean-limbed animals, placed saddles on their backs. This done, he glanced about, commandeered a greasy, wide-brimmed hat and a bulging haversack slung to a broken branch.

Leading the two saddled animals and praying they would neither snort nor curvet, Cary met Lenore Duveen cautiously advancing in his direction. No longer clad in cumbersome wide skirts, she moved lightly, looked lithe and long legged in a pair of gray breeches and a blue uniform jacket.

On the edge of camp Cary nodded his satisfaction as he set up the girths. The owl was calling again, not far away, and up the mountain a she-fox barked once, twice.

He indicated what looked to be the quieter of the two beasts and was reassured by the ease with which his companion rose into the saddle.

On foot, he began feeling a course along a downward trail. It must eventually lead into the valley.

"Hi! Who's that?"

From a few yards in Cary's rear a startled outpost challenged.

As the fellow's challenge rang out Cary swung up into the saddle. Already Lenore had urged her horse ahead. From the camp sounded voices thick with sleep, snortings and tramplings.

To Cary's dismay both his mount and the English girl's proved very loath to leave the picket lines and the grain bags. They moved so reluctantly that Cary, in desperation, spurred his beast with the point of Archer's bowie. At the sting of the steel the horse lurched into a holly thicket. It made such a racket that instantly furious yells rang out.

"Thar they go!"

"Quick, we got to git 'em."

"They cain't git out o' the valley!"

"Stay close," Cary warned the English girl. He kicked his beast. It was snorting with fear now. He tried to see the trail, but it was a punishing task. Low-sweeping branches lashed his face, stabbed at his eyes and shed icy showers of raindrops over his chilled body.

When they had plunged downward some five minutes Cary reined in with such suddenness that Lenore's mount blundered into his.

The dim outline of her face loomed near. "What's wrong?"

"Thought I heard horses on the trail below. Not sure though. You listen."

From the gloom below arose an unmistakable snap and crackle of branches, the faint click of equipment.

"Quite right," muttered the Duveen girl. Her horse swung sharply about. "Archer's men seem to be coming down after us."

The mountain above them resounded to muffled yells, to the pounding hoofs. Cary estimated that at least eight or ten jawhawkers were in pursuit, probably riding bareback.

The burning question concerned the horsemen below. Would they be Confederate regulars? Or perhaps a detachment of Federal cavalry cut off from General White's retreating army and groping its way out of the valley? Or were the riders simply more jayhawkers homeward bound from a foray?

At this point the trail was following the narrow crest of a ridge which fell away so sharply to either side that to risk sliding to safety would be suicidal.

His voice came through the dark, short, precise and level: "We can't avoid meeting those people below."

From his pocket he snatched a damp and dingy handkerchief. "Tie that under your jaw. You've an abscessed tooth, understand? Can't talk. Take this." He passed over the felt hat he had seized with the second haversack. "Be ready to ride through if I give the word. For God's sake, don't fall off."

"I seldom fall off." The English girl shot him a swift look, held out her hand. "Give me the revolver. I don't intend to be taken alive again."

Riding a few yards in advance of his companion, Cary continued down the narrow and winding trail at a quick trot. Louder sounded the slow *clip-clop* of horses' hoofs. Who was waiting below?

Archer's men must be taking a faster pace, settling down to a pursuit. At any rate, no more yells resounded from the direction of the camp.

"Doing all right?"

"Famously."

Lenore Duveen, sitting her saddle with superb sureness, was readjusting the handkerchief knotted under her jaw. Already she had jammed her hair into the crown of the felt hat. Abruptly she became metamorphosed into a long-legged youth carrying a revolver tucked into his waistband.

Cary's nerves keyed themselves to meet the impending crisis when, after galloping around a bend in the trail, he descried a column of dim figures. They were jayhawkers, all right.

Clad in the usual miscellany of uniforms and civilian clothes, they gripped cocked carbines and, craning their necks, came trotting upward. Cary counted two, four— nine in all.

"Halt! Who's thar?"

For some reason the name of Calthorp sprang to Cary's mind. "Bill Calthorp—new jined along o' Luke Archer."

"Bide whar ye are, Calthorp!" rasped a nasal voice. "Who's that by yuh?"

"New boy, jined up yestiddy." Cary strove to make his accent that of the hills. "Archer ordered we-uns back to the W. & P."

"Come hyar, Calthorp—and you'd best not make no sudden motions." The leader of this second group, a lanky individual with the face of a hawk, lowered a shotgun. Then he kicked forward his shaggy mount. Others of his party quickly encircled the two fugitives.

It was a critical moment, Cary realized. Had he time to try to lie his way out? No. Archer's men were coming closer each instant; everyone could hear the hoofbeats above.

"Who's that?" came the sharp query.

"More o' the boys goin' out on a job."

"What for did Luke order you all back to the railroad?"

For an agonizing instant Cary was at a loss, then he said, "One o' the prisoners 'lowed as how he'd hid a hell's mint o' money in some bushes back thar."

Cary could feel Lenore Duveen's knee pressing in behind his. She was staying close, all right. Thus far she had not said a word. Narrowly he surveyed the shadowy figures around him, then all at once found but a single jayhawker between him and a clear trail.

"Mebbe, mebbe," grunted the hawk-featured man. "But how come you all ain't ridin' together?"

Other gruff voices commented on the hurried hoofbeats from up the trail.

"Now!" Crisp as the snap of an ice-laden bough came Cary's command. Simultaneously he used the bowie point again. His horse lunged violently sideward.

"Hi! What——" The sentence remained incomplete. Cary's mount rode the hawk-faced man and another of his party off the trail. Yelling, they disappeared into a black gulf to the left.

Crashing noises filled the night as Cary exerted all his skill to keep his frantic beast on the trail. Ahead of him Lenore Duveen bent low on her horse's neck, continually drove her heels against its barrel.

All was wind, lashing branches and dripping darkness until a sudden, louder uproar announced that the men from Archer's camp had ridden full tilt into the disorganized group of horsemen already on the trail.

The wind beat in Cary's ears, twigs drew livid lines on his cheeks, and pebbles flung up by the hoofs of the girl's horse stung his face like huge wasps, but he gripped the sweaty reins and fought for control. A dozen times he deemed himself lost when his animal slipped, stiffened and lurched.

If this kept up much longer, he must sooner or later be flung headlong into the unseen depths below the trail.

A new anxiety gripped him when the noise of swift and angry pursuit again filled the dim forest; more familiar with the terrain, the jayhawkers should have no trouble in closing in.

Gasping, groping furiously for a plan, Cary relaxed his

pressure on the reins, permitted his stronger horse to close up until its outthrust head was straining at the flank of Lenore Duveen's stumbling, slipping animal.

"Pull up—around—next bend," he yelled and hoped she had heard him. She made a dramatic picture bent low like that to avoid the whiplike branches.

Her hat was gone, releasing her hair to stream out like a ghostly gonfalon. A jagged boulder loomed up and eclipsed the trail ahead. Something had to be done. The pursuers were closing in faster than he had anticipated.

"Get set," he called and pulled his right foot from the stirrup as the English girl's horse vanished around the boulder.

CHAPTER SEVENTEEN

THE FUGITIVES

LENORE DUVEEN'S slim shoulders were still jerking with her efforts to halt her mount when, after brushing by the overhanging rock, Cary flung himself off. He had her bridle in an instant.

"Off!" he gasped. "Slide off!"

When, trembling with weakness, the English girl delayed he reached up and hauled her bodily from the saddle. He almost flung her into the shrubbery.

The thunder of hoofs was now so close upon him that he could hear stones, kicked off the trail, go rolling and crackling down through wet underbrush on the mountainside. Fearful that his ruse might fail, he used his bowie to sting Lenore's horse. Snorting, it went racing on down the trail in pursuit of Cary's own mount.

Trying to appraise the situation, the Federal wound arms about Lenore's waist, dragged her flat in a dripping laurel thicket. His pulses were beating like the fists of a prisoner against a cell door.

"Don't move," he breathed. Above them was a vista of ragged black pine tops, of a silver-gray cloud which, thinner than its fellows, was striving to let through some moonlight.

On the trail an enormous horseman appeared, another and another. Bent far forward, they flashed by amid a jangle of stirrup irons and a creaking of leather. Pebbles rattled into the leaves of the laurel clump. Sparks, struck by a flying hoof, sketched brief pin points of fire. More sinister figures blotted out the sky—nine or ten at least.

"They all gone by?"

"Can't tell. Stay still."

Cary again became aware of this girl whose violent breathing shook her whole slim figure.

After the pursuit was definitely over he took her hand and, silently as possible, led her down to the floor of a steep ravine. There they rested among velvety shadows cast by a clump of enormous firs, panting like hounds after a hard run.

High up on the mountain distant voices still could be heard. The girl lay, spent and gasping, on the fragrant needles.

Gently he lifted her head and shoulders onto his lap. Warm and faintly scented currents of air were rising from her damp hair to arouse reminiscent twinges.

"You were magnificent."

Lenore Duveen said nothing, only fought for breath, eyes closed and limbs limply outstretched.

"You aren't hurt?" he demanded.

"N-n-no. I fancy not."

Slowy pallid eyelids slid back and her great eyes gazed up into his strongly modeled features. How wild, grim and disheveled he looked. This Hubert Cary little resembled the jaunty young cavalry officer she had encountered long ages ago on a terrace at Philomont Manor.

"I—I'm really all right," she murmured with a faint smile. "Only out of breath."

"I've never seen such—such superb riding!" His voice conveyed an admiration beyond the power of words.

"I have hunted stags in Devonshire—foxes too—since—little girl."

A while longer she lay quite still, her bright head pillowed on the knee of his wet and grimy civilian suit, then she sat up and began fumbling to secure buttons on the front of her blue cavalry jacket.

"Feel all right?"

"Quite, Captain. You're not wounded?"

He laughed quietly. "I haven't taken a complete inventory, but I don't think there's any serious damage."

"Why, you *are* hurt!" She bent close, the damp masses of her hair showing up faintly in the gloom. "Oh dear, there's —there's a cut on your forehead."

"It's a trifle; a stone hit me."

"But it's bleeding. Let me look at it." Because of the faint light the alluring oval of her face was now but a scant inch or so away. Her lips became parted in an expression of pity.

[201]

Quite before he realized it his arms went about her and his lips pressed hers. It was an odd kiss—intended as an expression of exultation at having escaped, as a tribute to her courage, rather than for a lover's caress.

Lenore Duveen did not struggle. She merely lay lax and leaden in his arms. Instantly he released her, commenced to stammer an apology. The English girl cut him short with a gesture and said in a strained voice:

"You are an admirable strategist, Colonel Redspurs, and make a better soldier than you do a gentleman." Her lips curved in a bitter smile. "How clever of you to realize that I am too tired to——"

"But—but"—he stammered to explain his impulse—"you don't understand. I was only so glad that you—we were safe. I only——" Words withered before her rigid scorn. It spoke from every line of her body.

He shrugged. "It's no use," came his weary conclusion. "I honestly meant no affront, but it seems we were never intended to understand each other."

"So it appears," she agreed stonily. "I was told that old Redspurs"—she injected a world of contempt into the nickname—"was like you. If he couldn't have a girl one way—well, he devised others."

"You are too generous, Miss Duveen," he muttered and, sinking back on the pine needles, he began to realize how close to utter exhaustion he was. "You can rest assured I shan't touch you again."

His exultation over their escape, over her calm incredible courage, evaporated. He felt, instead, immeasurably discouraged. What a mess he'd made of things: the raid a failure, his companions already dead or doomed to early hanging, himself a fugitive existing in the shadows of the gallows. Somehow, to endure further contempt from this girl would be intolerable.

Stifling a groan, he sat up, held his head between his hands and tried to forget his bruises.

At last he began to talk, not to his companion but thinking aloud.

"Must be somewhere in the Blue Ridge between Winchester and Catoctin Creek. If I stick to the mountains I'll travel slower but ought to be in less danger of meeting rebel troops.

"If I can cross the Potomac—um—somewhere between Berlin and Harpers Ferry, I might reach Frederick. Um— yes, that's the ticket—might even find Meade's corps."

Unexpectedly the Duveen girl spoke. "Don't let me hinder your going, Captain; you have a long way to go. I fancy I can find some village before long."

"Don't be a fool about everything," he advised. "I'm planning for the two of us, but I've got to be careful. I'm living with a noose around my neck."

"A noose? What do you mean?" Dawn could not be so far off. Now Cary could see the Duveen girl more distinctly as she clumsily braided her hair.

"A Union officer found inside rebel territory and not in uniform counts as a spy," he said tonelessly. "You can very easily earn the hearty thanks of the first Confederate you find.

"Well, it's time we were moving."

He arose, offered her the lighter of the two haversacks.

"Better take this."

She got up too, very boyish and slim.

"Shan't I carry the other too? You can make me, you know."

Too weary to resent her gibe, he only shrugged, said somberly, "We might have to separate. It would be wise for you to carry some food."

"Oh!"

"Now, my dear Diana, let's have a look at you." He might have been addressing a recruit. Critically, impersonally, he surveyed her from head to foot.

Lenore Duveen still wore her own low-heeled shoes, and the ripped remains of gray cotton stockings had been dragged up over the lacings of a Confederate trooper's breeches. The blue uniform coat fitted her tall figure well enough, save that its sleeves were too short. Where a shirt should have covered her drooped a most unmilitary flurry of ribbons and lace.

Had she not looked so tired, dirty and woebegone, he could have laughed. Lenore resembled nothing so much as a character in some play at a girls' finishing school. As it was, he gathered the pistol belt tighter about him and replaced the useful bowie in its sheath.

"It will be light before long. Since we know their hideout, the jayhawkers won't let us go so easily."

Through the early hours they further descended the mountain. Neither of them spoke. Cary merely helped his companion whenever he could. It was hard going, and the terrain, instead of becoming more civilized, was becoming increasingly desolate and wild.

Normally the cavalryman would have reveled in a series of magnificent vistas opening up between the straight-trunked pines, would have exulted in the warm sun. But not today.

The country abounded with game. Now a gray deer flashed its white semaphore of a tail, now a partridge or a great bronze turkey burst from the underbrush like a feathered bombshell. Once they startled a black bear feeding on the edge of a blueberry patch. High overhead turkey buzzards wheeled and turned endlessly on motionless five-foot wings.

Of mankind they saw nothing. In the late afternoon the fugitives entered a narrow little valley down which cascaded a clear brook. Here for the first time Cary gave indication that they would take more than a brief breath-catching halt.

"It will be dark before long," he explained. His eyes, deep-sunk with fatigue, looked red, dull.

"You had better decide what you want to do."

"Do?" Lenore slumped onto a log, fell to sucking a blackberry scratch across her hand.

"There's smoke rising above the next valley. If you wish, I'll see you to civilization. There I must leave you."

"Leave me?" Her lashes, long and black against her cheek, flickered up.

"I must report my failure with the railroad bridges as soon as may be."

Lenore Duveen's sunburned face remained lifted to this man so different from the dashing, debonair officers she had known.

"And the alternative?"

"We can camp out. If so, I must be getting busy."

The girl heaved a weary sigh. "I'm dead tired, can't go much further—no matter what. How can we make out in such a wilderness?"

"We wouldn't be too uncomfortable. I can fix you a bed of sorts—maybe a lean-to. I think we can even risk a fire."

"Then let's camp," she pleaded faintly. "I'm famished and I—I really can't go on."

"Why didn't you tell me you were so fagged?" Cary demanded, but she made no reply.

Brambles had ripped off the remains of her stockings, had cruelly slashed her knees. A scarlet line also marked her cheek. Some of his resentment at her long contemptuous silence departed, and he suggested in gentler tones than he had used all day:

"Suppose you get a drink and wash those scratches. I'll make camp."

"I must look a sight," she admitted. Limping, she set off for a miniature waterfall above which spray hovered in the lazy air like jewel dust.

Hardened by two years of campaigning, he planned to sleep on the bare ground, but for his companion he fashioned a bed of pine boughs beneath a crude lean-to.

Presently he heard Lenore returning and was vastly surprised by the change in her manner and appearance. Her body was held straight once more and she walked almost lightly.

When the English girl drew near he could see how the hair which had given her her sobriquet had been neatly plaited into twin braids which made her look more than ever like a boarding-school Thespian.

"I've had a dip in a little pool down there," she announced lightly. "Really, Captain, I feel like a female Alexander. Bring on a world for me to conquer!"

"You look more like Diana."

Her dark brown eyes danced and she even attempted a curtsy. Because of her breeches it was a grotesque effort.

"Prettily said. I see you know my undeserved nickname. Who told you?"

"My lieutenant, Tom Blake. He's a gay rascal." Expertly he flung the bowie at a near-by tree. Stuck into the trunk, it glimmered like an embodied moonbeam. She shuddered a little and looked curiously at the tall figure before her.

"That is you—expressed in a gesture."

"Me?"

"Yes, you are bright, efficient—and dangerous."

As if to rob her assertion of any sting, her laugh rang like a crystal goblet lightly touched. "And now, sir, be off for the bath. You have no idea how dirty, hot and tired you look. Besides, a bath may"—she dropped her eyes—"clear your head. It did wonders for mine."

"Yours to command, goddess. I'm so dirty I creak."

"I will see what can be done about getting dinner." She checked herself, smiled at her use of the formal word. "Supper, I mean."

Turning away, he missed seeing a sudden rush of color flood her face.

Delighted that she had apparently understood and had forgiven him, Cary brushed by and before long was splashing in water so clear that he could see bright, terror-stricken minnows scurrying back and forth over the pool's rocky floor.

How wonderfully soothing the water was! It drew the ache from his bones, cooled his skin, lent him a new strength. Really idyllic was this secluded little valley—a lovely private world secure from hideous realities. He'd like to linger here—with Lenore.

But the inescapable fact remained: he must report his failure. Somehow, God only knew by what means, the threatened garrison must be warned that their last fleeting hope was gone. If they still were to win free, it must be by the dint of bullets and bayonets.

Returning, flushed and glowing, to the lean-to, he found Lenore bent over a little campfire; she was toasting bacon on the point of a long willow switch. Sweet potatoes, he saw, were baking in the ashes; some apples, two pieces of corn pone, very yellow and appetizing of appearance, were spread on a strip of birch bark.

"A most bounteous repast, Diana."

The girl made no reply, did not even look up.

"What's wrong?" he demanded, his light mood dying.

"Nothing, save that once again I have been given cause to remember the type of gentleman you are."

"What in the world——"

"What use to talk?" demanded Lenore Duveen in a strained monotone. "I regret I forgot myself a while back."

Why should she so suddenly have reverted to her hostility? He stood quite still with water dripping slowly from red hair. Under the effects of his swim it had gathered into short curls. The injustice of her attitude stung him into a cold rage, and pleasant phrases which had risen to his lips were not said.

Seating himself beyond the fire, he moodily watched her complete her cooking. The yellow stripe down her breeches shone bright in the sunset. Angrily he selected the smaller piece of corn pone, fell to munching it. Bah! It was coarse, unsalted, tasteless.

By every rule they should have been happy, joyously happy, to have escaped the terrors of the night before; yet everything was wrong. They should be enjoying to the fullest this brief vacation from practicalities.

Hang it, this stage was set for companionship. Here were peace, beauty, fragrance. The sweet scent of the pines was mingled with a comforting aroma from the sizzling bacon. Pleasant flicks of wood smoke reached his nostrils.

"Look here," he began uncertainly, "please, Miss Duveen, won't you try again to let bygones be bygones? By now you must have understood that what I did at Philomont——" He got no further, so withering was her glance.

"Our master strategist is at work again, it seems," she observed, dark red lips bright in the firelight.

"Oh, for heaven's sake, listen—you've got to——"

"Listen? And why should I? Your conduct at Philomont was a mere introduction to your character." Though it did not rise in pitch, her voice quivered with the intensity of her emotion.

"Yes, my gallant sir." The vivid lips became curved in a mocking smile. "From now on I am quite prepared to meet you on your own ground."

[209]

"My own ground?" He gaped at her; his thin cheeks grew leaner yet. "Your meaning is obscure."

"Why fence? Your intentions are obvious as—as *that!*" She nodded at the lean-to and the solitary bed within it. "No doubt you pride yourself on aping old Harry Redspurs, whose chief ambition in life, I've been told, was to break a colt each morning, to kill an Englishman each noon and to bed a wench each night."

"Have you gone crazy!" he burst out.

"No, merely wary. For once you have guessed wrong, Colonel Redspurs."

Cary put down his morsel of pone and, if it was possible, his features flushed a deeper red. Again she misunderstood.

"Well you may blush; I marvel that so accomplished a rake can still summon one."

What was the use? Twice, thrice, he had tried to explain, to justify himself. Hadn't he saved her silly life for her? Hadn't he risked his neck to get her away? Yet invariably she was almost eager to believe the worst of him.

This cold, cutting contempt was too damned much. Angry voices clamored in his brain. "She's lost to you so take some kisses."

Cary stood up smiling. He bowed elaborately, sunken eyes bright and menacing.

"Since it is rude to disappoint a lady," he began, "I shall try not to fail in the role you have appointed for me."

Though he strove to keep his voice light and mocking, there crept into it a certain poignancy which checked her, made her draw back.

"Why—wha—what do you mean?"

Idiotically he swept another bow and declared, "I mean, my dear Diana, that we will exit Captain Cary and enter the Redspurs that you seem to insist on."

Tautly smiling, he started around the fire, then halted. From behind her Lenore Duveen had produced Luke Archer's barreled revolver.

"Alas for your little drama, Colonel; here is one wench who fails to be captivated."

"Put that down," he snapped with really devilish lights at the back of his eyes, "and permit me to observe that a comb or a mirror would look much better in such lovely hands."

When he advanced another step Lenore cocked the weapon. It was loaded, all right. He could see the sunset play redly on a circlet of copper percussion caps.

All the world resolved itself into a measureless interval across which he and Lenore Duveen faced each other. More than ever he loved her, yet the very hopelessness of his love goaded him on, as a tide running on top of a strong current creeps upstream against itself.

Though this round-eyed girl gave no further warnings, he very well knew that she would shoot. Shoe soles creaking faintly on the needles, he took two slow strides, then as the barrel swung up he ducked with the speed of a kingfisher diving on minnow.

The revolver's flat, incisive report drew so many echoes from the sunset-reddened slopes that it seemed as if a skirmish were raging.

CHAPTER EIGHTEEN

THE GOLDEN DIANA

A THREAD of blue smoke curled slowly upward from the revolver's muzzle. It hadn't been hard for Cary to wrench it from Lenore Duveen's grasp. With one arm he held her tight against the damp bosom of his checkered shirt, imprisoned her so effectively that a cable might have secured her.

When, by thrusting a hand beneath the delicate point of

her chin, he forced her to look up, a maddening exhilaration seized him. In it was blended an elemental satisfaction, rage and a maddening consciousness of his superior strength. A grin hardened on his cracked and sunburned lips.

"Well, Mistress Lenore, it appears you are still a poor shot—and a poorer judge of human nature. So you honestly thought I intended the lean-to for—for *both* of us?" he demanded.

"Nothing would be too vile for me to believe of you," the English girl panted. Suddenly she began struggling again, her feet digging dark furrows in the forest mold. It gave him an excuse to hold her closer, to test the firm softness of her body.

"Go ahead," he mocked. "This is really fun."

At length she relaxed, her whole lithe figure palpitating.

"I loathe you too indescribably to——"

"Really, my dear?" he inquired with cruel gentleness. "Now that makes it easier. Why, now I can take a real pleasure in living up to your opinion. So——" He bent, pressed a fierce, lingering kiss on the soft brightness of her mouth. "So—and so!"

At every contact of his lips the long-legged girl quivered as though stung by a steel point. Then he held her at arm's length and viciously shook her until she swayed, her eyes closed, quite helpless.

Ecstatic currents circulated in Cary's brain. "Damn you —you've no right to be so lovely!" Over her upturned face crept a vast bewilderment as he released her.

"Oh, Lenore, Lenore! Why wouldn't you listen?" Again he caught her in his arms, more gently this time.

From his lips tumbled a torrent of endearing words impounded within him ever since he had beheld her that silvered hour in the moonlight at Philomont. Why should he say such things when everything was so desperate, so hopeless between them?

All at once he was aware that the girl in his arms had relaxed. As his impassioned outburst continued her eyes opened. When, sharply, she shook her head and recommenced her struggles he kissed her so hungrily that he bruised her lips. The tenseness of her body gradually altered. Dear God above! She was straining *toward* him.

"Oh, Hubert, hold me, close—closer!" she gasped fiercely. "Thank God you have the courage, the love to—to force—to rule me. Oh, my dear, if you hadn't been such a masterful devil just now, I—I think I never would have known how desperately, how madly I love you. I suppose I—I've ruled men too long for my own happiness."

A play for time, this? No telling. Recklessly he drew her closer.

"Lenore, beloved, ever since we met I've adored you."

In the deepening twilight her arms crept about the muscular pillar of his neck. Her cheek pressed itself to his rough, unshaven one.

Suspicion was not longer to be tolerated, not with her lips seeking his so sweetly, so eagerly.

"Hubert, my darling, you need never doubt me again," she murmured. "I know now why I tried, why I fought to forget you. I—I—wanted to conquer! But now I—I don't care."

Timidly her finger tips crept up and, after brushing his cheek, pulled lower his reckless red head.

"You will be kind, loyal?" she sighed a little later. "Always?"

"Always—always."

Exquisitely lovely even in that stained blue jacket with its tarnished brass buttons, she sat beside the fire. Even yet Cary could scarcely credit that Lenore Duveen—the Golden Diana—had given him her love. He, of all the men in the world! The realization was somehow humbling.

"You understand about Philomont?" he inquired presently. "It was the garrison, the lives of ten thousand men that I sheltered behind you."

"Yes," she admitted. "I saw that after a while, though at first I was furious."

By the glow of the firelight his strong features softened. He started to speak but stiffened, held up a hand for silence.

"What is it, Hubert?" she breathed.

"Voices," he whispered. "Thought I heard voices in the distance."

She struggled to a sitting position. "Where?"

"On the other side of this ridge. Might be a road there."

"I hear nothing." She gazed fixedly at him. "I don't want to. I only want to be with you—to rest, to forget this unhappy, cruel world we live in."

"Perhaps I was wrong. I hope so."

After a little he got up and stamped out the fire. "It's getting dark, and the glow might show. No point inviting visitors."

"Two *is* company, isn't it?" Playfully Lenore's lips

brushed his ear. As if struck by a new thought, she looked up suddenly. "Darling, if—if the Confederates caught you, would they—really——?"

"Hang me? Oh yes, with the greatest of pleasure. I've no intention of pleasing them, however." He got up, led the way to the lean-to. "Tomorrow, I expect, will be a full day. Better take the revolver."

She slipped once more into his arms, and an eternally memorable hour passed before he left her lying on the pine-tip bed with his love words still singing in her ears.

Building wonderful dreams for the future, Cary sought an already selected hollow and extended himself on the still-warm pine needles.

By God, Lenore was worth having, worth planning, fighting for. Lacing hands behind his head, he gazed through a dark tracery of spruce boughs at stars shining white hot against a purple-black background.

Incredible that such mental and physical courage should be combined with so much charm and beauty. After this campaign he ought to be made a major. Could two live on a—major's pay? Brownell of Philadelphia would make a new dress uniform—Tom Blake would be best man; a nice touch of humor, that. An arch of swords for—Lenore.

Cary fell into that deep sleep which Shakespeare described as "Death's half sister."

Only training gained through two years of active campaigning could have aroused him from his abysmal slumber, but in obedience to some indefinable warning he awakened. Five minutes or five hours might have elapsed, but because the moon was still very low Cary decided his sleep had been of short duration.

Carefully the seeming sleeper's eyes searched the surrounding darkness. Otherwise the cavalryman moved not a muscle.

"Bad dream," he was thinking, when his ear, pressed to the pine mold, detected a series of faint but distinct and stealthy impacts. His breath quickened. Not fifty yards away a twig snapped, completed his alarm.

Lenore! Was this a panther on the prowl? Damn! He shouldn't have given her the revolver.

Moving with that silent sureness which had rendered successful many an assignment, he approached the lean-to.

An icy hand squeezed his heart. Though it still bore the imprint of Lenore's body, the pine bed was deserted, empty.

Had she taken alarm, slipped quietly away? Racked by anxiety, he listened. The devil! Noises now came from another direction, from another and another. It was men he had to deal with, several of them. Quickly a realization was brought home that this hollow was very probably surrounded.

With the monotonous tinkle of the waterfall beating in his ears Cary hesitated. Could he break through this slowly constricting circle?

Where had Lenore gone? He peered intently in all directions but could see nothing indicative of her fate. Meanwhile the ominous noises were drawing inexorably closer. Now he could catch the soft panting of men, now a faint crackle of underbrush.

There seemed no choice but to gamble. Speeding to the largest near-by spruce, he swung silently up onto its lower limbs and exercised great care not to chafe the bark. He climbed quickly until the moonlit earth was blotted out. Soon he was immeasurably alone at the top of the great pine and looking out over a wide vista of wooded mountains.

How very still it was. Not a breath of air fanned his face, and the splash of the mountain brook sounded like the roar of a huge waterfall.

Below a deep voice called out, "Rush 'em. Hands up in there!"

Body pressed tight to the pitchy trunk, Hubert Cary merged with the shadows, listened to the stamp and rush of feet.

"Hell's fire! Ain't no one heah!"

"Look around—can't have gone far!"

More trampling in the underbrush. Cary's heart hammered like a bass drum. *Where was Lenore?*

"This is the wrong place. Told you so, Sergeant."

Sergeant? A measure of relief filled Cary. These, then, were regular Confederate troops.

"No, no, 'tain't either, suh. Look, thar's the lean-to. Must be the place, Lieutenant, just like the gal said."

As the girl said? Shooting up from his vitals a searing pang soared into Hubert Cary's brain, burst like a rocket at the zenith of its flight.

Clever, clever Lenore Duveen! She'd fooled him; how well she had nullified his brief assumption of mastery.

Disillusionment shook him with such a force that he all

but loosed his hold on the treetop. Louder and louder infernal inner voices roared in his ear, "She betrayed you—and she knew *you'd hang if caught!*"

On his misery impinged more damning remarks.

"Yep, thar's the fire she spoke of. Let's have a light."

A match sputtered and a scroll of birch bark flared. By its light Cary made out half a dozen big men in butternut uniforms. They were infantry with long thin faces and black beards. Magnificent rangy soldiers of the type which had made of the Army of Northern Virginia a *corps d'élite.*

"Say, Lootenant, d'you suppose he's treed up?"

Cary held his breath; a spasm constricted his throat as if a noose already encircled it.

"Maybe so," the officer agreed. "Won't do any harm to take a look."

Another roll of birch bark sputtered, sent sweet, resinous smoke drifting into the spruce tops.

"See any skinned places?"

"Nary one on this tree. How about that big one?"

"Cain't see nothin'," said the sergeant's voice. "Jim, boy, just you shin up it a piece."

"Shin yo'self, Dave. I'm dawg tired. I ain't goin' less'n Lieutenant Clay so orders. How about it, sir?"

Hubert Cary's heart dangled frozen in his chest until he heard the officer's softer voice say:

"I reckon it's no use. There's no one here; must have been scared off. We'll head back fo' camp. We are in for a long march tomorrow."

The birch-bark flares sputtered out and underbrush crackled and voices faded. Soon all was quiet save for the mournful plaint of an owl in a tangle across the little valley.

"Close," Cary muttered to himself. Stubbornly he strove to achieve that frame of mind with which in the past he had dismissed such worries. He'd damn well waste no thought—not now at least—on Lenore. There were other more vital claims on his attention. Suppose he hadn't waked though? Damn! As he swung down his bowie slipped from its sheath and rattled off among the branches.

Once he regained the ground he tried to decide his course.

"Got to try to steal a horse. Mounted, I ought to reach Harpers Ferry sometime tomorrow."

As he had half expected, he encountered a cart track at the foot of the mountain. It was very rough and marked the end of the valley in which he had, in so brief a time, tasted happiness and the dregs of disillusionment.

Tight-lipped, the cavalryman began striding off down the moonlit track and resolutely fixed his attention on his immediate future. But before he knew it he was once more watching the slow curl of Lenore's red and shiny lower lip; he was hearing again the rich tones of her voice.

Damn! He'd never before let a woman get under his skin so badly. Of course Blake was right. Lenore Duveen was, after all, just the Golden Diana—but oh, she was a grand rider.

When in the distance a rooster crowed, Cary quickened his pace, felt dew-wetted grass lick about his ankles. With plenty of little farms all about he should contrive to steal a horse or at least a mule.

His sleep, short as it had been, was infinitely refreshing. Though he walked with the usual discomfort of a cavalry-man afoot, he covered a lot of ground. Steadily the pines and other conifers grew scarcer and oaks, elms and beeches became more plentiful.

Before long this track joined a wide, well-traveled road upon which the moon revealed the imprint of many hoofs, the miniature gulleys of iron-tired wheels. The fugitive's brow puckered. Beyond a doubt many units of field artillery had passed this way.

Why should they be riding *west*ward?

He was still seeking an explanation when, in a hamlet lying off to the left, a hound began to bell. Dogs at varying distances answered him. Was this where Lenore Duveen had gone? Lenore? Lenore!

"Halt!" The command impacted against Hubert Cary's consciousness with the force of an exploding bomb. Obediently he halted. Looking up, he descried, in a deep shadow cast by a beech tree, a man astride a mule. He was leveling a shotgun.

Had it been a rifle he faced, Cary might have risked a desperate leap into the underbrush. But yonder was a double-barrel probably containing eighteen or more deadly buckshot. It was too long a chance.

"Hello," he drawled. "What's wrong?"

"Come hyar," directed the stranger, "and keep yo'r dad-burned hands up."

CHAPTER NINETEEN

SLAVE PATROL

STEP into yander patch of moonlight."

Captain Hubert Cary had no choice but to obey and stood there, silently cursing his negligence. Should have seen this solitary fellow. Why had this civilian been sitting quietly under a tree? Umm-m. And at this hour of the night?

Studying the lanky figure sharply, he saw that the fellow wore a broad-brimmed felt hat, a long-tailed coat and homespun trousers crammed into the top of shapeless cowhide boots. He was powerfully built too, worse luck.

The man with the shotgun kicked forward his furry white mule, peered through the half-light, then sat straight.

"Sorry, friend," came the stranger's surprising remark. "Yer burnt so dark I couldn't tell if'n you was white or not."

Moonlight glinted along the gun barrels as he lowered it.

White? Instantly Cary understood. He with the shotgun was riding slave patrol—the padero so hated of the Negroes. It was his duty to travel country roads by night, to take up any slave found abroad without a satisfactory pass from his owner.

"Yep, you was moseyin' along so quiet, I sure took you for a nigger," the padero explained. He spat into the white dust muffling his mule's splintered and unshod hoofs. "There's a lot o' black bastards tries to run away just because the damned Yanks comes this-a-way now and then."

The slave patrol's eyes, pale and set beneath bushy eyebrows, continued to search Cary's face.

"Yes, I reckon there's a lot of 'em traipsin' off these days," Cary agreed solemnly. "Ain't no gratitude in a nigger."

A set of handcuffs secured by a string to the slave patrol's saddle clinked softly as he again sent a parabola of tobacco juice sailing through the air. "Say, friend, you goin' or comin'?"

What the correct answer should be Cary had no idea; accordingly he evaded the question, inquiring in a soft Virginian drawl:

"Lot of soldiers about, ain't they?"

While his mule sleepily canted its ears forward the

padero grinned, kicked one foot out of his rope stirrups and otherwise relaxed.

"Reckoned you'd ask that, mister. Reckon you're dodgin' conscription. Well, don't fret yo'self. My job's keepin' track of niggers. I won't say I'd stop at pluggin' a stray Yank that came my way. Yes, sir, they's a heap o' night raiders and spies gallovantin' round.'"

Did the moonlight reveal a hint of suspicion in the speaker's square-jawed visage? Cary could not decide, and since those gaping gun barrels remained quite still he idly collected heavy white road dust with the side of his shoe.

"Any Yanks in this neck o' the woods? I wouldn't admire gettin' took up by 'em."

"Mought be a sprinklin' o' their blasted cavalry about. Yanks is a hard lot, friend, mighty hard. Why, only last week a passel o' bluecoats stole every last one of Bill Peglar's shoats. Mistreated an old feller in the valley—name o' Calthorp—somethin' scandalous. Burnt his feet off, so they say. Damn blue-coated bastards!"

For the first time Cary felt he could get answered a question that had been ceaselessly gnawing in his imagination. Trying to keep his voice casual, he drawled:

"Heard tell was a passel of Yank cavalry burned some railroad bridges below Winchester. 'Tain't nowise true, is it?"

The world seemed to hesitate as he waited for the padero's reply. With a wholly human yearning to believe what he wanted to believe, he had been sure that at least one of the bridges had been rendered useless.

"Laws," grunted the padero, rubbing his bristle-covered

chin, "it shore beats time how news travels. We-uns at Hillsboro only heard 'bout that raid tonight."

"News?" Hope soared into Cary's weary being. "Then they *did* cut the railroad?"

"Naw," said the man on the mule, biting off a fresh chew. "They set fire to a couple of the W. & P.'s bridges, only the rain saved 'em. And it warn't no cavalry neither. 'Twas a bunch of goddam Yankee spies. Big rewards is up fer catchin' 'em—three's been took already."

Instantly Cary perceived his error in bringing up the subject. A subtle contraction was visible in the rider's hard, unshaven features.

Hurriedly Cary changed the subject.

"I'm on my way to jine up. Whereat is the nearest recruitin' deppo?"

"Reckon you could jine over to Hillsboro, friend. What's yo'r name and where 're you from?"

"I'm Luke Prouty; been share farmin' down below Snickersville."

"Farmer, eh?"

"Sure 'nough."

The patrol then asked a few more questions concerning Snickersville and its environs which Cary answered so glibly and accurately he felt sure he had banished any suspicions.

"Yes suh," Cary went on, "I heard tell them Yanks was onery cusses. Reckon I'll take a crack at 'em."

"Well, you can do that when you get to Hillsboro. You'll find plenty o' company. They's a whole army passin' through."

The words so surprised the weary, bareheaded man in the road that he almost uttered a betraying exclamation.

Troops at Hillsboro? Great God, why, that was *in the rear of Harpers Ferry!* A Confederate force then must be moving up the Potomac Valley as well as down it. If Colonel Miles were to stand the least chance of evacuating his men, he must be warned with all possible speed.

Truly disaster was being piled on disaster.

"A army?" he drawled unintelligently. "You mean they's one o' our posts there?"

"Post! *Haw-haw!* General Walker's hull army was pullin' in, come sundown."

Cold chills shot through Cary's body. Great God! Walker *must have recrossed the Potomac* and was now marching to bar Miles's last avenue of escape! The Federal drew himself up and tightened the belt over his stomach. He must hurry, use every bit of resource to reach Harpers Ferry.

His thoughts so occupied him he failed to notice the slave patron straightening in the saddle, absently rubbing his long and unshaven jaw.

"Well, Mister Padero, if I'm to git to Hillsboro by sun-up," Cary drawled, "I reckon I better be fixin' to move."

"Reckon you had, mister," agreed the ill-dressed figure. "Iffen you spy any loose niggers, jes' leave two sticks crossed in the middle of this road with the long one pointed the way he went. I'll be ridin' this-a-way later on." The padero offered an enormous hand. "Well, heah's luck."

Even as Cary took his hand he felt the other's finger tighten. In a flash he perceived his error. His hands, though hard from long campaigning, lacked the heavy callouses of a farmer's. In the shadowy face above him he read a deadly menace.

"Put 'em up, you damn' lyin' Yank spy!"

With his left hand the padero tried to slew the shotgun round to bear. Cary, however, clung to the patrol's right fist and, by flinging his weight violently backward, commenced to haul the other down from his mule.

At first the slave patrol resisted furiously, then, abruptly abandoning these tactics, he flung himself from the saddle upon his dismounted assailant. He landed with crushing violence on Cary's chest. Amid the frightened snorting of the mule and the clatter of the falling shotgun the two fell and rolled over and over amid a flurry of moon-silvered dust.

Only the fact that he was in condition enabled the cavalry officer somewhat to recover himself. Right away he could tell that the padero was heavier and stronger and, no doubt, very much more adept in the arts of rough-and-tumble—that primitive mode of combat in which biting, gouging and kneeing were legitimate instruments of offense.

On the other hand, Cary sensed himself to be quicker; certainly he was less encumbered by clothes.

Cary, as he struck the earth, managed to twist sidewise and rolled to the right. Successfully pinning the padero's right arm beneath him, he drove a short right at his enemy's bearded jaw. Stung, the padero, emitting a howl, heaved himself over and tried to drive his knee into Cary's stomach. Failing in this, he sank teeth into the cavalry captain's shoulder.

His cotton shirt afforded no protection and the pain was agonizing. Viciously Cary smacked the biter's head side-wise, but this move freed both of his enemy's hands. Immediately broken nails and grimy fingers began gouging at the Federal's eyes.

Rearing his head back as far as possible, Cary clamped hands over his assailant's throat. He hung on with a strength developed by the continual handling of half-broken horses and by drilling with a heavy cavalry saber.

Now under, now on top, Cary squeezed and squeezed at the flesh and muscle pulsing under his grip. Nothing must break his hold on the other's bristle-covered wind-pipe.

The slave patrol's arms proved longer, and his fingers clawed closer and closer, grazed Cary's eyelids. With a lit-tle more reach the padero would be able to blind him. The moonlight was blotted out.

Without loosening his grip the Federal heaved mightily and found himself on top again. Those rending fingers, however, were still at his eyes. Accordingly Cary smashed his forehead full into the contorted face below.

Sharp pains told him his brow had impacted on the other's teeth. He had hoped to stun the man beneath him but had failed.

He knew he possessed strength enough to hold on until his enemy lay strangled, but any instant a clawing finger-nail might rip his eyeballs from their sockets. It would accomplish nothing to kill this enemy at the cost of his own eyesight. A blind man could never find his way into Har-pers Ferry.

Abruptly Cary let go the padero's throat, tried to spring clear. The slave patrol thrust out a foot which so flung the Federal off balance that he fell short of the shotgun he had been expecting to capture.

Snarling, wheezing for breath, the padero was up. Yellowed teeth and bloodied mouth clearly seen in the placid moonlight, he was murderous of expression.

The padero's throat was evidently too bruised to permit an outcry, but he leaped at the Federal like a rabid dog. Cary, a fair enough fencer, leaped sidewise and, as the padero lurched by, drove a stinging right to the side of the fellow's neck. The blow landed just below the other's ear. Surely he must fall.

The slave patrol, however, seemed to be fashioned of steel springs and rawhide. He only staggered, then wheeled, a knife gleaming in his fist. Damn! The shotgun, Cary found, was still out of reach. Long before he could reach it he would be flung to the ground with the padero's razor-sharp blade in his vitals.

Cary realized that death walked very near. For an instant he courted the idea of trying to dash in under the knife, of accepting a slash on his left arm.

The padero, evidently an expert knife fighter, was carrying his blade low. When the moment offered he would stab with an upward movement into his opponent's belly— a blow infinitely more effective than the often-pictured downward thrust.

A scant three yards of moonlit road separated the gasping, sweat-blinded antagonists. Intently Cary watched that murderously twinkling point. Any attempt to turn and run would be fatal, yet if he stood to meet the attack he must quickly perish.

The padero was gathering himself and for a split second Cary could see a row of moonlit trees, the mule standing a few yards away with furry ears cocked forward. The padero's wide hat sketched a black blot in the trampled sand of the road.

The slave patrol rushed, wheezing, jaws working above his collarless shirt front.

Cary recalled a hooligan trick described by Tatnall, that war-hardened veteran, as an unarmed man's best defense against a knife attack.

Pivoting swiftly on his left leg, the cavalryman presented his back to the padero, then suddenly bent over until his finger tips touched the earth. At the same time he exerted every ounce of strength in driving his right heel upward.

His heel impacted on something that gave with a dull crunching sound. Then the evil-smelling weight of the padero pinned him flat and he agonized for breath.

He'd lost. Cary bit his lip against the searing thrusts which would end everything.

Lenore! He'd never again see her lovely, treacherous face. Lenore. No stabs—— Why? Dazedly the cavalryman realized that the padero lay limp and motionless across his legs.

Fighting for breath, he began to free his legs from the other's bulk. Panting, on the edge of nausea, he twisted about and beheld the padero's unkempt head lolling loose.

Reaching backward, the Federal wound fingers in the fellow's shock of greasy hair and hauled his head aside.

It was not a pretty sight. The moon revealed the padero's jaw as sagging loose, bloody and crushed. His eyes, half open, were fixed, vacant and expressionless.

Cary's numbed mind gradually formulated a realization. "Heel caught him square—broke his neck."

A streak of silver attracted his attention. It was the padero's knife. It lay on the far side of the road beside a clump of ragweed.

How flat the patrol looked when Cary loosed the dead man's head. The white mule dropped its head, commenced to browse on dusty grass by the roadside.

PART II

The Potomac

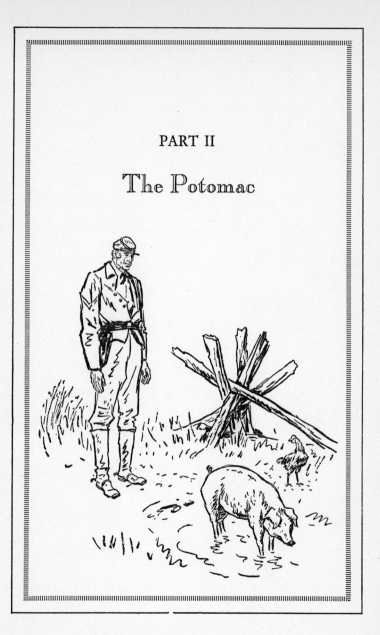

CHAPTER ONE

HILLSBORO

IT REQUIRED considerable effort to think, to make plans, yet Captain Cary knew he must. Harpers Ferry lay, he judged, nearly seventy miles distant to the northwest. To get there he must traverse a bitterly hostile countryside. Judging by what the slave patrol had said, whole Confederate brigades, divisions and corps, aside from cavalry detachments and minor infantry units, were on the march.

He stood, still sweating heavily, rubbing a scratched eyelid and wondering if he had ever been half so weary, uncertain and discouraged before. Somehow what Lenore had done seemed to disorient him the most. She needn't have gone to such lengths, especially when aware of what would inevitably follow if he got caught.

To drag this padero off the road was essential. Some rebel commanders, wise with experience, preferred to march their commands in the cool of night.

Cary's efforts to move the dead man's heavy body failed. The mule, however, gave him an idea. Speaking in an undertone, he approached the ribby animal, had no difficulty in catching it.

Conscious that the passage of each second lessened his chances, Cary hastily untied one of the crude rope stirrups. Throwing a hitch about the pommel of the padero's ancient, scrofulous saddle, he knotted the free end about the dead man's ankle and dragged him, for all the world like a misshapen bag of meal, into a clump of alders.

This accomplished, he explored his late enemy's pockets, eagerly seized a brace of sandwiches wrapped in greasy newspaper. Also he found a sheath for the padero's knife.

Retying the stirrup, he returned to the road and retrieved the slave patrol's hat. Inspecting the shotgun, he found it to be an archaic flintlock fowling piece converted to a percussion cap. It was so old that copper wire had been wrapped to reinforce weak spots in the barrels. The weapon, however, might do in a pinch. Secured to the saddle alongside the handcuffs hung a bag containing buckshot, a flask of powder and a tin box of percussion caps.

Once he had mounted up and had headed the mule down a sandy, weed-covered road he couldn't help a hard smile. Good God, suppose his troopers could see him astride a shambling, lop-eared mule and posing as a chaser of runaway slaves.

The smile faded when the mule took up a slow, bone-racking trot in the direction of the forces encamped about Hillsboro.

How far would he travel before he would find himself challenged by some gray outpost? Painstakingly he proceeded to fabricate and to rehearse a story. God knew he'd better be letter perfect. These days it didn't take many mistakes to get a man hanged.

Almost before he knew it dawn was silhouetting those familiar rolling hills marking the course of the Potomac.

A wide, well-traveled road now opened up. Many troops must have passed this way, for scattered along its edges lay the varied and distinctive jetsam a marching army leaves in its wake. Here lay a worn-out boot; there a punctured gray canteen; yonder a bandage, spotted with dried blood, draped a laurel bush. Fence rails, too, were gone, and the ashes of many campfires sketched white spots by the roadside.

He commenced to overtake increasing numbers of stragglers, stamping silently, wearily along. They were from all branches of the Confederate service, and details of their uniforms and equipment revealed a great deal to the hollow-eyed padero so placidly riding his furry white mule in the direction of Hillsboro.

The stragglers, he noted, were for the most part undersized men or boys in tattered, ill-fitting uniforms of homespun, dyed with butternuts to every shade from light tan to deep brown. Their hatchet-sharp faces appeared thin to emaciation. Most of them looked sick and many went barefooted, carried their shoes slung over their shoulders or on their muskets' barrels.

A few individuals, furtive of expression, seemed better fed. These, the Federal guessed, were the habitual stragglers and malingerers such as inevitably afflict an army of any size.

Cary's role of padero proved effective beyond his fondest hopes. Hardly a man in the Southern service but was familiar with the slave patrol who, year in and year out, could be seen riding roads after sundown. They accepted his presence without question.

He felt less easy, however, when a squad of unshaven gray cavalry on provost duty came cantering down the road in an effort to round up stragglers.

"Heyo, friend, cotch any loose niggers last night?" demanded the gangling sergeant in command.

"No, Mister Sojuh, cain't do much these days. Damn Yanks is still too nigh."

"Well, you'll have plenty of work before long. This time we-uns aim to whip them Yank bastards to a frazzle."

To Cary's immense relief the detachment presently moved on, sabers rattling in dented scabbards, gaunt bodies swinging in saddles.

Gradually the Federal's nerves tautened. Each yard he traveled in the direction of Hillsboro by that much increased his peril. In the village, of course, lived dozens of persons familiar with the white mule and its original owner. Let but one such person see him and all would be lost. It behooved him, therefore, to pass through Hillsboro in a hurry—when few of its inhabitants were astir.

Of course there would be other hazards—officers from his cousin's troop, its N.C.O.s too, knew him by sight. This, he surmised, was a very definite danger, for logically

Craig's troop would be used in reconnaissance operations covering an advance on Harpers Ferry.

A third menace threatened—the fact that during the railroad raid dozens of people had cause to recall his face.

Goading the mule into a reluctant trot, he entered the environs of Hillsboro. He found outlying elements of General Walker's division lying under a pall of blue campfire smoke.

A succession of dog-tired pickets challenged as he rode by, but his function was so familiar that they passed him through the lines. Soon the mule's chipped hoofs were *clip-clopping* past rows of ramshackle Negro cabins lying on the outskirts of the village.

Hundreds of soldiers were bivouacked on near-by fields; in regular clumps their stacked muskets and cased colors towered above the sleeping host. Here and there a campfire still sent skyward a feeble gray thread.

How much like dead men the sleepers seemed, sprawled in their blankets with hard, sun-darkened faces turned toward the graying sky. These ragged battalions seemed utterly exhausted.

The men around him were the 27th North Carolina, if an insignia stenciled on the top of the forage wagon meant anything.

Three other North Carolina regiments—the 46th, the 48th and the 49th—the false padero recognized before he entered into the outskirts of Hillsboro and the zone of his greatest danger. He tried to urge his stolid mount to a faster gait.

The need for speed was great. Already the sun was hovering below the horizon and might at any moment appear to evoke reveille. On the far side of the village he hoped to locate a cavalry picket line from which he might steal a real mount.

Only in the neat red brick town hall was there any semblance of enemy activity. Here, apparently, Brigadier General John G. Walker had established his headquarters. A dozen couriers squatted on the town hall's well-worn steps. Some smoked, others nodded beside tired horses and seemed completely uninterested in the appearance and disappearance of other aides and dispatch riders.

To Hubert Cary's practiced eye it became clear that this corps had marched fast and far. Without exception the staff horses looked tired and thin. Dust lay thick on coats which would normally have been smooth and shiny.

The tree-shaded main street—there were not half a dozen streets in the whole pretty little village—was still destitute of white civilians. Only a few dogs wandered aimlessly around and sniffed at slaves shuffling about on early morning duties.

Cary, on his white mule, was riding past the town hall

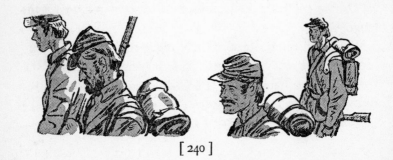

when a bugler appeared on its steps. Hardly more than a boy, the musician rubbed eyes with grimy fists, then momentarily warmed his instrument's mouthpiece.

Cary's anxiety soared when the lad commenced to sound reveille. Arrogantly, insistently, the bugle's brazen notes echoed among the frame houses of Hillsboro. Somewhere down near the Potomac another bugle took up the call. Another and another and another joined in, until it seemed as if Judgment Day were at hand.

In the shade of the padero's hat Hubert Cary's gaunt brown features contracted. Desperately he hammered heels against the mule's bony barrel. It was useless. The animal's stable must have been located down a little road to the left for, to the impostor's dismay, no amount of wrenching at its bridle or kicking could turn it aside. Slowly, inexorably, the mule kept along its self-appointed course.

"No," the stubborn, loose-drooping ears seemed to announce. "I put up with a heap of nonsense last night. I'm going home to bed."

A red-bearded Confederate signal corps officer, yawning and still digging sleep out of his eyes, appeared at the door of a near-by dwelling. He paused to grin broadly at the spectacle of man and mule matching will power.

"Ornery critter, ain't he? Reminds me of my wife," he laughed.

Windows commenced to rattle up so, venting an exasperated curse, Cary surrendered, let the mule amble on toward a ramshackle hut lying some few hundred yards distant from the village proper.

To allow the mule to reach its home would, of course,

mean disaster. The Federal therefore dragged his now tractable beast into a thicket and anchored it by its bridle.

Slinging the padero's shotgun over his shoulder, he commenced shuffling off toward the northern limits of the village. Faintly came the familiar whinny of a horse scenting morning rations. Lord, but the rebels were thick in and about the town. No doubt now that General Walker was driving up behind the Ferry!

Cary had covered barely two hundred yards on the Harpers Ferry road when his fears seemed realized. A mounted picket beheld the rustic figure plodding along, yelled, "Hi, stop thar!"

An eternal, critical second Cary hesitated. A thick growth of bushes led continuously up to a wooded hill. Should he make a dash for it? No, the gray vedette was already too close.

Foolishly he gaped at the picket and drawled, "Mornin', mister. Was it me you was callin'?"

The rider, his weary, flat-looking face glazed with dirt, pointed to the right.

"It wuz. You kin put down yore gun and go down to the cavalry camp yander. They need help waterin' horses."

The command came as such an anticlimax to his fears that Cary almost laughed.

"Sho' now, I reckon them rabbits kin wait. Whereat did you say I should go to?"

"Down by the stone farm yander."

Three minutes later Cary was shambling uncertainly up to a farmhouse and viewing the familiar spectacle of cavalry preparing for another day. A few troopers, pinkly naked to the waist, were sluicing themselves at the farm's watering trough; others were blowing on embers, and still others—the wise ones—were currying their horses' backs.

A sergeant spied him and called, "Hey, Bub, take the lootenant's hoss to water."

"Yes suh, I'd sure be pleasured to."

Despite himself Cary's jaw dropped. Tethered to a twisted apple tree stood Eclipse, unsaddled, but the same black demon.

Eclipse's presence could mean only one thing. He'd reasoned correctly. Craig Carey's command *was* accompanying this movement. It couldn't be far off either—already he'd recognized a trooper here and there.

"Say, you lost your wits?"

"No, mister," Cary grinned, "I ain't. Only 'tain't often you sees so pert a lookin' hoss." A passionate hope surged through him. "Is that the lootenant's hoss?"

"Naw—it's the cap'n's. You water this one. Don't argufy."

Aware that recognition might come at any instant, Cary dared not play for a chance to water his own charger. With a seemingly eager hand he took the bridle reins of a powerful bay thoroughbred and, slouching shamelessly, joined a long line of horses being led down toward the river.

How grotesque. With one hand Fate placed him in the deadliest of peril and with the other offered him means of escaping it.

Pulling the slave patrol's hat low over his brows, he kept his eyes busy. Men and horses alike looked thin and tired but far from exhausted. What tough, wiry individuals these men were. Most of the gray troopers were enjoying their morning "chaw." They cursed their rations, their government and the world in general, as soldiers have since shaggy cave men first caught up weapons with the intention of exterminating a neighboring tribe.

It was not until he had watered the lieutenant's charge and had begun a return trip to the picket line that opportunity offered to lead the animal aside under pretense of readjusting the cinch strap.

He was, Cary found, still quite close to the Potomac. Better still, clumps of willows and alders partially screened him. So, little by little, he guided the bay thoroughbred upstream until the watering party was quite lost to view.

After calmly adjusting the stirrups he swung into the thoroughbred's saddle. God, but it was *fine* to feel a saddle under him once more!

Bending, twisting, to avoid low branches, he paralleled the river between it and a road leading to Harpers Ferry. Momentarily his peril increased. The awakening army was encamped all about. Twice he was forced to ride boldly through watering lines.

His situation became acute when an impassable little gorge, descending to the Potomac, forced him again up to the road where a bridge crossed it.

"Once across I'll go back down beside the river," he told himself. "The rest shouldn't be too hard."

A mean turn of Fate to have come so near to recovering Eclipse! The black had been mighty useful down in the Wilderness; on the Peninsula too.

Riding with brazen assurance, the Federal headed for the bridge. At the near end of it a small knot of gray cavalry were halted. Craig's men? Maybe. This was where they'd be posted. He straightened himself in the saddle. The next few moments might easily prove the most critical of his attempt to pass through Walker's corps.

When he trotted straight toward the bridge the guards turned, looked in his direction. The sun suddenly climbed above the heights on the opposite side of the river, began to sketch long black and gold patterns across the road. Damn! Yonder flashed the yellow sash of an officer. Bad luck. Officers were so much harder to satisfy than enlisted men.

Would the yellow sash believe his cock-and-bull story about taking this horse back to its owner after having it shod in town?

The interval to the bridge had shortened to a scant twenty yards when, to his consternation, Cary recognized the yellow sash as young Lieutenant Chambers of Craig Carey's troop. Postponing recognition to the last unforgiving second, the Federal bent, pretended to fumble with a stirrup leather.

At the first alarm he'd drop flat on the charger's neck and ride for it. This was his only chance—and a reasonable one; the beast between his knees had breeding.

Swiftly yardage to the bridgehead decreased. Cary felt the breath grow short in his throat. What did it feel like when you got hit by a bullet? Some men claimed a shot wound didn't hurt much—not to begin with.

Ten yards to the bridge now. A voice called, "Halt!"

Still bent, he pretended not to notice, rode on.

Then more sharply, "Halt there! You, halt!"

Cary set his jaw and dug his heels into the bay's flanks. Outraged, the thoroughbred bounded forward so furiously that he was plunging by the bridge guards before Cary realized it. Too startled to do more than yell, the gray troopers remained inactive during a priceless instant. Then they began clawing at holstered revolvers and slung carbines.

Faintly he heard young Chambers' voice: "My God! It's that Yank cousin o' Craig's. Get him! Fifty dollars for whoever brings him in!"

The bay charger's hoofs drummed hollowly over the worn planking of the bridge, then beat more quietly on solid earth.

Shouts and yells were rising in all directions. Behind, a number of carbines cracked spitefully and bullets screamed past Cary's ears. Bent low, he wrenched his mount off the road into a field and set him at a four-foot hedge. Up, up, soared the stolen charger. Wind tore at Cary's hair. The bay landed like the steeplechaser he must once have been.

To Cary's blank dismay he blundered squarely into a company of butternut infantry in the act of falling in.

Frantically the Federal swerved his mount toward a woods further to the right. Damnation! Soldiers seemed to sprout from the earth in all directions. A squad with fixed bayonets barred his path; he veered left, making for a gap between a platoon and the rest of its company.

From nowhere materialized a red-faced soldier. Deliberately the rebel raised his piece, sighted a long-barreled musket. Cary very distinctly saw the infantryman's left eye close, saw his brown fingers tighten around the weapon's grip.

Crash! Flame beat full in Cary's face. His mount gave a terrific convulsive leap; then, like a vast sponge, a blackness seemed to erase Hubert Cary from the face of the earth.

CHAPTER TWO

COURT-MARTIAL

"THE PRISONER will arise."

Not unkindly a swarthy infantry corporal standing at Cary's left repeated the command.

Across the low-ceilinged schoolroom Craig Carey started as though he, and not his cousin, was facing death by hanging.

Handcuffed and under the guard of four sunburned privates, the Federal got to his feet and stood, a grimy, disheveled figure, among school desks marred by the penknives of generations of young Virginians.

The court-martial board were indeed a grim-looking lot. Obviously they hated being here. There was a Georgian, a couple of North Carolina Scots with intense black eyes and restless ways, a stranger with a tawny beard—the rest Virginians.

No use deceiving himself. Ever since Vance Chambers' troopers had pulled him from beneath the dead thoroughbred and had brought him back to Hillsboro, dazed

[248]

and helpless, he'd known what was going to be done.

Strangely, the imminence of death did not seem to matter—he was too tired, sore and soul-sick. From the gay, dangerous adventure he'd pictured and expected back in '61, war had degenerated into a drab, exhausting turmoil, bestial in its execution, horrible to contemplate.

Woodenly he stood listening to a dull rumble beat in through the schoolroom's cracked windowpanes. It was rather like distant thunder. Yet it wasn't thunder. It was a bombardment getting under way across the river, somewhere in Maryland.

His captors were commenting on it, were speculating. Some reckoned a fight was making up near Cramptons Gap. Wasn't McClellan known to be pushing north? *Grumble. Grumble. Rumble!*

Momentarily the distant guns boomed louder.

Heretofore Cary's blood had quickened to the sound of artillery fire, but not now. He had, it seemed, failed for a second time, and because of this failure Harpers Ferry was probably doomed.

And always at the back of his mind gnawed the conviction that Lenore Duveen had coldly, deliberately attempted to betray him to a certain death.

Blinking in the ruddy rays of sunset, a scholarly looking military clerk put away the penknife with which he had been improving the point of his quill pen. He jumped to attention, however, when the court-martial board jingled and clanked in, one by one.

Cary's judges were cavalrymen mostly—though their uniforms varied. All showed effects of the hard campaigning before Richmond. Tarnished braid and buttons bespoke many nights spent beneath the open sky.

Van H. Manning, colonel of the 3rd Arkansas and president of the board, halted behind the teacher's desk serving as a tribunal. The sunset tinged his heavy brown beard with minute flecks of fire.

A penetrating silence ruled when Colonel Manning cleared his throat and fixed fine, sad-looking eyes on the manacled prisoner.

"Captain Cary, I believe you do not deny that you were captured within our lines in civilian clothes?"

The speaker's tones were not deep enough to drown the shrill yapping of a puppy in the street outside.

"That is correct, sir."

"You are conversant with the Articles of War?"

"I am familiar with them, sir." Cary could quite clearly visualize the ivy-clad walls of the Point and old Colonel Drew lecturing on military law, droning on and on.

"You do not deny that you led a party of spies in an attempt to ruin our line of communication?"

"No sir." The prisoner spoke with flat detachment, as if restating a tiresome fact.

"Have you anything to say before the sentence of this court is pronounced?"

Cary shook his head. Across the room someone caught his breath with a hiss. Craig Carey's face had gone gray and faded, like a Chinese lantern with its candle burned out.

His cousin, Cary felt sure, was suffering more than himself. Toward the close of the trial Craig had given his testimony in a noticeably unsteady voice.

[250]

"Then, Captain Cary"—Colonel Manning's voice was flat and toneless—"it is the duty of this court to sentence you to death. You will be hanged by the neck until dead—as provided by the Articles of War. Sentence will be executed at the moment of sunrise tomorrow—and may God have mercy on your soul."

Boots shuffled, a sword scabbard clashed softly against a desk, spurs clinked. The military clerk, having carefully closed his small lead ink bottle, commenced to collect his papers and to place them in a portable field desk. Surprisingly soon the schoolroom was deserted save for the prisoner, his four guards and his cousin's bowed figure.

"Parris is the capitol of France," some child had written across a blackboard above Craig Carey.

"This way, suh," the infantry corporal said. "We have permission to use the town jail; you won't have to keep those damn things on your wrists, suh."

"That will be pleasant." The prisoner's cheerful tone made his guards stare.

Craig Carey started to come forward, then, as if unable to carry out some intent, wavered, wheeled about to gaze fixedly out of a window until prisoner and guards had marched out into the sunlight.

Gray battalions were still moving through Hillsboro in the direction of Maryland and Pennsylvania. By tens and hundreds Confederate infantry were swinging by with the loose-kneed, space-eating stride of veterans. The clothing of some were grotesque tatters, a far cry from the gay panoplies worn at Bull Run. Their weapons were bright though, and their cartridge boxes dragged hard at their belts.

"There's the spy!" children squealed when Cary was led out. "There's the Yankee spy!"

A half-witted boy kept mumbling, chanting, "He's a-goin' to hang, a-goin' to hang. Hang! Hang! Hang! De-de-dang!"

The jail, located in the rear of the town hall, proved to be a stout stone structure fitted with iron bars and heavy padlocks. Its one cell was large though. Probably in all of Hillsboro's hitherto uneventful history it had seldom confined more than two or three prisoners at a time.

"Thank you," nodded the prisoner when the swarthy corporal unlocked his manacles. "Quite a fight beginning over yonder."

"She sho' ain't no measly skirmish. All them cannons means a real ruckus. I'll try to get you some food, suh." He hesitated, then added: "Maybe you'd like to write some letters? Reckon I might come across a pencil and paper."

"No need." Somber-eyed, Craig Carey appeared, waited before the cell door. He held gauntlets in one hand and black-plumed hat under his arm. "I have brought paper."

"Yes suh."

"You may go, Corporal."

"But—but—suh, it's——"

"You may lock the door outside, but you will leave us alone. I will assume the responsibility."

Striving to appear unconcerned, Hubert waited. Why had Craig come? To reproach him for his conduct at Philomont? To inquire for Lenore?

The Southerner approached the bars, put a hand to his

cousin's shoulder. Though the Confederate said not a word, the gesture was infinitely eloquent.

"Little Grandma—is all right? I—— Oh hang, Craig, I've been mighty worried about her. I—I—tried to make her go upstairs on the night of—of the raid; but you know Little Grandma."

"Yes," the Southerner nodded. "I heard about that and"—blue eyes, red rimmed with fatigue, sought Hubert's—"I want to tell you, Hubie—about the matter of—of Lenore Duveen." He paused, jerked at the fingers of the gauntlet, "I—well, I understand why you did what you did—even if it looked cowardly to some people."

"Thank you, Craig, glad you understand. I imagine no one else does."

"Little Grandma does, but Melissa's hot against you—so are my officers."

"I expect they are." Hubert motioned to a small bare bench. They seemed so alone in the center of the big cell.

"Hubie"—Craig Carey made a small futile gesture—"I don't know what—how——"

"It doesn't matter so much as you might figure, Craig. I end here and you—over there perhaps." The Federal's dirty red head inclined in the direction of the distant engagement. "We knew such things might happen when we joined the army, didn't we?"

"But to *hang!*" Craig's voice broke, and his features quivered like those of a man being operated on without an anesthetic. "To hang like a common felon! It ain't right—damned if it is. Here." Hurriedly he pressed a small cold object in the prisoner's hand.

[253]

"Only a penknife. Ain't big enough to hurt anybody or anything—except—except a blood vessel."

The anguish in Craig's voice was deep, poignant. For some instants Hubert looked steadily into his cousin's well-remembered eyes. Seemed hard to realize that they'd never again cry on the hounds of a crisp winter's day. That they'd never again shoot canvasbacks on the Susquehanna Flats, thrill to the roar of a rising covey. A trifle ironic that Craig's farewell gesture should be the boon of a private, less dishonorable extinction.

"Better clear out and pour yourself a drink, Craig," the Federal suggested. "Forget this whole stupid business if you can. It's just like facing a bad operation—after all. One that can't be ducked. Really. Don't think me afraid; I'm not."

"You wouldn't be. You never were afraid of anything much." His whole body shook as he passed a hand over his eyes. "Oh God, if only we hadn't turned aside at Catoctin Bridge. That would have been a heap better than this."

He steadied, drew himself up and forced a smile. "My troop is moving out in a few minutes," Craig muttered. "If there is—anything I can do?"

Hubert felt prompted to dispatch an ironic farewell to Lenore Duveen. Redspurs to the Golden Diana—— No. To hell with that!

He said lightly, "I'd like some blankets, Craig—haven't slept warm for a coon's age, and a pipe of tobacco, maybe."

A muscle in Craig's cheek jerked spasmodically when he held out his hand.

"Good-by, Hubie. There's going to be hell and repeat

[254]

over in Maryland before long. We may meet again soon—
sooner than we know."

Once his cousin had gone Cary went over to the iron-
barred window and looked down into a pleasant elm-
shaded street. Presently a group of curious children collected and stared open-mouthed at him. He waved, went
back into the cell and, smoothing the letter paper Craig
had brought, commenced to write.

The guns in the distance finally fell silent as the twilight
deepened and the sky over the Potomac became a glowing,
inverted bowl of purple gold. A brief letter to his family;
another, briefer, to Corliss, his commanding officer.

He wandered over to the window again.

His last evening. Fate was kind. Billowy, faintly roseate
clouds hung poised incredibly high over those purplish
heights across the Potomac. Above them was drawn a band
of the deepest blue he had ever seen. It reminded him of
Melissa standing in the doorway at Philomont. Her dress
had been that color.

To either side of his face his hands tightened on the bars.
It looked mighty still and peaceful up there. No war, no
heartache, no tired body.

He was dimly conscious of people moving on the road
below, and once he vaguely heard a little gasp. His thoughts
were too far away, though, to pay any heed to its origin.

The jailer, a hangdog fellow in patched homespuns, appeared at the door. He had a cocked revolver thrust into a
wide leather belt and carried a brass ring of keys.

"Heah you are, Cap'n—a fryin' chicken, compliments of
Cunnel Manning. And Cap'n Clay sent you this."

Somewhat regretfully the jailer thrust between the greasy iron bars a pint bottle of bourbon whisky.

Cary had not realized he was hungry but now he recalled that, save for a chunk of meat and a slab of corn pone, he had not eaten since he and Lenore Duveen had camped beneath the stars. How many lifetimes could be packed into twenty-four short hours! Last night at this same hour they had been together talking, dreaming of a future. That made him laugh.

When darkness had blotted out the street a spectacled young guard brought in a pair of lanterns. He hung these outside the barred-off space, then seated himself on a wooden bench facing the prisoner.

"You must forgive me, suh," he apologized. "I have orders to keep you under constant observation. I imagine the authorities intend to make sure you are not going to get away."

"Get away?" Emptily Cary's laugh resounded in the big, sour-smelling cell. "That's a rare one! Behold, my friend, three of this room's walls are of stone. The fourth of heavy iron bars, which—poets to the contrary—do a prison make."

Escape! The only escape for him lay through the blade of a pocketknife. Craig—so damned decent.

A warm wind was rising, blowing up through cracks in the jail floor as the prisoner made up a bed of blankets in one corner. For the first time in forty-eight hours Cary really relaxed.

He was dozing off when a voice recalled him from the threshold of sleep. Beyond the lamplit bars he made out a pale blur. A woman—a kindly village matron? The scholarly guard had disappeared.

Cary got to his feet, pushing the disordered red hair from his eyes. What he saw held him motionless and incredulous. Lenore Duveen, exquisitely lovely—more desirable than ever.

"Then it *was* you at the window?" she murmured hurriedly. "I couldn't believe——"

Cary remained in the center of the cell, faintly outlined by the lantern's glow.

"How very kind of you to come," he observed in brittle courtesy.

The slim figure extended slim arms through the bars. "Hubert, Hubert dearest—what dreadful——"

"There's really no need for you to exercise your undeniable charms again, my dear. This time I'm so securely trapped it's hardly worth the trouble."

Lenore's arms sank. Her eager look faded to one of bewilderment. Skirts rustling softly, she pressed herself to the bars.

Where had she come across this dress? If only she hadn't looked so lovely. The deep red of her lips at a moment like this was maddening.

"Don't look at me so. I—I can't bear it."

"And how would you prefer your victim to look?" Cary checked himself. "No, that's not fair; I'm not really your victim. I'd the good fortune to escape the gentleman you sent to capture me."

Had he suddenly exchanged English for an unknown tongue, Lenore Duveen could not have appeared more surprised. She stared at him uncomprehendingly. Her dark eyes became incredibly large and tragic.

"Nice of you to stop by," Cary continued with a mirthless laugh. "A pity it's not *de rigeur* to invite you in. In fact I——"

At the anguish stiffening her features his voice failed. Tears began slipping down the pallid luster of her cheeks.

"You must forgive me," he said in a gentler tone. "Somehow I never seem to know what to say or to do when you are around. I'm a stupid fool."

"Hubert, Hubert! Don't look at me like this!" She shivered as though suddenly stripped bare. "I've been in agony ever since you disappeared."

"Disappeared?" The condemned man stiffened, asked very slowly, "What do you mean?"

Her hands tightened over the greasy bars, marking small white intervals in their length.

"Last night," she said rapidly, "after you left me in the lean-to I was thirsty. I went down to the pool. After I had drunk I stayed to watch the moon on the waterfall, to think how happy I was. I fell asleep; when I awoke it was dawn. I rushed back to our camp, found the lean-to knocked down and you gone. Hubert, my darling, I—I nearly went crazy then."

Guiltily he recalled that those men at the foot of his tree had referred only to "the girl." Any inhabitant of the neighborhood might have said as much.

In rebellion now at the thought of what would soon be done to him, Cary reached through the grille.

[258]

"Lenore!" When he clasped her through the bars her mouth was ever so eager and fragrant.

After a time Lenore Duveen gently disengaged herself. The cold pressure of iron along her cheek was a reminder.

"I'm going now, Hubert," she told him over her shoulder. "I will find General Walker. He—they can't—must grant at least a stay. I won't let them——"

In her flushed excitement she was again the girl of those fearful hours in Luke Archer's camp.

His hard hands closed over hers. "There's no use, darling, absolutely none. They have tried me fairly enough. After all, I am what they say, so, dear, we must face the situation squarely."

Lenore came back to the bars, clung to him, rained kisses on his cheeks, his brow, his lips.

"I *can't,* I *won't* let you go! They shan't—hang——" The word stuck in her throat like a thing of tangible dimensions. "God won't permit such a frightful thing!"

He could feel her cold hands shaking like those of an exhausted runner.

"Steady, dear—steady," was all he could find to say. Then, uncertain of his own ability to restrain himself, he took her flushed face between his hands, deliberately memorized each gracious curve. Such a mental portrait might be fine to recall.

"Guard!" he called. "Guard!"

When the scholarly private came running in Lenore Duveen recovered herself in a measure.

The soldier saluted, pointed down the corridor leading to the front of the jail.

"I regret to remind you, Miss. Your pass called for a five-minute interview. I've already allowed you ten."

A sensitive, well-spoken fellow, this; looked as if he might have been a schoolteacher or a theological student.

CHAPTER THREE

THE PENKNIFE

WIND had begun to rattle the leaves of some elms just outside. It came beating up through the cracks in the floor in puffs strong enough to stir Cary's hair. But he was quite unaware of it. Those ten minutes with Lenore had altered his attitude.

Great God, never again to hear her rich laughter, never again to watch those glowing brown eyes rise to meet his, never again to feel the warm pressure of her lips! The thought was intolerable.

He must think—must try to solve this predicament.

Lying on the rough, sour-smelling blankets, he felt an absurd impulse to jump up and try, by main strength, to tear the bars from their setting. Easy on! This was a waste of valuable time.

His hand felt for the penknife. It was fragile—its blade hardly more than a half inch of very thin, very sharp steel. Admirable, no doubt, for pointing a quill, but hardly a useful tool.

Cautiously Cary raised his head. The guard was bent over a book, his lips moving slightly as he read. He had rested his bayoneted musket against the wall.

In rising hopelessness Cary cast about for an idea. Minute after minute ticked by. Could he dig the cement from a window bar setting? No, the penknife's blade was much too fragile—also the guard would notice him at work.

While the prisoner considered ways and means rats began to scurry through the walls. Any chance of tricking the guard, of overpowering him? No, that would accomplish nothing. The key to this cell was kept by the sergeant of the guard.

Ever more distinctly before his eyes materialized the outline of a noose. Voices in the street momentarily distracted Cary's attention.

Someone was saying, "I wouldn't go through that again for a fortune."

"A bad business, all right. But what could Manning do? A spy's a spy, and there's no two ways about it."

"Dammit, if he don't hang, we'll be overrun with Yankee agents." The speaker paused, evidently lit a pipe. "Bit of a beauty, wasn't she?"

"Loveliest I've ever seen. Couldn't bear to see her so—so desperate." Boots scuffed along a board sidewalk, began to fade.

"What does Manning intend to do?"

"She lives up near Sharpsburg somewhere. I imagine he plans to send her home soon's we've crossed the river and gobbled old Davis' command."

[262]

"To hell with Harpers Ferry! Dammit, Harry, war ought not to be like this—hurting nice people. War's a dirty game when——" The voices faded.

The restless wind began hissing so strongly between the floor boards that at length it stirred Cary's blankets. Struck by a sudden inspiration, he rolled over and examined the floor.

It was solidly constructed of worn white-pine planks.

Keeping one eye on his guard, the prisoner ran fingers along the wide cracks to either side of what seemed to be the widest board. Um. Didn't seem too long.

Further groping and probing revealed that a pair of ten-penny nails at each end secured this board to its floor beam. How wide was it? A generous eight inches wide. Hope began to glimmer.

Opening the penknife, Cary first drew up his top covering, then pulled down the lower blanket until the nail-heads were exposed.

He opened the penknife's blade again, then, without permitting himself definitely to hope, he commenced to cut at wood surrounding one of the nailheads. It was hard work since he must labor by sense of touch alone. Presently, however, the moon arose, cast a bright zebra-striped pattern over the floor.

Though the village clock clanged out ten strokes, the guard still read on. Before the sweating prisoner realized it eleven was sounding. He'd have to lay off 'til a new guard came to relieve the old. He appeared presently, evidently appalled at the prospect of keeping a deathwatch.

"How—how is he?" the newcomer stammered.

"Asleep," the relieved guard replied. "Damned if I could."

When the clock struck midnight, and drowsy reverberations were flung back by bold bluffs rising in Maryland across the river, quite a pile of pale whittlings lay beneath Cary's blankets.

Half the length of the nail now was freed. At half-past two he had entirely freed the first nail and had disclosed a good half of the second. Sweat rolled down Cary's brow in acid rivulets. His fingers were numb and aching, but the now seriously dulled knife rasped steadily away at the edges of the hole. It made a noise very like that of the gnawing rat.

At four o'clock a hint of dawn grayed the sky. Only a little more remained to be done when jaded muscles caused the knife to slip. Horror-stricken, Cary tested the blade. It had snapped off close to the handle!

Despairingly he thrust a trembling forefinger down along the shaft of the nail in an effort to estimate just how much wood remained uncut. No telling.

To maintain his self-control was difficult. If he couldn't lift the board, he would die at the end of a rope inside of two more hours.

Trembling, his bruised fingers tested the plank's corners in search of a purchase. He managed at length to get a fair grip because the floor planks were badly fitted. Heart in mouth, he gave a tentative pull and a flood of joy swept through him because the board end gave perceptibly.

The cavalryman lay still a minute, listening to roosters

[264]

on the outskirts of Hillsboro crow sleepily. Since he must stand or fall by a single effort, he must foresee everything. What lay below? An air space, or a cellar from which escape might be impossible?

Summoning a realistic yawn, he stirred and from beneath lowered lids studied his most recent guard. The man, slouched on the bench, was staring fixedly at a broad big toe which was protruding through the split end of his boot. When Cary sat up and began to stretch the fellow started nervously.

"I'm mighty thirsty," Cary said. "Think you can find me a drink?"

"Reckon so."

The guard, the third that night, was more suspicious than his fellows and, before going down the corridor, unhooked one of the lanterns to peer in through the bars. Seeing nothing but a gaunt, hollow-eyed wretch squatting amid a heap of blankets on the floor, he turned and stalked out, his loose boot sole softly scuffing.

At once Hubert Cary scrambled to his knees and grabbed at the loose end. When he pulled the plank yielded a little, then suddenly snapped free, tearing his fingernails. With the strength of despair he tried again and succeeded in forcing two fingers under the plank's end. With this better purchase the prisoner was now able to lift the plank free of the nails which had secured it. Grunting, he forced it back much as one lifts and bends back the board cover of a packing case.

A musty wind rushed up through the black parallelogram he had created. Below was only blackness—how much of a drop? No time to speculate. The guard would be back any instant.

He slid his legs into the aperture and wriggled through until only head and shoulders remained above the cell floor. In convulsive haste he jerked the blanket over the uptilted board, then stretched his legs downward until, mercifully, they encountered an uneven surface. Squeezing head and shoulders through the gap, he reached up and drew the board back into position as best he might.

This was no cellar, thank God, only an air space under the floor—such a place as is used for the storing of odds and ends of lumber. A few feet away a glimmer of moonlight indicated open ground. He commenced to crawl toward it at all speed, for, like the tread of doom, the guard's loose boot sole could be heard slap-slapping back down the corridor.

Quickly the hot and dusty fugitive crept out from beneath the jail and crouched behind a water barrel to get his bearings. Very distinctly he heard the guard's first bewildered shout of:

"Hey! Why—where——"

Casting stealth to the winds, Cary raced out onto a street which appeared to lead toward the not-distant Potomac. Behind him the jail guard fired his musket. At once sentries posted in and around Hillsboro began discharging theirs.

Running as only a man can run when death snaps at his heels, the cavalryman sped past the last black and silent houses.

A mongrel, spying the fleeting figure, rushed to the end

of its chain and set up a furious clamor. Was any cavalry left in Hillsboro? Cary figured he could outrun any unmounted pursuit. The thought of Lenore was enough.

Deserting the road as unsafe, the fugitive diagonaled across a big field of standing corn and, reaching the middle of it, paused to determine the nature and direction of the chase. Men were running hotfoot down the same road he had followed, were forming to sweep the cornfield.

Refreshed by his comparative inactivity in the jail, Cary put on a respectable burst of speed which carried him the width of the cornfield; then he hurdled a rail fence and continued pelting across a pasture.

No sooner had he emerged into the open, however, than a picket posted on the riverbank saw him and raised a view halloo. This forced Cary to sheer away and run parallel to the riverbank.

The picket proved to be a mounted one, so the first instant Cary judged himself out of sight he leaped down into a myrtle tangle leading to the Potomac's edge.

The riverbank was steeper than Cary had imagined, and he fell heavily, clutching futilely at trees and bushes.

His head banged against a stone and thousands of lights soared before his eyes, but he got up again and went plunging down toward the mist-veiled river. A minute more and his feet were cooled by the Potomac.

Reckless of commands to halt, he splashed across a rocky shallow in search of the river's main course. Once the water reached his waist Cary stopped wading and struck out into the stream as silently as he might. Then, only mouth and nose clear of the surface, he floated.

After a safe interval Cary turned over and struck out for the Maryland shore with slow and powerful strokes.

He had, however, not taken a dozen strokes before he abruptly altered his course. A regiment of cavalry of some kind was watering horses on the Maryland shore.

Temptation to risk a landing in Maryland was well-nigh irresistible, but it was too much of a gamble. Both banks of the Potomac seemed to be swarming with enemies.

Cary swam back to the Virginia side and sought shelter of a rocky, boulder-strewn point where alder clumps grew right down to the water's edge. Flat as any Indian, he worked along the shore until he found a hiding place in a hollow formed by the roots of a big overturned sycamore.

A morning mist descended, then presently lifted to reveal the unidentified cavalry as Confederate. For over an hour, therefore, Cary remained huddled, shivering and tortured by mosquitoes which, making capital of his helplessness, stabbed him unmercifully.

The sun was well up when the last of the horsemen opposite had finished watering. It was a vast relief to hear the regimental bugler sound a call and to see a color sergeant ride up the bank with the Stars and Bars flaunting in the new sunlight.

Cary held an inward consultation. What to do? He remained as far as ever from Harpers Ferry, but there seemed still time to bring a warning. All along, the conduct of Walker's corps had suggested that speed was being sacrificed to secrecy.

It was infinitely exasperating to realize that his objective lay within easy striking distance upstream. Where would

Lenore have gone? Up to Sharpsburg? Certainly she would
not be permitted to cross the river until Harpers Ferry had
fallen. Most likely she was somewhere between Hillsboro
and the besieged post.

Watching the last gray horsemen go scrambling up from
the river to be momentarily silhouetted on the opposite
heights, Cary smiled grimly. But for that little penknife——

As if to stir him to action, a sound of very distant rifle
fire came from across the Potomac.

Presently he recognized a sound much like that of a
bowling ball as it goes rolling down an alley; it meant that
a battery of artillery was going into action. Whose? What
in blazes *was* going on? The cannonade going on today
sounded far closer than the dull reports heard the night
before.

Gradually an explanation evolved that the armies of Lee
and McClellan had begun to feint and thrust at each other
among the rich, rolling hills of northern Maryland.

He was deliberating his next move when, on the bluff
above him, he recognized the soft thump of horses' hoofs.

"Reckon hyar's a likely place, Bill," a voice said. It
sounded not fifty feet away. "Danged if I don't git in that
pool and drown a few divisions o' my graybacks."

"Sho' enough," drawled another. "I'm so dirty I creak
every time I move. Fer a fact, I'm scairt o' mebbe gettin'
wounded. Pa says dirty clothes don't help when they rub
agin a hurt."

"Think we've got time?" demanded a third and unexpectedly cultured voice. "The lieutenant will give us blazes
if he finds out."

"Why the devil should he? He's 'way over by the pike and it wun't take us twenty minutes."

The fugitive pressed his body flatter among the sycamore's roots. He hardly dared breathe. The three riders were dismounting almost above his head. He could hear every word of their conversation.

"Got airy soap, Dave?"

"Just a mite."

"Hey, Loosh! Don't tie your hoss so near my mare. She's jest come in heat and she'll shorely kick the daylights outer him."

The hollow-eyed fugitive heard objects being thrown onto the ground; then a naked form made its way by the sycamore. Next appeared a thin trooper with short yellow chin whiskers, then a well-built young man who carried a soiled shirt in one hand, a scrap of yellow soap in the other.

All would be well, Cary realized, until the swimmers started back up the bank; then they could not help but see him. How near were the other members of the bathers' unit?

Once splashings came from the river Cary crawled out of his retreat. All three troopers were up to their waists in the river, busily soaping themselves. Two of them began washing their heads, and suds streamed over their faces.

When the third Confederate turned his back Cary swept up an armful of clothes and cast loose the strongest appearing of the three horses.

THE MISSISSIPPIANS

IN A HOLLOW not too distant from the river Captain Cary reined in and dropped onto the ground his miscellany of stolen clothes. Certainly some garments in the armful must come close to fitting.

After making a cautious survey of his surroundings he hitched the stolen horse to a sapling. It was a sturdy half-bred gelding—apparently the property of one David Burton.

Rapidly Cary divested himself of the padero's coat and the filthy civilian trousers and shirt he had worn ever since, long ages ago, he had boarded that local for Mount Jackson. "Um, let's see what we've got to work with."

In a pair of dusty saddlebags strapped to Corporal Burton's cantle—he must have been a gentleman, judging by the saddle's quality—he found a razor among other toilet articles.

At a brook purling by only a few yards away he moistened his stubbly beard and, not without many groans, first shaved, then removed the short red sideburns. As an added precaution he shortened his eyebrows at both ends. His hair, he felt, remained the worst danger.

"By this time, horse, the rebs will be throwing every red-head in Loudoun County into jail," he solemnly informed his browsing mount. "What can we do about it?"

Charcoal? That might help some—but for a time only. Besides, to light a fire was to invite disaster. Puzzled, he darted quick glances about. Inspiration came from a lone black walnut tree not far away. Clinging to its spreading branches were hundreds of pulpy covers.

He kicked off his boots and ran toward the tree. It stood majestically aloof under a sky now quivering with the thunder of the engagement taking place over in Mary-land.

Later the crushed husks of a dozen walnut fruits went bobbing off down the brook as there rode out of the gully a corporal of Confederate cavalry with a skin so bronzed that he might easily have passed for an Indian. A wide felt hat garnished with a blackbird's wing covered hair turned a streaky dark brown.

As the rider cantered out onto a road lying hot and yellow beneath the noonday sun he sang:

> *"The years glide slowly by, Lorena,*
> *The snow is on the grass again;*
> *The sun is low down in the sky, Lorena,*
> *The frost gleams where the flowers have been——"*

Corporal David Burton—*soi-disant*—of the 10th Virginia Cavalry, on his way back from "remounting himself" in lower Loudoun County, with a secret smile changed the lady's name to Lenore and became vastly more pleased with his vocal efforts.

Using considerable pains, the rider circled Hillsboro. When, from a distant hilltop, he glimpsed the stone façade of the jail a chill crept down his spine.

No use tempting Fortuna. Of late she had smiled too sweetly. How empty the countryside appeared now that Walker's army had disappeared slogging slowly, steadily in the direction of the Ferry.

"Mustn't look worried," he warned himself; so, ever keeping a wary lookout, the corporal dusted off wide chevrons, swallowed a refreshing draught from a silver flask discovered in the gentleman ranker's saddlebags.

Presently Cary's spirits rose so high that with hardly a tremor he trotted out onto that same bridge which caused his downfall.

Heigho! What with a good mount, arms and a good dollop of bourbon beneath his belt, war again was becoming a gallant and a fascinating game; life, a glorious adventure. Had not Lenore Duveen given him her trust—her love?

Here and there the solitary rider overtook barefooted stragglers who cast envious eyes at the tall chestnut between his knees.

All went well until, in a patch of woods, a squad of the tallest and thinnest rebel troopers he had ever seen came riding onto the road. They were, with one exception, bearded, hawk-featured and deeply sunburned. The letters J. D. L. had been branded on the wooden canteens hanging over their hips. Despite their shaggy and undisciplined appearance the newcomers rode horses such as any Federal officer might envy.

"Heyo, friend," called the leader, speaking with a curious nasal twang. "Real ruckus beginnin' crost the river, ain't it?"

"Right smart skirmish, all right."

"You all headed fer the main army?"

"Stuart's command."

They were eying him very sharply, these hatchet-faced troopers; otherwise they seemed friendly enough.

"That's fine, we're for Stuart too. We-uns been back remountin' and cain't nohow come up with our outfit."

"Where d'you belong?"

"The Jeff Davis legion out o' Mississip'—Cunnel Martin. Somebody 'lowed our people had done gone on 'crost the river."

These were the first Mississippians Cary had ever encountered. No wonder they had seemed dissimilar to the graceful Virginia riders; they more resembled mountain men.

"Well, mebbe I can help you all."

"Know this heah country?" drawled the leader, who wore a red fox's brush fastened to a low-crowned straw hat.

"Sho' do. I hail from lower down this county."

"Well, hain't that luck? We-uns are lookin' fer a place called Maddox's Crossroads. Know it?"

"Sho', it's only an hour's ride ahead."

"We're fixin' to meet some o' our boys there," the leader announced, yellowish eyes following the river.

Gradually the dull cannonade across the Potomac swelled in intensity—like a summer storm coming nearer.

The uncertainty of its significance was reflected in the faces of stragglers on the road. Steadily the road was becoming more thickly peopled—strays, small detachments and messengers.

The quick-eyed Mississippians rode close, uncomfortably so. Were they becoming suspicious?

Cary was still wondering when, at a fork of the road, a weather-beaten fingerpost indicated Maddox's Crossroads as lying some two miles off to the left.

Long since, Cary had decided that he stood some chance of success if he attempted the last three miles of his journey into Harpers Ferry after dark. To ride with these Mississippians over to Maddox's Crossroads would use up time. Besides, the crossroads seemed to lie away from the most active zone of operations. In that direction he would run less risk of blundering into a provost patrol which might ask embarrassing questions.

Accordingly he rode off the main road in company with the Mississippians and observed that this portion of the countryside seemed to have been very little traveled by armed forces.

"Who's the leader of this detachment?" Cary presently inquired of a man at his left.

"Luke Hawks, but he air with the boys we aim to meet at Maddox's."

Instantly Cary's thoughts reverted to another Luke—and that brought him back to Lenore. Where would she be? Probably within a few miles of him, unless she had traveled down instead of up the troubled Potomac.

When the Federal's eye noted a complete and surprising

absence of gray troops along the Maryland shore he began to hunt for a reason.

"Probably," he assured himself, "the rebs on the other side of the river are traveling north—in the direction of Hagerstown."

His pulses quickened at a thought which came to him. "By God, if our garrison could get across into Maryland tonight—and moved *fast*—they might circle the rebel right flank and join McClellan."

The more he studied the idea the more he cursed the hours which must pass before nightfall.

"Is this heah Maddox's Crossroads?"

The man with the foxtail in his hat jerked a bony thumb at a substantial frame house standing alone beneath two towering elms.

"Yes, this is it."

"Hi-yi! For the Lawd's sake, look at all them fat shoats!" One of the riders started to unsheath his saber. "Mah Gawd, I could do plenty with a rasher of hawg meat."

"Git back in ranks." The leader, by the others called Abell, scowled so ferociously that the would-be forager vented a disappointed snarl and slid his saber back into its scabbard.

Uneasiness concerning these hungry-looking strangers grew in Cary's mind. Though they rode well, the Mississippians carried a weird assortment of weapons; pistols, bowies—even carving knives worn in homemade sheaths. Further, they lacked any iota of discipline or military bearing, and they certainly seemed in no great hurry to rejoin their command. But then the rumor ran that most of the

Western Confederate cavalry was hardly more than armed civilians.

The little cavalcade presently rode into the barnyard, where a full-bosomed woman in a starched calico sunbonnet was tossing grain to a flock of hens.

"Howdy, boys," she greeted. "Rid' far?"

"Fur enough, ma'am." Abell lifted his cap. "Reckon we'd like to camp heah fo' a while. We're fixin' to meet some of our boys heah."

The housewife beamed. "Reckon you can; any boys in gray are welcome. And what's more, I'll give you some eggs."

"Eggs? Hell!" growled a horseman behind Cary. "Who yo' savin' all them hens for? The Yanks?"

"Well, of all the pert, ungrateful scalawags!" The farmer woman glared. "Just you touch one o' my hens and I'll smack your sassy face!"

"Don't pay him no mind, ma'am," Abell drawled while swinging off his horse. "Tom's got a holler leg. We'll pay fo' anythin' we take."

Uneasiness crept into the woman's ruddy, good-natured countenance.

"Pay with what? Greenbacks?"

Abell's manner became sardonic. "Why, I'm right grieved, ma'am. Yo'd take money from pore fellers fightin' to keep you free? Howsumever, we'll pay you in good secesh bills." Abell winked ponderously in Cary's direction. "That's right, ain't it, Virginny?"

Cary nodded. "I reckon so. These boys won't harm anything."

Though the Mississippians unbridled and watered their mounts, they made no attempt to remove their saddles. Wary birds.

For reasons of his own Cary quietly led his own horse behind a big white barn. There he found a freckled lad feeding an ancient mare.

" 'Lo,. Bub. Ain't it gettin' on toward your suppertime?"

"Reckon so, mister," grinned the lad, eying him with frank curiosity, "but I got to finish my chores. I'm late tonight."

"Late? Been listenin' to the battle, eh?"

"Naw, they's always battles round here. Ma Gordon, she's come to visit—brought a sick friend too, dum it. If you've a mind, you kin loose your hoss in the box stall."

The boy measured out some oats and grinned again. "That's a nice hoss you got, mister; give him this, but don't tell them others. They're powerful hungry lookin' and their hosses looks just like 'em."

When Cary, after having rubbed down his horse before resaddling, came out into the sunset he found six gangle-legged Western troopers busy at the Maddox haycock. Helping themselves to huge armfuls, they were flinging the hay down before their mounts though the owner raised shrill protests. Next they helped themselves to cordwood and built a fire on the edge of the farmyard.

"Don't you dast take any more wood," wailed Mrs Maddox. "I ain't got enough to last next week."

"Hush yo' fuss, ma'am; heah's a thousand dollars." Abell whipped off his hat and, bowing deeply, offered a great wad of Confederate bills. "They can keep you warm, any-how, if they don't make you rich fo' life."

"Look here," Cary protested, "you know well as I do that money's next to worthless."

"In this Confederacy it's legal tender, so jest you shut up, Virginny. Who asked yu to open yer trap, anyway?"

Unhappily Cary made his way toward the tearful farm wife.

"Where's your husband?" he demanded.

"Dead. I got only the boy left."

"These fellers seem a hard lot, ma'am, and since there ain't no provost patrols about you'd best not anger them," he advised earnestly. "I'm riding on soon and I'll see if I can't send some provost guards out to make 'em behave."

"They're scoundrels—worse than the Yankees ever were." The woman's red cheeks paled a little as she de-manded uneasily, "D-do you figger they'll want drink?"

"It's likely," Cary admitted. "If you've any liquor about the place, you'd better hide it."

"Life's hard these days. 'Twouldn't be like this if James hadn't gone away to the war and got killed at First Manassas. Come into the kitchen and advise me what to do," pleaded the agitated woman. "Yo're Virginian, so I reckon you'll act right."

"Thank you, ma'am."

"Oh, sakes alive"—Mrs Maddox made a distracted ges-ture—"ain't this just too bad? My friend Mis' Gordon came over from Emory this afternoon 'cause the place there is full of troops. She's brought along a young female—must have had bereavement. Poor thing was takin' on so we put her to bed." The brown, toil-hardened face contracted. "She don't know what it is to lose her man and a son though."

"I'm right sorry, ma'am," Cary murmured. "Can't you get that girl out of the house? This is sure an ornery-actin' lot."

"Don't see how. Like I said, Mis' Gordon's friend is asleep—gave her a few drops of laudanum—in the spare room above the kitchen. Plague take those thieves!"

The shrill, despairing squawks of a hen stirred Mrs Maddox to such a frenzy that she caught up a flintlock fowling piece.

Hastily Cary put down a cup of sassafras tea and barred her path. "No use, ma'am; there's too many of 'em."

Night, warm even for a Virginia September, had fallen, and the flare of the cavalry campfire in the barnyard was casting an unsteady glow through the kitchen windows when Cary pushed back his plate.

"Thank you kindly, ma'am."

"Yo're welcome, I'm sure. Reckon I'll go and see how that gal's makin' out." Mrs Maddox sighed. "Oh, this war is a turrible, turrible business—ain't anythin' ever goin' to be like it was?"

Mrs Maddox caught up a tray of food and, holding a candle in one hand, went waddling up the back stairs. Hardly had she disappeared when in the barnyard a rattle of hoofs sounded and cries from the Mississippians. From the window Cary watched a fresh contingent of gray cavalry dismounting before the stable.

Who might these newcomers be? Provost guards? Or

possibly some stray patrol of Virginia horse? Tight-lipped, the Federal studied the firelit group. Then Hubert Cary's breath went out in a sharp hiss.

Yonder, greeting the members of Abell's party, was Luke Archer. Undoubtedly it was he, scar, great black beard and all!

Turning over his mount to an underling, the guerrilla leader came striding toward the farmhouse.

AT MADDOX'S CROSSROADS

FOR THE THIRD TIME Hubert Cary and Luke Archer found themselves face to face. Apparently the jayhawker failed to recognize him. Had he really? Seemed so. After all, their first encounter outside of Calthorp's farm had been of the briefest. On their second meeting the guerrilla had ridden at the head of the column during daylight, and it had been only after nightfall and by uncertain firelight that he had inspected his captives with any attention. The disguise was a help too.

Quickly Cary deduced that Archer, intimately familiar with the whole vicinity, had appropriated certain districts for himself.

"Waal, Virginny," he drawled, easing one hip onto the kitchen table, "we-uns may be a mite late gettin' up to the fight, but we shore forages good."

"Reckon so," Cary returned shortly and fell to picking his teeth with a supple forefinger. "You fellers aim to cross the river tomorrow?"

[283]

Luke Archer winked as he fell to munching a biscuit from a pan atop the oven. "Mebbe, mebbe not. Me an' Abell—he's from Tennessee—ain't burnin' out our hosses in no rush to stop Yankee bullets. You familiar with these hyar parts?"

The dark-faced corporal admitted that he was.

"Waal, ain't that a hawg's own luck? Listen, Virginny, you ride along with us an' when the dust settles ye'll have somethin' more to show for this war than bullet holes or six foot o' ground."

Mindful of Mrs Maddox, Cary smiled genially and undid tunic buttons to produce a plug of tobacco.

"Real niggerhead; have a chaw, Captain—Captain——" He hesitated, waiting for the name.

"You kin call me Cappen Hawks, count of I'm so cute with chickens," rumbled the black-bearded marauder. Outlaws, crowding in the dark little kitchen's door, bellowed, "That's a good one, Abell. Hain't it?"

"Sho' is, Luke."

"How's ev'thin' been down in Ten'see?"

"Tol'able, Luke, tol'able," grinned the pseudo Mississippian. "We air hopin' for fatter pickin's up this-a-way though."

"Heyo! Come down, Maw!" The jayhawker's summons made the windows rattle. "Rustle some grub."

Wide-eyed, Mrs Maddox reappeared and made a courageous if unwise attempt to assert herself.

"Clear out, you no-count rascals!" she shrilled. "I won't tolerate you all trampling yore dirty boots through my kitchen."

"Keep yer hair on, Maw." Archer grinned, pinching the angry woman's plump stern. "But mebbe yer right. Come on, Jed, le's go to the parlor. Maw"—he spoke sharply—"yu kin tote our vittles in thar. Come to think on it, I'm powerful dry."

"There ain't no liquor in this house," stated Mrs Maddox promptly.

Irregular yellow teeth revealed, Archer suddenly clamped down on Mrs Maddox' arm.

"Ef yu don't lie, maybe we'll git on better," said he. "There never was a farm in Virginny 'thout a kag o' corn liquor somewheres about."

"I tell you there ain't any. We don't—— Oh-h——"

Cary had hard work to remain impassive when the jay-hawker gave Mrs Maddox' arm such a vicious twist that she screamed and tears started from her eyes.

"It—it's in the root cellar," she whimpered. "Oh-h—let me go! Please let me go."

During the next hour the guerrillas of both Abell's and Archer's gangs drank, stuffed themselves with what food they could find. They swarmed through the ground floor of the farmhouse. Between long pulls at a cobwebby jug found in the root cellar they pocketed whatever suited their fancy.

"Waal, now, Virginny, ain't this turned out to be a right sociable occasion?" Archer demanded between huge mouthfuls of ham. He turned to the youngest of the jayhawkers. "Freddie, jest wet yer whistle and give us a stave."

Grinning, the boy produced a jew's-harp and, beating

[285]

time with his heels, performed "The Arkansaw Traveler" and "Goober Peas."

Increasingly Cary was torn between the necessity of moving on and that of protecting Mrs Maddox and her sick visitor. Long since, the widow's younger son had caught a cuff on the ear and had run whimpering to hide in the barn.

"Yes suh," Abell drawled, "I allow they's richer pickin's roun' hyar than in Kaintuck'. Plenty of silver and some gold too, shouldn't wonder."

"Right you air, Johnny, ef yu knows how to coax hit out into daylight!" said Archer, emitting a loud belch. "Just now we'll lay on back o' the army, an' comes there a battle, they's always rings an' watches waitin' finders."

Suddenly the black-bearded leader set down his cup of bourbon.

"Hi, Jonas, you all find out anythin' 'bout that gal?"

"Larnt she bides near Sharpsburg and her paw's name is Albert Dooveen. We-uns trailed her fur as Hillsboro last night. Folks thar 'lowed someone lookin' like her had druv out o' town in a buggy early this mornin'."

"Up river or down?"

"Toward the Ferry, Luke."

"The Ferry? Hell's fire! What road?" Archer got up, black beard quivering. "How you know she for sure went thar?"

Jonas cringed. "Don't know for sure. Warn't no more to be larned, Luke."

"Thought I told yu to bide thar 'til yu got sure info'mation. Stand up on yer hind laigs——"

"Oh-h, don't hit me, Luke——"

There sounded a blow, and Cary, rigid in the kitchen, heard the crash of overturned furniture.

"Mebbe that'll larn yu to obey orders."

"But, Luke," objected Abell's voice, "'twarn't no use Jonas' hangin' 'bout Hillsboro. What's ailin' ye lately? You all ack mighty queer. Sho' now, one yaller-haired wench ain't wuth hangin' round——"

"Shet up! Gawd boil my body! No wench, no matter how purty, can cozen me and brag about hit. Johnny, you never seed sech a female. Ain't none o' that dog-run cabin stink 'bout her. I mean to have her. What the blue flames o' hell yer think I trailed her half acrost the Blue Ridge fer?"

"Dunno," was Abell's uneasy reply.

"Speakin' o' gals"—a voice thick with drink suddenly dominated the twanging of the jew's-harp in the front hall—"hear tell they's a gal hyar in this house. Le's get her to sing for us, Luke."

"Now that's a smart idyah."

"Get her up, Maw." One of the jayhawkers came swaggering out into the kitchen where the terrified farm woman sat in company with the Virginian.

"I won't!"

"We need cheerin' up. Go and fetch her, Maw. Le's see the filly."

"No. She's in bed."

"Now ain't you a ornery ol' bitch? Reckon I'll have to haul her out o' the sheets myself."

Cary did some fast thinking. "Don't do that, friend," he interposed good-humoredly. "She'll come down lookin' like the wrath of God on a hayfork. Mis' Maddox"—he winked at the terrified woman—"just you mosey along and tell her to pretty herself up."

"Sho', git along on, old gal, git along."

As the widow scuttled away a drunken outlaw slapped Mrs Maddox on the buttocks as though she were a cow, and she emitted a little squeal of fear.

"Sure to be 'nother jug in the cellar," Archer rumbled. "Be back in a minute and larn that gal a few mountain steps."

Recalling the last time a woman had been taught "a few mountain steps," Cary thought fast as the other swayed off down the cellar stairs.

He must not linger here an unnecessary instant—a garrison of thousands rated more importance than these two women. Yet in his mind's eye was an impression of Mrs Ross's naked, rain-wetted corpse lying in the pine grove. At the foot of the kitchen stairs he overtook Mrs Maddox, caught her by the arm.

"You've got to get away," he advised in a low voice. "These aren't rebs—er, our boys—they're jayhawkers."

"Jayhawkers?"

"Guerrillas, some people call them."

"Oh, my God!" Mrs Maddox turned a dirty gray and clutched at the stair rail. "What can I do?"

"Run to the next farm and get 'em to send word to our troops camped below Loudoun Heights."

"What about Mis' Gordon's gal? She's sound asleep."

"I'll try to get her out," the pseudo Virginian promised. "Where 'll I take her?"

"To Judge Gordon's house at Emory. She'll know the way. Reckon these thieves won't dast follow in that direction. Oh, Gawd, my furniture, my poor furniture!"

"Get going." Cary gave her a push. "Don't let them catch you."

The outlaws in the parlor had started an obscene hillbilly ballad when Cary, on tiptoe, reached the top of the back stairs. Damn! He should be riding quietly away now. The bedroom door, he found, was unlocked, and the dark-haired girl within was sleeping soundly despite the uproar below. Candle in hand, he hesitated, but heavy and uncertain footsteps re-entered the kitchen.

"Hey, Maw," Archer bellowed, "git a wiggle on."

Cary stepped quickly inside, shook a shoulder showing pale above a "blazing star" patchwork quilt. The girl was small, smaller even than Melissa, and her hair was just as dark. Right now she slept the sleep of one utterly exhausted.

When he shook her gently the girl awoke with a start and would have screamed had not Cary clapped a hand tight over her lips. He began talking in an urgent undertone.

"Guerrillas below. Coming up for you. Trust me!"

"Hey, Maw"—Archer's guttural voice was becoming insistent—"trot down that gal!"

Eyes ringed with terror met his, then she nodded and hurried to pull up an enormous nightgown sizes too large.

"Come quick, Miss——"

"Ruth Hazen, I——"

It was clear the Hazen girl was still too dazed by sleep to think clearly, but the clamor below brought conviction

[289]

of her peril. Already Luke Archer's heavy tread was thumping up the kitchen stairs.

"Cl'ar the parlor, boys; she'll dance for us."

Time was desperately short, and to Cary's dismay the bedroom door lock looked of little use. Hurriedly he jammed a chair back under the knob in an attempt to delay the jayhawker's entry.

A fist banged on the door panels. "Open up in there. Gawd boil my body, why don't ye answer?" Silence, heavy breathing outside. "I'll larn ye in a minute, yer ornery old sow!"

A window opening onto the kitchen roof seemed to offer the best—indeed the only means of escape. The moonlit barnyard, moreover, seemed deserted save for a row of horses hitched to the fence.

"Open up, gal." A series of blows made the door rattle even as Cary flung up the back window.

"Come up heah, some o' you razorbacks, and bust this down."

"Out!" Cary commanded.

"I—not strong," gasped the Hazen girl when she stepped out of bed, swaying.

Beside himself with anxiety, the cavalryman helped her toward the window. Booted feet were kicking savagely at the lower door panels.

"Open up, yer damned sassy piece! Open up or I'll frale yer good an' proper!"

Long-skirted nightgown billowing in the warm night wind, Mrs Maddox' guest slid sidewise through the window, paused like a frightened specter on the moonlit roof.

As Cary was crawling through the window he saw a door panel splinter, saw yellow slivers fly far and wide.

"Jump!" he ordered the instant he had dropped from the easily slanting roof. He caught the invalid in his arms and, running as lightly as possible, made for the barn. There'd be no time to saddle another horse. Already Archer's furious curses rang from the window.

Scared by the ghostly figure in Cary's arms, the half-bred snorted with fright, tried to back away. Cary quieted the animal and in a tearing hurry jerked tight its cinch strap.

Voices sounded loud in the barnyard and doors slammed back.

Shivering, Ruth Hazen waited in the center of the barn.

"Oh, please hurry!" she whimpered, clutching at the voluminous nightgown which kept slipping off her shoulders, revealing small well-formed breasts. "They're coming into the barnyard."

Cary needed no urging. Archer's furious commands of "Ketch 'em! They must be in the barn!" filled the night.

It would be a near thing, the Federal realized. His horse was becoming so frightened as to be nearly unmanageable.

The black-haired girl gave a gasp and shrank back when, framed in the barn's wide doorway, a pair of shadowy, running figures materialized. Bending low in the saddle, Cary with a powerful heave lifted her to his pommel. Good job she wasn't heavier—never could have managed it with Lenore.

Cruelly he spurred the chestnut. Utterly outraged, the half-bred bounded into the air, then plunged headlong through the stable door. A jayhawker who foolishly attempted to catch the fluttering reins got knocked flat.

Two—four shots drew vivid orange streaks across the background. Cary bent low and gave the horse its head until he came to a road. Immediately the chestnut extended himself in a powerful headlong gallop which set the night wind to roaring in Cary's ears.

The jayhawkers, it appeared, were either afraid or unable to follow. When Hubert at last reined in there came no sounds of hoofs from behind. He lifted the Hazen girl's scantily clad white form to a more comfortable position which enabled her to pass an arm about his neck and so help to support her own weight.

Next he unbuckled from Corporal Burton's cantle a cloak and wrapped her so efficiently that only her feet remained unprotected.

"Where shall we go?" he asked. "You will have to direct me."

The girl before him stopped shivering, made an effort to collect herself. "You are very kind. I don't really understand what—you see, I—well—I'm still so dazed—terribly hurt. Andrew and Lucian—my brother, both were reported killed——"

"Confederates?"

The dark-haired girl shook her head. "No, they were Union. My family all is."

Momentarily Cary debated a confession but thought better of it. Everything was all right as it was.

"You are from near here?"

"We live near Sharpsburg. I—I suppose, as a Unionist, I oughtn't to let you——"

"Uniforms don't matter in messes like these." Cary let the horse follow the road.

"Sharpsburg? Do you know anyone of the name of Duveen there?"

The Hazen girl's eyes flickered up. "You mean Mr Albert Duveen, the Englishman?"

"Yes."

"No, you don't." The ghost of a chuckle escaped her. "You mean Lenore Duveen's family. I declare, half the armies are mad over her, and I don't blame them." She sighed. "It's wonderful Lenore isn't rotten spoiled, but she isn't——"

The Hazen girl's eyes broke away suddenly. "Lucian was insane for Lenore—— Oh dear"—she began to tremble again—"there's going to be another battle—everybody says so. There 'll be more Andys and Lucians—dead—dead——"

CHAPTER SIX

HARPERS FERRY

LAMPS were still glowing in Judge Gordon's house on the outskirts of Emory Village and fireflies were whirling in a gaudy display over deep banks of magnolia and laurel.

Following the Hazen girl's directions, Cary rode up to the edge of a wide lawn on the far side of which stood a big clapboard house. Troops still were moving down a road beyond it.

"Please don't come any further. You can leave me here," Ruth Hazen said heavily. "I can walk to the house."

"Grass is wet." Cary shook his head and trotted up to the edge of the Gordon's wide porch. When he eased the small figure onto it he hesitated.

"Who's in the house?"

"Mrs Gordon, her overseer and the servants. I will be perfectly safe, thank you.

"I can't begin to thank you," said she soberly, "so I won't attempt it—but Papa, well, he's the leading lawyer at home—if only——" She gathered the cloak tighter about her.

The ungreased axle of an artillery caisson screeched monotonously in the distance.

"Is there anything at all I can do—or say?"

"Yes," said he quickly and began to finger his gray kepi. "How would I find Mr Duveen's place?"

She peered up at the square-shouldered figure sitting so easily in the saddle. The horse reached down, commenced to crop at a row of nasturtiums.

"Her home is not really in Sharpsburg but about two miles outside of town." Ruth Hazen spoke slowly, as if trying to recall details. "It lies between Sharpsburg and the river, on the road to Showman's Corners. Let's see now—the house is square, of red brick, has six narrow white columns across its front. Yes, and there's a double row of chestnuts leading to it.

"You'll have no trouble finding it; everyone in Sharpsburg knows the Duveens. God send that you cross the Potomac in peace—I'm afraid the smell of death blows over the river."

"Good-by, Miss Hazen—and thanks." He started to collect his reins, then paused. "In case you see Lenore again—and I don't—please tell her that—well, there will never be anyone else for me."

"Your name?"

"Hubert Cary of the 1st Rhode Island."

"Then you're Union! Oh, God preserve you——" Bursting into tears, the girl in the military cape suddenly turned and ran into the house. Softly her bare feet sounded on the boards.

Cary gathered his reins. Frightened by the flowing gown beneath her cape, the chestnut had shied. Hurriedly Cary wheeled and rode out through the front gate toward a multitude of blinking fires which, to the south of Loudoun Heights, marked the presence of John G. Walker's Confederate corps.

Familiar with the terrain, Cary circled Loudoun Heights to the southwest and soon was putting his horse to a steep footpath running along the west side of it. By the moonlight he discovered that many guns and caissons had been hauled to the summit of the heights not many hours ago.

More indications that an iron ring was being forged about the strategically vital Union citadel were not lacking. If the garrison were to be saved, prompt action must be taken.

Presently he saw the roof of the Harpers Ferry arsenal gleaming whitely across the river.

To his vast surprise he was not challenged as, cautiously, he descended the Shenandoah River just above that point at which the Potomac joined with it to form the promontory on which Harpers Ferry was located.

Soon he was able to discern the tracks of the Winchester & Potomac on the far shore. What aeons had not elapsed since he had fled for life along the lower reaches of that same railroad?

The Federal garrison, he deduced, had been very busy with the work of destruction. Tracks had been ripped up; culverts had been blasted into crumbled heaps of stone; and everywhere strands of telegraph wire dangled forlornly from poles.

He rode boldly down to the blackly flowing water, for now the moon had become eclipsed by clouds over the tall heights in Maryland. An uncanny stillness ruled over the whole deep valley. That gap below Walker's corps—possibly Miles might already have learned of it? But if not——

He strained every sense to avoid falling into an ambuscade. What irony if he were captured within sight of the garrison he had striven so hard to save. It was not until his horse had splashed all the way across the Shenandoah's shallow stream that a deep voice challenged:

"Halt! Who goes there?"

"Friend."

"Dismount, friend, and advance to be recognized!"

When Cary halted and dismounted two blue-clad pickets rose from a near-by bush with muskets leveled. Blue soldiers again! He could have hugged them. As he led his mount forward Cary offered silent prayers of thankfulness.

"Well, gol durn me, if 'tain't a reb yellow-leg out for a stroll! Reach for apples, Johnny, and keep reachin'."

"I'm not a rebel. I'm Captain Hubert Cary of the 1st Rhode Island; I must see Colonel Miles immediately."

The foremost picket grinned derisively. "Yeah, and I'm 'Little Mac.' Frisk him, Hank."

But the other private lowered his musket and, stepping closer, demanded, "You ain't the Captain Cary what stole the train, are you?"

"I am."

At this the first picket nodded. "Pass, friend; Private Donelson will escort you in." Then, turning to his companion, he said: "Shake a leg, Fred; H.Q. wanted to see the captain the minute he showed up."

Harpers Ferry, with silent and shell-plowed streets, seemed unfamiliar. Apparently some of the firing he had heard had been a preliminary bombardment of the post. Serious damage had been done, and the ruins of two married officers' quarters glowed redly at the end of Fillmore Street.

Discouragement and gloom were written large in the faces of everyone who passed. Maybe they'd brighten when they learned of the gap below Maryland Heights.

In front of headquarters the sergeant of the guard saluted joyfully.

"Welcome back, sir! Tatnall made out you'd been killed, sir."

"Thank you, Sergeant. Is Colonel Miles inside?"

"Yes sir. He has been wanting to see you."

Quickly the dark-faced man in the gray cavalry uniform was conducted into the depths of the building. In his mind's eye he began to visualize the disconsolate blue regiments forming in stealth and darkness—swinging quietly across the pontoon bridge into Maryland—on their way.

The H.Q. door loomed before him.

The colonel commanding, haggard and worn, was seated in the room surrounded by his staff. Cary's heart skipped a beat when he drew himself up and saluted. By God, they certainly looked miserable, these gold-laced officers.

"Captain Cary reporting, sir."

Colonel Miles spun about, his mouth a colorless slash.

"Oh, back at last?" he rasped. "By God, sir, for sheer effrontery you are astounding."

A hot tide swept into Cary's dyed cheeks. "I'm sorry, sir. I did the best I could."

Livid, Colonel Miles sprang to his feet, and his staff fixed baleful looks on the new arrival.

"That will do. You will consider yourself under arrest."

The room spun around Cary's head. What was Miles saying? Arrest?

Stiffly the commandant turned aside.

"Major MacKenny," he directed, "see that the prisoner is held in close confinement."

When a guard touched Cary's arm he shook the fellow off. Said he in metallic tones, "Sir, I do not understand this. I demand to know with what offense I am charged."

"You are charged"—Miles's heavy red face thrust itself far over the council table—"with disobedience in the face of the enemy, with insubordination, with having deserted your post without orders!"

Like the blows of a fist beating on Cary's brain, Miles's words impacted.

"On my honor, sir, there has been some mistake. Such charges are preposterous! Why, you yourself granted me permission to undertake the raid."

The commanding officer's ruddy features darkened to an apoplectic hue.

"Goddam it, sir, don't you dare put words into my mouth! I recollect perfectly what I said. I said that, provided you could secure volunteers, we would then consider *if*"—he emphasized the word—"your plan was possible of success. Am I right, Major?"

"Those were your exact words," came MacKenny's prompt corroboration. "I remember them very distinctly."

A chill current commenced to trickle down Cary's spine. He held out an appealing hand.

"But, sir, I'm positive you didn't use the word 'if.' I remember exactly what you said—'We will consider the plan is possible of success. You may go.'" He peered at the hostile circle hemming him in. "I can prove it by Major Corliss. He was there."

"A thin dodge, Captain," rasped Miles. "You are no doubt aware that your friend escaped with the cavalry earlier tonight."

"*Know,* sir? How could I know? I've just come back."

"In any case, Major MacKenny heard your boast to Corliss. What was it Cary said to Corliss? Come on, man, repeat his words."

The adjutant readjusted his sword belt as he got to his feet. "I heard Captain Cary say to Corliss, 'That makes no difference, I'm going to do it anyhow.'"

"Do you deny having said those words?"

"Why, no," came Cary's prompt response. "But Major Corliss could tell you what it was I referred to."

"Major Corliss again!" snapped the commandant. "Ser-

geant, conduct this officer to the guardhouse. Permit him
to communicate with no one."

Cary looked stonily about.

"Gentlemen, I've just been through a lot. I've tried my
best to inform this garrison of a way to retreat. You *must*
believe me. Colonel Miles has made a mistake."

"There is no mistake." MacKenny's voice was harsh as
the scrape of steel on stone. "I heard every word which
passed between you and Corliss."

Colonel Miles nodded. "In due course, Captain Cary,
you will be required to answer a principal charge of insubordination in the face of the enemy."

The guards closed in.

"Wait! Wait, Colonel!" furiously Cary struggled. "Let
that go for the moment. I came—back—Colonel Miles,
you can still—there's a gap in the enemy line below Maryland Heights!"

"Take Captain Cary away," MacKenny flung at the
guards. "How many times need you be told?"

Desperately Cary tried to make himself heard. "Colonel
Miles, for God's sake, listen—you can retreat—saw the gap
with my own eyes."

"Cary," snapped a gray-haired artillery colonel, "we've
listened to you before—to our cost."

Neither Miles nor the rest would listen. Bitterness ate
like acid into Cary's soul. Damn these stupid fools! Twelve
thousand good blue troops would pay for their obstinacy.

If only Augustus Corliss and his testimony were avail-
able. Cary stood quite still when, in the guardroom, the
sergeant of the guard unbuckled the Virginia corporal's

pistol. In Sergeant Haines's long, sun-darkened features he detected the only touch of sympathy he had met with since his return.

Two privates with fixed bayonets fell in to either side of the prisoner, and a moment later he was marched out into the moonlight on Cliff Street. Everywhere loitered troops discussing casualties and the hopelessness of their situation.

Hollowly the sound of his boots resounded among the empty houses. Thanks to the humanity of General Jackson, the civilian inhabitants had been afforded an opportunity of fleeing.

Far away some pickets were exchanging shots.

"If you can, Sergeant," Cary murmured when the cell door clanged shut, "find Sergeant Tatnall; send him here."

"I'll try, sir. I ain't forgotten you helpin' me at that summary court."

"Don't get yourself in trouble, Haines," was Cary's caution.

It was not surprising, therefore, that when the midnight relief went on duty a bowlegged figure appeared in the corridor, passed a hand through the bars. It contained a key.

"Mighty glad you pulled through too, sir," whispered Tatnall. "Be waiting by the enjinehouse. Better shake a leg, sir."

"Why?"

"Sure as God's above, Colonel Miles aims to surrender come morning."

PART III

The Battle

CHAPTER ONE

IN MARYLAND

CARY DISCOVERED not one but a pair of shadowy figures lurking among shadows cast by that same enginehouse in which "Old Ossawattomie's" futile, criminal attempt had come to grief. Three horses stamped, pricked ears toward a hospital occupied by men wounded during the fight of the day before.

"That you, Cary?" called the taller of the two figures. A handgrip closed over Cary's.

"God, Blake, but I'm glad to see you," whispered the red-haired captain. "You too, Tatnall. Glad you gave the jayhawkers the slip."

"Thanky, sir. It weren't too hard."

Blake shoved forward some dimly discernible objects. "Here's your sword, a hat and a spare tunic. Look better than reb regimentals. Tatnall and I figured you wouldn't want to stay—to get yourself surrendered in the morning."

"You figured entirely correct."

Hurriedly Cary ripped off the gentleman ranker's yellow-chevroned gray tunic, donned his own blue shell jacket. Blake held out the sword belt and side arms, and observed:

"You're sure in a peck of trouble. Your friend Mac-Kenny's been working overtime."

"I'll fix him."

"Not for a while," grimly corrected the lieutenant while Tatnall checked girths and bridles. "MacKenny's got the strongest kind of a case. Colonel Miles has already prepared and signed charges against you. He's really convinced he never authorized you to leave Harpers Ferry. He's an honest fool."

In the dim moonlight Tatnall's anxious face showed up surprisingly sharp. "Cap'n, I cal'late we'd do well to tie these rags over our critters' hoofs; did it once outside o' Mexico City."

"Good idea," Cary agreed instantly. "We'll put them on by the pontoon bridge."

Unusual activity in the streets of the beleaguered citadel enabled the three horsemen to escape attention. It needed only Lieutenant Blake's brief explanation that he and his companions were departing on reconnaissance duty to pass the fugitives through the last cordon of blue sentries.

Once the muffling rags had been applied the three rode

silently down toward a swaying, gurgling pontoon structure which had replaced a permanent bridge burned earlier in the war.

On shadowy heights rising above the Potomac on all sides, the fugitives could hear ringing of axes and sounds of voices. No doubt now that McLaws on Maryland Heights was making his final siege preparations, that Jackson and Walker, respectively on Bolivar and Loudoun Heights, were engaged in similar occupations.

Nearer at hand bullfrogs in various backwaters kept up a continual grunting and booming.

"Which way did Colonel Davis and his cavalry go?" Cary asked.

"Upstream, I think," Blake muttered as he bent over his charger's feet.

"Then we'd best head downstream," Cary decided. "The passage of Davis' column must have stirred up some rebs. We'll follow the Maryland shore. There's a place we can get up on the plain about a mile below here."

Hearts in mouths, the three rode out onto the dully resonant planking of the pontoon bridge. How far would they get before lurking gray pickets opened fire? In Cary's imagination the hollow thudding of the rag-muffled hoofs sounded loud as the beat of as many kettledrums.

Yard by yard the Federals neared the Maryland shore. Still no rifle fire. Was luck or Confederate tactics to be thanked?

After a night of narrow escapes Cary, Blake and Tatnall found themselves traveling warily across a terrain only

recently occupied by a retreating Confederate brigade un
der R. H. Anderson.

"Must've been a stiff bicker at Cramptons Gap yesterday," Blake observed when they reined in on the edge of
some woods. It is wise to look about before starting across
a succession of open fields.

"Then you heard the cannonading all the way up to
Harpers Ferry?" demanded the red-haired captain.

"Yes, but we couldn't tell where it came from. Too busy
firing, ourselves. Must have been Cramptons though."

"Johnnies must have taken quite a licking round here,
sir," Tatnall presently remarked. "Notice that there pile
of stiffs?"

The branches of a near-by oak were crowded with buzzards—repulsive brown-black birds. Hideous scaly heads
outstretched, they were studying a row of boots protruding
from a low mound of boughs. The air, too, was filled with
the lazily wheeling scavengers.

"Listen! There goes McLaws!"

The gray sky commenced to resound to a furious cannonade. "That will be Walker." Louder grew the distant
thunder as battery after battery began to hurl shot at the
Federal stronghold.

"If they'd only listened!" Cary cried bitterly. "Poor
Miles—and the rest."

Blake gripped his companion's arm. "Easy on—horses—
coming this way!"

Jerking out revolvers, the three blue riders reined back
among some scrub pines. Presently a party of Confederate
cavalry came pouring through a gap in a snake fence. They

were herding before them perhaps two dozen fat cattle and half as many horses. On the fringes of this herd sweaty troopers armed with switches rode by not fifty yards away.

"Dismount—grab ears," Cary warned. "They mayn't notice——"

"Quiet! Something's up!" Blake's eyes were wide.

A sudden spatter of pistol shots echoed through the woods from the Confederate left.

Uncertain as to what impended, the three bluecoats watched the raiders hurry along the edge of the field. They had to work hard to urge their stolen farm horses into a gallop. Presently a body of gray horsemen appeared in the wake of the cattle guards.

"Johnnies are goin' to make a stand," predicted Tatnall, his thin nostrils opening and shutting like the gills of a fish.

The veteran was right. Once the last of the enemy riders had passed through the fence gap they wheeled to form a long double line on the far edge of the field.

"Draw sabers!" piped a boyish lieutenant, and out swept some sixty blades.

Cary's heart leaped as always to see the morning sun play on those bright arcs of steel.

"Line! Line!" the Confederate noncoms kept bawling. "Close up—close up, you bastards, close up, fer Gawd's sake."

The gray line tightened; restless hoofs trampled late daisies and bluebells.

"There's what they're lookin' fer." Tatnall's gnarled fore-finger pointed through the tree trunks.

Through the gap in the snake fence was trotting a

column of dusty blue riders. They were bent low on their horses' necks, already had their sabers out. An officer riding well out ahead of the guidon bearer reined in and with his sword signaled his men also to form a line. A chunky little bugler mounted on a gray horse repeated the order in a series of brazen wails.

Deep in the woods sounded the noises of the stolen livestock being driven off.

Spurring their mounts, the bluecoats deployed steadily enough behind their red and white guidon. Cary, blood singing once more, scrambled back into his saddle. Blake was a little white as he drew his sword. Almost simultaneously both bodies of cavalry began to trot across a field all yellow with late hay and brown-eyed Susans.

"Oh, my Gawd," chortled Tatnall, "this is shapin' to be the purtiest skirmish *I* seen since Boona Vista."

Perhaps sixty troopers rode on each side. Manes and tails began to toss once the horses of both sides were urged to a gallop.

"Hi-yah! Hi-yah! Yah!" Rebel yells, indescribably savage and piercing, were raised.

"Hoo-raw! Hoo-raw!" Deeper-pitched, a Yankee cheer went ringing back across the field.

Lower on their horses' necks dropped the charging troopers; each thrust his saber as far out ahead as he could. Only subconsciously did Cary realize that Tatnall was having difficulty in remounting his horse, that Blake was cursing in repressed excitement as he began adjusting the leather sword knot about his wrist. More rapidly the two lines thundered at each other.

A huge yellow-headed Confederate officer went racing out ahead of his men. He stood in his stirrups and charged straight at the thick of the Union formation.

Incredibly quickly the interval between the two lines diminished.

Blake gasped, "Look out!" as, with a resounding, dull impact, the two lines merged. Dust arose in dense swirls through which beat sudden brief gleams of steel. The clang of blades, an occasional revolver shot, yells, shouts and screams pierced the air. Both guidons rocked and flashed.

Quickly the main skirmish dissolved into a dozen minor ones. All over the meadow troopers in blue, brown and gray were wheeling and backing, astride rearing mounts. They slashed and thrust at each other like demons.

"Come on!" Cary called to his companions. "Yell like hell!"

"Hoo-raw! Hoo-raw!" At a dead run the three Federals came bursting out of the woods whirling sabers above their heads.

The Confederate saw them, became fearful that this sortie might be the prelude of a flank attack; they wavered. At once the red-faced Federals sensed their advantage, pressed their enemies with renewed vigor.

With the earth flashing by under his mount's hoofs Cary raised another series of shouts.

His practiced eye selected a big freckled corporal with a bunch of goldenrod tucked into his hatband. Extending his sword well out in front, he sighted along its blade, aimed at the second button of this corporal's tunic.

His horse tripped a little and staggered off-stride. Steel whirred past his ear and a revolver banged, but Cary kept his eyes concentrated on that small bright button. His mount recovered, surged on.

His opponent saw him, vented a hoarse yell and whipped up a long-barreled Colt. The Confederate's shot whizzed past his ear. The whole world swayed before him. That gleaming button.

As Cary braced his shoulder for the impact an impression came to him that he was stationary, that the gray figure behind that button was rushing at him.

The corporal's pistol exploded a second time—just a split second before Cary felt a jarring wrench at his sword point. He tried to disengage by turning his wrist, fingers uppermost—but the blade had become too deeply embedded in the enemy's chest. The blade buckled, and a strap securing it to his wrist broke.

Meanwhile his horse staggered, halted and commenced to shudder—it had taken the corporal's bullet squarely in its chest.

The stricken animal's collapse was so gradual that Cary was able to jerk free his revolver before stepping from the saddle without so much as losing his balance.

Immediately he crouched, waiting for a chance to get in a shot. All was confusion; mounted men, riderless horses were dashing back and forth through the sifting dust. He fully expected to be ridden down.

To his amazement he was abruptly left quite deserted except for fallen men and animals. Gasping, he stood up, saw the gray riders in full retreat. Pursuing them was a ragged line of blue cavalry.

"Hell an' damnation, ain't *this* a mess?" Near by a young trooper was, with his fingers, trying to check a flow of blood from an artery severed in his upper right arm. A dismounted companion was cutting a bandage from the shirt-tail of a fallen enemy.

"We'll fix that, Bub," Cary said, cutting the reins of his dying horse.

"I ain't scared, sir," the boy declared. But he was. He was terrified to see his blood streaking the grass and the yellow stripe on his breeches.

"We'll twist this—so. It 'll check the blood; but don't keep it tight for over twenty minutes at a stretch."

A major, red-faced and with his shirt open at the neck, trotted up.

"Thank you, Captain," said he, wiping his face on his sleeve. "Your coming out of the woods like that helped matters. Name's Whiting, 5th United States Regulars. We've been driving Munford's men all morning." He raised a curious brow. "Where are you from?"

"We escaped—three of us—from Harpers Ferry last night. See anything of our cavalry?"

"No," returned the other, mopping his face again.

"What's been happening?" Cary demanded. "Haven't had any news in Harpers Ferry for five days."

Enthusiasm lit the major's heated features. "A great deal. Seems as if luck's turning our way—at last. Somehow Little Mac—McClellan—has learned that Lee has let his elements become scattered all over northern Maryland.

"Little Mac's pressing him so hard there'll likely be a great battle sometime today—or tomorrow, maybe. This time, pray God, we're going to win."

"It's about time," was Cary's sober rejoinder. "Anything I can do?"

"Yes. We need to know more about the units we're facing. Suppose you go over and take a look at that reb lying yonder—the one by the stump."

While the men of Major Whiting's command collected their more gravely wounded comrades Cary strode off on his mission. So a great battle was brewing?

A pang of anxiety pierced him. Great God, suppose Corliss got killed? He stared blankly before him. There'd be no one to speak for him before the inevitable court-martial. He guessed he'd better try to find 'Gustus Corliss as soon as possible.

A movement on the ground aroused him. The gray body by the stump had sat up suddenly, was aiming a heavy revolver.

"Here, fer you—yer bum-blistered Yank!"

The report beat in Cary's face, and his head was jarred as if a mailed fist had punched it.

He stood rigid, gazing foolishly at the shamming Confederate a long instant; then Cary's vitals seemed suddenly to dissolve, leaving a cold void in his body. Despite frantic efforts to remain erect he toppled forward onto his face and lay very still among the blood-sprinkled daisies.

CHAPTER TWO

THE HAY BARN

HUBERT CARY guessed at first he must be aboard
ship, his body swayed so. Soon, however, he perceived various objections to this theory. For one thing, the
air outside of his feeble semiconsciousness seemed hot and
heavy. Further, a wailing and yammering sound persisted
—rather like the whining of a ship's yards under heavy
canvas—yet dissimilar too.

Puzzled, he tried to gather an arm under him in order to

sit up and to look about. Surprisingly his body remained quite motionless. What was wrong?

Finally he decided to open his eyes. A most amazing scene met his gaze. Overhead glowed dozens and dozens of kerosene lanterns. They really were lanterns; he could smell burned coal oil. They illuminated what seemed to be the interior of a huge barn. Dizzily the lights spun and whirled before his eyes.

An experimental groan achieved no visible result amid the turmoil of sound and activity all about.

A sudden confusion overpowered him. Was he conscious? Was he alive? Was he a prisoner? A Joyce MacKenny ten feet tall glared down—dozens of Joyce MacKennys dragged him before a court-martial—wasn't fair—wasn't right—Colonel Miles *had* granted him permission to undertake the raid—only trouble was he'd failed—*failed*—FAILED.

Where was Colonel Miles now? Why, it wasn't Miles at all—just—silent marble bust—or was this an apparition? 'Gustus Corliss, maybe? Corliss a marble bust? No—it was Tatnall. If the raid had succeeded, those marble busts would have called him a hero. Damned small-souled—most men.

Fogs. Whirling mists. He stood in the middle of a regiment drawn up in a hollow square; a grinning MacKenny was cutting his buttons away.

"No!" he protested. "No! MacKenny—I never told on you——"

"Hello." A voice spoke beside him. "Thought you'd never come around."

"What's happened?" demanded Cary, suddenly sane.

"I'd say a bullet's grooved the top of your head," replied the unknown. "You've lost plenty of blood too."

"Wh—where am I?"

"In a barn, among the wounded from Burnside's IX Corps." The voice was barely audible amid continual gales of groans and screams. "Me, I'm out of Rodman's division. Just in case you want to know everything, it's three in the morning, September seventeenth, 1862."

A sudden breathlessness cut short the speaker's voice. Cary wished very much he could see him, but the effort to turn his head was quite beyond his strength. He could only lie still, staring up at the dusty lantern-strung beams.

He watched a bearded man in a red-splashed apron stalk by—another, an impossible creature carrying in one hand a naked human leg which ended just above the knee in a mass of red tatters and pale pink strings.

Cary's head began to ache so intolerably from the screaming and groaning all about that he stopped trying to think.

"Who are you?" the voice demanded presently.

Cary told him. Then, feeling a trifle stronger, he managed to turn his head. By the amber lantern light he made out a brown-whiskered lieutenant lying on a pile of hay right alongside. His putty-colored face was dreadfully sunken and it twitched spasmodically every now and then.

"Who are you?"

"Lieutenant Peters, 5th Regular Artillery."

"You badly hurt?"

The other uttered a hollow, wheezing laugh. "Not bad.

Only minus my left leg above the knee and a Minié ball through my left shoulder."

"Too bad." It seemed an inadequate thing to say. "What's happening?"

"Cursed if I know," the other replied. "Except there was a heavy skirmish this afternoon outside of a place called Sharpsburg. I look for a big fight—soon as it's light. But it won't hold much interest for either of us."

"Who brought me in?"

"No idea," the wounded artilleryman replied, helping himself to a chew of tobacco. "Must have fetched you in late last night; one of the orderlies said they came damn near leaving you for a burial detail."

"What time?"

"Don't know. I was too busy having my leg taken off." The other sighed, chewing steadily. "It ain't much fun without chloroform. Four big hospital stewards just hold you down. The surgeon, if he's a gentleman, gives you a corncob to bite on before he gets busy with his knives and his little saw."

The other's voice sank. "You know, it's the queerest sensation feeling that saw at work on a bone? Think that was when I bit clean through the corncob." A faint smile flitted over features shiny as if varnished. "Damned near swallowed the nub. Hell of a joke on old sawbones if I'd suffocated, wouldn't it?"

The recital had a beneficial effect on Cary. After all, his own wound was nothing. If the regular survived he'd be a life-long cripple.

"Ever hear of an officer called Corliss? He was a regular," Cary asked once a series of hair-raising howls of some wretch on the surgeon's table had subsided to shuddering moans.

"Who?"

"Augustus Corliss. He's a major in the 1st Rhode Island. He escaped with most of the cavalry from Harpers Ferry."

"What class would he have been at the Point?"

"Fifty-eight."

"No. I wasn't out till sixty-one."

Lieutenant Peters, with his one good hand, pulled a muddied blanket higher while Cary stared, wide-eyed, at a dreadful faceless apparition being led by. His entire head seemed swathed in bloody bandages and he mumbled unintelligible nothings as an orderly guided him to another long pile of hay.

"You talked about this Corliss fellow enough," Peters remarked. "Come to think of it, I *did* hear something about the Harpers Ferry cavalry having captured a wagon train—one of Longstreet's. Heard that they had been ordered to join——" The artilleryman hesitated.

"Yes! Yes! Go on!" Cary pleaded. "Join who? What became of them?"

"Sorry, can't remember. Maybe it was the Kanawha division of the Ninth Corps or Rickett's division of Joe Hooker. Maybe it will be coming back to me."

As he lay on the hay with his nostrils filled with hospital stenches Cary engraved the names of those two units on his memory. Kanawha division, Rickett's division. Oughtn't to be too hard to locate.

"You want to find Corliss pretty badly, don't you?"

"Yes."

"You are in trouble of some kind, I gather."

Briefly Cary outlined his situation while the other listened, catching his breath every few minutes.

"You're in a mess, all right." Peters sighed. "Rotten—way things sometimes go in the army. Remember Miles—stationed at Savannah. Brave enough, but a poor judge of men. If your friend MacKenny backs him up, he can see you cashiered—ruined."

"You see, then, why I need to find Corliss? It's on account of——"

"Lenore?" The other attempted a pallid smile.

"I must have raved plenty," Cary admitted. "When do you suppose I'll be able to get up?"

"In about five days, the surgeon said—*if* you're strong!"

"Five days! Nonsense—I'm strong as an ox right now." God above, suppose 'Gustus Corliss got killed?"

"Strong as a hen rabbit with the pip!" Peters joked feebly and listlessly sank back. "You've a regular trench across the top of your skull.

"Well, 'pears we've got the Johnny Rebs cornered at last. They claim Little Mac somehow got hold of Lee's general orders. Everyone knows the reb army is scattered from Dan to Beersheba."

Peters stopped talking and Cary dozed. Slowly strength crept back as he lay immobile on the pile of hay, covered with a blanket that was marked with dreadful reddish-brown spots.

"I'm d-d-damned cold." Peters was speaking again. It was amazing how weak his voice had grown in such a short time. "Hate to t-trouble you, but could y-you reach an extra b-blanket?"

Cary felt about. "None here. I'll try to get an orderly." Several times he signaled, but the hard-worked stewards were too busy depositing more dreadfully mangled bodies on the rows of hay. "Here, take mine," Cary said. "Really, don't need——"

When the artilleryman made no reply Cary turned weakly onto his side. Lieutenant Peters was lying with eyes fixed on a ratty old horse collar hanging from a beam far above. His brown whiskers showed up in sudden silhouette against the waxen pallor of his skin.

"Peters!" he cried. "Peters! What's wrong?"

He summoned all his strength to arouse the other, then, quite horrified, he saw that the hay beneath the bandaged stump seemed to have been freshly spattered with red paint. The bandages on the artillery lieutenant's leg had slipped.

"Orderly! Come here, for God's sake!" Cary tried to raise his voice. No use. He reached over and shook the inert figure. Maybe Peters wasn't dead yet. Maybe he could still tell him with which corps Corliss' and Davis' men had gone.

"Orderly! Orderly!" He tried to get up, but the effort proved too much and he sank back, semiconscious, on the sour-smelling hay.

When he had recovered enough to open his eyes once more, his mind was clearer and his body once more obedient to his command. Lanterns were still moving back and forth. He still lay upon a pile of hay, and in his ears still was a sound like the lowing of many thirsty cattle.

Lieutenant Peters had disappeared, and now a greenish faced private lay in his place.

Cary sat up uncertainly. More lanterns had been strung about; they lent this dreadful place a theatrical air, making of the red-splashed orderlies figures out of some crude melodrama. Hospital smells were stronger in the air.

Cary turned to the new patient on his left. He could not have been over seventeen years of age and lay quite still, staring up at the cobwebby beams of the roof with the wide eyes of a bewildered boy.

Cary asked, "Where were you hurt, soldier?"

The boy turned his head and smiled faintly.

"In a big fight around Dunker's Church above Sharpsburg, sir. I think we licked the rebels, but no one seems sure."

"Is the battle over?"

"Oh no, sir," the boy replied. "Cap'n said both armies are still gathering, even if Harpers Ferry has surrendered."

"Surrendered?"

"Yes sir, so they say. Twelve thousand men, the arsenal and all. It's a bad blow for our side, sir."

A bad blow indeed. If only the rain hadn't come. If only Miles and his staff had listened, how very different everything would have been.

"Today, Cap'n figures, will come the real battle," the soldier continued. "Do you want something to eat, sir? There's lots in my haversack here."

"You'd better save it for yourself."

"Not hungry, sir. There ought to be a flask of brandy in it too."

[322]

"But you'll need it yourself."

The boy shook his head. "I guess not—wouldn't do much good down—down there!" With a trembling hand the private stripped back a blue overcoat which lay across his stomach, revealed a hideous blue-gray and red abdominal wound.

"You see," he explained quietly, "I couldn't possibly use it."

Cary found no words to meet this calm assurance. He ate some pieces of sausage, a slice of cheese and chewed on a piece of hardtack. After taking a deep gulp of the dying boy's brandy he felt more like his old self, tested the bandage about his head, found it to be neat and not too bulky.

"Thank you." Cary gave the boy a friendly smile. "I'm going now—is there anything I can do? Now or later?"

"Oh, I'm all right," murmured the lad. "It—it don't hurt much—and, well, I guess Zeb, with the Lord's help, will take care of Mom all right—Zeb's a mighty capable boy for his age."

SEPTEMBER 17, 1862

JUST BEFORE SUNUP Hubert Cary arose, mingled with a line of "walking cases" and crept from the barn out into a humid darkness. Below the ridge on which stood the barn was a wide, gently sloping valley. As far as the eye could reach it was dotted with tiny, jewel-bright campfires. Beside one of them Augustus Corliss might be resting. It was not easy to shape ideas, but Cary held this one clearly enough in mind.

He must find the major before he could be captured or killed. When he realized how far away those bivouac campfires were twinkling he was staggered. To find one man in such a host would be—well, rationally he wouldn't ever have attempted it.

So Harpers Ferry had surrendered. For all the efforts of the Pocahontas and her crew. The surrender, however, furnished a fresh incentive to his quest. Folks said General Jackson had paroled the Harpers Ferry garrison.

There must have been serious skirmishing over this area,

[324]

Cary realized as he walked uncertainly along. Everywhere debris littered the ground. Among the dew-brightened bushes lay tangled heaps of pallid dead—from both armies. Rigidly arms were raised above nodding goldenrod.

Cary kept rehearsing what Peters had said concerning the cavalry escaped with Colonel B. F. Davis from the Ferry. They must have joined either Hooker's command in the First Corps or Rodman's of the Ninth. His immediate object, he reminded himself, was to locate these units.

Like a scarecrow he trudged toward a cluster of camp-fires, unaware of the dramatic picture he presented in the yellow-striped gray breeches of a Virginia cavalryman, in his own blue coat and wearing a crown of bandages.

Everywhere bugles were blowing reveille. A surly N.C.O. informed him that the two units he sought were separated by the whole length of the battlefield.

"Sure, it's just as I said," he grunted. "Ol' Joe Hooker's outfit's 'way around on our right; Burnside's is furtherest left."

"What division is this?" demanded the hollow-eyed wanderer.

"Sykes' of the Fifth Corps. You can always tell us by this." The sergeant touched a brass pattée cross set in his kepi top. "The First Corps has a circle—the Second a trefoil and the Fourth a Greek cross."

"And Burnside's?"

"He ain't sportin' none yet. New corps."

It seemed as if all the men in creation had put on blue uniforms and were swarming into northern Maryland. Thousands upon thousands of them were rolling up blankets or munching hardtack from their haversacks. Others were forming up behind guidons and regimental colors.

"Hi, yellow-legs, have a bite?" called a group of officers seated on a broken-down caisson. "You look kind of petered out."

"No, thanks, already eaten."

Corliss! Now that he wasn't fit or able to handle weapons or to command men—only the locating of Augustus Corliss mattered. That—and Lenore.

Dawn began breaking in earnest, rosy gray, with vermilion-edged clouds flicking the horizon. It was the last dawn that four thousand and more soldiers—North and South—would ever behold. Such a daybreak as this would dwell forever in the memory of one hundred and thirty thousand men mustering on the dewy fields to either side of Antietam Creek.

Activity commenced everywhere. Orderlies and well-dressed staff officers began to gallop back and forth, coordinating the blue host. A column of field artillery overtook and rattled past an infantry brigade which, cursing, left the road and halted. A clatter of heavy wheels, the pounding of big hoofs and the cracking of whips filled the air.

An unforgettable sight. All the length of this valley artillery units were climbing to the top of a ridge. Drivers, swaying from the fatigue of an all-night march, lashed forward weary teams. Gunners walked behind pieces and caissons held on for support, moved like automatons. So thickly coated with dust were they that they seemed to be uniformed in yellow instead of blue.

On they rattled, battery on battery, with pails and ramrods rattling on the limbers and with red guidons hanging limp. Now a stand of colors—national and regimental flags—trotted past. Horses, straining and panting to haul forward sleek tubes of death, endlessly went by.

Corliss? Where was Corliss?

Fortune extended a helping hand. In a thicket the wanderer came upon the corpse of a cavalryman whose stiffened hands yet clutched the reins of a bony bay horse.

By drawing recklessly on his scant store of strength Cary managed to mount just as a battery of artillery—Von Kleiser's—unlimbered and, sharply silhouetted against the rose-gray sky, went into battery along the crest of the ridge.

Promptly the blue gunners began to dig pits for their gun trails; others removed sponges and rammers from racks on the caissons. Still others ran to a near-by brook to fill buckets while red-eyed officers gathered to compute firing data. The horses hung their heads, nibbled wearily at the dew-sodden grass.

Everywhere long columns of infantry began to move, to disappear over the summit of a bold line of hills.

Because Burnside's corps must be the nearer of his objectives, Cary accordingly commenced to ride to the left—crossing the rear of the Union army. His present mount, he soon discovered, was both lame and weak; still he was making better time than he would afoot.

Soon he entered a zone in which many Federal regiments lay hidden amid ripe cornfields and in orchards heavy with fruit.

The flowing movement toward Sharpsburg continued. For a while a white-topped ammunition train barred Cary's path, so perforce he watched an endless succession of men and beasts go staggering along, drunk with fatigue.

Like the first few raindrops which prelude a threatened storm, a faint patter of rifleshots sounded far away to the right.

"There she goes!" Sunburned soldiers turned kepied heads to stare in that direction; other units, which had but recently come into position and had seated themselves, began to get up. Knots of officers standing on the ridge top leveled field glasses, peered about. The distant crashes of musketry increased until the noise resembled that of coal tumbling down a metal chute.

"Fightin' Joe Hooker's gone in," Cary heard a nervous lieutenant call.

As a note swells on an organ, so the sound of conflict gradually grew in volume; another and another battery added its thunder to the general uproar. Still intent on his quest, Cary watched the emplaced gunners of Weed and Durell fidgeting, their officers craning sun-reddened necks for the arrival of an expected courier.

"Burnside?" a courier replied to Cary's query. "Oh, he's lyin' straddle o' Antietam Creek below the bridge. Sure, there's cavalry with him. How would I know what cavalry?"

The conflict to the north grew steadily more thunderous. Above the distant spires of Sharpsburg a curious white haze could be seen gathering.

"They're burning buildings over there," Cary solemnly informed himself. "Military stores," he amended when the white smoke became streaked with black. "Hooker must be closing in."

Near at hand more and still more columns were on the move. When Cary's horse, only half controlled, shambled to the summit of the ridge he saw, through a curious film in his eyes, the main battlefield-to-be.

Some three hundred yards below this ridge wandered the Antietam, a pretty little stream spanned by a mossy, three-arch stone bridge. Not over half a mile distant the roofs and steeples of Sharpsburg glistened in the newly risen sun.

On the far bank of the creek Cary could make out a series of compact gray columns moving into position. Those distant toy batteries and guns were still maneuvering when suddenly a cluster of gigantic cotton balls bloomed briefly among them. On yonder easy green slope was a spectacle of fallen figures, kicking horses and shattered caissons.

Cary's horse wabbled in feeble fear when a shell screamed by and with a deafening report burst right alongside an ammunition train he had noticed—it had halted to issue cartridges to a New York regiment.

One wagon team became panic-stricken and, kicking and plunging, careered crazily off down the hillside, scattering a column of halted infantry. Canvas powder bags rolled right and left until the runaway wagon struck a stump and finally upset. The four-horse team was knocked from its feet into a struggling heap.

Zo-o-oe-ee! A series of projectiles from Confederate batteries howled overhead. At a trot the blue infantry retreated under the brow of the hill.

Hazily Cary watched a courier on a lathered horse pound up, salute and thrust a sheet of paper into the hands of an artillery colonel who stood studying the slope opposite. How long and blue his shadow looked in the new sun!

The officer read the order carefully once, twice, then put away his map and glasses. When he called a brief command his gun crews ran forward to take post about their pieces.

Cr-r-ash! A rifled Parrott gun sent a charge of canister screaming over to the far side of Antietam Creek. Number Two gun went into action—Number Three, Number Four. A dense white fog of burnt powder smoke began drifting slowly down into the valley; coughing, the gunners sponged out their barrels then, reversing rods, rammed home fresh charges of powder. Wads followed, then, on top of that, roundshot.

"This Burnside's corps?" Cary demanded of an unshaven captain.

The other stared at this apparition with bloodied bandages crowning his head. "No—over on our left."

Still quite dazed and finding it hard to think, Cary rode on through a dim acrid mist which made his sunken eyes smart and water. The artillery duel was still raging in full fury when he arrived at last on the left flank of General Burnside's position.

Now that the roar of the guns was loud in his ears the

cavalry captain's blood began to stir. He *would* find Corliss, of course, he assured himself; but first he'd better try to take a hand in this business.

When the sun rose higher the artillery battle gradually slacked away and, as though motivated by a single control, dozens of infantry columns in parallel lines began marching down toward Antietam Creek.

Bayonets fixed, faces bright with sweat and with heavy ammunition pouches dragging at their hips, they slogged along; nothing of a parade-ground swing was in their gait.

Behind the lines provost guards had already begun to round up stragglers. They sent them forward, cursing their cowardice. A rain of shells from across the stream began to burst among the Federal columns, littered the ground with human debris.

The advance halted for some reason.

"Yes, this is Burnside's corps," an angry infantry captain told him. "Rodman's division? How the hell would I know? Might be over on our left; there was some cavalry over there."

The gray-faced cavalryman, warmed by the sun and feeling more than a little lightheaded, rode among acres and acres of sour-smelling soldiers in blue. They waited sprawled on the ground and chewing tobacco or grass blades. The younger ones spat nervously at near-by targets.

"Some fight coming up, sir," grunted the grizzled sergeant major Cary next addressed. "All the rebs in creation are over yonder, and more comin' up every hour. Guess there'll be a lot of people goin' shoutin' home to heaven t'other side of Sharpsburg."

"Seen any cavalry? Rodman's?"

"Cavalry? Yes sir, round an hour ago we seen a passel of cavalry down beyond Willcox's division."

"*Where?*" Cary sat straighter, focused his eyes. A nice-looking fellow, this—long yellow hair and blue eyes.

"On t'other side o' that brook. Yes, sir, it looks like we'll be gettin' into quite a fight. Excuse me, sir—we're movin' at last, 'pears like."

With the speed of a grass fire the general conflict spread rapidly from the Union right toward the center. Brigade after brigade became engaged in heavy infantry fire.

Cary rode on, assuring himself that Corliss must be with Rodman's division. "Better find him before they go into action," he told himself. "Might find me a decent nag and some side arms, too."

"Forward-ho!" Voices took up the command and, like the soldiers of Cadmus, blue troops leaped up from the tall, flower-sprinkled grass and fell in. Lean, bearded faces tensed, they readjusted pack straps, made other final preparations.

All along the line battle flags commenced to gleam, but the wind was so slight that regimental colors, tattered through hard campaigning in Virginia, were but lazily displaying their designs. Simultaneously the Confederate batteries opened up again, made the air quiver with the terrific reports of bursting shells.

Worried, Cary urged his sorry beast to a painful, jolting trot and so passed through the next to the last division of Burnside's corps—this he identified as Willcox's division. The next, therefore, must be Rodman's. He uttered a feeble croak of joy, when, on the edge of a little wood, he spied some red and white guidons and many brown horses grazing. Hundreds of blue-clad riders had dismounted beside them.

Following Cary's course past the infantry came a bareheaded staff officer. He'd his sword out and, with brass buttons glinting like fiery eyes, was riding at an extended gallop.

On passing each group of regimental commanders he yelled a command. At once the Federals raised a cheer, swept over the ridge top and, with bayonets flashing, commenced to trot down toward that pretty little stream.

One after another more elements of the Union left began surging forward, a vast composite dagger thrusting at

the gray legions opposite. Momentarily confusion reigned on the ridge. Moving men, bursting shells, drifting smoke weaved a crazy pattern.

When Cary looked again for the cavalry they were gone. Well, Corliss or no Corliss, it was time he went along to the fight. He felt strong again—or thought he did.

After readjusting his stirrup leathers Cary tried to forget the pounding pain in his scalp and, spurring his feeble animal, started after the advancing infantry for all the world like a child left behind by larger playmates.

Already blue-coated bodies were beginning to dot the brown earth.

Buoyed with excitement, he drew a saber tucked through the saddle's quarter straps and, quite alone, rode slowly after the infantry of the IX Corps.

ANTIETAM CREEK

SUCH CAVALRY as Rodman commanded would probably be employed on the extreme left flank, or so
Captain Cary reasoned. Therefore he reined to that direction, headed after a division a wounded signaler told him
was Rodman's.

The hot, early fall air grew more and more resonant with
the crash and roar of bursting shells. On a slope below Cary
the grass seemed to come alive because of so many spent
musket balls plunging into it.

Battles Cary had been in before—some of them important—but these paled to insignificance beside the conflict
taking shape along the crescent-shaped course of Antietam
Creek.

Off on the far flanks and emerging from a cornfield Cary
glimpsed dense columns of blue-coated cavalry. Real, or
only a will-o'-the-wisp? Was he really ahorseback? Or was
this fearful panorama the product of a fevered wound?
For the life of him Cary couldn't be sure.

He rode by a blown-up Union caisson. All about lay the mangled bodies of its crew. The carcasses of the gun teams were pouring crimson streams down the hillside. A mangled wheel horse tried to come over to him with its entrails scraping over the dry earth.

Though Cary now kept his attention chiefly on the Union cavalry, he noticed, nonetheless, that some Federal infantry had begun to ford the stream.

"Must find a stronger horse," he advised himself as he went splashing across the ford by which Rodman's cavalry had crossed. "Damn foolish to stay on this brute; too weak."

Hardly was he out of the water than the battle pounced down upon him. Bullets skittered, glanced through near-by treetops. By the hundreds leaves came scaling down. Red-faced Union infantry, previously hidden in the thicket-covered ditch on the far side of the creek, suddenly sprang up, uttered wild yells and started up the slope.

Coincidentally figures in gray arose, formed a long steel-tipped line higher up the same hill. Bugles brayed breathless commands all about. Cary was forced to abandon his pursuit of Rodman's cavalry.

A hissing tornado of sound struck. Trees went crackling over.

"Rebs is settin' a pretty tune!" sang out a first sergeant of engineers.

Instinct told Cary that if the enemy movement gained weight there'd be a general retirement.

An infantry captain was struck in the chest by a cannon ball—his lieutenant fell too, commenced to struggle crazily about on the long grass like a great blue beetle fixed on a pin.

The men's advance slackened; many halted, looked over their shoulders to see what lay behind. A few faced about, began to retreat toward the creek.

"Steady!" Cary began to yell and wave his saber. "Go on —meet them. If you run, they'll fix you!" But nobody seemed to hear or heed him.

"Hi-yah! Hi-yah!" Successfully a rebel yell pierced the din. Through gaps in the battle smoke solid masses of gray infantry could be seen swarming down to meet the attackers. The Stars and Bars of at least three regiments shone red above the jogging ranks.

Lacking officers, a Federal company began to fall back.

Aware that for rods around he was the only mounted man, Cary raised his voice. If these men really began to retreat they would be driven into the Antietam—leaving the flank of Rodman's division exposed.

His horse, stung by a bullet, carried him out in front of the shaken blue troops. They were in a bad case now—falling by twos and threes—tens. Some died silently, some screaming.

Hardy individuals, however, were still firing. The glimmer of ramrods whirled above their heads, shone in a thin sparkle. Their lips grew black from biting the ends off of cartridges.

"Look out! More rebs comin'," warned a scared voice. "What 'll we do, sir?"

"Stand steady!" Cary yelled over the snarling musketry

and tried to control his pain-maddened mount. "Wait—wait! Lace 'em at point-blank."

Experienced, he noted an encouraging fact: these troops —they were the 16th Connecticut—were discarding their packs, getting ready to resist unencumbered.

"Hi-yah-h-h!"

Toombs's Georgians, bayonets deadly bright in the sun, came running to sweep the Federals back into the creek. Despite deadly gunnery from Union batteries across the Antietam they rushed down upon the New Englanders.

"Steady!" a crippled major began to call. He limped along using a musket as a crutch. "Close up! Fix bayonets!"

Because he was on a horse and his bandaged head was easy to see, the Connecticuters listened to Cary—for all he was crazy as any coot. Wavering ranks stiffened; a new light shone in their sweaty faces—a stubborn pugnacity inherited from English ancestors. Musket balls hissed past Cary's head.

"Hoo-raw!"

In a double rank that swayed, straightened and bent again, the Federals surged forward, bayonets held well out in advance. Behind this line strode the sergeants; they hurried up stragglers, helped up men who had tripped or who had been knocked off their feet by some minor wound.

The din became overwhelming. The two forces met, tangled amid ragged banks of gray powder smoke which now hid, now revealed the enemy. Rifle fire, like noise of ten thousand sheets being ripped at once, beat in Cary's eardrums.

Curiously he was quite able to appraise the significance of this apparently commonplace infantry struggle.

The 16th Connecticut, he realized, occupied the extreme left of the Union position. Should they be driven, Burnside's whole corps must retire in order to protect its flanks. This, in turn, would force the Federal center to follow suit. And then——

He shouted incoherent encouragement at a swaying, supple blue line. The sensation possessed him that these men were a part of his body—that one could thrust and punch with them as if they were fists.

"Cha-a-r-rge!" shouted the crippled major. "Go get 'em, you terriers!"

The New Englanders set unshaven jaws, began to run heavily. Only a few yards now separated the two lines—a few feet. Whirling smoke, dust and flame.

Cary's horse was hit again and staggered in trying to keep its footing. A towering Georgian bunched his body behind his musket and lunged savagely. Convulsively Cary twitched aside his leg, and the bayonet's point only grazed his thigh but sank smoothly into the saddle flap. The horse screamed and reared. Somehow Cary brought his saber down, and to his surprise the Georgian reeled away with bloodied hands holding his split scalp together.

Back and forth the men struggled amid a choking smoke; clutching hands, staring, yelling faces appeared and vanished.

The scene became kaleidoscopic. Cary caught glimpses of straining faces, of blackened lips flecked with the foam of effort, of clubbed muskets swung with the energy of despair.

Presently the tide of combat carried him into a vicious struggle eddying around the colors of the 15th Georgia. The chunkier, short-legged New Englanders were thrusting at a knot of tall, flat-faced Georgians defending their red standard.

A succession of blue troops rushed up out of the murk, and the gray knot was overridden by sheer numbers. The Stars and Bars fluttered frantically, and hands clutched at it until the battle flag swayed and sank. Another swirl of gray figures was flung into fight, and the colors tottered upward. A pair of Union sergeants ran up, emptied their revolvers into the thick of the defenders. Like puppets with their strings cut the new color guard collapsed, and the flag with thirteen stars vanished from sight.

Whether it was captured or not, Cary couldn't tell. Shouts arose from the rear, and in overwhelming numbers more Federals, still dripping from the creek, came up and drove off the valiant but heavily outnumbered Confederates.

Cary, feverish but clearheaded, noted an abrupt change in the course of the retreating Georgians. Some Federal cavalry was cutting in at them from the rebel right.

"My God, what keeps this crowbait on its feet?" Too spent, too weak to do more than laugh crazily, Cary sat where he was, watching the struggle recoil up the hill toward Sharpsburg.

Abruptly he remembered his quest. That cavalry over yonder. 'Gustus Corliss?

Cary turned and at a limping pace commenced to ride

back to the Antietam. His wounded head hurt like a broken tooth and the pain glazed his vision.

A cavalry column headed back toward Antietam was escorting a large body of bedraggled prisoners. For this reason the lone rider was able to come up to them though his horse's wavering legs threatened collapse.

He passed a small drummer sitting beside a broken drum, his immature body racked with convulsive sobs.

"You hurt?" croaked Cary.

"N-no sir. But th' d-d-damn—rebs—have—b-b-broke my drum."

With painful slowness Cary rode nearer to the prisoner column. Vainly he tried to read the brass insignia on those rakish blue kepis.

It was hard to see details; officers were realigning their men, and clouds of brown dust obscured the further units. Wasn't there a single familiar face anywhere? A captain with enormous side whiskers turned aside to meet him.

"You have dispatches for the 6th New York?"

"No."

The blond captain squinted at this gaunt scarecrow of an officer.

"You'd better dismount!" he called. "That goat is about ready to cave in. You too. You'd better go to the rear."

Dazedly Cary shook his head. "I—I—looking for cavalry —got away from Harpers Ferry—must find them."

"You mean 'Grimes' Davis' outfit?"

Cary's haggard face lit. "Yes, yes! For God's sake, where are they? Davis' command is with you, isn't it?"

"Davis? Lord, no!"

"Not—not here?"

"Why, no. Old 'Grimes' gobbled one of Longstreet's ordnance trains, then rode in above Sharpsburg—on our other flank. I expect they'll have been brigaded with Hooker's corps."

Cary groaned, gripped the pommel.

The blond captain hurriedly pulled out a flask. "Take a pull of this, and for God's sake get off that wreck 'fore he falls on you."

Cary dismounted, let the poor creature limp off, head down.

The other said, "If you came out of the Ferry you were damned lucky not to be with Davis." He dropped his voice. "They say Hooker has been taking a terrible beating. Nearly *fifty per cent casualties!*"

"Lucky?" Cary wanted to burst into wild laughter.

"I've got to find a Major Corliss," said he in what he hoped was a normal voice. "I must get over to Hooker's corps."

"You can't! Don't be a goddam fool, man; you can't possibly! Why, the whole battle's being fought between them and us."

He called to a sergeant who, after an interval, appeared leading a horse. "Boone, adjust stirrups for the captain." He spoke persuasively. "You'd better stick with us—if you won't go to a hospital."

"Thank you."

For an interval Hubert Cary lived in a dim haze interspaced with lucid spells. In later days he recalled riding

endlessly on, guns thundering. He remembered that toward sundown a final skirmish had taken place which
drove in the Confederate flanks rapidly enough to free a
throng of Federal prisoners.

"When was you captured?" a corporal of the 6th New
York bawled at a rescued prisoner.

"Early this morning—'twas when old Joe Hooker made
his first attack."

Hooker! In Hubert's sluggish brain the name kindled a
tiny flame. He roused himself.

"You from General Hooker's corps?"

"Yes sir—what's left of it."

"Where was Hooker's cavalry?"

"Running as usual," came the stock answer. A derisive
chorus rose: "Who ever saw a *dead* cavalryman?"

Once this ritual had been observed the released prisoner
added, "Matter of fact, the yellow-legs got pounded. Some
of them was captured along with us."

"Where are they?"

"Back in the column somewhere."

Cary rode back among the ex-prisoners, alert for yellow-
striped breeches. Must find out before he became engulfed
by a chill, weakening tide rising inside of him.

There were several hundreds of men in the column, and
the task was not easy. Cary was drooping in the saddle
when suddenly someone called his name.

The jolly brown features of Lieutenant Tom Blake were
set in lines of deep astonishment.

"Is it really you? My God, Cary, I simply can't credit my
eyes. You've been reported dead and buried."

"Might as well be," Cary sighed.

Blake remembered, looked about anxiously.

"You heard the news? The prisoners from the Ferry came in, said Miles has been killed."

"Miles was *killed?*"

"Yes. Just before the garrison surrendered. You're in worse trouble now. Cross-examination might have shaken the commandant's testimony—now there's only his written word. You can't modify that."

"I see. There's that and the spoken word of Joyce Mac-Kenny."

"Hi!" A voice from among the shuffling column hailed the two mounted figures. Blake waved.

"Charlie Russell!" He turned to Cary. "You remember him. He was at the Ferry with us."

"Yes." Cary only vaguely recalled him as a captain of Maryland cavalry. "What happened to 'Grimes' Davis?"

"We got out, passed right through the reb lines—rode all night and captured an ordnance train." Russell broke off. "Heard you were in trouble, Cary."

"I am."

"I wouldn't worry too much. 'Gustus Corliss told me he knows plenty about that business. He'll clear you."

"Captain Russell——" The Rhode Islander's bloodshot eyes fixed themselves.

"Is Corliss still alive?"

He could feel Blake's anxious scrutiny, was dimly aware of a river of faces moving beyond Russell.

The Marylander said quietly, "Corliss ought to be safe—he was ordered to escort the captured train to Greencastle."

CHAPTER FIVE

THE HOUSE BY THE RIVER

DID YOU HEAR THAT? 'Gustus Corliss isn't captured, isn't dead! He's safe!" Cary turned twitching
features. "Did you hear what Charlie Russell said? Did you
hear?"

"Yes. Damned glad to, too. It'll be a real disappointment
to MacKenny."

"No court-martial," Cary said slowly. Strength began
welling back into him like a warm and healing tide.

Briefly the Maryland captain described how the cavalry
at Harpers Ferry had refused to let themselves be surrendered, had elected to attempt to escape. Under Colonel
"Grimes" Davis the detachments had ascended the northern bank of the Potomac, had ridden by night through the
Army of Northern Virginia until, just after daylight, they
had been able to pounce upon a gray ammunition train.

Later the Union cavalry column had split, some turning off to join the Federal army at Sharpsburg. The balance, under command of Corliss, continuing northward to escort the captured train into Pennsylvania.

Continually details of troops of all branches passed, plodding doggedly on toward that conflict which still rumbled and grumbled beyond the hills.

A sorrier procession flowed the other way. Walking wounded, grimacing as they limped along; prisoners still sullen and dazed from the impact of battle and the imminence of death; long lines of farm carts in which badly wounded men groaned on the hay. Often a distinct pattern of scarlet drops followed these improvised ambulances.

Both sides of the road were littered with discarded or broken equipment: carbines, bits of harness, blankets, broken shoes, bloodied bandages. And everywhere birds sang. The butchered carcass of a cow was watched over by a pair of weeping towheaded children.

As the sun started down, the battle gradually diminished and much of Cary's fever left him.

What had happened back there by Antietam Creek? He would never be sure. Strange, he should have come out alive from a struggle like that, should have gotten hurt in a silly little skirmish. Still, war was like that.

So Corliss was alive and safe. That changed everything. His word and Corliss' against MacKenny's. Relaxing, he wondered where Lenore might be. He wanted to tell her the good news—that he'd fought once more and still had survived. How long would his luck last?

"You for a dressing station right away," Blake urged. "You look like death warmed over."

"Dressing station? All right. Expect I could stand a cleaning up."

Russell reached up to shake hands.

"You'll have no trouble finding Corliss," he said. "Best of luck to you. You deserve it. Everyone is saying your attempt on the Washington & Potomac was the nerviest thing they'd ever heard tell of. Damned shame it had to rain."

By the time that Cary had found a dressing station, had got his head freshly bandaged, a warm still night had fallen. On the horizon the ruddy glow of houses burning near Sharpsburg town beat against the sky. Fighting had died to occasional bursts of musketry exchanged by isolated detachments which, in endeavoring to find their way back to their lines, had blundered into the enemy.

Blake touched his arm as still another creaking line of ambulances came up and, by the light of pine-knot torches, commenced to discharge its miserable freight.

"Let's clear out of this. Thank God you look more like a man now and less like a ghost. Come on. We'd better report in."

"Not yet," came the red-haired captain's reply as they hurried away from the ghastly sights and sounds of the dressing station.

"My fiancée lives somewhere on this side of the town. I'll report in the morning."

"*Your fiancée?* My God, you aren't engaged!" In the starlight Blake's eyes widened ludicrously. "Why—when——"

[347]

"Remember my speaking of Philomont—my cousins there? Well," grinned Cary, "that's where it began. Then I saw her again, but that's a long story. We fought like a pair of strange wildcats to start with, but after a bit we got on pretty well. Figured we might as well get hitched."

The lieutenant raised hands in mock despair. "Good God, Cary, what next? And here's me figuring on you for a shining example of practical bachelorhood."

They were drawing near the grove in which they had left their mounts in charge of a stray company of horse artillery.

The wounded man cheerfully grinned. "You never can tell." He chuckled inwardly—no point now in telling Blake everything.

"Good God in heaven," Blake burst out suddenly, "did you mean to say your intended lives near all this?"

Cary sobered. "That's what I need to find out. I was told she and her family live about two miles out of town—down near the river. There's an avenue of chestnuts. A red brick house—it's quite a way off from any others. That's what bothers me most."

In the cool of the evening and with food inside of him Cary felt ready for considerable exertion.

"But you can't go riding about." Blake used the tone of an elder remonstrating with an unreasonable child. "The whole country's swarming with Stuart's rebel patrols. Everyone knows that A. P. Hill's corps has crossed the river below Sharpsburg. There'll be stragglers everywhere."

"Nevertheless, Tom, I'm going."

[348]

"Oh, don't be a damned fool," pleaded the lieutenant. "All the civilians cleared out of this country yesterday and the day before. You aren't strong enough, anyhow."

The crown of bandages glimmered as Cary shook his head. Probably Blake was right; most likely Lenore would have remained in Virginia—but again Lenore was unusually courageous and determined—and her home was in danger.

"I'm going, Tom," he announced, gathering his reins. "I can't rest easy 'til I know."

The lieutenant suddenly mounted his charger. *"Be* a big idiot then." He laughed. "When the day comes that Hubert Cary falls under the spell I want to take a look at the girl. By the by, who is she?"

Cary chuckled as cautiously they set off toward the Potomac. "Tell you later. Maybe you'll recognize her from this description—'she's the most divine, the loveliest and the most glorious girl——'"

"Maybe," sighed Tom Blake. "Wait until you see the divine Diana. Hi! For God's sake, man, look where you're riding."

Half an hour's ride along a shadowy little country road left the horrors of Antietam field far enough behind to erase all manner of sad sounds troubling the gathering twilight.

"What did you say her pa's place looks like?" Blake presently inquired.

"Square and of brick, with six narrow white columns along its front, and there'll be a double row of chestnuts leading up to the front door."

"Let's hope it is still that way," Blake grunted. The

lieutenant's sharp profile kept swinging from right to left. Frogs boomed in a little pond and an opossum frightened both horses as it lumbered off this winding country road which, more often than not, led through tall woods. Here deer, scared down from the northern part of Maryland, stepped restlessly back into the underbrush. Here, too, were signs of encampments, of the passage of troops.

"Better face possibilities," Blake presently advised. "The house may not still be there. When reb irregulars forage they *forage!*"

Beneath the new bandage Hubert Cary's brow wrinkled. "I've noticed some of these German-born troopers of ours aren't slouches at picking up loose property either." He spurred his mount.

"Her home ought to be off the path of Lee's invasion. I —I'm sure nothing's happened."

As if to belie such a probability, flotsam brought in on the tide of war grew thicker on all sides. They moved in silence past a shattered forage wagon, past a pile of broken muskets; further on an abandoned blanket roll lay coiled like an immense snake in the center of the sandy road.

As if sent to re-establish normality in a distracted world, stars came out by tens, hundreds and thousands. A whippoorwill complained softly in the darkness.

Gripped by a growing uneasiness, Cary hurried his horse until presently Antietam Creek glistened before them. Quite silent now, the two shadowy riders splashed across a pebbly ford and, after scrambling up the far bank, came upon a grassy crossroads where a faded old finger post pointed: "To Showman's."

"That's it," Cary announced. "That Hazen girl spoke of Showman's. We're going right."

Even while they paused in the dim starlight both men stiffened in their saddles.

Blake demanded softly, "Hear that?"

"Hear what?"

"Hoofs, going somewhere damned fast."

Cary's heart commenced to pound when the trampling of horses could be distinctly heard in a patch of woods lying ahead. Immediately both Federals reined off the road and listened intently until it became evident that the other party was riding away from, not toward, this crossroads.

More cautiously Cary and his companion entered the cool of a sweet-smelling but mosquito-infested woods but surprisingly soon came upon a wide clearing. Yonder a handsome brick house stood at the end of a long line of trees. Outlined against the starry sky, it seemed square as to its proportions.

A dim light, burning in one of the downstairs windows, gave the only sign of occupancy.

"She's there!" Cary cried.

"Someone's there, all right," Blake corrected softly. His kepied head shook sharply as he laid a detaining hand on his friend's arm. "Take it easy, man. May be a parcel of rebs in yonder; let's not barge into a trap at this late date."

At a safe distance both Federals circled a stately, shadowy mansion with six white pillars across its front. This must be the Duveen home—there was a truly English reserve and conventionality both as to architecture and grounds.

Presently Cary made the interesting discovery that a pair of horses stood tethered at the porch rail. They were fitted with military saddles, saddlebags and blanket rolls.

Sharp misgivings flooded Cary's being when he noticed how many windowpanes were smashed, that several shutters were broken or missing altogether. The big house seemed deserted; no dogs barked, no lights moved, and a pair of barns standing off at some distance also seemed empty.

"Hadn't we better dismount?" Blake suggested.

"Yes."

Five minutes later the two, revolvers drawn, commenced a stealthy advance up a driveway. Treading with care, they drifted on between a double rank of tall chestnuts standing like crack troops drawn up on parade.

"Cary!" Blake's staccato undertone checked the other in his tracks. "Look—look at this!"

Cary hurried across the drive, found himself looking at a pair of spurred boots which, on a level with his eyes, hung swaying a little in mid-air. Stepping swiftly back, the Rhode Islander peered up into the shadows and was barely able to glimpse contorted hands bound behind the dead man's back.

"Reb or ours?" breathed Blake from where he crouched by the tree trunk.

"Can't tell—too dark."

The leaves of the big chestnut cut off the starlight so completely it was impossible to distinguish either the dead man's features or even his uniform. All Cary could make out was the indistinct outline of a head canting sharply to the left. A pungent latrine odor in the cooling air brought back a sense of reality to the incredulous cavalrymen.

Cary's wounded head began to throb again, and his throat suddenly felt dry and tight. If this had happened outside of the house—what had gone on, or was going on, within?

"We'd better ride back, fetch a detail," Blake advised.

"No! No! I'm going to find out what's happened. I've got to."

"Don't be a fool," came the lieutenant's harsh whisper. "Fellow hasn't been dead long."

Disregarding Blake's urgent protests, Cary reconnoitered the lawn and, with every nerve on edge, peered into a window of the lamplit room. The furniture was in wild disorder.

"There's at least one reb," he murmured. "I can see part of a gray coat."

"There 're *two* horses outside," Blake reminded. "Where's the other?"

"Can't see," Cary muttered. "Watch their horses. I'm going to other side—then go in. If anybody tries to get away, shoot. If I don't come out in five minutes, come in after me."

When he tiptoed across the wide veranda Cary's spur chains grated softly. The horses at the far end of the piazza snorted, cocked suspicious ears. The Rhode Islander tried the bullet-scarred front door, found that it gave easily. Studying every shadow, he advanced down a darkened hall. He circled an overturned chair and paused when his boots grated on a number of empty cartridge cases.

Had anyone heard? He listened. God above! Lenore Duveen was talking. Her voice sounded hurried, shaken, and came from a room to the right.

Poising his revolver, Cary groped for a doorknob. His fingers hesitated over the cold brass surface. What was going on? He didn't like the implication of that over-turned furniture, of those bullet holes in the front door.

There was at least one man inside, no doubt of that. Gathering himself, he suddenly pushed the door wide open. When the Confederate wheeled toward a pistol gleaming in the candlelight Lenore's slim figure flashed in front of the enemy.

"Don't! *Don't!*" Her great eyes flew wide. "He—he's——"

"Lenore! Stand aside!"

"Cary, by God!" This time it was not Lenore but the Confederate who spoke.

For an eternal second all three remained poised in the paralysis of complete astonishment. Gradually Cary's re-volver muzzle sank.

"Well, Mr Chambers——" He got no further. Lenore, with a smothered gasp of joy, had flung herself onto him.

"Oh, Hubert! Hubert! Thank God—poor Craig—is—is——"

"He's hurt?" The brilliance of the moment paled.

"Oh, Hubert, he—he's gone. A charge through—near a cornfield." Tears streaked her smooth cheeks. "But you—oh, my dear, what have they done to you?"

Sobbing, her whole figure shaking, Lenore pressed her-self to him, bruised her cheek against the buttons of his bedraggled uniform. Awkwardly Lieutenant Chambers passed a dirty hand over his fine features; he looked a thousand years too old.

"Yes, Captain—Craig, yo' cousin, is—is gone." He studied the pattern of the rug beneath his dusty jack boots. "It was the way he wanted——"

Cary could only look his grief.

The lean youth in gray choked. "Suh, Craig was mighty pleased you—that you got away from Hillsboro. He was all-fired—pleased. He loved you, suh—tol' me so this mawnin' when—when he was goin'. He hoped there 'd be no bitterness in yo' heart."

"Bitterness? Bitterness?" Cary repeated. "Never! If only —he should have lived."

"Oh, Hubert, why? Why must these things be?"

Gently he stroked her pale hair. "I don't know—except, well, when a new life—a new nation comes into being there's bound to be pain—danger. Maybe there 'll be two nations—maybe one, when this is all over"—Cary spoke softly, but his voice filled all the great shadowy room—"but they'll have been fought for hard and honestly. Your pardon, Lieutenant—I'm sorry, I hadn't noticed—you're wounded."

The Southerner smiled wanly. "Only slightly. Miss Duveen was tying it up."

"But that's a fresh wound!"

"Reckon so." Lieutenant Chambers' eyes hardened. "Yesterday Craig—yo' cousin, sent some of our people to see if Miss Duveen or her family was here. They reported this lady present." Chambers' teeth glinted and his sharp dark features relaxed. "So, as we all weren't but a few miles away, I brought a message from Craig." He drew himself up. "It was lucky we came along."

"That man in the tree——"

The Southerner's dark and sensitive eyes flashed. "Caught him robbin' an' scarin' "—he loaded the trivial word with meaning—"Miss Duveen.

"My boys hanged him. They've ridden on. They need their rest powerful bad." He half smiled. "When Miss Duveen offered to fuss over this silly little wound I—well, I said I'd catch up."

Cary asked, "Who was that—out there?" Lenore shuddered and clung even more tightly to his dark blue shell jacket.

"A jayhawker—Miss Duveen said."

"One of Archer's?"

"Y-y-yes," stammered Lenore. "Archer himself. He—he traced me—followed me all the way from Hillsboro."

"War breeds a lot o' brutes," Chambers observed. "War ain't much like what we thought it was—is it?"

Cary remembered the private dying in the barn, waiting so patiently for death. "Not much, Lieutenant."

"I pray it will end *soon*," Lenore murmured.

"Can't thank you enough, Mr Chambers," the Northerner said presently. "I feel there is no need to—well, to be practical. You must want to—to find your men!"

"Yo' are very generous, suh." The Southerner's body inclined in a deep old-fashioned bow. "One last thing. Craig said"—Chambers swallowed painfully, and his teeth glinted in the lamplight—"he wished yo' and Miss Duveen his duty and—and his hope that when all this is done——"

The sound of a cautious step outside made the Southerner start, whirl. With his unwounded hand he reached for his revolver. Then his gaze flickered to Cary.

"Yours?"

"Yes."

"Then I'm yo' prisoner, suh?"

Cary's bandaged head shook. He smiled faintly.

"That is Mr Blake, my lieutenant. He is coming to pay a bet——"

Lenore stared. "A bet? I declare, Hubert! The idea of betting at a time like this!"

They faced the door, watched Blake appear cautiously in the entrance. When the lieutenant beheld his captain standing easily, talking with a Confederate, his eyes grew round. When he sighted Lenore Duveen they grew rounder still.

"Miss D-Duveen!" he stammered. "Why—what——"

Lightly Cary kissed Lenore on the lips.

"Your fiancée?"

"What would you say?"

Blake flushed, then, remembering, laughed. "You win. See you payday."

Chambers picked up his plumed hat and turned to the Federal lieutenant.

"Lieutenant Blake, yo' captain has decided I ain't worth taking prisoner. So, suh, if you will be kind enough to set me on the river road . . ."

Blake read Chambers' glance and nodded. "I can't find my way around at night either."

Lenore held up a hand.

"Wait——"

When they halted she turned, looked up into Hubert Cary's face.

"Darling, since you are ever so clever—tell me—how in the world are we going to get both of these gentlemen to our wedding?"